THE
REBEL

Center Point
Large Print

Also by Marta Perry and available from
Center Point Large Print:

Susanna's Dream
The Rescued
Search the Dark
Abandon the Dark

**This Large Print Book carries the
Seal of Approval of N.A.V.H.**

THE REBEL

Keepers of the Promise
—Book Three—

Marta Perry

CENTER POINT LARGE PRINT
THORNDIKE, MAINE

This Center Point Large Print edition is published in the year 2016 by arrangement with The Berkley Publishing Group, an imprint of Penguin Publishing Group, a division of Penguin Random House LLC.

The text of this Large Print edition is unabridged. In other aspects, this book may vary from the original edition. Printed in the United States of America on permanent paper. Set in 16-point Times New Roman type.

ISBN: 978-1-62899-970-9

Library of Congress Cataloging-in-Publication Data

Names: Perry, Marta author.
Title: The rebel / Marta Perry.
Description: Center Point Large Print edition. | Thorndike, Maine : Center Point Large Print, 2016. | ©2016 | Series: Keepers of the promise ; book 3
Identifiers: LCCN 2016003500 | ISBN 9781628999709 (hardcover : alk. paper)
Subjects: LCSH: Large type books. | GSAFD: Love stories. | Christian fiction.
Classification: LCC PS3616.E7933 R43 2016b | DDC 813/.6—dc23
LC record available at http://lccn.loc.gov/2016003500

This book is dedicated
to my husband, Brian,
with love and thanks
for his unfailing support

List of Characters

PRESENT DAY:
Barbara "Barbie" Lapp
Benuel Kauffmann, his children: Abram, 4,
  Libby, 2
Moses Kauffmann, Benuel's father
Mary Kauffmann, Benuel's sister, 16
David Lapp, Barbie's younger brother
Ashlee Anderson, Barbie's Englisch friend
James Lapp, Barbie's oldest brother
Terry Gilliam, Barbie's Englisch friend
Rebecca Byler, Barbie's cousin
Judith Wegler, Barbie's cousin
Elizabeth Lapp, Barbie's grandmother

LANCASTER COUNTY, 1960:
Elizabeth Lapp
Reuben Lapp, Elizabeth's husband
Mamm Alice, Reuben's mother
Isaac Lapp, Reuben's brother
Becky Lapp, Isaac's wife
Daad Eli, Reuben's father

Glossary of Pennsylvania Dutch Words and Phrases

ach. oh; used as an exclamation

agasinish. stubborn; self-willed

ain't so. A phrase commonly used at the end of a sentence to invite agreement.

alter. old man

anymore. Used as a substitute for "nowadays."

Ausbund. Amish hymnal. Used in the worship services, it contains traditional hymns, words only, to be sung without accompaniment. Many of the hymns date from the sixteenth century.

befuddled. mixed up

blabbermaul. talkative one

blaid. bashful

boppli. baby

bruder. brother

bu. boy

buwe. boys

daadi. daddy

Da Herr sei mit du. The Lord be with you.

denke. thanks (or *danki*)

Englischer. one who is not Plain

ferhoodled. upset; distracted

ferleicht. perhaps

frau. wife

fress. eat

gross. big

grossdaadi. grandfather

grossdaadi haus. An addition to the farmhouse, built for the grandparents to live in once they've "retired" from actively running the farm.

grossmutter. grandmother

gut. good

hatt. hard; difficult

haus. house

hinnersich. backward

ich. I

ja. yes

kapp. Prayer covering, worn in obedience to the Biblical injunction that women should pray with their heads covered. Kapps are made of Swiss organdy and are white. (In some Amish communities, unmarried girls thirteen and older wear black kapps during worship service.)

kinder. kids (or *kinner*)

komm. come

komm schnell. come quick

Leit. the people; the Amish

lippy. sassy

maidal. old maid; spinster

mamm. mother

middaagesse. lunch

mind. remember

onkel. uncle

Ordnung. The agreed-upon rules by which the Amish community lives. When new practices become an issue, they are discussed at length among the leadership. The decision for or against innovation is generally made on the basis of maintaining the home and family as separate from the world. For instance, a telephone might be necessary in a shop in order to conduct business but would be banned from the home because it would intrude on family time.

Pennsylvania Dutch. The language is actually German in origin and is primarily a spoken language. Most Amish write in English, which results in many variations in spelling when the dialect is put into writing! The language probably originated in the south of Germany but is common also among the Swiss Mennonite and French Huguenot immigrants to Pennsylvania. The language was brought to America prior to the Revolution and is still in use today. High German is used for Scripture and church documents, while English is the language of commerce.

rumspringa. Running-around time. The late teen years when Amish youth taste some aspects of the outside world before deciding to be baptized into the church.

schnickelfritz. mischievous child

ser gut. very good (or *sehr gut*)
tastes like more. delicious
Was ist letz? What's the matter?
Wie bist du heit. How are you; said in greeting
wilkom. welcome
Wo bist du? Where are you?

Chapter One

Barbie Lapp came to a sudden halt as her Englisch friend Ashlee reached out to open the door to the bar. Ashlee turned with a flip of her shoulder-length auburn hair and sent a mocking glance in Barbie's direction. "Not going to chicken out now, are you?"

It was all very well for Ashlee Anderson to casually drop into a bar on a Friday night, but she couldn't possibly understand how huge such a thing was for Barbie. From an eighteen-year-old Amish boy with a touch of rumspringa wildness, it might be understood, if not condoned, but attitudes were different toward a twenty-four-year-old unmarried Amish woman.

Still, she was the one who'd wanted to see what a night out would be like if she were Englisch; this was her chance. "Of course not. Just nudge me if I say anything stupid, okay?"

"It'll be so loud nobody will hear you anyway." Ashlee grabbed the door and yanked it open. Loud talk, loud laughter, and even louder music seemed to hit them in the face. "Let's go."

Right. Her fingers brushing the unfamiliar denim jeans on her legs, Barbie followed Ashlee inside.

The noise was even worse when the door closed behind them. Barbie tried not to gawk while Ashlee threaded her way between tables as easily as if she were in the café where they both worked.

Following her, Barbie realized the truth of what Ashlee had said. How could any of these people possibly hear what anyone else was saying? This was certain-sure no place for a good Amish girl.

Maybe that was the point. Maybe she wasn't a good Amish girl any longer. Maybe she was a rebel, a fence-jumper, like her brother James. She felt the familiar constriction in her heart at the thought of James. He'd vanished from her life completely when she was eight, but she still missed him. Still wondered why—why he'd left, why he'd cut all ties to the Amish world so completely, why he'd deserted her.

James must have had the restlessness, too—that sense she had too often that life was passing her by. That there was something waiting for her out there, somewhere, beyond everything she'd experienced.

"Hey, here you are!" Ashlee motioned Barbie to slide into an already-crowded booth and squeezed in next to her, shoving her against the guy on the other side. "Everybody, this is Barbie."

People nodded and went on with their conversations, apparently not feeling the need to do more. But they were friendly enough, easily including her in their talk.

They didn't seem to care who she was. If she'd been introduced to a group of Amish she didn't know, the first thing they'd have done would have been to play what some Amish called "the name game" of trying to place her in the complicated genealogy of the Lapp family tree.

The man next to her gave her a friendly grin. "Loud, isn't it? How do you know Ashlee?"

She thawed under his casual friendliness. "We work together."

"Yeah? I can see I'll have to start going to the café for lunch. I'm Terry Gilliam. No point waiting for Ashlee to introduce anyone."

"Nice to meet you, Terry."

If he did come by the café, he'd have a shock when he saw her in her usual Amish garb instead of the jeans and cotton sweater she'd borrowed from Ashlee. Still, he was likely just being polite. The only reason she'd agreed to come to this place was because it was well away from Brook Hill, with its large Amish population.

You won't see anyone you know, Ashlee had said. *What are you worrying about? You're a grown woman, aren't you?*

True enough. Everyone around her was having a good time. So could she.

Someone plopped a glass of beer in front of her. She picked it up gingerly and sipped it, trying not to make a face.

Terry chuckled, his blue eyes crinkling with

amusement. "Not a beer drinker, are you? Listen, you don't have to drink it. How about a glass of wine? Or a soft drink?"

She wavered, not wanting to look different from anyone else. But then, that was why she was here —because she was tired of looking just like everyone else. "A cola would be great, thanks."

He waved to a server and ordered it. "No problem. So what do you do when you're not serving coffee at the café?"

She shrugged. "Nothing very exciting. My cousin takes guests on her farm during the summer, and I help run it."

"Two jobs. I'm impressed. One is enough for me." He was bending toward her, his laughing, open face attentive. "I work for the power company, keeping the lines clear. You owe your electric light to me."

She could hardly say she didn't rely on the power company for electricity. But he didn't expect a real answer, anyway. This was just flirting, and she'd always been able to flirt.

"Think of that—climbing all those poles just for me." She gave him the wide-eyed glance that usually had the boys stumbling over themselves.

He grinned. "Mostly I go up in the bucket. It's more fun."

Someone interrupted to tell a joke, followed by an incomprehensible, to her, discussion of the baseball season. Meanwhile, the women started talking about spring clothes. She was reminded of the early years of her rumspringa, when her gang of girls had clustered together, swapping secrets and talking about anything and everything, including which of their exactly-alike dresses looked best on them.

All those girls were long since married and mothers. When they got together, they seemed separated from her by an unimaginable gap. They'd compare remedies for teething pain and colic, while she sat feeling left out.

What would they think if they saw her now? She could just imagine the sidelong glances and disapproving murmurs. Fortunately, as Ashlee kept assuring her, she wouldn't see anyone she knew here.

Except that Ashlee had been wrong. Barbie's heart thumped when she spotted the group coming through the door. Several young Englisch men, and one girl, trying to look Englisch, just like Barbie.

She wasn't succeeding. Surely anyone who looked at her would know she was Amish, and underage as well.

Mary Kauffmann wore what were undoubtedly borrowed Englisch clothes, too—tight jeans and a shirt snug enough to show off her curvy young figure. The three boys were older, but surely not old enough to drink.

And they undoubtedly had been drinking.

They'd reached the stage of being boisterous, swaggering their way to a table as if they owned the place. As for Mary . . .

Barbie's heart sank. Mary was glassy-eyed, stumbling a little as one of the boys shoved her into a chair. How on earth had she managed to get into such a state? And what was Barbie going to do about it?

Nothing—that was the quick and easy answer. Mary was, after all, just doing what she was, sampling the Englisch life. But Mary was sixteen, not twenty-four. And she didn't have a buddy with her. She was alone with a group of guys too old for her, and too drunk for any girl to be safe.

Barbie tried not to stare, looking down at her drink while her mind whirled. It wasn't her business. Mary wouldn't thank her for intervening. But at least she could keep an eye on the girl as long as she was here.

One of the boys swaggered to the bar. Barbie held her breath. The bartender wouldn't serve them, would he?

He didn't. Barbie watched as he shook his head and the kid flushed angrily. The boy shouted something, thankfully drowned out by the music but turning a few heads. Then he returned to his table and grabbed Mary's hand. In a moment they were all headed out the door.

It was no use. She couldn't sit here while Mary Kauffmann headed straight for disaster. She doubted anyone heard her murmured excuse, but when she nudged her, Ashlee moved to let her out.

The group had already reached the door, and Barbie wiggled her way through the mass of humanity that blocked her way. Urgency pushed her forward, and she went the last few yards at a run and burst through the door, praying Mary wouldn't be in a car before she could reach her.

At first Barbie thought she'd missed them. Then she saw movement by the rank of parked cars. One of the boys had Mary pressed up against the vehicle, kissing her, his hands tugging at her jeans. Mary struggled feebly, swatting at him without any effect. The kid was too drunk to notice or care.

Barbie flew across the parking lot. Grabbing the boy by the shoulders, she yanked him away. Taken by surprise, he let go of Mary.

"Leave her alone." She tightened her grip, murmuring a silent prayer for help.

The boy jerked free of Barbie, glaring at her. Boy? Man? Whatever he was, he exuded an air of danger that chilled her.

"What's it to you?" He added a few words she'd never heard applied to herself before. "Get out."

One of the others—tall, skinny, with a tattoo that ran clear down his arm—nudged him. "Maybe she wants to party with us, too."

"That's right." The third pressed in, too close. "Come on, sweetie. We'll show you a good time."

Barbie put her arm around Mary, and the girl sagged against her. Did she even realize what was happening? One thing was certain—Barbie couldn't expect any help from her, and the three boys were drunk enough to have shed any inhibitions they might normally have.

"She's underage." She kept her voice firm despite the quaking inside her. "You've already broken the law by getting her drunk. You want to be in worse trouble?"

"We can handle a little trouble," one said, and the others snickered.

"Really?" She tried to sound as cool as Ashlee might in this situation. "All I have to do is let out one loud scream, and my friends will come running. The bartender is already calling the police."

That was probably wishful thinking, but if that bartender had a conscience at all, he wouldn't ignore what was right in front of his face.

The guys exchanged glances, a little less certain of themselves.

Instinctively she pressed her advantage. "If you're still here when they arrive, you'll be arrested. I'm a witness. You tried to molest an underage girl. Do you want to end this night in jail?"

A car pulled into the parking lot, its headlights sweeping over them, radio blaring. That seemed to be the deciding factor. Uttering a few more profanities, the three jumped into the car.

Barbie pulled Mary away as they backed up and then spun out of the parking lot, spraying gravel behind them.

Relief swept over her, but she couldn't relax yet. "Mary, are you all right?"

The girl roused enough to glare at her. "Leave me alone."

Barbie gritted her teeth, trying to hold on to her temper. "If I leave you alone, what will you do? Walk home? It's a good twenty miles."

Mary looked away, deliberately ignoring her. Barbie suppressed an urge to shake her. That wouldn't help, no matter how satisfying it might be. Clearly she had to find a way to get Mary home, where she belonged. They were on foot and alone in the dark. She'd have to ask Ashlee to drive them.

Tugging the sulky teenager along, Barbie headed back inside. It was louder and smokier than before, and just getting Ashlee's attention was a challenge.

"Leave? What do you mean, leave? The party's just starting. Terry wondered where you went. He wants to get to know you."

Barbie clutched Ashlee's arm. She wouldn't mind shaking her as well. "Look at this kid. She's drunk, she's only sixteen, and she doesn't have a way home. Come on, Ashlee. We can't just ignore her."

Ashlee sighed, but she was too good-hearted not

to respond to a need that was right in front of her.

"Okay, you're right, you're right. Let's go. I just hope we're not going to end up in more trouble when we get her home."

That was exactly what Barbie was thinking, except that she knew there was no hope at all. Mary lived with her father and her brother, Benuel, both widowers, and Benuel's children. And Benuel Kauffmann just happened to be one of the ministers of Barbie's congregation.

"The Kauffmann farm is about a half mile on the right." Barbie leaned forward to watch for the mailbox marking the lane. Ashlee had already been vocal about how dark it was out in the country, and naturally an Amish farm didn't have all the outside lighting an Englisch property might have.

Ashlee slowed a bit. "Just say when." She cast a glance toward the backseat and rolled her eyes.

Barbie knew what she meant. She had tried to talk to Mary a couple of times, but her efforts had been met with stony silence. The girl stared out the window, face averted. At least, thank goodness, she hadn't been sick in Ashlee's car.

"Just ahead," Barbie said as the pasture fence on their right came to an end. "See the mailbox?"

"Got it." Ashlee made the turn, tires biting into the gravel lane past the sign that read *Kauffmann Buggy Repairs*.

Barbie looked toward the backseat again. Mary had her hand to her face. If she was crying, she didn't want them to see her tears.

Barbie's heart twisted in sudden sympathy. The girl was bound to be worried about how she'd be received at home.

"It probably won't be as bad as you think," she said quietly.

"You don't know anything. Leave me alone." Mary's snarled response didn't give any indication that she appreciated Barbie's support.

"Put a sock in it," Ashlee snapped. "The least you could do is act a little grateful, you selfish brat."

"Don't, Ashlee," Barbie said softly. "Just pull up by the back porch and wait for me, okay?"

Ashlee nodded curtly. By the time this night was over, she'd no doubt regret the impulse that had made her befriend the new Amish server at the café.

Barbie got out and waited silently as Mary fumbled with the car door. There was a light on in the kitchen, and she could see movement inside. They'd be wondering why a car was coming down their lane at this hour.

Mary's father probably thought she was spending the night with a friend. After all, that's what Barbie's own parents thought. Shame flicked at her conscience. She'd lied to them. No point in putting up a fancy excuse for it, not to herself.

Mary stopped at the bottom of the porch steps, gripping the railing. "You don't have to come in with me." She sounded very young and uncertain. "I won't tell on you."

So maybe she did realize the cost Barbie would pay. For a moment she considered taking Mary up on the offer, but only for a moment. Whatever she was, she wasn't a coward.

"Come on." She put her arm around the girl's waist. "We'll face them together."

The door was already opening. Moses Kauffmann peered out, face questioning. "Who is it?" He spoke in Englisch, apparently thinking he saw two Englisch women coming to his door.

"It's Barbie Lapp, Moses. My friend and I brought Mary home."

His gaze, fixed uncertainly on her, shifted to the slight figure next to her. Barbie saw the shock hit him, tightening his weathered face, sending him back a step with its impact.

"Mary." His voice shook. "You'd best both come in."

Barbie felt Mary tremble. In another moment she'd be weeping, but that might be the best thing she could do.

"Daadi . . ." she began.

Benuel Kauffmann appeared behind his father, taking in the situation with a glance. "What have you been up to?" Anger edged his voice. "Mary, I thought you could be trusted."

Apparently Ben hadn't thought the same of her. Well, maybe that wasn't surprising. No doubt there were some in the church who thought Barbie Lapp was leaning too far on the other side of the line between Amish and not Amish. And Ben Kauffmann was well-known for his strict interpretation of the Ordnung, the agreed-upon rules by which their congregation lived.

Moses brushed past his son to come and grasp Mary's arm. She clung to Barbie, and so the three of them went together from the cool spring darkness into the warm, lighted kitchen. Despite the lack of a mother in the home, it was as clean and orderly as Barbie's mother's kitchen.

"Are you all right, Daughter?" Moses's tone was gentle, but his eyes behind his glasses were so filled with pain that it hurt Barbie to look at him.

"She's not all right. She's been drinking." If Ben was similarly pained, he certainly hid it well. He glared at Barbie before focusing on his sister. "Where did you get those clothes? You are supposed to be with Sally Stoltzfus tonight. Don't tell me she took you out to some beer party."

Mary shot a resentful glance at him. "I wasn't with Sally."

Barbie felt a tremor go through the girl. Her face was white, and if she didn't lie down, in another moment she'd probably be throwing up.

"Mary's feeling pretty bad, I think. Maybe this could wait until tomorrow." She addressed her words to Moses, figuring he was the more reasonable of the two.

"They won't listen!" The words burst out of Mary. "Nobody will listen!" Her pale face took on a greenish tinge. She clapped her hand over her mouth and raced for the stairs. They heard the thud of her feet on the steps.

Barbie would just as soon be out of here, but if Mary was indeed being sick upstairs, she might rather have another woman there. She took a tentative step. "Do you want me to help her?"

Moses straightened. "I'll go to her. How did you . . ."

"I saw that she was out of her depth," Barbie said quickly. She had no desire to be the one to tell him exactly where his daughter had been or with whom. That was up to Mary. "I thought it best to intervene, and my friend and I brought her home."

Moses nodded, apparently accepting the things that she didn't say. "Denke, Barbie. I'll go to her now."

There didn't seem to be anything else useful she could do, so as he left the room, Barbie turned toward the door.

Ben's voice stopped her. "Where did you take my sister?"

She surveyed him, trying to keep a tight rein on her anger. Ben was tall for an Amish man, and he could be an imposing figure when he preached in worship despite his relative youth. His thick, reddish-brown hair was echoed in the beard that didn't hide his firm, uncompromising mouth. At the moment, she could plainly read condemnation in his brown eyes.

Well, she wasn't going to be intimidated by him. "I didn't take your sister anywhere. I saw her by accident."

"Because you were in a place no self-respecting Amish woman should go. Is this how you spend your spare time now that you're working at that Englisch business, bringing shame to your family?"

His gesture took in her sweater and jeans, making her uncomfortably aware of how the clothes clung to her figure. The embarrassed heat in her cheeks lit the fuse to her anger.

"It's lucky for your sister that I happened to be where I was tonight." She snapped the words at him, head up, and saw him blink as the truth of them hit him. "You'd best save your concern for your own household. And what's more, if you carry on like this with Mary, you'll probably drive her to even worse behavior."

Before Ben could come up with another condemning remark, she stormed out of the house, welcoming the air against her hot cheeks.

Fuming, she yanked the car door open and slid inside. "We can go now."

"Making a fast getaway?" Ashlee swung the car

around on the grass and headed back down the lane. "What did they say to you?"

She took in a breath, reminding herself not to involve Ashlee any further in something she wouldn't understand. "Mary's father was okay. Her older brother was a bit touchy."

That was putting it mildly. Her stomach churned. What would Ben do now? As her minister, he'd probably consider it his duty to speak to her parents about what he saw as her out-of-bounds behavior.

Well, be honest. It was out-of-bounds. But that didn't mean she wanted her parents hurt by it.

It had seemed such a silly thing at the time that Ashlee suggested it—just to spend a few hours pretending to be Englisch to see what it was like. But the consequences in the hands of Benuel Kauffmann could be painfully serious.

The next afternoon, Ben reluctantly climbed down from his buggy at the café on the edge of town. He'd rather be almost anyplace but here. And on any other errand. But given what Mary had told Daad this morning, he had no choice but to speak to Barbie Lapp. Not just speak to her—apologize to her.

Daad had managed to get Mary to talk, and Ben saw how he'd struggled not to show the pain and shock her revelations caused. Ben gritted his teeth in frustration. He should have been able to spare Daad that task. Besides, as a minister of the Gmay, the local church district, chosen by God, it was his duty, wasn't it?

It occurred to him, not for the first time, that God might have been mistaken in choosing him. When Donna was alive, they'd faced the consequences of his choosing together. Without her, he seemed to fail more than he succeeded.

As he was doing right now. What he should do, as a minister of the church, was discuss the situation with the other ministers. Then two or three of them should call on the family of the offending party and seek a confession of the wrongdoing and a promise to change.

But he wasn't doing any of those things, because it was his own sister and father who would be affected, and he couldn't bear to hurt Daad any further. Which meant, like it or not, Barbie also escaped the consequences of her wrongdoing.

He'd made the decision, and he'd better get on with it. Gripping the handle of the door, he pulled it open and went inside.

As he'd hoped, the café wasn't very busy in the middle of the afternoon. Barbie, standing behind the cash register in conversation with an Englisch server, looked up at the sound of the door opening. When she saw him, the welcoming smile slid from her face. She murmured something to the other woman, who looked at him with interest. Then Barbie came toward him.

"Benuel. May I help you?" Barbie contrived to act as if she were busy despite the fact that only two tables were occupied.

"We have to talk." He clenched his teeth. That certain-sure didn't sound polite, but his embarrassment at his task didn't spare him any energy for idle chatter.

"Here?" She lifted her rounded chin as if in defiance. "This is my workplace. Can't it wait until later?"

"I think it best if we get this out of the way now. You can surely spare a few minutes to speak with me." He gestured toward the empty tables.

Barbie's face tightened, but she nodded. "Very well." She gestured toward a booth as far as possible from the occupied tables. "Sit down. I'll bring you a cup of coffee."

"I don't want—"

"If you must talk with me here, you'll have to look like a patron." The words contained a snap. "I don't want my boss coming down on me for entertaining people when I'm working."

Entertaining was hardly the word, but he understood her point. She owed it to her employer to give a day's work for a day's pay. Besides, it wouldn't be fair to get her in trouble with her boss just because he didn't think she should be working here.

Benuel jerked a nod and went quickly to the booth she'd indicated, aware of eyes following him. The café, located as it was on the far side of town from most Amish farms, was mostly patronized by Englisch customers. An Amish person was apparently rare enough to be stared at.

Why, then, had Barbie chosen to work here, when she could as easily have gotten a job at an Amish-run business? A sign of restlessness on her part? Sliding into the booth, he ignored the stares and began mentally to rehearse the words he'd say to her.

Barbie returned quickly, putting a mug of coffee in front of him with a smile that was probably automatic. She slid into the bench on the other side of the booth. "I only have fifteen minutes for my break."

"This won't take that long." He stared down at the coffee, discovering that the prepared words had vanished now that the moment had arrived.

Barbie stared at him, her bright blue eyes vaguely disapproving. "Are you sure? Have you timed your lecture?"

He gaped before realizing what she meant and then raised one eyebrow, feeling an unwelcome smile tugging at his lips. "Now you are the one jumping to conclusions, ain't so? Just as I did last night."

She blinked, her lively features frozen. Then she nodded. "I take it Mary told you what happened."

"She told our father." Barbie couldn't possibly guess what that admission meant to him. "If you hadn't come to the rescue, those boys might have . . ." He stopped, not wanting to put it in words, and the anger he thought he'd conquered raised its head again.

Her expression sobered as she evidently remembered those moments. "There were three of them, all cocky and drunk. It's a bad combination."

"Mary said you risked your own safety to help her."

Barbie shrugged. "I don't think they'd have done anything to me, but if they'd made a move, I was ready to scream the place down, even if . . ."

He could fill in the rest of it. "Even if that made the whole thing public."

"Ja." Her full lips pressed together for an instant. "I would hate for my parents to know where I was. Do you intend to tell them?"

"That should be my duty as your minister, ain't so?" He gripped the coffee mug. "But Mary's action has made it more complicated. I've already seen how it's affected my father. How can I inflict more pain and humiliation on him?"

"I'm sorry." Sympathy filled her eyes. "It hasn't been easy for him, raising a teenage girl without a woman in the house."

"Ja. Mamm's death and then my Donna's . . . that changed everything. And obedience to the Ordnung is not as simple as I thought it on the day I was ordained."

Barbie nodded, her lips lifting slightly. "Sometimes I have that feeling about growing up. It's not nearly as easy to tell right from wrong as I once expected it would be."

Her understanding startled him. Ben had always thought Barbie as frivolous as a butterfly, flitting here and there and unable or unwilling to focus on religious duties.

Still, it was his duty to at least try to awaken her to the dangers of her present course.

"You were wrong to dress up in Englisch clothes. Wrong to go to a bar."

Her gaze met his without flinching. "If I hadn't been there, I wouldn't have been able to help Mary."

"Ja. I know." He said the words heavily. God did indeed work in mysterious ways. He sucked in a breath, accepting the inevitable. "I won't tell your parents about it."

She gave a quick nod. "Denke, Benuel. You don't need to worry that anyone will hear of what happened with Mary from me. I'm just thankful she's all right."

He frowned, the worry weighing on him. "I wish . . . Ach, it's not right to question God's will. But if Donna were here, I can't help but think she'd be able to deal with this . . . this rebellion of Mary's better than Daad or I."

"I know." Sudden sympathy filled Barbie's voice, and she leaned toward him. "Donna has left a big gap in so many lives. Your kinder . . ."

Pain made him grimace. "Abram and Libby don't even remember her. Well, they wouldn't. Abram was only two when Libby was born, and Donna passed two weeks later."

He pressed his lips together, not wanting to talk about his loss, not wanting her to see his emptiness. He'd have to marry again, of course. It had been two years, and folks were wondering why he hadn't done it already.

"We do the best we can, Daad and I," he said. "And my sister Sarah helps, but she has her own family to worry about. Besides, she and Mary have never gotten along too well."

Barbie looked as if she were picturing his oldest sister, with her noisy laugh and bossy manner. "No, I guess not. Maybe . . ."

"I wasn't asking for advice." His voice became stiff. Did she really think he'd ask someone who was teetering on the fence about being Amish for advice?

"Meaning I'd better concentrate on my own behavior?" The blue eyes snapped. Barbie was as capricious as a dandelion blown by the wind. "I haven't been baptized into the church yet, remember?"

"Maybe you won't be, the way you're going." He hadn't intended to lose his temper, and he was aghast that he'd spoken the words aloud.

Barbie just stared at him for a moment. "Maybe I won't," she said deliberately.

"I should not have said it, Barbie." His voice was stiff with mortification. What kind of minister was he? He'd better get away from her before he made matters even worse. "I must go." He pushed his cup away and put money on the table. "Don't worry about Mary. She won't get into that kind of trouble again. I'll be keeping a strict watch on her."

He could almost see her temper rising. "If you do that, I can practically guarantee she'll find some new way to rebel."

Ben stood, looking down at her. From somewhere the thought flickered into his mind that she was a wonderful pretty woman, sitting there looking up at him with every emotion showing on her face.

"Are you sure you're not talking about yourself?" he said, and then strode away before he could make matters any worse.

Chapter Two

Barbie was still fuming over her encounter with Ben when she reached her grandmother's place after work. She stopped often to visit with Grossmammi, who now lived in the grandparent house attached to the farmhouse of her eldest son, Barbie's uncle, the father of her dear cousin Rebecca. Today she might have skipped the visit, afraid her grandmother's sharp eyes would pick up her bad mood, but Grossmammi particularly wanted to see her.

She drew up to the hitching post at the end of the farm lane, waving to Rebecca's two children as they came running from the barn. Rebecca and her family lived on the adjoining farm, and her kinder were here nearly as much as they were at home. With the warming weather, Rebecca would soon be opening the farm-stay she ran for folks who wanted to enjoy a weekend in the country and see what Amish farm life was really like.

Last season, Barbie had been Rebecca's trusted partner as she'd gotten the business going, but Rebecca had remarried in the fall, and Barbie wasn't sure how that might affect her work. They ought to talk soon. She'd have to figure out how to juggle helping Rebecca with her job at the café.

Going to the side door that led directly to the grossdaadi haus, Barbie tapped once and walked in. "Grossmammi? It's Barbie."

"In the kitchen." As always, her grandmother sounded delighted at her visit. Grossmammi managed to make each of her many grand-children feel as if he or she was the most loved person in the world when they were together.

"Don't get up." Barbie hurried to hug her grandmother, sitting in her favorite rocking chair near the stove. "If you need something, I'll get it for you."

Grossmammi's arms tightened around her, and love seemed to envelop her. "Ach, you young ones fuss too much. I can get up and get you some cookies and a cup of tea, ain't so?"

"You can, but let me do it instead. It keeps me in practice for my job." And indeed, the teacups and cookies were already set out on a tray and the kettle was steaming gently on the stove. All that remained was to fill the teapot and carry the tray to the small table next to her grandmother's chair.

"There, now." She pulled one of the chairs over from the table and settled herself. "This is wonderful nice. I'm sehr glad to relax with you."

She glanced around the kitchen as Grossmammi poured out. It was smaller than the kitchen in the old farmhouse where Grossmammi had spent most of her married life, but Barbie's onkels and her daad had done a fine job of building a new, convenient home for her.

The cookies were freshly baked peanut butter ones, their aroma filling the room, and seeds were sprouting in pots on the windowsills. Grossmammi always had to have her flowers and herbs, no matter where she was.

Did she still miss the old farmhouse, with all its reminders of a long marriage? Barbie eyed her grandmother's wrinkled face, soft as the skin of a peach, the blue eyes still sharp behind her wire-rimmed glasses. The hair pulled back from a center part was as white now as her kapp.

"Why are you so quiet today, my Barbie?" Grossmammi seemed to be studying her as well. "Usually you're talking away a mile a minute about all your doings."

Barbie's mind flickered to the most recent example of her "doings," which she hoped her grandmother would never learn of. And to its unfortunate aftermath. Tension tightened her nerves at the thought of Benuel Kauffmann. Would he keep quiet, or would his rigid conscience eventually get the better of his discretion?

She shrugged, realizing her grandmother was still waiting for an answer. "I guess I'm a little tired today."

Grossmammi studied her face so intently she might be looking right into Barbie's inner thoughts, and Barbie felt her cheeks grow warm in response.

"Something is troubling you, I think. Will you tell me about it?" The question was gentle, but somehow Barbie suspected no one ever failed to respond to it.

"It's nothing," she said quickly. "Well, it's foolish anyway." Maybe a little part of the truth would be best. Grossmammi had a delicate ear for falsehoods. "Benuel Kauffmann stopped by the café while I was working today." She made a face. "I don't think he approves of me."

"Maybe he fears it's not a gut place for you to work," Grossmammi suggested.

"Well, maybe so, but he didn't need to act as if I'd committed every sin in the Bible." Her annoyance was like a prickly rash, impossible not to scratch. "Anyway, he's not my daad. It's not his business."

Grossmammi didn't speak. She just looked at Barbie until Barbie couldn't handle that clear gaze any longer.

"Ja, I know he's one of the ministers. I guess he means well, but everyone knows how strict he is. You'd think a younger man might be more flexible, but not Benuel Kauffmann."

Somehow she didn't think Grossmammi was going to join in her criticism of Ben. Sure enough, she didn't.

"I think, my Barbie, that you wouldn't be so annoyed with Benuel unless there was some truth in what he said, ain't so?"

No matter how long she delayed, her answer would have to be the same. Grossmammi saw too much. "Maybe so. But I don't need him pointing it out to me."

Grossmammi reached out to pat her hand, the touch as gentle as the brush of the spring breeze on her skin. "Ach, Barbie. So restless and eager. I trust that soon God will lead you to whatever it is you are seeking."

The words went right to her heart and settled

there. How could God know what it was she sought, when she didn't know herself? But Grossmammi seemed confident.

She nodded, afraid her voice might wobble if she tried to speak.

"Now, let's get to the reason I wanted you to stop by today." Grossmammi's voice became brisk. "Komm. We'll go into the living room, and I'll show you."

"Show me what?" Barbie moved the tray out of the way as her grandmother got up. With her grandmother's heart problems, she was supposed to take it easy, but that never seemed to slow her down at all.

"You'll see." Grossmammi led the way, her small body in the black dress somehow indomitable. "You must have thought I'd forgotten to pick out a family gift for you, but I haven't. Here it is."

She stepped aside, leaving Barbie confronting the object that sat right in the middle of the living room floor. A dower chest. But not just any dower chest. It was Grossmammi's own, the one that had come to her from her own grandmother.

"But . . . you shouldn't part with something you treasure so much, Grossmammi. Something else will be fine for me, that's certain-sure."

Since last spring, Barbie and her two cousins, Rebecca Byler and Judith Wegler, had been helping Grossmammi to dispose of the collection of objects belonging to the Lapp family—objects that seemed to summarize the history of the Amish in America. Grossmammi had always been the family's storyteller, keeping the stories alive, and she was determined that Barbie and her cousins would take over that role. She had given family pieces to Rebecca and Judith already, but not to Barbie, until now. Barbie had begun to wonder if Grossmammi had forgotten about it.

Grossmammi sat down in the corner of the sofa, her small figure dwarfed by its high back, her gaze resting on the chest. It was large even for a dower chest—big enough that an Amish bride would be able to store all the linens she'd need for her new home. Chests were usually either passed on in families or built by fathers for their daughters, so that from the time Amish girls hit their teens, they'd begin acquiring the things they'd need for their married lives.

Amish married lives, of course. The idea seemed to stick in Barbie's throat. The last thing she ought to have, given her current uncertainty about her future, was a dower chest.

"This is for you." Grossmammi's tone was firm.

It was clearly useless to argue. "Denke, Gross-mammi," she murmured, her throat tight.

"I pray it will be a blessing to you, just as Rebecca's and Judith's gifts were to them. They each found an understanding they needed from the previous owners of their objects."

"This was yours, so I already can rely on your

wisdom, ain't so?" She tried to speak lightly, not wanting to think of a time when Grossmammi wouldn't be with them.

Her grandmother smiled, her gaze softening as it rested on the dower chest. "It holds such memories for me. All the important reminders of my life were in this chest at one time or another."

"All the more reason not to let it go," Barbie said quickly.

But her grandmother shook her head. "No. It's time. We'll go through the things in it together, you and me. There's no hurry. Then I'll know that my stories won't die with me, ain't so?"

"None of us will ever forget you. And you'll be with us for a gut long time yet." Surely Grossmammi knew what an influence her love had been on each of her grandchildren, didn't she?

Grossmammi just shook her head. "Open it."

Barbie knelt on the braided rug in front of the chest, taking a moment to trace the faded painting on the front. Two stylized birds faced each other, surrounded by hearts, the colors paled almost to invisibility. Then she raised the latch and lifted the lid, letting out the scent of the lavender Grossmammi had put in with her treasures.

The trunk was full to the top. Clearly this was going to take some time, if Grossmammi intended to tell her something about every item in the trunk. She hesitated a moment and then lifted out the object that lay on top—something soft wrapped in a section of an old sheet, faded to a soft ivory color with age and as thin as paper.

Carefully, not knowing what was inside, she unwrapped the fabric. Her breath caught. Inside was a tiny baby gown, made in the softest of cotton to the same pattern baby gowns were made to this day. She lifted it, spreading it out, and it struck Barbie that something was wrong.

Baby gowns were normally worn and frayed from frequent washings as they passed from one baby to the next . . . inevitable in an Amish family. This one looked brand new.

"Grossmammi?" She looked up, a question in her voice.

Her grandmother's eyes had filled with tears. She held out her hands, and Barbie put the gown in them, speculations tumbling in her mind.

Grossmammi stroked the fine stitching with gentle fingers, as if each stitch contained a memory. A tear dropped on the material, and she blotted it away.

"This I made for my first babe," she said softly. "We were going to name him Matthias. He never lived to wear it."

Lancaster County, Spring 1960

Elizabeth Lapp folded the sheet over the baby gown, her heart wincing as the precious garment vanished from view. For an instant everything in her rebelled. It wasn't right. It wasn't fair. Why should she and Reuben be denied the right to watch their firstborn live and grow?

It is God's will. The answer was clear, but so very hard to accept. She'd never realized how hard. Nothing in her life thus far had prepared her for the pain of losing little Matthias.

Amish thrift insisted that the gown should be saved and used for another baby, but Elizabeth knew she would never do so. She'd sewn it while feeling the boppli kicking inside her, laughing a little in sheer joy when the vigorous effort had actually made the fabric bounce as she held it. No, she wouldn't put it on another baby. She placed it gently into her dower chest.

Would there even be another babe? The fear seized her. She and Reuben had waited over a year for a pregnancy, only to lose the baby in the final months. What if she didn't conceive again?

Ach, these are foolish thoughts, Elizabeth. Her mother's voice seemed to sound in her ears. It was only to Mammi that she'd confided her fears. Only Mammi who had been able to comfort her.

It struck her that it was disloyal to Reuben, and she quickly closed the lid of the chest. Of course Reuben was a wonderful great comfort to her. But some things only another woman could understand. How could she possibly have gotten through the past year without having her mother and her sisters so close at hand?

The farmhouse belonging to Reuben's father was unusually quiet this afternoon. The men were out repairing pasture fence, while Mamm Alice, Reuben's mother, had gone shopping with Becky, the young wife of Reuben's brother Isaac. The family filled the place to overflowing, but no one really minded. After all, it took a lot of hands to run a dairy farm.

Still, Reuben said they must think about getting a place of their own. Isaac, the youngest, would stay here on the family farm when his parents moved into the daadi haus they spoke of building, and his and Becky's children would be the ones to grow up here. That was how things were done, and Elizabeth didn't have any argument with it. She just prayed Reuben would find a farm to buy somewhere very close. She didn't want to have to hitch up the buggy every time she wanted to chat with Mamm Alice or her own mother, just down the road.

Closing the door to their bedroom behind her, Elizabeth headed downstairs. Since Mamm Alice was out, she'd go ahead and start the chicken for supper. Everyone would be hungry after a busy afternoon.

As she passed the living room window, she saw a car turning into the long lane that led to the farmhouse. Frowning a little, she hurried to the back door. Someone from the dairy to talk to Reuben's father? If so, she'd have to run out and find him, unless the men happened to be working within sight of the lane.

But when the car pulled up to the back porch, Elizabeth felt sure she'd been mistaken. This looked more like a family seeking directions, with a man and woman in the front seat and two children in the back.

After a brief conversation with the driver, the woman got out. Englisch, probably nearing her forties, although it was difficult to tell with Englisch women. She wore a pair of bright red slacks with a red-and-white checked blouse and had a camera slung round her neck. Visitors, then, not locals.

"Can I help you find something?" Elizabeth so seldom spoke anything other than Pennsylvania Dutch that she had to concentrate on getting the words right in Englisch.

"You're Amish, aren't you?" The woman broke into a smile and turned toward the car. "Look, kids! See? This is an Amish woman."

For all the world as if I were an animal in the zoo. Elizabeth tried to keep her smile from faltering. "Are you folks lost?"

"I'll say we're lost. We've been driving around for ages looking for a real Amish farm. The man at the motel said we'd be able to tell because of there not being electric lines, but every place we stopped, we didn't see anyone."

Since just about every farm along Dahl Road

was Amish, they must have been visiting each one. "It's the middle of the day," she said. "The men are out in the fields. Did you need to see them about something?"

"Well, we came all the way from New Jersey because the tourist bureau said we'd see real Amish people here in Lancaster County. We didn't want to disappoint the kiddies. How about showing us around the house?"

Elizabeth couldn't find her voice. She'd heard tales from other church members of pushy tourists now that the county was becoming such an attraction, but she hadn't dreamed she'd experience it herself. What should she do? She glanced toward the pastures, seeing the men working at a distance. They weren't even looking this way, apparently thinking she'd handle whoever had come to the door.

The woman, her eyes on the door Elizabeth had left open behind her, seemed to take her silence for assent. She moved forward, gesturing to her family, who piled out of the car. Elizabeth gathered her scattered wits and stepped in front of her.

"I'm sorry. It wouldn't be appropriate for me to show you the inside of our house."

"Now see here." The husband, pudgy and sunburned, looked affronted. "The only reason we came here on our vacation was that the wife thought it would be good for the kids to see real live Amish. The least you can do is show us around the house. We want the kids to see how you live without electricity or anything."

Elizabeth felt the heat rising in her cheeks and wished fervently for Reuben, for anyone, to intercede. She didn't know how to handle these people. They were acting as if she owed them something.

The older of the two kids, a girl of about twelve, gave an elaborate sigh. "You dragged us all over that colonial village last year. We saw enough history. I don't see why we can't go to the beach like everybody else. This is dumb."

The complaint just seemed to deepen the man's irritation, but he didn't correct the girl for her sass. Elizabeth couldn't imagine an Amish child speaking to her parents that way, but at least maybe it would deter the rude parents.

"We came to see Amish, and that's what we're going to do. Either you show us around or the tourist bureau is going to hear about it." He said that with the air of someone giving orders from on high.

Elizabeth shook her head, fearing she was going to trip over her words. "I don't understand. We don't have anything to do with this . . . this tourist bureau."

His face reddened, but before he could speak, his wife patted his arm.

"It's okay. Maybe this is a day off or something.

Come on, kids. Go stand with the Amish lady and I'll take your picture." She raised the camera.

This just went from bad to worse. Elizabeth backed away, holding her hands out. "No, please." They really did speak a different language, and she couldn't seem to get through to them.

"It's against our beliefs to have our pictures taken." She hadn't seen Reuben and his father coming, and she sagged with relief at the sound of Daad Eli's calm tones.

Reuben touched her arm, drawing her back as his father took over. A quick glance at Reuben's face showed her his tight jaw and compressed lips. Angry, but trying to overcome the feeling, she could tell.

The tourist was pouring out all his complaints to Daad Eli, who listened with his usual patience, his gray-bearded figure attentive but somehow unyielding, too.

"Go inside," Reuben said softly in dialect. "We will deal with them. I'll come in a minute."

It was considerably more than a minute. She busied herself at the stove, unable to keep from glancing out. Daad Eli must be soothing them down, because the man's irritation seemed to disappear. Eventually Reuben's father led them off toward the barn, and Reuben came inside.

He crossed the kitchen quickly, putting his arms around her, and she could feel his tension. "I'm sorry you had to handle those Englischers on your own. I'd have sent them on their way, but Daad is letting them take some pictures of the animals."

"Ach, it's fine. I should have thought of that instead of standing there like a dummy." She managed a smile, hating to see him so upset.

"You weren't being a dummy." He grasped her arms so he could look into her face. "Never say that. It's these . . . these tourists." He said the word with disgust. "What do they think they're going to see? They act as if we're putting on a show for them."

"Not all of them." She patted his arm. "And times are changing, ain't so? Some of the Leit are even making money by selling things to the tourists."

"The change certain-sure isn't for the better, money or not." Reuben's straight brows drew down, his normally cheerful expression gone entirely. With his strong jaw and firm mouth, he could look forbidding when his usual smile was missing. His blue eyes were icy at the moment, not soft and dancing as they often were when he looked at her.

It almost frightened her, this look at a Reuben she didn't seem to know. She'd seen him grieved, and his pain at the loss of their baby had been a terrible thing. But she'd never seen this almost implacable anger.

"Don't take it so seriously, Reuben." She patted

his arm. "I'm not. Next time I'll know better how to handle them."

"There shouldn't be a next time. We ought to be able to live our lives the way we believe, without people acting as if we're something on display."

Since she'd thought that herself, she had trouble arguing, but she'd best tease him into a better mood if she could.

"Komm see the elephants and zebras and Amish," she said, making her voice light. "Ach, they're just foolish. Or not understanding our ways the way the Englisch who live around here do."

"They're probably the ones who will benefit from the county bringing in visitors to gawk at the Amish," he muttered, "not us." But she could feel his initial anger seeping away.

"Maybe that's what God wants for us," she suggested. "To be an example of people living according to His word."

Reuben shook his head, unconvinced and still frowning. "It will just keep getting worse and worse, that's what folks are saying. Just like land prices keep going up and up. Seems like Lancaster County might not be the best place for Amish any longer."

His words struck her, leaving her speechless for a moment. Then protests sprang to her lips. "But, Reuben, there have always been Amish in Lancaster County, ever since the very first ship came over from Europe. You know that."

"Like you said, times change." He was looking at her now, an expression she couldn't interpret in his eyes. "Maybe it's time for us to move on. Go someplace where we can have peace."

He was serious. He was actually serious, and fear struck Elizabeth's heart. She wanted to put her hands over her ears, like a child blocking out something she didn't want to hear.

"No, no." She seemed to be shaking inside. "We can't do such a thing. This is our home. It always has been. It always will be."

Reuben just looked at her, not speaking. He didn't need to speak to make his views clear. He really was thinking about this terrible idea. He really thought it would be possible for them to move away from everything and everyone they knew and loved.

Chapter Three

Barbie cut slices of peach pie as her mamm set dishes in the sink. Daad and David, her two-years-younger brother, were engrossed in a conversation about the upcoming livestock auction, but David broke off to grin at her.

"What, no ice cream?"

"In a minute." She ruffled the hair that was as

blond as hers. With their identical blue eyes and closeness in age, their older brothers liked to tease them about being twins—the runts of the family, coming along some years after the next older brother. "If you put on too much weight around the middle, the girls aren't going to bat their eyes at you anymore."

"Ach, I think Sally King would overlook a few extra pounds," Mamm teased, obviously glad to see that David, at least, was showing signs of fixing his interest on a possible mate.

"I wouldn't be so sure." Barbie managed a mock-serious tone as she took vanilla ice cream from the gas-operated refrigerator. "Seems to me there are a lot of guys interested in her."

"She just likes me," David said, plunging his fork into the pie. "I'm irresistible. She told me so."

"She should have known better," Barbie retorted. "I'll have to have a talk with her."

"You leave her alone." David tried to sound fierce, but his eyes danced. "No stories about what a cute little boppli I was, mind. It's bad enough when Mamm starts that."

"I'm sure I never interfere," Mamm said, and her children exchanged laughing glances.

"Right, Mammi. We know that." Barbie flicked her brother's clean-shaven cheek and sat down to her own pie. "Since you're all spiffed up, I'd guess you're taking off in the courting buggy again tonight."

David glanced at the clock and bolted his last bite of pie. "I have to get going."

"Mind you're not late getting her home," Daad said, pushing back his chair. "I'll walk out with you. I want to have another look at Belle. Wouldn't be surprised if that foal came along sooner than we expected."

The two of them went out, leaving Barbie and Mammi with the remains of supper. Barbie took another bite of pie. "This is wonderful gut, Mamm."

Her mother hid a pleased look behind a shake of her head. "Always hard to get the filling right when I use our canned peaches, no matter how I try. Warm as it's been, the rhubarb will be ready by next week, I think. Then we'll have something fresh at last."

Their meals always revolved around what was in season, and Barbie knew the progression of pies as well as Mamm. Rhubarb first, then strawberry. Then the black raspberries would be ripening, followed by blueberries. To say nothing of the tree fruits—plums, then peaches, then apples.

"You're making me feel stuffed, talking about rhubarb pie when we've just finished a big meal." She carried the last of the pie plates to the sink. "Want me to wash tonight?"

"My turn to wash, yours to dry," Mamm said briskly, bringing the coffee cups to the sink. "It's wonderful gut I don't have to rely on David to help me. He breaks more dishes than he dries."

"He probably does that on purpose so he won't have to help." She took out a clean dish towel as Mamm ran water into the sink.

"Ach, he's a gut boy." Mamm's indulgent smile said it all as far as how she felt about her youngest.

Somehow that reminded Barbie of that unexpected revelation from her grandmother earlier.

"Mamm, did you know that Grossmammi Lapp had a baby that died before the other kinder were born?"

Her mother looked startled. "Ja, I knew it, but only because your daad mentioned it once. She never talks about it. Did she tell you?"

Barbie nodded. There hadn't been time to discuss her visit with Grossmammi, but she could always count on chatting over the dishes. "I stopped to see her after work today. She showed me the piece of family furniture she's giving me—her own dower chest."

Again she felt that odd cringing. Was it that she didn't think her grandmother should part with it? Or because she didn't want something that might seem to ensure her own inevitable Amish marriage?

"She did?" Mamm let a dish slide from her hands into the dishwater. "Ach, that's wonderful kind of her. That dower chest is a treasure. I'm thinking she said it was her own grandmother's."

Barbie nodded. "It was. It seems to mean so much to her that I felt strange accepting it. I told her she should keep it, but she's determined."

"We'll have to find some space for it in your bedroom." Mamm looked ready to fly upstairs and start rearranging furniture right now.

Barbie smiled, shaking her head. "No rush. The chest is full of things, and she wants to go through it with me first. That's how she came to tell me about the lost baby." Her throat tightened. "There was a gown in it she'd made for her first baby—never used. They were going to name him Matthias." She had to clear her throat to go on. "She cried a little when she told me, and I . . . I didn't know how to comfort her."

"You couldn't." Mamm's voice sounded strained. "You never forget the babe you lost, no matter what the cause."

"Mamm?" She reached out to touch her mother's wet hand, clutching the edge of the sink. "What is it?"

Her mother shook her head. "Just remembering." She took a deep breath. "I had two miscarriages between Zeb and you."

"I . . . I never knew." She'd never even wondered at the gap between her and her next older brother.

"Ach, it was a sad time. For a while I feared

there wouldn't be any more babies. But then you came along, just when I'd begun to give up hope." Her smile was like the sun coming up. "A precious girl after all those boys. Just what I'd dreamed of."

Once again she didn't know what to say. This had been a day of surprises. She settled for giving her mother a quick hug.

"How ferhoodled we're being." Mammi wiped away a tear with the back of her hand. "I'll have you all wet before we're done."

"I don't mind." She hesitated. "I'm glad you told me."

She felt as if she'd been admitted to a private company of Lapp women—those females who were old enough to be let in on the secrets.

"Anyhow, I'm wonderful glad your grossmammi is going to entrust that dower chest to you. Some girls would say they wanted a brand new one, but I'm sure she knows you'll treasure it."

Barbie could practically see her mother's thoughts. She was imagining Barbie taking another step toward her place as a married Amish woman.

"When Grossmammi told the three of us cousins that she wanted us to carry on the family stories, I never thought . . ." She hesitated, wondering what she *had* thought that day nearly a year ago when her grandmother had talked to her and Rebecca and Judith. "Well, I guess I didn't think about there being sad stories, as well as happy ones."

Mammi looked at her, seeming to study her face for a moment. "But that's what life is, my Barbie. It's a mix of all the happy times and sad times, sometimes coming right on top of one another. Good and bad, light and dark." She smiled gently. "It's like that quilt pattern I'm working on now: sunshine and shadows. That's what life is."

Again, Barbie didn't know what to say. Maybe she wasn't ready to be admitted to so much knowledge. She dried a plate slowly, trying to find a way to turn the conversation to something less serious.

"I had thought I'd stop and see Rebecca after I saw Grossmammi, but it was getting too late. I'll have to do it another day. We should be firming up plans for the farm-stay for this season."

Mamm brightened. "Just what I was thinking myself. If this warm spring weather lasts, she'll be getting some reservations soon, ain't so?"

"I guess she will." Barbie hesitated. "Now that she's married, I'm not sure how much she's going to want me to do."

"She'll probably need you more than ever now," Mamm said. "Especially if she's . . ."

Mamm let the sentence die away, flushing a little.

Barbie looked at her for a long moment before it sank in. "Is Rebecca pregnant?"

"Hush," Mamm said quickly. "She's not saying

anything yet. But sometimes—well, sometimes you can just tell from how a woman looks. She has a glow about her."

Barbie considered. "Maybe that's just because she's so happy now that she and Matt are married."

"We'll see," her mother said with an air of knowing that annoyed Barbie. "In any event, I think she'll need more help than ever. Once you quit your job at the café, you'll have plenty of time to help."

Barbie stared at her mother, aghast. Quit the café? "What makes you think I'm going to quit working at the café?"

A guilty look crossed her mother's face. "I . . . well, I don't know, but I always thought it was just a stopgap until the farm-stay opened again. Surely you'd rather be working with your cousin instead of working for strangers."

Non-Amish strangers, that was what she meant, Barbie realized. Mamm had been worrying about her, out there among the Englisch. "Mamm, I don't know that I want to quit the café. I'll need to find out what Rebecca has in mind. And even so . . ." She stopped, because she could read the expression in her mother's eyes too clearly.

Fear. Her mother was afraid of what might become of her working in the Englisch world. The words her mother had spoken earlier seemed to take on a new meaning. *You never forget the child you lost.*

Mamm had also lost her firstborn, James—not to death, but to the outside world. That was what her mother had meant. She'd been mourning James, gone as certainly as if he'd died.

And now she feared losing Barbie in the same way.

When Ben went into the house after closing up at the buggy repair shop, he was surprised to find Daad stirring something in a pot on the stove while Mary set the table. Before he could comment, four-year-old Abram ran toward him, grabbing his pant leg. "I'm helping make supper, Daadi."

"You are? That's wonderful gut." He rested his hand on his son's thatch of straight blond hair. "You're a big help, ain't so?"

"Libby help, too." Two-year-old Libby waved the spoon she held in her small hand, and it promptly fell on the floor. She looked down at the spoon, her round face puckering, but Mary swooped down and retrieved it.

"Put this one on the table for Daadi." She handed his daughter another spoon. "He'll like this one."

"That's right." He scooped her up into a hug and then set her down by his place at the table. "That's just the spoon I want."

Libby plopped the spoon onto the table upside down and beamed.

"Gut job," he said. He shared a smile with his son, wordlessly encouraging the boy.

"Gut job," Abram echoed.

It was good. Not just that his kinder were learning to help, but that Abram was finding out what it meant to be the big bruder.

Ben straightened, glancing around the kitchen. "I thought Sarah was here." His sister had stopped by earlier that afternoon with the intention, she said, of fixing supper for them.

"I sent her on home to tend to her own family." There was a warning note in Daad's voice that alerted Ben. "She shouldn't be fussing around here when she ought to be taking care of her kinder."

"Daad means that Sarah was fussing at me." Mary put a plate down with unnecessary force. "She decided it was her job to lecture me about my behavior. Well, it's not! And what's more, I told her so!"

Ben could imagine how that had gone over. Sarah always thought she knew best for everyone. He looked at Daad, who shook his head slightly.

"Ach, I forgot to shut the chickens in," Daad said. "Mary, would you run out and do that before we dish up supper?"

Mary looked as if she were considering whether to make an issue of it, but then she put down the plates she was holding. "I know what that means. You want to talk to Ben."

Daad just looked at her with that steady gaze that always seemed to require obedience. Mary held his gaze for a moment before she shrugged and went out the back door.

Crossing to the stove, Ben inhaled the aroma of chicken potpie. "I suppose Sarah didn't say anything to her that wasn't true."

"Probably not," Daad said. "It's the way she says things. And the fact that she thought she ought to speak at all."

Ben was reminded of Barbie's reaction to his sister Sarah when they'd talked. Sarah's bossy manner and sharp tongue did raise people's hackles even when she had the best of intentions. "She means well." That was all he could think of to say.

"Sarah was after me again to let Mary live with her. Seems to me that's the worst thing that could happen, so don't you encourage her if she brings it up to you. I'm not so old I can't raise my own daughter."

"If Sarah could be a bit more tactful . . ." He couldn't help but think that his sister understood adolescent girls better than he and Daad did.

"She won't. She can't." Daad gave a reluctant smile. "I love her dearly, but she drives me crazy with her bossiness, and it would drive Mary into something even worse."

He was afraid that was true. "Ach, I should get married again." He glanced toward the kinder, hoping they hadn't heard his outburst, but Libby was helping Abram build a block tower, probably with a view to knocking it down.

Daad chuckled. "Maybe you should, but not just to provide Mary with a woman to confide in."

"No, but . . . I can't help seeing that it's what we need." He frowned down at the tabletop. "It's been two years, and as gut as Mary is with them, the young ones need a mammi of their own. And I need someone to help. It's hard enough to be a minister even with a wife at your side. Alone . . ." He let that trail off.

Daad watched him, his faded blue eyes cautious and maybe a little amused. "Well, if you want a wife, then you should get to work on finding someone."

"It's not that easy." He replied seriously, even though he suspected Daad was teasing him. "It has to be someone mature, first of all. Someone who's willing to be a mother to my kinder. To take over the work of the house, to help me in ministering to the church. Someone wise and kind."

Daad's mouth twitched. "You have left something out. What about you? It should be a woman you love, ain't so?"

"I'm past the stage of falling in love. That's for teenagers."

He remembered the feeling, and very uncomfortable it had been. Wondering whether Donna cared about him at all, eager to see her and yet afraid of giving away too much too soon, the ups when she smiled at him and the despair when she let someone else drive her home from singing . . .

"You don't want to behave like a teenager again, but that doesn't mean you shouldn't look for love in a wife," Daad said. "You would be in for a long lifetime of getting along without it."

"I know." He struggled with his feelings, not wanting to let them out. "I just can't imagine loving anyone else the way I loved Donna. Besides," he said hurriedly, "how can I find someone? If I so much as nod to an unattached female after worship on Sunday, half the Gmay has us married."

Daad shook his head. "You are worrying too much about how to do it, Benuel. Maybe it would do you good to fall in love again. You love with your heart, not your mind."

"What are you talking about?" Mary came back in just then. "Or should I say who are you talking about?" Her challenging expression said she assumed they'd been discussing her.

Daad chuckled. "We were talking about finding a wife for your brother. Do you have any ideas?"

Standing back, hands on her hips, Mary looked him up and down, probably relieved that the focus was off her. "Ben's not a bad catch for someone his age. He ought to be able to find *someone* to marry him."

"Denke," he said, sarcasm lacing the word. "I'm not tottering on the edge of the grave yet."

"I know. Isn't that what I was just saying?" Mary's eyes lit suddenly. "I know what you need. You need someone like Barbie Lapp."

He stared at her, aghast. "What? Are you ferhoodled? Barbie Lapp is the last woman in the world who should be a minister's wife."

"Maybe that's what the church needs," Mary retorted. "Maybe that's what you need. Someone who'd lighten you up."

Daad chuckled and then tried to turn the sound into a cough when they both looked at him. "You like Barbie, ja?" he asked Mary.

Mary shrugged, the defensive look forming on her face. "Barbie's sympathetic. She's full of fun. And she can tell you what's what without scolding and making you feel small."

"Maybe that's because she's just as reckless as you are," Ben snapped.

Before Mary could respond in kind, Daad intervened. "Enough from both of you. There's no reason I know of to talk about a sister in the faith that way, Benuel. Mary, let's get supper dished up and feed these hungry kinder."

Abram punctuated the words by knocking over the block tower before Libby could, which led to tears on both sides. By the time Ben got them both calmed down and seated at the table, he felt as if he'd been through the wringer. He did need a wife. But he could never replace Donna, so where did that leave him?

Lancaster County, Spring 1960

Reuben Lapp made an effort to shake off his low spirits as he drove the gelding up the lane toward the barn. It wouldn't do to let Elizabeth see how concerned he was about their future. He was the man of the family. Elizabeth and any children they might have were his responsibility. He must take care of them.

The thought of kinder sent a spasm of pain into his heart, sharp as any knife. Little Matthias, the son they'd dreamed of, had gone before he'd taken his first breath. He blinked back tears. He couldn't let Elizabeth see his weakness. He had to be strong for her.

There would still be kinder—strong boys to help with the farm and sweet girls who would look like Elizabeth. He had to believe that, and he had to help Elizabeth believe it.

He could do it. But what he couldn't do was protect her from the changes that were coming to their way of life. Nobody could protect any of the Leit from the headlong drive of what the Englisch called progress.

Daad came out of the barn and stood waiting as Reuben approached. He'd be eager to hear Reuben's news and hoping it was good.

Reuben planted a smile on his face as he drew up. Daad took hold of the harness, looking like the Englisch notion of St. Nicholas with his curly white beard and round cheeks. He smiled back at Reuben, but his blue eyes were grave as he studied Reuben's face.

"How did you make out? Or isn't it gut to ask?"

Reuben shrugged. Moving together with the ease of long practice, they began to unharness the horse. "Wish I could say I had encouraging news, but I don't."

"Not about either place? Not the Harrisons' farm or the one that belongs to that Englisch family over toward Lancaster?"

"Nothing."

Reuben's jaw tightened as he thought about giving Elizabeth the news. Not that she'd have wanted to move over toward Lancaster anyway. She continued to believe he was going to find a farm to buy in their church district, even though she must know how unlikely that was.

Trouble was, she wasn't thinking reasonably on this subject. She was reacting with her heart, not her mind.

"Isn't Fred Harrison selling after all? I was certain-sure he'd put his place on the market this spring." Daad led Brownie clear of the buggy shafts.

"He's selling, all right. In fact, he's already sold." Reuben could hear the grim tone of his voice and wanted to soften it. But what was the use? Daad knew him too well to be fooled. "He sold out to some company that's going to break the farm up into half-acre lots and build houses on them. Another fine farm gone for good."

Daad made the complicated sound in his throat that expressed disapproval and disappointment at the same time. "Ach, I never thought a gut farmer like Fred would do such a thing."

"He was sorry. Maybe even regretting it, I'd say. But like he said, he doesn't have sons to take it over, and his daughter lives clear up in New York. Married to a doctor, she is. They're not going to farm it."

"You'd still think he'd want to sell to someone who'd farm the land. I hate to think it of him."

"Seems his wife's health isn't good, and the doctors want her to move out to the southwest. That takes money, and I guess the folks who run the building company have plenty to spare. More than anyone who was buying it for farmland could afford to spend."

Daad turned the gelding into the paddock and came back, shaking his head. "It's not for us to judge, that's certain-sure. What about the other place you heard about?"

"That's no good, either. I might as well have saved myself the trip." He grasped the shafts and pushed the buggy into place with a little more effort than he needed. "The owner decided not to sell now after all. It seems there's talk of a big new four-lane highway cutting right through the county. He figures his land would become real valuable if that happens, and he's willing to hang on to it until then."

Daad's forehead furrowed. "There was talk of that at the lumber yard when I went in. Some folks sounded pretty sure it would happen, and if it does, it would cut right through the settlement—splitting us in two, likely. After all, we can't take buggies on a four-lane highway."

"I hear there are those who think it would be gut, because it would bring more tourists in to gawk at us." Reuben's hands worked futilely, as if he could grasp the situation and bend it into place the way he would with a piece of chicken fence. "Some of the Leit are saying we should fight against the government building it."

"Ja, I've heard talk like that. Foolish talk." Daad sounded severe. "It's not our way to fight against the government. If we can't settle it any other way, we move on. We don't fight."

"I know." That was their history, after all. The Amish didn't fight. They took the Lord's teachings seriously. And they'd learned the futility of trying to stay where they were hated when their people were hunted down and killed in the time of persecution in Europe. Still, a man couldn't help the anger that welled up sometimes, even knowing it for a sin.

"I've heard rumors." Daad's expression was questioning. "Talk that some of the younger families are thinking of moving on. Starting a new settlement someplace else."

Reuben nodded slowly. He hadn't meant to tell Daad yet, but maybe it was for the best. "Johnny Stoltzfus, for one. Daniel King. And the younger Esch boys. They're all in the same boat I am— needing a farm and finding none available they can afford."

Daad didn't speak right away, and Reuben sensed he was measuring his words and trying to be fair. Finally he put a hand on Reuben's shoulder.

"You don't need to think about doing something right away. There's plenty of work here on the farm for all of us."

"That wouldn't be fair to Isaac and Becky. It's been settled for ages that Isaac would have the farm when you were ready to take it easier."

"That was before we knew how hard it would be to find farmland for you. Your mamm and I saved so we'd be able to help you buy a place. We didn't count on land being so dear. If you or Isaac wanted to do something other than farming . . ." he began.

Reuben shook his head. "That's something I won't do, and Isaac feels the same way. Farm life is what's right for Amish—the whole family working together, not having the father go off someplace else to work all day and hardly see his kinder."

"Ach, I can't argue with you there. Taking care of the Lord's earth is as close as a man can get to Heaven in this world. It's what I want for my kinder, that's certain-sure." He hesitated. "But I don't know how the women are going to feel about the notion of you moving away."

There it was, the thing he didn't want to think about. Elizabeth's reaction to the idea of leaving. "Elizabeth won't want to leave her family."

His voice was flat. He knew, only too well, how she felt about it. She'd always been close to her mother and sisters, and especially so since she lost the baby.

"Well, I guess that's the way it's always been," Daad said slowly. "I don't doubt our ancestors left the old country with the women looking back over their shoulders at what they were leaving behind. Still, if it has to be, they'll accept. You'll just have to help Elizabeth understand."

Daad gave him a final clap on the shoulder and turned away, leaving Reuben standing there, struggling with himself. Daad was right, that was certain-sure. He'd have to help Elizabeth understand.

But what if that was impossible? Then what?

Chapter Four

Barbie took a deep breath and forced herself to open the door to the café kitchen. She'd put off talking to her boss until after the morning rush, but she couldn't delay any longer. She hoped he'd agree to change her schedule now that she'd be juggling this job with working at the farm-stay.

When they'd finally had a chance to talk it over the previous day, Rebecca had been definite. Her marriage wasn't going to make a difference in having Barbie work with her. She'd insisted she couldn't care for the guests without Barbie's help. After all, Barbie was the outgoing one who actually liked entertaining the Englisch visitors.

She and Rebecca had come a long way in the past year. She knew perfectly well that Rebecca had thought her reckless and irresponsible, just as she'd thought Rebecca a shy stick-in-the-mud. Well, they'd both found out differently when Grossmammi pushed them into working together on the farm-stay, and Barbie knew she'd always be grateful. But at the same time, she didn't want to give up the little bit of freedom she experienced working here at the café.

"If you're coming in, come in and shut the door." Walt Tyler, the café owner, had a brusque, snarling manner that was like the bear he resembled —big, paunchy, and hairy. He was an excellent cook who kept an immaculate kitchen, though no one would think it to look at him.

She let the door swing closed behind her. "Do . . . do you have a minute, Mr. Tyler?"

He gave her a grudging smile. "Yeah, I guess so. What's up, Barbie? And don't tell me you're going to give me an excuse why that Ashlee didn't make it for the breakfast shift, because I wouldn't believe one of them."

"I won't . . . I mean, I don't know what happened to Ashlee. Maybe she's sick."

Ashlee had been showing up late too often, with Barbie and Jean, the elderly Englisch server, trying to cover for her.

Tyler's snort told her he didn't think much of Ashlee's likely illness. "Don't tell me you're going to quit on me. You and Jean are the only reliable servers I have."

"Nothing like that," she said, and plunged into her request. "I just hoped that for the next few months, you might schedule me for times other than Friday and Saturday."

"Are you sure you wouldn't like a three-course dinner thrown in?" He slammed a spatula on the cooktop. "I hired you because you claimed you'd be responsible, and now you want special treatment. Between you and Ashlee, pretty soon nobody will want to work."

Barbie refused to quake when he yelled. He didn't seem to think any less of people who stood up to him—in fact, she thought he preferred it.

"I've been very responsible," she said, keeping her voice firm. "All I'm asking is a change in the shifts. Jean would rather work more on the weekends and have off during the week, because she watches her grandkids. And I'd rather work weekdays so I can help my cousin on weekends. Doesn't that make sense?"

He glared at her, brows lowering, for what seemed forever. Then he gave a curt nod. "Okay. You and Jean fix up the schedule between you. Just make sure all the shifts are covered."

Barbie let out a breath of relief. "Thank you. We won't let you down."

"You better not." The scowl was back. "And if Miss Ashlee ever decides to show up, tell her I want to see her."

"Ja—yes, I will." She escaped, letting the door swing shut.

Poor Ashlee. It sounded as if she was in for it.

She rounded the corner from the kitchen and found herself face-to-face with Terry Gilliam, sitting on the end stool at the counter. He grinned at her, jerking his head toward the kitchen.

"Sounds like trouble in the kitchen. You okay, Barbie?"

"I . . . yes, I'm fine. Mr. Tyler always sounds that way." She could feel her cheeks growing warm. "I'm surprised to see you here."

His lips quirked. "I'll bet I'm more surprised." He nodded toward her dress. "Or is that a costume you wear for work?"

"No. No costume. I'm really Amish. I thought Ashlee might have told you." Her cheeks must be bright red by this time.

"So what was the other night? An experiment?"

Was he angry? She didn't think so, but it was hard to tell since she didn't really know him.

"No. At least, not exactly. Ashlee and I got to talking about the differences between Amish and Englisch, and, well, she sort of egged me on to see what a night out was like for her."

"You must not have liked it. You didn't stay long." He actually sounded disappointed.

"It wasn't that," she said quickly. "I enjoyed meeting you. And your friends. But there was a girl there I knew who was obviously headed for trouble, and I thought I'd better take her home."

He tilted his head to the side, considering. "That's all?"

"Yes, of course." Had he been offended that she'd hurried away when they'd been talking? She'd never thought of such a thing.

"Too bad you had to rush off." He touched her fingers where they rested on the countertop.

"We were just getting to know each other. You couldn't let the girl take care of herself?"

"She was only sixteen." Startled, she gave him a look to see if he really was as flippant as he sounded.

He shrugged. "Plenty of sixteen-year-old girls can take care of themselves."

"She couldn't." She was irrationally disappointed in him.

"Hey, don't be mad. I'm a great believer in letting people do what they want, that's all. If you felt like you had to interfere, that's okay by me. I hope that doesn't mean you won't be around in the future, though. We need to finish our conversation."

She found herself nodding, responding to the twinkle in his eyes. Maybe there was a lot to be said for being easygoing. At least he wasn't as stiff-necked as Benuel.

She caught a sidelong glimpse of Mr. Tyler, moving by the pass-through on the kitchen side. If he glanced this way, he'd think she was wasting time.

"Would you like something?" she asked quickly. "Coffee?"

Terry nodded. "Black, two sugars. And a cruller."

"You have a sweet tooth," she teased.

"Goes with my sweet personality," he said.

With a ripple of laughter, she went to get his

order. She'd just set the coffee and cruller in front of him when she spotted Ashlee slip in the side door.

"Ashlee. Thank goodness you're here. Are you okay?"

"Fine." The word came out as a snarl. Ashlee yanked off her sunglasses and blinked as if the light hurt her eyes. She was pale, her lipstick put on crooked, and she stared blearily at Barbie. "Did you cover for me?"

"We tried, but it didn't work." She glanced toward the kitchen. "He wants to see you."

"Sounds like you didn't try very hard," Ashlee snapped. She marched off to the kitchen.

Barbie blinked. What did Ashlee expect? The small café wasn't crowded today, and all Mr. Tyler had to do was glance out of the kitchen to see that she was missing.

"I wouldn't take anything she says seriously. She's hungover." Terry sent a doubtful look her way. "That means—"

"I know what it means," she interrupted. "Just because I'm Amish, I didn't grow up under a rock. I saw my brothers in that condition a time or two during their rumspringa."

Terry nodded as if the word meant something to him. "Time to run wild, right? At least for the guys."

Barbie shook her head, wondering if it was worth it to try to correct the common myth. "It's not that at all. Rumspringa is a time when Amish teens have freedom to mingle with others their age, to start figuring out who you're going to marry. Some kids do get carried away, and there's a certain amount of drinking."

Her own teen years had been happy but uneventful, but there were always stories of Amish kids who took a wilder track. She glanced toward the kitchen, wondering how Ashlee was doing.

"I wouldn't worry about Ashlee," Terry said, correctly interpreting her look. "She always lands on her feet."

"I hope so." Ashlee liked to have fun. There was nothing wrong with that, but she'd hate to lose her job.

But when Ashlee came out a few minutes later, she was putting on her apron. Apparently she'd smoothed things over with Mr. Tyler, one way or another. She paused by Barbie.

"Hey, I'm sorry. That was my headache talking earlier."

"No problem." She echoed the words she'd heard Ashlee use often. "Maybe some coffee would help."

Ashlee nodded carefully, as if her head might slip off. She headed for the coffeepot.

"See? All settled," Terry said. "Now, when are you coming out with Ashlee again?"

"I don't know." Much as she enjoyed talking

to Terry, her first excursion had left a bad taste in Barbie's mouth.

He raised one eyebrow. "Maybe you and I could go someplace together. Do something quieter, like dinner or a movie."

He looked very appealing, sitting there with that easy smile on his face. She felt her enthusiasm rise and nearly said yes. But she'd better think this through.

Besides, it never hurt to let a guy wonder.

"Maybe," she said lightly, and turned away as the bell rang on the door.

They grew busy enough that there wasn't another chance for any private exchanges with Terry. But he caught her eye as he left. Grinning, he winked at her.

By the time her shift was over, Barbie was relieved to find things had returned to normal with Ashlee. In fact, Ashlee hurried to catch up with her as she started to leave.

"Hey, wait up." Ashlee thrust an envelope into Barbie's hand. "Jean says someone left this for you by the cash register." Her eyes sparkled. "Maybe it's a note from Terry."

"I doubt it." She studied Ashlee's face. "Are you sure you're all right?"

"Fine." There was an edge to the word that warned her off. "I better get back to work. I said I'd do an extra shift to make up for being late today. Let's go out again soon. You owe me a whole evening, remember." She hurried back inside.

Barbie went slowly through the motions of harnessing the mare to the buggy. Go out with Ashlee again? Go out with Terry? She wanted to explore that new world, and she didn't want to lose the friendship she'd started with either of them, so why did she hesitate?

Maybe Grossmammi had been lucky to grow up when she did. She'd had her sorrow, but at least she hadn't had to juggle two worlds and try to decide where she belonged.

It would be nice to think she could talk the whole issue over with someone who wouldn't judge, but she didn't know anyone who didn't have a bias when it came to being or not being Amish.

As she climbed into the buggy, the envelope crackled, reminding her. She settled on the seat, ripping it open. Maybe somebody had chosen this odd way of leaving her a tip.

But no money fell out. Just a small piece of lined paper that looked as if it had been torn from a notebook. The message on it was printed in pencil.

Don't think you'll get away with leading innocents astray. Someone is always watching.

Lancaster County, Spring 1960

Elizabeth forced herself to keep smiling as she entered the front room at her sister Lovina's house for the quilting frolic. Not because of the quilting, but because today they had met to complete a crib quilt for Cousin Jessie's baby.

Her heart twisted. The last time she'd come to a quilting frolic, they'd been doing the crib quilt for Matthias.

This is Jessie's time. It would be unkind not to celebrate with her or to draw attention away from the joy of the day.

"Here we are," Mamm announced. She'd insisted on stopping to pick up Elizabeth today. Maybe she'd thought Elizabeth would need a little support. "You didn't start without us already, did you?"

"We've been gossiping," Lovina said, her cheeks pink with pleasure at having them all at her house. She hugged Mamm and then pressed her cheek against Elizabeth's, holding her close for an extra moment.

"That's as much fun as quilting." Anna, Elizabeth's other sister, hurried over to get her share of the hugs. "You'd think we didn't see one another for a month instead of most every day."

Anna and Lovina were very alike, with only a little over a year between them. They both had soft brown hair that persisted in curling no matter how severely they pulled it back. They had identical hazel eyes, but where Lovina's chin was softly rounded, Anna's came to a point like a heart. And they both regarded Elizabeth as their baby sister, to be chided and encouraged and helped along the way.

There had been a point in her life when Elizabeth had resented their big-sister bossiness, but now she felt nothing but gratitude. She could never have gone through the past year without them.

Cousin Jessie, heavy with the last months of pregnancy, blew Elizabeth a kiss. "I'd try to hug you, but something keeps getting in the way." She patted her belly, face curving in a sweet smile, her gaze seeming to go inward. The forthcoming baby would never be mentioned in mixed company, but among women, it was another story. How could they help it?

Elizabeth's smile faltered. She remembered the feeling Jessie had now—that time when the life inside a woman occupied so much of her attention that she hardly had any to spare for the world outside her own body.

"Well, let's get to work," Lovina announced, starting toward the quilting frame. Maybe she'd noticed Elizabeth's reaction, but if so, she would be tactful. Lovina was always so quick to think of others' feelings.

There was a shuffle of pulling up chairs around

the frame. It was an adjustable frame, shortened to fit the crib quilt. The five of them were plenty around the small quilt. Any more people, and they'd have been getting in one another's way.

Everyone exclaimed at how fine the quilt top had turned out. It was a traditional log cabin design, but done in pale shades of pink and yellow and green instead of the deep, saturated colors common to Amish quilts. Lovina had done most of the piecing, with some help from Anna. Now the layers of top, batting, and back were put together like a sandwich and stretched out on the frame, ready for the quilting stitches.

Each woman's movement echoed the others' as they threaded needles, slipped thimbles into place, and readied themselves for the first stitch, right hands on top, left hands underneath. Mamm smiled at Jessie as if in silent acknowledgement of her babe. Then she took the first stitch and the others joined in, each one working on the space directly in front of her.

Elizabeth swallowed the lump in her throat and focused on the hands, dipping and swooping like so many birds over the surface of the quilt, making tiny, even stitches. No one would admit to pride in her work of course, but on a project like this, a person certain-sure didn't want her stitches to be larger or more uneven than her neighbor's.

The talk began to flow again—about babies, naturally. Anna began it, innocently enough, with the mention that her little Jonah was teething. From teething remedies to feeding problems to sleeping issues—everyone had something to contribute. Everyone but Elizabeth.

I will not spoil this time for Jessie. But despite her intentions, the lump in her throat was getting to unmanageable size. With a muttered excuse about getting a drink of water, she fled to the kitchen.

She was gripping the sink with both hands, forcing the tears back, when Mamm joined her a moment later. She heard her step and then felt Mamm's work-worn hand patting her back, just as Mamm had done when she'd been a tiny girl frightened by a bad dream.

"I'm sorry," Mamm said. "You didn't have to come."

"I thought I was ready. I want to be ready." She brushed away a tear. "Surely I'll start another baby soon, ain't so?"

"I pray it every day," Mamm said gently. "But it is in God's hands. When the time is right, it will happen."

Elizabeth nodded. Sometimes it was hard to accept what happened as God's will, but there was no other choice. She filled a glass with water, drained it, and took a deep breath. "I'm all right. Let's go back in."

Mamm gave her a searching look. She seemed satisfied with what she saw, because she nodded.

Together they went back to the quilting frame.

Maybe Lovina had said something to the others while she'd been in the kitchen. In any event, the talk had left the subject of babies and turned to chatter about the community's young people. That was an endless source of fascination as each rumspringa group began making the first tentative steps toward matching up with each other.

Everyone had something to contribute, whether it was a rumor about who had taken whom home after a singing or who had coaxed his parents into a new courting buggy.

"All I can say is," Lovina declared, "that some of those boys are more interested in buying a new buggy than in doing the courting that's supposed to come with it."

"Ach, don't tell me that," Mamm chided. "Didn't your Sam talk his folks into a new buggy when the two of you started courting? And weren't you pleased as could be to sit up beside him in that new rig?"

Even Lovina chuckled at that, though her cheeks were pink.

"Why is it men are so fascinated by a new piece of equipment or a vehicle?" Elizabeth managed to sound normal. "If somebody gets a new cultivator, half the men in the church district will make an excuse to stop by so they can look at it."

"And the time they spend over a piece of equipment," Jessie said. "You'd think it was the prettiest thing in the world instead of a farm tool."

Anna nudged her. "Not like us, when you came over to see the fabric I got when I went to that big new fabric store over toward Lancaster."

A ripple of laughter circled the quilting frame—the sound of women working together, laughing over the differences between the sexes just like women had been doing for countless generations. Elizabeth's gaze swept from face to face, her love welling up. This had to be the best part of the day—to be here in her sister's familiar front room, surrounded by the women who had been part of her life since before she was born.

"Well, whatever you say, I still think men get excited about the silliest things," Jessie said. "My Eli came home from the mill all upset because there's talk again about the state building a big highway right across the county."

"If it took some of the cars off the roads we use, that might be a gut thing," Anna said. "Somebody near sideswiped our buggy on the way home from worship last week."

"Eli says it would split the community in half," Jessie said. "I didn't understand it all, but it seems like we wouldn't be able to get across the new road with horse and buggy. Imagine having to go miles out of your way to get to worship."

"Ach, it will probably come to nothing in the end," Lovina said. "That's the way with a lot of the fancy plans the government makes."

"Well, and if they do, we'll adjust." Mamm's voice was calm. "We always do, no matter how the Englisch world changes."

They all nodded, but Anna looked troubled. "Seems to me there's more to be worried about with the farmland it would eat up. Like all those building projects. Progress, they call it, putting up houses and stores right on land that should be growing food to feed people."

Jessie nodded. "Eli says that, too. Eli says that if the price of farmland keeps going up the way it is, we might not be able to buy farms for our kinder when they're grown."

Jessie was prone to quote Eli on any and every subject, as if he were the wisest man she knew. Elizabeth saw her sisters exchange glances and knew they were thinking the same thing she was—how did Eli get to be such an expert?

"Ach, I'm sure prices will always go up some," Mamm said comfortably. "At the same time, we're getting more for our milk, so maybe it evens out in the long run."

Jessie shook her head—surprisingly, since she wouldn't normally disagree with her aunt. "I don't know. Eli has heard that some families are already planning to leave Lancaster County to start a daughter community somewhere else."

"Are you sure?" Lovina spoke what Elizabeth was thinking. "I can't imagine any of our brethren up and moving away."

Jessie looked nettled that her Eli's word was being doubted. "Eli says so. He says John Stoltzfus actually went out to the valleys beyond Harrisburg looking at land. In fact, he says—" She stopped abruptly.

"He says what?" Anna leaned toward her, needle suspended as if she'd forgotten it.

Jessie colored. "He says John told him some others were interested, too. He mentioned the Esch boys and Daniel King and . . . well, and Reuben."

Elizabeth stared at her, trying to take in the words. Reuben? Her Reuben? Surely not. He would never consider such a thing. Would he? She remembered his fruitless search for a farm, the way he'd talked about the future, and there suddenly seemed to be a weight on her chest, pressing all the air out of her.

Reuben wouldn't expect her to move away from everything she knew. He couldn't.

From his seat at the front on the men's side, Benuel glanced around at the Gmay assembling for worship in the Esch family's barn on Sunday morning. They had filed in as always from eldest to youngest, taking their places in a silence that somehow seemed intense after the chatter of voices outside where the women had drawn together, greeting one another, while the men did the same, shaking hands all around.

The group of young boys who were finally considered old enough to sit with their peers instead of their daads were the last in, taking their places in the front row where they were under the eyes of the whole congregation. Ben vividly remembered the first worship when he'd been able to join them, the mingling of pride and nervousness at what was yet another recognized step on the road to becoming an adult.

He could see the women's side easily from here, not that he would stare. But he glanced at Mary, noting that she sat with hands folded and eyes downcast. He could only hope she was considering her wrongdoing and repenting it.

Barbie Lapp was in the row behind Mary, sitting between the unmarried younger women and those who were newly married or young mothers. Most likely they were members of Barbie's rumspringa gang, all married and with kinder already.

Even as he watched, she leaned forward to murmur something to Mary, who responded with a quick smile and a sparkling glance. Ben's stomach churned. It would suit him far better if Barbie had nothing at all to say to his sister. What kind of example was she setting for the younger girls with her behavior?

The Voorsinger glanced at the three ministers. Apparently satisfied that they were ready, he raised his voice in the opening hymn, the rest of the voices joining in on the long drawn-out notes.

Ben automatically stood with the other two ministers as they filed out for their time of consulting with one another over who was to preach the sermons today. In the absence of the bishop, who was visiting another church district, two of them would speak.

Given the turmoil his thoughts were in, he'd be just as pleased if he wasn't picked. He looked from Ezra King to Jonas Fisher—the one bent and gray-bearded, the other ruddy and comfortably rotund, firmly settled into his middle years. They'd taken on more than their fair share of the responsibility for the church district since his wife's death, and he'd been grateful to have their strength and example to support him.

His thoughts returned, willy-nilly, to Barbie Lapp. Ordinarily he'd have confided his discovery of Barbie's activities to them. Together they'd have prayed over the situation, consulted the bishop, and then two of them would have called on the Lapp family to confront the backslider and bring her to repentance.

He hadn't, and that decision still ate at him as they grouped up at the paddock gate for their consultation. He kept having second thoughts. It wasn't too late. He could tell them now, seek their guidance, and shift the responsibility to them.

No, he couldn't. To do so meant exposing Mary as well, and while that might be the proper course, he couldn't do that to Daad. How could

Ben add to his father's burdens by letting the whole church district know about Mary? Because that's what would happen. No matter how firmly they kept silent, folks would know they'd been to call and would put two and two together to make ten, most likely.

"Ben, you are very quiet this morning." Ezra's creaky old voice was husky. "Thinking about a sermon topic?"

Ben blinked, trying to come up with a reasonable excuse. But even as he delayed, Jonas clapped him on the shoulder.

"Gut. I've a thought I've been mulling over that would be just right for the short sermon, I think. Ezra's fighting a cold, so how about you take the long one? We'll give him a rest this morning, ain't so?"

What could he do but nod? In normal circumstances he'd have been preparing all week, just in case it came to him to speak. But this week he'd been totally occupied with his fears for Mary's future, his concern for Daad, and his growing frustration over his inability to bring Barbie to a realization of the dangerous road she was traveling.

A thought struck him, so sudden and clear that maybe it was a sign from God.

"There's a duty that's been weighing on me this week—our responsibility to act in such a way that we don't cause a weaker brother or sister to stumble."

Ezra studied him solemnly for a moment. Then he nodded. "If that's on your mind, the Lord must intend for you to speak to it, ain't so?"

The weight he'd been carrying seemed to slip away, like a draft horse shedding the heavy harness and trotting away from the plow. He should have realized sooner that scripture would have the answer he sought. He could say everything that should be said, and if Barbie felt herself accused, maybe that was the way it should be.

Chapter Five

Since it was a warm spring day, the men and boys had set up the lunch tables under the trees behind the King house, and people had hung around longer than usual, enjoying the sunshine and catching up on all the news. Barbie waited, watching for her chance, not caring how long it took. She was going to have it out with Benuel Kauffmann.

The idea of it—preaching a sermon that had been directed at her. No one else could have known, but that didn't make it any better. He'd actually looked right at her when he'd spoken the words from scripture. Well, she intended to tell him exactly what she thought of him, taking advantage of his position to scold her that way.

If he thought—

A green ball rolled bumpily across the grass and bounced against her ankles. She bent to grab it and found little Abram Kauffmann running toward her, arms outstretched for his ball.

She couldn't help smiling at the wide grin on his face. Abram had a look of his father about him, but it was certain-sure she'd never seen Ben look that carefree.

"Here it comes, Abram." She bent to toss the ball gently toward the child. "Catch it."

"I will. I'll get it." He held out both hands and by some miracle actually closed them around the ball. He looked at it with astonishment.

"Gut catch." She sent a quick glance around. Nobody would thank her for encouraging him if he hit someone in the head with it. Especially Benuel, not that his opinion mattered to her. "Roll it to me." That would be safer.

Abram nodded. He bent, his small face crinkling with concentration as he eyed the distance between them. He gave the ball a mighty push. It came straight, bounced on a tussock of grass, and veered off. Grinning, she ran after it, catching it before it rolled into a chattering group of older women.

"Here it comes." She rolled it back, beginning to wonder how she was going to ease herself out of this game so she could have words with the boy's father.

As Abram scrambled after the ball, his little sister toddled toward them.

"Me, me," she cried. She sent a ravishing look at Barbie with a pair of huge, bright blue eyes.

Barbie grinned. If Benuel thought he was having trouble with Mary, wait until this little charmer hit rumspringa.

Abram, meanwhile, was showing a tendency to hold his pleasure to himself. He wrapped both arms around the ball and shook his head, eyebrows lowering. "Mine," he announced.

"Three is more fun than two," Barbie said quickly. "You roll it to Libby, she rolls it to me, and I roll it back to you. It makes a triangle, right?"

Apparently struck by that way of looking at it, Abram rolled his precious ball to his little sister, who crowed with joy and ran after it.

Moses, who must have been looking after his grandchildren, walked over to watch, smiling. With Libby involved, the game took on a more erratic turn, since the ball seldom went where she wanted it to. Barbie saw Abram growing restive.

"Kick it to me this time," she said, hoping to distract him. "Go on, give it a boot."

Abram placed it carefully in front of him, drew back his leg, overbalanced, and fell on his bottom. His lower lip puckered, probably more in embarrassment than hurt. Barbie ran to scoop him up in a hug.

"You're okay. Let's try again." Hands on his small shoulders, she steadied him as he kicked again, connecting firmly this time. Letting go, she ran after the ball.

It bounced crazily over the grass and fetched up against a pair of legs in black broad-fall trousers. Barbie skidded to a stop. Benuel. It would be, just when she was acting like a child.

He picked up the ball with a brief nod. Was there a trace of embarrassment in the way he turned quickly away toward his family? If there wasn't, there should be, she decided.

"We should be going soon. Where's Mary? I thought she was watching the kinder."

Moses ambled over. "What's the hurry? I told Mary to run off and talk to her girlfriends. The young ones have been having a grand time with Barbie."

"No doubt Mary and her girlfriends are comparing notes on what they'll wear to the singing tonight," Barbie said. "I see the King boys are putting the volleyball net up already."

She nodded to the level field beside the barn where several teenagers were erecting the net. They'd look forward to a game later before moving into the barn for tonight's singing.

"I suppose." Ben clamped his lips tightly, no doubt to keep from saying that he didn't think

Mary should be joining the other teenagers for tonight's fun. "All the more reason for us to get home before it's time to turn around and bring her back."

Now or never, Barbie thought. "I'd like a few words before you leave." She could be just as firm as he could.

"No, no." Abram grabbed Barbie's skirt, and Libby hurled herself at her legs. "Play more."

Moses bent to peel them away before Ben could speak. "We'll take a break for some lemonade. That will taste fine, ain't so?"

Talking gently, he eased his grandchildren away, leaving Barbie to stare up at Benuel.

She knew just what she wanted to say to him. Instead, she found her thoughts on his attitude toward the singing. "I take it you think Mary shouldn't be coming tonight."

He bent a forbidding look on her. "It doesn't matter what I think. Daad made the decision to let her attend."

"Lucky for Mary her father has more sense than you. If you don't want her looking for fun and excitement someplace else, you'd best let her find it in the community."

Ben appeared to grit his teeth. "She ought to be punished for what she did." *And so should you,* his expression said.

Barbie made an effort to speak calmly. "If you do that, everyone will be wondering why she's not allowed to be there. They'll probably come up with something much worse than the truth."

"Nothing could be worse than the truth." Anger flared in his eyes, setting a match to her own.

"You are impossible. I suppose that was why you decided to preach a sermon aimed directly at me this morning. I'm surprised you didn't call me by name as a terrible example."

His jaw hardened, if that was possible. "I didn't say anything that wasn't true."

"There's a difference between telling the truth and interfering." She glared at him.

"I am a minister. It's my job to interfere when one of the Leit is drifting away." He returned the look doubly.

Much as she wanted to hold on to the anger, Barbie couldn't help seeing how ridiculous they must look, standing here glaring at each other. Her perverse sense of humor bubbled up through her anger.

"I know," she said. "That's why I'm so mad at you."

His surprise gave way to an answering gleam of humor in his eyes, startling her. Benuel was actually attractive when he almost smiled.

"Truth has a way of doing that," he agreed. "I expect that's why your words about Mary and the singing annoyed me so much."

She nodded, accepting what might have been a slight apology.

The next instant the rare warmth disappeared from his eyes. "All the same, I'd rather you stay away from my little sister."

Barbie's chin came up. "Fine. I'd be delighted if it will save me from any more lectures from you."

She thought he'd snap back at her. Instead, he spun and walked away.

Lancaster County, Spring 1960

Reuben ran his hand down the pony's cannon bone, and Dolly obediently lifted her hoof. The hooves were badly overgrown after a winter in the pasture with nothing to wear them down. She'd be more comfortable with them trimmed back a bit.

He'd put her in cross-ties in the barn, not that it was necessary. Dolly knew perfectly well what he was doing.

The shaggy black-and-white pony had taught all of them how to drive the pony cart. He had an inward smile for the thought. Oh, Daadi had given the instructions, but it was Dolly who knew what to do. He'd tried to persuade her into a gallop once when Daad wasn't watching. She'd turned her head, looked at him, and trotted patiently on, ignoring his urgings.

Over twenty now, she was. Ponies lived a *gut* long time, but he doubted she'd be around when his and Elizabeth's *kinder* were ready to learn to drive the pony cart. Dolly deserved a peaceful retirement.

The thought flickered through his mind to start looking for a suitable pony, but he dismissed it. There was little point in doing that until their future was determined. If they ended up moving—well, then it made more sense to wait until they were settled.

The worry that hung heavy on his mind reared up again. Time was moving on. Ideally he hoped to have the matter settled by fall. That was a gut time to buy, giving him the winter to plan the planting and prepare the fields for the next growing season.

If only . . . The thought slid away as a shadow crossed the shaft of sunlight that lay on the barn floor. He glanced up to see Elizabeth coming toward him.

"Back from the quilting frolic, ja? Did you get Cousin Jessie's quilt finished? And find plenty to talk about with your mamm and sisters?"

"It's done, ja. As for the talk . . ." She drew in a breath, and as quickly as that Reuben realized something was wrong.

He straightened. "Elizabeth? Was ist letz?"

She stared at him, her eyes wide and somehow almost frightened. "It's Cousin Jessie. She said she'd heard that John Stoltzfus and some others were thinking of starting a daughter settlement elsewhere. And she said you were one of them."

Reuben clenched his teeth. Drat Jessie. He'd

been trying to keep things quiet until he'd broken it to Elizabeth in his own time.

And when would that time have come? his conscience murmured. He didn't have an answer, and that added to his annoyance.

"Your Cousin Jessie is a blabbermaul," he muttered. He'd like to stay focused on the pony's hoof, but he suspected that wasn't going to work. He set the foot down, dropping the nippers he'd picked up, and Dolly turned her head to give him an inquiring look.

"Jessie was repeating what Eli told her. Is he a blabbermaul, too?"

The edge in his gentle Elizabeth's voice took him by surprise. It was foreign to everything he knew about her.

He patted Dolly's graying muzzle, buying time to arrange his thoughts. "All right. Now, don't be upset, but I have talked to John a little about his plans."

"Without telling me." The hurt in her face reproached him.

"I didn't want you to start worrying about it until I knew a little more, that's all. Nothing's been decided. So far Johnny and the others are just thinking about it. There's no harm in talking about their plans, is there?"

"I guess not, as long as it's just talk." Some of the rigidity seemed to leave her, and she stroked the pony's back absently, as if hardly aware of what she did. "Then you're not really wanting to go away."

He was tempted to assure her that he wasn't just to get to the end of this conversation. But that wouldn't be fair. Elizabeth had a stake in any decision.

"We have to find a place of our own," he said. "Isaac and Becky will be starting a family of their own before long, and this place will go to them. It's best if we get settled before that time comes, ain't so?"

She nodded, and he wondered if he'd imagined that she'd winced when he'd spoken of Isaac and Becky starting a family.

"I understand all that, but I always thought we'd be finding a place somewhere close. Maybe even a little nearer to my folks. Why can't we do it that way?"

"Because there's nothing available." He heard his voice rise and reined it back. "You know I've been following up everything that might be for sale. Either the farms are already earmarked to stay in the family, or they're being sold to outsiders for outrageous amounts of money. If things keep going the way they are, pretty soon nobody will be able to afford farmland in Lancaster County."

Elizabeth was shaking her head, seeming unable to take it in. "But . . . how can that be? Our people have always farmed here. Even the Englisch think that's a gut idea, the way they're advertising for tourists to come and visit to see the Amish."

"I know." The contradiction wasn't lost on him. "It wonders me what they're thinking, inviting people to come here because of the Amish with one hand and making it too hard or too expensive for us to live here with the other."

"But surely they'll see it. Something will happen to turn things around. It has to."

He wished he could believe it. "I don't know what. You can't stop progress—that's what I hear everyplace I go."

Elizabeth pressed her fingers against her temples. He thought she was within an inch of putting her palms over her ears, like a child desperate not to hear unwelcome news.

"I know you don't want to accept it." He reached out to touch her arm, half-wanting to draw her into his arms and half-afraid that if he did, he might not be able to say what he had to. "But we must look at things the way they are. If we can't find farmland here, I don't see any choice but to move."

"You could do something else. You don't have to be a farmer." She blurted the words out.

Reuben stiffened, his hand dropping to his side. "I'm a farmer, Elizabeth. It's what I've always been and what I've always wanted. Our kinder must grow up on a farm the way we did, working the land, caring for the animals, all of us working and sharing together."

She didn't answer, and he tried again.

"There's nothing wrong with moving on. It's what the Amish have always done. If living a separate life becomes impossible where we are, we don't fight and we don't change. We move on to where we can live the way God calls us to."

Elizabeth shook her head, and he wasn't even sure she'd taken it in.

He tried a third time. "Those who are thinking of it aren't talking about going far away. Just maybe down to Maryland or out to the valleys in central Pennsylvania. It's not like going to the other side of an ocean."

"Don't!" She shook her head again, tears welling in her eyes. "I can't. I never thought you would do such a thing."

He stiffened, feeling as if they stood on either side of a chasm that was getting deeper with every word they spoke.

"Elizabeth, I will do my best to find a place here in the county, close to family. But if I don't succeed, I'll have to think of leaving. I'm your husband, and I have a duty to take care of you and any children we have."

Elizabeth stood staring at him. Then she turned away. With a muffled sob, she stumbled toward the barn door and out of his sight, leaving him berating himself.

He shouldn't have said it that way. He should

have comforted her, reassured her, and tried to win her over.

But he'd only said what was true. He was the head of the family. The decision and the responsibility were his, and he couldn't shirk them.

A quiet Sunday evening at home gave Barbie more time to think than she appreciated. She'd rather be playing a lively game, but no one would join her on the Sabbath.

Did Benuel feel he'd discharged his duties toward her with that pointed sermon that morning? Or should she be ready for further repercussions?

She put away the last few dishes from supper as Mamm sat down at the table, automatically picking up a patch from the quilt she was piecing. Mamm never could just sit. She always had to be doing something.

Daad was just the same. He sat at the end of the table, whittling a small toy animal for one of his grandkids—probably a goat for young Sammy, from the look of it. Sammy was crazy about goats and couldn't wait until he was old enough to raise them all by himself.

That reminded her of Grossmammi, showing her a crib quilt she'd made with her sisters and cousin. Quilting frolics never went out of style among the Amish, at least. Grossmammi had seemed to gaze into the past, to a time when her family had been close by instead of far off in Lancaster County. Funny that she'd never thought, until Grossmammi had started telling her stories, how hard it must have been to move here. And even funnier that Barbie found the place so boring that sometimes she longed to be anywhere else.

The sound of wheels drew her attention to the lane outside. A buggy drew up to the back door, and her heart sank when she recognized the driver. Benuel Kauffmann.

This was it, then. Ben had decided that his sermon wasn't enough, probably because of her angry reaction to it. No doubt he had come as minister to inform her parents of her misdeeds.

Barbie's heart clenched. This would hurt them so much. Why, oh why, had she let herself get involved with Mary?

"Who is it, Barbie?" Mamm was already picking up the coffeepot, weighing it in her hand to see if there was enough left from supper for visitors.

Daad swept wood shavings from the table into his palm and dumped them into the trash can. "One of the kids, most likely."

"It's Ben Kauffmann," she said reluctantly. "And his daad."

That was odd. If Ben had come on an official call, she'd expect him to have one of the other ministers with him, or even the bishop.

"Well, let them in," Mamm said impatiently. "Don't stand there mooning, Barbie."

"Right." She went to the door, opening it and surprising Ben with his fist raised to knock. She met his gaze with a pronounced glare, then stepped back from the door. "Komm in."

Nodding curtly, Ben walked into the kitchen, followed closely by his father, who had a smile for Barbie that took the edge off her mix of fear and anger.

Moses's friendliness argued against a confrontation, but why else would they be here? Taking a steadying breath, she closed the door and followed them, barely noticing Mamm and Daad's greetings and Mamm's inevitable insistence that they must be hungry and thirsty.

"Denke, but just the coffee, please." Moses settled himself at the table, folding gnarled hands in front of him. "We're here to talk to Barbie, mostly, but to you as well."

Mamm looked startled, but she finished pouring the coffee and sat down while Daad laid aside his whittling knife.

"We're listening, Moses. What can we do for you?" Daad glanced at Barbie, and she slid into a chair.

"Well, it's this way." Moses stared at his hands. "Ach, this is difficult to say."

Barbie's heart sank. So it would be Moses who would tell her parents. He'd been hurt by what

106

his daughter had done, but now he'd cause her parents that same hurt.

"Just take your time," Mamm said, casting a swift glance at Daad. "We're listening."

"It's our Mary." Once the first words were out, Moses seemed to find it easier going. "The thing is, we're having a lot of problems with her."

"Is the child ill?" Mamm asked with quick sympathy.

"No, no." Moses shook his head. "Not ill. Just . . . rebellious. Ach, well, I suppose the truth is that she needs a woman to talk to. She's a teen-ager now, and it seems all she can think about is arguing with the way things are and even breaking the rules."

Barbie's stomach seemed to clench.

"She needs a woman to talk to, like I said. If her mamm were still with us . . . But try as we do, Benuel and I can't seem to get through to her." He glanced at Mamm. "I know you're thinking that it ought to be her older sister she's turning to, but the truth is that she and Sarah have never gotten on well."

Mamm nodded. "We'd be wonderful glad to do anything we can." There was a note in her voice that seemed to ask what that might be.

"I've thought about it and thought about it, and the thing is that our Mary has developed an admiration for Barbie."

"For me?" Barbie's voice came out in a squeak.

"But I . . ." She stopped, not wanting to betray anything she didn't have to.

"So I was thinking that maybe if Barbie would take Mary under her wing, like, it might be a big help to my girl."

"Of course, of course," Daad said before Barbie could find her voice. "Barbie will help."

"Um, ja, for sure," she mumbled, wondering how on earth she could get out of this. "I'm just not sure what I can do."

Glancing up, she caught the full glare of Benuel's eyes. He was hating this even more than she was, obviously.

"Just make a friend of the child," Mamm said, and there was a warning in her voice. "That's not hard."

"How? I can't just walk in on her and invite her to talk to me. That would turn her off for sure." Didn't they see that? But Mamm was giving her the frown that said she didn't want to hear objections.

"I thought maybe Mary could help out at the farm-stay if you and your cousin are willing," Moses said, appealing directly to her. "She'd like getting away from home, and she's a fine worker. But we wouldn't expect you to pay her."

She was well and truly trapped, with Mamm and Daad looking on approvingly and Moses appealing to her. Ben was the only one who might object, but he apparently wasn't going to, no matter how he hated the idea.

Barbie tried to sound upbeat. "There's plenty to do getting the place ready for guests. And we'd certain-sure want to pay her something for helping. But will Mary want to come?"

"I'll tell her you asked for her," Moses said quickly. "Just talk to Rebecca and let us know when you want her."

He rose as he spoke, as if eager to get away before she could change her mind. Or maybe he was embarrassed at having admitted Mary's problems to her parents. If so, that was ironic.

"We're sehr glad our Barbie can help you." Daad glanced at Mamm. "She'll do everything she can."

Barbie nodded, but her heart felt like lead. Why, knowing what he did, would Moses think she'd be a good influence on his daughter? And how could she advise the girl when she had such questions herself?

She jerked her attention back to the moment. Moses was turning down Mamm's renewed offers of food, and Benuel strode out the door with a quick good-bye as if he couldn't get away fast enough.

With a glance, Daad gathered them to go outside to see Moses and Ben off. Barbie suppressed the urge to disappear.

Chance put her close to Ben while her parents

and his father were saying their good-byes. She couldn't resist saying something.

"You're hating this, aren't you?"

His strong jaw clamped, looking as if it had been formed of iron. "My father appreciates your efforts." He ground out the words. "I will be watching you."

The words jolted her with their reminder of the anonymous note she'd received. "Did you send me that letter?"

As soon as the words were out, she knew he hadn't. He stared at her blankly for a moment.

"What letter?"

She shook her head, sorry she'd mentioned it. "Nothing. Never mind."

"It's not nothing. What letter—"

"Ready, Ben?" Moses was climbing into the buggy.

"Ja, coming." Ben sent her a look that promised a renewal of his question at the earliest opportunity.

How had she gotten committed to this crazy scheme? Didn't Moses realize how foolish it was to ask a woman who was already skating dangerously near the line of being Amish to act as guide to a rebellious girl?

And if something bad happened to Mary now, she had no doubt she'd be the one to get the blame. She was really and truly stuck.

Chapter Six

The perfect solution occurred to Barbie the next day as she drove down the lane to Rebecca's house. Why hadn't she seen it sooner? The plan Moses had come up with didn't depend solely on her. Rebecca would have something to say about it as well.

On second thought, maybe that solution wasn't so perfect. Her cousin Rebecca was a generous, openhearted woman with a maternal streak a mile wide. Rebecca was more likely to be mothering Mary instead of turning down her help.

Everything about Rebecca's home was as welcoming as she was. Daffodils along the porch steps looked ready to burst into bloom, and the tulips were already several inches high. And Rebecca was setting out pansies in the planters along the edge of the porch, the cheerful pansy faces bobbing in the breeze.

Barbie drew up at the hitching rail, returning Rebecca's wave. By the time she'd hopped down and flipped the lines over the rail, Rebecca was there to sweep her into a hug.

"Barbie, this is so nice. I wasn't expecting you. Aren't you working today?"

"I have the supper shift." She held her cousin at arm's length, scrutinizing her.

"What are you looking at?" Rebecca's words trembled on the edge of laughter. Her eyes sparkled, and there seemed to be an extra bloom on her cheeks.

"Just checking. Mamm says you've been looking especially glowing lately."

The color came up in Rebecca's face. "Oops. And I thought I was hiding it."

"You mean it's true? You and Matt are expecting?"

"Shh." Laughter bubbled out of her, her joy so obvious that it was as if she wore a huge sign. "No one is supposed to know. But I can't help how I feel, can I?"

"Ach, Rebecca, I'm wonderful glad for you." She pressed her cheek against Rebecca's. Was that actually a tinge of envy she felt? Ridiculous.

"Denke. I have been hoping, you know. I don't want there to be too big a gap between the kinder. And to think a year ago I didn't believe I could ever be truly happy again."

"Well, that just shows how foolish you were." Barbie put her arm around her cousin's waist as they headed toward the house. "Somebody like you was made for marriage and family."

Rebecca gave her a challenging look. "And what about somebody like Barbie?"

"Don't start," Barbie warned her, keeping it light. "I hear enough of it from my mamm."

Rebecca chuckled, but she desisted. "Komm. We'll go in and have coffee."

"I don't want to interrupt. Let me help you finish the pansies first."

She eyed Rebecca covertly as they settled on the edge of the porch by the long planters. Rebecca looked so happy, so—contented. A year ago at this time she'd been overburdened with the weight of trying to raise her two kinder alone and make a go of the farm the way she thought Paul would have wanted. Then, grief had hollowed her cheeks and set worried lines between her eyes. Now she seemed to have come into the sunshine.

Rebecca handed her a pansy, holding the root ball in the palm of her hand. Barbie set it into the planter, pressing the soil down firmly with the trowel. "Where's Matt today?"

"He's off with his onkel and cousin, helping them with a kitchen they're doing. The home-owner wants a built-in breakfast area, so Matt is building it for them."

Matt's furniture business was thriving, but he still managed to find time to help his family, to say nothing of farming the property with Rebecca's father and brothers.

"He's not going to have much space in his schedule to help with the guests, is he?"

"He says he will. And with my brothers pitching

in and your help, we'll manage." Rebecca seemed to look inward for a moment, pressing her palm against her still-flat stomach. "But you can see why your help is so important now."

This was the prime moment to bring up having Mary work with them, but she didn't want to.

"Grossmammi is wonderful glad you've been spending so much time with her lately." Rebecca's words gave her a respite.

"It doesn't take any urging to make me want to be with her. Did you ever know anyone who could make you feel so . . . well, so special?" That idea didn't really fit in too well with the Amish value of humility, but Rebecca would know what she meant.

In fact, her cousin was already nodding. "She has a gift for it, ain't so? Not that my mamm doesn't spend a lot of time and attention on my young ones," she added quickly. "But Gross-mammi isn't so busy, not like Mamm with the boys still at home. Anyway, it's sehr gut that she's been sharing her stories with you." There was a touch of curiosity in Rebecca's face.

"We've been going through the things in her dower chest." Barbie hesitated. "Some of her stories—well, I didn't realize how difficult things were back before the family left Lancaster County. Leaving must have been a hard decision to make."

Rebecca's fingers slowed as she pressed another pansy into place. "Big decisions are always hard, ain't so? When Matt came along—well, it wasn't like it had been with Paul." A spasm of pain crossed her face, a cloud passing over the sun. "If I'd known everything that was going to happen with Paul when I was eighteen . . ." She let the words fade.

"Maybe it's best not to know," Barbie suggested, realizing her cousin must be thinking of those difficult days when Paul became ill and they realized he wasn't going to get better.

"Ja." Rebecca nodded, her serenity returning as quickly as it had vanished. "If we knew the future, we'd never move on. But God only lets us see far enough ahead for the next step."

The words seemed to strike a chord in Barbie's heart. Where was the vision that would illuminate her future? Maybe she hadn't been paying enough attention.

In any event, she couldn't delay the inevitable any longer. She had to talk to Rebecca about Mary.

She focused on the nodding pansies. Sound casual—that was the idea. "By the way, I happened to be talking to Moses Kauffmann. He said that if we needed any help with the farm-stay, Mary would be interested in working for us."

Silence for a long moment.

"What do you think about it?" Rebecca sounded cautious.

She knew Rebecca was watching her, but she

didn't want to meet her eyes, fearing she'd give away too much. "Well, I . . . I'm not sure . . . That is . . ."

She'd been living a lie with her parents, hiding her fascination with the Englisch world. Why should it be so difficult to tell Rebecca she didn't like the notion?

"Barbie." Rebecca's voice was so serious that Barbie had to look at her. "I know something is wrong. I've heard rumors."

"About me?" She flared up in an instant.

"About you, ja. But about Mary Kauffmann, too. Can't you tell me what is going on?"

"You're getting as bad as Grossmammi. One look, and she sees far too much." She tried to decide what, and how much, to say to her cousin.

"I've known you all your life. And I hope we are friends, as well as cousins." She clasped Barbie's hand. "I want to help, but how can I, if I don't know the truth? Why does Moses want Mary to work for us? And why don't you?"

Barbie studied her face. Rebecca was safe. But she would be trusting her not just with her own secret, but with Mary's.

Finally she let out a long breath. "No one else can hear this," she warned. "Not even Matt."

Rebecca nodded. "I understand."

"Mary got in trouble the other night. Out with some Englisch kids who got her drunk."

"Ach, the poor child. And her without a mother

116

to turn to." Pity filled her eyes. "No wonder Moses wants something to occupy her. Of course we must help."

She could just let it go at that—let Rebecca assume Barbie was only motivated by wanting to provide guidance for the motherless girl.

No. She couldn't stop there and be able to face herself in the mirror.

"That's not the whole story." She realized that she was plaiting her fingers together. Realized, too, that Rebecca had noticed. "I saw Mary at a bar out on the Jonestown road. I couldn't just leave her, so I got my friend Ashlee to drive us to the Kauffmann place to take her home."

Silence again. Finally she looked at Rebecca. "Aren't you going to ask me what I was doing there?"

Rebecca's eyes were grave, but she didn't shy away from the challenge. "I think I know already. You were out with an Englisch friend, trying to be one of them."

"Not . . . not that, exactly." She stumbled over the words. "I mean, I just wanted to see what it was like to be with Ashlee and her friends."

Rebecca didn't say anything. She just waited.

Barbie clenched her hands together. "Anyway, you can imagine how Benuel Kauffmann reacted. He immediately assumed I'd been the one leading his sister astray."

"You explained, didn't you?"

"I did, but I'm not sure it helped. Anyway, I certain-sure never expected them to ask me to influence Mary, but Moses says she admires me, and he thinks working here with us would be good for Mary." She grimaced. "Ben didn't agree."

"Well, it's up to Mary's father, after all." Rebecca paused, her gaze on Barbie's face. "You are reluctant to do it."

"Can't you understand why?" The words burst out of her. "If Mary gets into trouble now, I'll get the blame. Anyway, I'm the last person who should be asked to guide a rebellious teenager. I'm not exactly the model of a perfect Amish woman."

That brought Rebecca's smile back. "Ach, Barbie, don't you see? That's exactly why you are in a place to help this girl."

"But . . ." The objections died on her tongue at Rebecca's expression. It was no use. Whether Rebecca was right or not she didn't know, but if she was . . .

Well, then, Barbie had to go through with it.

Ben, glancing up from the buggy wheel he was working on in the shop behind the house, started as movement caught his eye. A buggy, with Barbie Lapp driving. He'd been expecting her to show up, since Daad had asked her to let them know about Mary working at the farm-stay.

He didn't like it. Daad seemed to think he would

become reconciled to the idea, but he wouldn't. Still, he had no choice but to accept.

But Barbie could find a way out if she really tried. Maybe that was what she'd come to tell them. And if not—well, if not, he'd seize the opportunity to make it clear that he held her responsible for Mary.

Apparently not noticing him, or maybe not wanting to notice him, Barbie headed for the back door. Reluctantly he stepped out into the sunshine and called to her.

"Barbie! No one is here but me."

He saw the movement of her bonnet as she nodded, and she started walking toward him. He had a moment of thinking that with her black bonnet and dark sweater she looked like every other Amish woman. And then she was close enough that he saw the lively face and pert dimples and knew she'd never look just like everyone else.

At least she was decently covered, not like the night she'd appeared in the jeans and sweater that showed off her slender figure. That image seemed stuck in his mind no matter how he tried to ignore it.

"Have they all gone off and left you today?" She smiled, but there was wariness, as always, when she looked at him.

"Mary went with the kinder to Sarah's house, and Daad is picking up a part we need at the hardware store. If you want to talk with him, he should be back in about half an hour."

She hesitated, and he could almost see her reluctance to trust in him. He turned back to the wheel, deliberately letting her stew about it.

After a long moment, she let out her breath in a tiny sigh. "I suppose I may as well tell you, ain't so?"

He straightened. "If it's about Mary, I hope you've come to say that it doesn't suit Rebecca to have Mary working there."

The color in her cheeks deepened. "I thought of that already, but it wasn't any use. We should both have known Rebecca better than that—of course she said yes."

"Maybe you could have tried harder to dissuade her." It probably wasn't fair to blame her for that, but since he already blamed her for so much, it was easy to pile a little more on.

"Maybe you could have tried harder to dissuade your daad," she snapped back.

"All right." He spread his hands in surrender. "We neither of us could prevent this happening."

Her lips twitched, the ready humor coming into her eyes and the dimples at play. "See, that wasn't so hard, was it?"

He tried not to return the smile, but he couldn't seem to help himself. Much as he disapproved of Barbie's actions, he could see why Mary admired her.

"It's Mary I'm worried about. Seems to me Daad ought to be tightening up after what she's done, not giving her more freedom. She's too young to be responsible."

He didn't expect Barbie to agree with that opinion, and of course she didn't. He could see it in her eyes. But she paused before speaking, as if determined to reply calmly.

"She is young, but not younger than most Amish girls when they start taking on jobs. I began working in the bakery in town when I was about her age." She seemed to look back at that younger self. "I was probably less mature than Mary is, but my job taught me responsibility."

He didn't speak, but she shot him a defiant look.

"I suppose you're thinking that I haven't been showing a lot of responsibility lately."

He bit back the impulse to reply sharply, forcing himself to think before he spoke. "How can I think that when you were responsible for rescuing Mary from the results of her foolishness?"

Barbie blinked, as if for once he'd taken her by surprise. "No matter how foolish she was, I'd like to have held those boys responsible. I don't suppose their parents had any idea what they were up to."

"Ja." He braced his hands against the buggy. "It would be easy to condemn the parents, but we didn't know what Mary was doing, either." He hesitated. "That's what hurts me most—that I had no idea. I should be closer to her. I know how difficult it is for Daad, trying to raise a young girl without Mamm to rely on. If I'd been closer to Mary . . ."

"No matter how close you were, that's not the kind of thing a girl confides in her brother. Maybe a sister, but not a brother. They're too protective."

"You act like that's a bad thing." He guessed that meant she didn't confide in any of her brothers, either.

Barbie leaned back against the buggy, her face tilted up to him. Did she realize how appealing she looked? Most likely.

"Not bad, just inconvenient when you know you're going to break the rules." Before he could speak, she hurried on. "I'm not proud of deceiving my parents. I just . . ." She let the words die away, shrugging a little.

"You just what?" He leaned closer, intent on her expression. "Help me understand, Barbie."

"That's not so easy, when I don't really understand myself." She had a rueful look on her face. "I feel sometimes as if I want something different. Something challenging and exciting and . . ." Her momentary excitement died. "Maybe I'm too much like James."

For a moment the name didn't register, and then he realized. James, the oldest Lapp boy. The one who'd left the Amish and never been heard of since.

He clamped his lips closed on the words that wanted to rush out. As her minister, his duty was to help Barbie do right. That wouldn't come through condemning the brother she loved.

"Your family hasn't been whole since," he said slowly. "There is an empty place in it where James should be."

She nodded, not speaking, and her blue eyes glistened with tears. "I've never understood why he didn't stay in touch with us. The restlessness, the longing to have a different life—I could understand those feelings. But he never even wrote."

He spoke carefully, considering his words. Maybe he shouldn't say what was in his thoughts, but he'd never imagined that behind her bright, lively manner Barbie was hurting so.

"You were just a child then. Is it possible that your parents did hear from him but chose not to tell you?"

Her face grew very still. "I . . . I can't believe they'd let me think he didn't care."

"They might not realize. They might have thought they were doing the best thing for you." His own words seemed to ring in his ears. That was all he was doing, wasn't it? Trying to do the best thing for Mary? "I don't know," he added hastily, afraid of what he might have opened up. "It just . . . wondered me, that's all."

"If they know where James is . . ." A tear spilled over, glistening on her cheek. She wiped it away impatiently. "No. I'm sure you're wrong." She glared at him.

"Maybe so." This was what came of trying to do what he should as her minister. He failed more often than he succeeded. "I'm sorry, Barbie. I shouldn't have said anything about it."

"No, you shouldn't." She snapped the words, but then she bit her lip. "I'm sorry, too. I don't even know why we started talking about James. I came here to make arrangements for Mary, that's all."

He gave a short nod. "When do you want her?" They'd best stick to business and not stray off into the side roads of their own pain and loss.

"Friday afternoon." Barbie kept her voice brisk. "We'll do a trial run, just as if we were getting ready for weekend visitors. I'll pick her up around one, if that's okay."

"One o'clock," he repeated. "I'll tell Daad, and he can set it up with Mary. Denke, Barbie."

Now was the moment to do what he'd promised himself—to ensure that Barbie knew he held her responsible for anything that happened to his sister while she was in her care.

But something prevented him—the image of her face, suddenly pained and vulnerable, as a tear trickled down her cheek.

Lancaster County, Spring 1960

One good thing about living in such a busy household, Elizabeth decided the next afternoon, was that no one seemed to notice that she and Reuben had very little to say to each other. The trouble between them was difficult enough. It would be far worse if anyone else was aware of it.

She'd caught Reuben's mother watching her with a troubled expression once or twice, though. Maybe Mamm Alice had seen that Elizabeth's eyes were heavy today. She hadn't managed to get much sleep last night.

Reuben had lingered downstairs, talking with his daad, when she'd gone upstairs. And when he had come into the bedroom, she'd kept her eyes shut, trying to breathe as deeply and evenly as if she were asleep.

Reuben hadn't spoken. He'd undressed silently in the dark, and she'd felt the bed move as he settled into his side. She lay still, hoping he felt as miserable over their quarrel as she did.

But in a few minutes she heard his gentle snore. If he had been upset, he certainly wasn't showing it. She lay stiffly, unable to relax, feeling the distance between them in the bed.

It would be easy to reach over. If she touched him, she was certain-sure he'd draw her close.

But she couldn't. She could only lie there,

imagining the space widen and deepen until it was a terrible chasm no one could cross.

Elizabeth's eyes filled with tears at the memory, and she blinked them back furiously as Mamm Alice came into the kitchen. Picking up the clothes basket, Elizabeth started for the back door.

"I think it's coming on to shower. I'd best get the sheets off the line." She hurried out before Mamm Alice could offer to help her.

At least that was true. The clouds had been thickening all afternoon, and the air seemed heavy with the threat of a cloudburst. She glanced to the west, seeing the black sky over the distant hills. Rain for sure, and coming their way fast.

Dropping the basket in the grass, she began unpinning the first of the line of sheets she and Becky had hung out that morning, automatically feeling to be sure they were dry. They were, but they wouldn't stay that way for long if she didn't get them off the line.

She folded quickly and tossed the sheet into the basket, then moved on to the next. The breeze picked up, setting the sheets flapping and making her kapp strings fly.

"You're going to get wet." Reuben was suddenly beside her, snatching a sheet off the line. "Better hurry."

"I am," she protested, unable to keep from smiling at the sight of Reuben trying to fold the sheet. "Just put it in the basket. I'll refold them inside, where it's dry."

Reuben grabbed another just as the wind took it, and it fluttered around him like a cape. He batted at it, and she grabbed the ends, laughing now, and brought them up to his hands. He took them, managing to clasp her fingers at the same time.

For an instant she froze, unable to think of anything but the touch of his hands and the longing to be done with this quarrel. Then a sputter of raindrops hit her face.

"Hurry," she cried, grabbing sheets any old way, letting the clothespins fly as she rolled them up and stuffed them in the basket. "Here it comes."

Reuben snatched the last sheet. He took the basket in one arm and grabbed her hand. "Run for it."

Together they raced across the lawn to the back door, the heavens letting loose as they covered the last few steps. They stumbled inside, breathless and laughing, and leaned against the door.

Reuben looked down at her, the laughter wiping out all the strain that had been in his eyes. She couldn't look away, because she saw all the love that was there—love that had been overlaid with the grief and stress of the past months.

"Ach, my Elizabeth." His voice was deep and soft. "I don't want to fight with you. I love you."

She reached for him, hardly knowing what she did, and in an instant she was in his arms where she longed to be. Safe. Together. Surely, some-how—

The door banged against Reuben's back. "Hey, you two." Isaac was boisterous as always. "Let us in. You can cuddle later."

Flushing, Elizabeth backed up into the kitchen as Isaac and Daad Eli came in, shaking their hats free of rainwater and spraying it in every direction.

"You boys wipe your feet before you track anything onto my clean kitchen floor." Mamm Alice handed them a towel, shaking her head at the mess they were making. "Here, Elizabeth, let me take that basket before the men get the sheets all wet again."

Like a hen with her chicks, Mamm Alice ushered everyone into place until they were settled around the kitchen table, listening to the rain pounding against the roof as they had what Mamm Alice called "just a little snack to tide you over to supper."

Becky hurried to help Elizabeth fold the sheets. As they did so, Reuben caught her gaze, giving Elizabeth just the suggestion of a wink as if to say he'd like to be doing that instead of Becky.

"You won't believe what I heard when I was at the hardware store," Isaac declared, then stuffed an oatmeal cookie into his mouth.

"I think men only go to the hardware store to gossip," Mamm Alice observed. "They just don't want to call it what it is."

"Not gossip," Isaac managed to say around the cookie. He took a gulp of milk. "It's true all right."

"Well, and what is it?" Daad Eli said. "Either eat or talk, not both."

Nodding, Isaac plonked his glass onto the table. "The county is going to rezone a bunch of property from agriculture to commercial," he said. "Everybody was talking about it."

"That's nothing new. It's happening all the time." The lines between Reuben's brows formed again, and Elizabeth's heart sank.

"Ja, but this is different. It's up there along Fisher Road, where the Henderson farm is. Both sides of the road. Nobody knows what they're doing it for, but the surveyors were out already, and there's talk of what they call a strip mall on both sides of the road. You know what that means. More traffic than that area has ever seen."

Daad Eli's frown echoed Reuben's. "If that happens, how are we supposed to get to the produce auction? We always go up the lane and across Fisher Road there with the wagons. We can't stop all that traffic in both directions to get wagons to auction."

Isaac shrugged. "I guess we're going to have to find another way to get there. Or hope they move the produce auction site."

"If we don't have the auction to sell what we grow . . ." Daad Eli let that fade away and fetched

129

up a deep sigh. "We'll find a way. We always do. That's the cost of living separate."

Elizabeth's gaze flew to Reuben's face. She could see what he was thinking, and a cold hand seemed to grab her heart. For him, this was just another reason to leave.

Chapter Seven

"Did I do all right?" Mary's face was surprisingly anxious as Barbie drove her home after her first time helping at the farm-stay.

"All right? You were great," Barbie said quickly. "Rebecca was very pleased. Didn't you hear her say so?"

Mary blinked a couple of times, studiously watching the team pulling a plow through the field next to the road. "I thought maybe she was just being nice."

Barbie couldn't help smiling. "She's always nice, but she meant it. I could tell."

And why not? Barbie had been a little surprised herself by how quickly Mary had caught on to what was expected of her. Not that it was unusual for an Amish girl her age to understand how to clean and change beds and do laundry. But Mary had also showed initiative, asking questions and making careful notes on exactly what was to be put in each guest room.

"She is nice, isn't she?" Mary recovered her smile. "She's different from you, ain't so?"

Barbie bit back a grin. "You mean I'm not nice?"

Mary's lips formed an O of dismay. "Ach, Barbie, I certain-sure didn't mean that. You know, don't you?"

"I'm just teasing." She let the lines go slack in her hands, trusting the mare along this quiet back road.

All around them, spring was making its presence felt. The spring peepers sang their song along the banks of a boggy spot in the stream, and a willow near the stream had already leafed out. The fields looked greener than they had this morning, and even the ridges showed the beginnings of color. It was a day to make the heart expand.

"Gut." Mary was still for a moment. "I just meant that Rebecca seems like she might be a little shy." She darted a look at Barbie. "You could take on anybody."

"Not quite anybody," Barbie confessed. "I'm still a tad nervous about my boss. But I know he doesn't think less of people who stand up to him. I don't answer him back or anything, but I do tell him what I think."

Mary seemed to consider the words. "It's hard

sometimes to . . . well, to say what you want without sounding sassy."

This had to be a direct reference to Mary's family, and Barbie picked her words carefully. "I guess it's more a matter of how you say things. Like with my boss. Even if he yells, I certain-sure don't yell back. I keep my voice kind of neutral and try to stay focused on what I want to say."

A glance at the girl's face told her that she was digesting the words. Probably thinking about how they might apply to her family—maybe to Sarah in particular. There seemed no doubt that she and Sarah brought out the worst in each other.

Barbie was content to be silent and let her mull it over. She'd considered whether she should bring up the events of that night at the bar with Mary, but she'd decided their friendship was too fragile to bear the weight of that topic yet. For now, she'd do better to focus on just being there.

It was enough to see Mary without the sullen expression on her face. To see her laugh at the antics of Rebecca's young ones when they came in from school. If she could keep Mary in that happy frame of mind, that was a fine accomplishment for one afternoon.

But when they made the turn onto the Kauffmann lane, she could sense the girl tighten up, as if she prepared for criticism. Surely that was all in her imagination. After all, Moses wanted her to work at the farm-stay.

But Benuel didn't. Was Mary aware of her brother's disapproval? Maybe the mere fact that her brother was one of their ministers was enough to make their relationship difficult.

"You know," she said, keeping her voice casual, "I'd like to tell your father and brother how pleased Rebecca and I were with your work. But I wouldn't want to talk about you without your permission. Is that okay with you?"

Mary's expression was of surprise, or maybe gratitude at being treated as an adult. "I guess that would be all right."

They'd reached the hitching post, and the mare stopped without being asked. As the two of them descended from Barbie's buggy, Abram came Running across the grass to them as fast as his short legs would carry him. He threw himself at Mary.

"You're home, you're home!"

"Sure I am. I told you I'd come after you got up from your nap, ain't so?" Mary hugged him, her face lighting.

"Here's someone else to greet you." Moses stepped off the porch, Libby in his arms, and set her down in the grass.

For a moment the two-year-old just stood there, wiggling her bare toes in the grass, and then she toddled over, holding up her arms for a hug. Abram gave Barbie a shy smile, obviously remembering her from their ball game after worship.

"Want to play ball?" he asked hopefully.

"Ach, Abram, don't tease Barbie." Moses shook his head, smiling. "You started something, I'm afraid."

She ought to be heading for home, but Barbie couldn't resist the pleading look on Abram's small face. "Sure, for a few minutes. Where's the ball?"

In answer, Abram ran full tilt to the porch, making her wonder if the little boy had any speed other than fast. He was back in seconds with the ball, tossing it toward Barbie.

She had to lunge to catch it. "Wait a second until I take my bonnet off. I have to be able to see better to play ball."

She was happy to shed the black bonnet, stowing it under the buggy seat. Normally she might not wear it to go a short distance, but since she was coming clear over to the Kauffmanns', she'd thought she should.

Because Benuel might disapprove otherwise? She hoped that hadn't been in the back of her mind. No bonnet would change his opinion of her.

Tossing the ball gently to Abram, she clapped when it actually landed in his arms. He looked so surprised at himself that she nearly laughed out loud. What a cutie he was, with his straight silky hair and his round blue eyes and that funny intent look he wore when he prepared to throw the ball.

"Me, me!" Libby wasn't going to be left out.

She ran a few steps, fell down in the soft grass, and promptly hopped back up again, holding out her arms.

This time Abram rolled the ball to her without protest.

"Gut job, Abram," she said, and he beamed. "Next one goes to your aunt Mary, ja?"

He nodded, and they soon had the ball bouncing merrily among the four of them. Libby, of course, never actually caught it, but she seemed to get as much pleasure out of running after it as actually getting it.

Mary tossed the ball slightly off course to Barbie, and when it hit the ground, Libby chased it.

"Hey, that one's for me, Libby." Barbie took off after her, catching the little girl and swinging her up in her arms. "You're trying to take my turn, aren't you?" She grinned, bouncing the child.

Libby giggled helplessly, and then she threw her chubby little arms around Barbie's neck in a huge hug.

Barbie's heart swelled at the feel of the small body pressed against her so trustingly. To have a child of her own, to have her own little girl giving her a heartfelt hug—the longing welled up in her suddenly, astonishing her with its power. She'd never felt this with any of her nieces and nephews or her friends' babies. Why should it happen today?

●●●

Benuel crossed the yard toward the group, frowning a little. His young ones were shrieking with laughter as they chased Abram's ball back and forth with some help from Barbie and Mary. He'd hoped to have an opportunity to ask Barbie a question, but not with the entire family around.

What letter? He hadn't forgotten the moment when she'd flung the question at him like an accusation. She hadn't answered him then, and the words were like a burr under a blanket, prickling and demanding action.

Barbie raced Abram across the grass, both of them laughing. She was a different person today than she'd been that night when she came to the door with Mary—that was certain-sure. But which one was the real Barbie?

His father nudged him. "Barbie's gut with the kinder, ain't so?"

"Maybe," he said, grudging the word. "She's . . . frivolous."

"She's lighthearted," Daad corrected. "The world needs some lighthearted folk to balance out all the negative ones."

He didn't object to Daad's characterization, because he didn't want to start an argument. He couldn't deny that Barbie's laughing face was an enjoyable sight, but Barbie was a grown woman. It was time she started acting more serious.

The game came to an end with all four of them

tumbled in a heap on the ground. At a glance from him, Barbie swung herself to her feet and brushed off her apron.

"You two are just too good for me. I give up."

Ben's daad, smiling, put a hand on each child's head, hushing them. "So, Mary, we haven't had a chance to ask the important question, what with these noisy kinder. How did your first day of work go?"

Mary's pale, heart-shaped face seemed to glow from within. "Ach, it was wonderful gut. And I learned so much."

"You weren't the only one," Barbie said quickly. "Mary taught us a couple of things about bed-making."

"So she did all right?" Anxiety threaded Daad's voice. He wanted so much to hear something good about Mary that it caught at Ben's heart.

"All right? She was excellent. Caught on right away to how we like the rooms prepared and took the initiative in setting up." Barbie was beaming, so apparently it was true.

"Gut, gut." His daad's relief was plain. "I'm wonderful glad she can be of some help to you."

Mary smiled eagerly. "Rebecca showed me how to get the rooms ready, and Barbie taught me about the questions the Englisch might ask me. I'll have a whole list of answers ready for them, ain't so, Barbie?"

"You sure will." Barbie exchanged grins with

her, and for a moment it seemed to Ben that she was as young and inexperienced as Mary was.

"Did you thank Rebecca and Barbie for taking all this trouble?"

No sooner was the question out of his mouth than Benuel knew he'd made a mistake. Mary's smile vanished, transformed in an instant into that familiar sullen look. And Barbie—well, Barbie looked as if she was clenching her teeth to keep from giving him a rare scolding.

"Sorry," he said quickly, focusing on his sister. "I'm sure they know you appreciate the job."

He thought Mary was going to burst out with a retort, but a squeal from Libby had them all turning to her. Libby clapped her hands.

"Doggie! Komm, doggie." She held out her arms, and the shepherd-mix puppy he'd thought was secure in his pen pranced over to her, his tail wagging furiously.

"How cute he is. Is he your puppy?" Barbie knelt next to Libby and Abram, gently restraining the pup's efforts to lick Libby's face.

"His name is Shep," Abram said. "Cause Daadi says our farm dogs are always called Shep."

"Sounds like a good name for him." She stroked the puppy's head, and he turned his attention to trying to lick her face. She fended him off easily. "Good Shep. I don't want any kisses today."

Libby giggled at the idea of the dog giving kisses. Abram, eager not to miss out, rolled over in the grass and plopped the puppy on his stomach, only to have his sister dive on him.

"I thought I had the pen door latched." Daad shook his head. "Maybe he dug his way out. Komm, Abram. We'll take him back and check to see if the pen needs repair."

Abram got up willingly enough, but Libby started to wail at being left behind. Mary scooped her up.

"You'll help me with supper, ain't so? We should get started."

Sniffing a little, Libby nodded, and Mary carted her off toward the back door. He and Barbie were left alone together.

Ben braced himself for the criticism she was no doubt about to offer in regard to what he'd said to his sister. Not that it was any of Barbie's business, anyway.

"I should be getting home," she said instead. "Mamm will wonder what happened to me." She turned toward her buggy.

He'd have snapped back if she'd scolded him. The fact that she didn't made him all the more eager to justify himself, only he couldn't, not if he was being honest.

He fell into step with her. "I shouldn't have said what I did to Mary. That's what you're thinking, isn't it?"

"If you already know that, there's no point in my saying so."

Somehow the woman always seemed to get him in the wrong. Gritting his teeth, he put out a hand to stop her as she started to get up into the buggy. "What letter?" he said abruptly.

Barbie blinked, turning to look at him. Then the puzzlement in her face was replaced by wariness. "What are you talking about?" She glanced away, fumbling with the lines.

"That day we talked about Mary. You accused me of writing a letter to you."

She shrugged, evading his eyes. "It's nothing. I just thought what you said sounded like . . . well, like a letter someone left for me at the café."

It took a moment to process that information. "You are saying that someone wrote you an anonymous letter?"

"It's . . . nothing." She braced her hand on the edge of the seat to pull herself up, but he covered her hand with his.

"It can't be nothing if someone is writing you anonymous letters. Have you told your father about it?"

"No," she said sharply. "He doesn't need something to worry about. I threw it away, and there's an end to it."

"Barbie, wait. I know you think it's none of my business, but I am your minister. If one of the Leit is doing such a thing . . . or was it one of your Englisch friends?"

"Meaning they'd be more likely to do it?" A

spasm of annoyance crossed her face. "It was written in pencil on a scrap of lined paper. It didn't sound or look like an Englisch person wrote it."

He stood for a moment, frowning, mulling it over with his hand still clasping hers. "Can you tell me what it said?" At the objection he could see forming in her face, he hurried on. "The ministers and the bishop should know if one of our people is doing such a thing."

Barbie seemed to waver for a moment before giving in. "It was just a line or two, saying something about people knowing what I'm doing." She looked up at him, the blue of her eyes deep with distress. "It was ugly, getting something like that."

"Do you remember which of our people were in the café that day?"

She shook her head. "My station was away from the door and the register, and I was wonderful busy. I didn't have time to be looking around. Somebody could even have walked in and dropped the note and walked back out again." Her eyes flashed briefly. "I'd have thought you were in complete agreement with what it said. So why do you care?"

Why did he? He pushed away several possible answers to the question. "It's wrong for one of the Leit to do such a thing. It's divisive and unkind. Whether I agree with the sentiment or not, the person who did it should be confronted with his or her sin. Are you sure you don't have any idea who it was?"

"No." Her lips actually trembled for an instant before she firmed them. "I don't see any way to find out, and I don't want to know anyway. There's nothing you can do."

"I guess not." He conceded it reluctantly. He ought to be able to deal with such ill will arising in the Gmay. A local church district was like a large family, with everyone knowing everyone else well. Too well, maybe, in this case. "Promise me you'll tell me if you receive another."

"I don't think—" she began.

His fingers tightened on hers. "Promise me, Barbie."

He thought she'd argue, but she didn't. She gave a quick nod, freed her hand from his, and climbed into the buggy before he could assist her.

She didn't want his help with anything—that much was clear. He was left feeling annoyed, whether with himself or with her he wasn't sure.

Lancaster County, Spring 1960

Reuben tested the new hinge he'd just put on the stall door, making sure the door moved smoothly before putting his tools away. It seemed there were always things needing to be repaired on a farm. A farmer had to be a jack-of-all-trades, not calling in someone else to fix what went wrong.

Setting the toolbox back on its shelf, he moved through the barn door out into a warm spring day, blinking against the bright sunshine and watching with a smile as the buggy horses chased one another in the paddock. Spring made them act like foals again.

Too bad he couldn't say the same for the people around him. The Leit couldn't seem to talk about anything for the past week except the problems that might come with the rezoning proposal. No solutions, mind. Just problems. Everyone was worried.

That is, everyone except Elizabeth. His amusement vanished, his brow furrowing. Elizabeth had apparently decided to ignore the entire subject, as if that would make it go away.

Worse, he'd heard her talking to his mamm about the potential apple crop and how they'd have an apple-butter-making frolic come September. Making plans for the future as if their life here would continue forever. By September—well, by then, he hoped they'd be settled on a farm of their own, and the odds were growing that it would not be here in Lancaster County.

Those moments when they'd pulled sheets off the clothesline together popped into his mind. For just a little while, things had been the way they used to be between them. He loved it. He missed it. But he didn't know how to bring it back again.

Movement caught his eye, and he realized it was Elizabeth. She was stooping over the rhubarb patch, gently moving the fanlike leaves as she pulled weeds from around the plants. Reuben hesitated for a moment and then headed toward her. Maybe, if they worked together again as they had on the day of that spring shower, he could find a way of talking to her quietly about what was in his heart.

And he had to. Daniel King had found a lead on some good farmland for sale up in the central valleys, a place called Brook Hill. They were thinking they ought all to go and look it over, and he wanted her approval. Well, maybe not approval, exactly, but at least understanding.

"Looks like the rhubarb has grown a couple of inches since that last rain." He stepped into the row where she knelt, avoiding the large leaves.

Elizabeth looked up at him, and her smile was as warm as the sunshine. "Just look at the stalks. They're plenty big enough to pull some, ain't so?"

He squatted next to her, checking the pinkish-green stalks that were the edible part of the rhubarb plants. "I'd say so, as long as you don't take too many from the same plants. These are getting a little overgrown anyway."

"I was just thinking I should start a new bed. After all, it takes a few years to get it established." Her hands were busy among the plants, selecting the stalks to be pulled. "I'll make a dish of rhubarb sauce for supper. That'll taste like spring."

He nodded, using the knife she'd brought to cut off the leaf before putting the stalk in her basket. "It'll be a job to keep Isaiah from eating more than his share. It's just about his favorite thing, next to strawberry rhubarb pie."

Why was it so difficult to move the conversation in the direction he wanted it to go? Surely he could find a way to talk about the subject without putting her back up right off.

Elizabeth handed him another stalk. He fingered the smooth pinkish stem as he tried to find the right words.

"The men have been awful concerned about that zoning thing," she said suddenly.

It startled him, and he blinked. He'd thought she'd been ignoring the situation. Apparently not.

"It's worrying," he said, trying to be cautious in what he said. "It'll make it harder to reach the produce auction, that's certain-sure. And maybe other things, as well, depending on how fast that land is developed."

Elizabeth nodded, seeming to study the roots of the weed she'd just pulled up. "Your daad says there's nothing to be done. The Englisch will do as they want."

"Ja, I know." He felt his way slowly. "Just another thing that they call progress. Too bad they can't see that it's pushing us out."

She seemed to stiffen at his words, but she went on calmly enough. "Isaac and some of the other younger men think they can change things."

Instead of just leaving. She didn't say it, but he could tell she was thinking it.

"I don't see what they can do." He hadn't heard anything about it from his brother.

"Isaac says they're going to go to the zoning board meeting." She frowned, and he suspected she found the very words alien. "They hope they can show the people who make decisions how the farmers will be affected. Then maybe those people won't go through with it."

He shook his head. Given the money people stood to gain by the proposed rezoning, it seemed unlikely they'd give it up to satisfy a few Amish farmers.

"Funny that Isaac didn't say anything to me about his plans."

Elizabeth darted a quick look at him—a look he wasn't sure how to interpret. "Maybe he thinks you're so set on going away that you don't care anymore about what happens here."

That rocked him. "Of course I care. Isaac is my brother. I want things to work out for the best for him."

Now he could read her expression. It was challenging.

"So you'll help them? You'll join Isaac and the others in trying to change things?"

Reuben frowned, sitting back on his heels. He didn't like being pushed into things. "What's the point, when it's doomed to fail? The zoning board isn't going to listen to them."

"Maybe Isaac was right," Elizabeth said slowly. "Maybe you're so set on leaving that you've forgotten about the people here in our own place."

He wanted to object—wanted to say the hot words that came to his tongue, denying it. But he couldn't. Was it possible there was a little truth in what Elizabeth said? Had he been ignoring his own family's needs in his quest to find the right place for them?

Reuben sucked in a long breath and let it out slowly. All he'd thought, when Isaac had told them about the zoning issue, was that it was yet another reason to move elsewhere. How could he have been so blind to his own brother's needs?

"I do care." He said the words quietly. "Maybe I have been too busy thinking about my own problems to show it. I'll talk to Isaac right away." He hesitated, then said the rest of it. "I'm glad you made me see it, Elizabeth."

A smile trembled on her lips, and her blue eyes were bright with tears. "Denke, Reuben. Isaac will be wonderful happy for your help."

All he could do was nod. She was right. He certain-sure had to help his brother.

But how was it that he still hadn't been able to tell Elizabeth about the projected trip to Brook Hill?

Chapter Eight

Even while she was taking orders, Barbie found she was scanning the customers in the café. Which of them disliked her enough to have left that note?

Of course, it may not have been dislike. To do the writer justice, an Amish person fearful that Barbie was slipping too far away from the Leit might have thought to bring her to a realization of it. But even so, there'd been a hint of malice about the words—an implication that she was a bad example for others.

Ben's reaction, once he'd bullied the story out of her, had come as a surprise. He'd almost seemed sympathetic, but that couldn't be.

"Why are you standing there staring at the coffee machine?" Ashlee's voice startled her.

"I'm not." She grinned, shaking her head. "Well, maybe I was."

"Grab some coffee. It's quiet enough at the moment that we can take our break." Ashlee reached past her for a mug.

"Maybe we shouldn't—not at the same time." The last thing Barbie wanted was to see Ashlee in trouble with Walt again.

"Walt says it's okay." Ashlee's lively face wrinkled into a scowl that was probably meant to represent their sometimes-surly boss. "I'm being careful. Honest. I need this job."

Once they'd both filled their cups, they slid into a booth at the back where they could keep an eye on the whole café. They could jump up immediately if someone needed something or a new customer came in.

"Okay, spill." Ashlee planted her elbows on the table. "What's on your mind? You were a million miles away just then."

"Not that far," she protested. Was it ever possible to get away from Ashlee's questions? To be Ashlee's friend, a person had to put up with her insatiable drive to hear all the answers.

Why not tell her? Ashlee might have some insight into who left the note. Even if she didn't, she was safe. The Amish were the only ones who would care, and Ashlee didn't know them.

"Quit stalling," Ashlee prompted. "We only have ten minutes."

"You remember that envelope you gave me the other day? The one that had been left by the cash register?"

Ashlee blinked, as if to focus. "That? Sure, I remember. Was it a tip? If somebody left you a winning lottery ticket, I'd like a share."

"It was an anonymous note." Barbie lowered her voice, even though no one was close enough to hear them. The nearest occupied table had a group of four retired men who would sit there, nursing their coffee, for half the afternoon while they solved the world's problems in voices loud enough to be heard by the one who consistently refused to wear his hearing aid.

"No," Ashlee whispered. "Whatever about? Was it obscene?"

"Of course not." Barbie felt the color come up in her cheeks. Honestly, the things Ashlee thought of. "It was in pencil, not signed, saying something about me not getting away with what I was doing. That people knew."

"Knew?" Ashlee blinked. "Knew what? You live the most boring life I've ever seen. What is there to know?"

Did Ashlee really think that about her? Well, she supposed her life did look boring to someone like Ashlee, who wanted to be out every night.

"They might have been talking about going to that bar. Or I guess about Mary Kauffmann. Or even just my working here." She shook her head, getting more frustrated every time she thought about it. "If somebody saw me talking to Terry . . ."

"You mean flirting with Terry," Ashlee corrected. "What business is that of anyone else's?"

"If it was an Amish person, they might be worried that I was straying away from the faith." Now that she'd said it aloud, Barbie realized that was the most likely thing. "If it wasn't . . .

well, I don't know. Terry doesn't have a girl-friend or wife that I should know about, does he?"

"No. Anyway, not that I know of," Ashlee added.

"That doesn't exactly make me feel good. Still, he's a nice guy. I don't think he'd lie to me."

And yet, how could she tell? If he were an Amish man, even from another state, she wouldn't have to wonder. Someone would have a link to his home church and be only too eager to tell all about him. Ashlee's friends seemed to accept each other at face value, apparently without wanting to know more.

Ashlee seemed to dismiss Terry with a wave of her hand. "Anyway, this note. You didn't show it to your parents?"

"I couldn't. I'd have to tell them—well, things I don't want to." She'd told Ben, but that was an accident.

"Right. You're smart not to. The less our parents know about our lives, the better." Ashlee's expression puzzled Barbie about as much as her statement did.

"I don't know about that. I'm pretty close to my family. Ordinarily, I wouldn't keep things from them, but this—well, it would hurt them, and there's nothing they can do about it."

Ashlee shrugged. "My theory is that the more they know, the more they interfere. That's why I'm here, instead of in Baltimore, where my parents would be looking over my shoulder all the time, trying to push me into the mold they want for me."

The bitterness in her voice took Barbie by surprise, and she didn't know how to respond. "Is that where you grew up?"

Ashlee nodded. "It's not a bad place. Lots of jobs, lots of clubs and nightlife. But I had to get away someplace where I could be on my own." She looked around at the quiet café. "Didn't picture ending up here, but after I dropped out of college, I just sort of drifted. I knew a guy at school who was from this area, so . . ." She let that trail off, as if she didn't really have a reason why she was here instead of anywhere else in the world.

"Don't you miss your family and friends? There must be people you grew up with who you want to stay in touch with."

Barbie's thoughts flickered to the girls from her rumspringa group. Maybe their interests were different now, but they were still important to her.

"Nope." Ashlee glanced toward the door and grinned. "Look who's here. And I don't think it's because he likes the pie."

Terry, pausing in the doorway, saw them, smiled, and came straight toward them. "Hi. Funny thing, running into two of my favorite people in the same spot." His gaze, resting on Barbie's face, was warm and admiring.

"Never mind about me," Ashlee said, sliding out

of the booth. "I'm done. You can sit here with Barbie."

"I can't." Barbie glanced at the clock. "Our break is over."

"Guess I should have come in sooner," Terry said easily. "So is this table in your station?" He smiled at Barbie as she slipped out of the booth.

Okay, flirting she understood. It was the same in the Amish or Englisch world. So she smiled back. "It is. May I help you?"

He sat down. "You bet. Bring me a coffee, black, and a piece of whatever kind of pie you think is the best today. And don't be in a hurry. I tip better if the server chats a bit."

"I bet you do." Smiling, she headed for the counter.

Amazing, how much it improved her mood to have a personable man look at her so admiringly. It contrasted very nicely with the disapproving scowl she usually received from Ben Kauffmann.

When she returned with the slice of cherry pie and the coffee, she contrived to set them down slowly, arranging the fork and spoon, the napkin and plate, with care.

"I thought you'd like the cherry today. It's fresh this morning. The owner's sister makes them. I've never met her, but she has a light hand with pastry."

"So, can you bake a cherry pie, Barbie?"

"I do a pretty fair one, though I shouldn't brag.

My mother taught me when I was no higher than this." She gestured to a spot about three feet off the floor.

"I can just picture you. Long blond braids, big blue eyes, and a smile that would light up the room. Right?"

Now she did blush. "I don't recall anyone ever saying that about me."

"Then they just haven't been noticing." He brushed her fingers lightly with his.

Barbie let them linger for a moment before she drew back. Walt could be unpredictable, and she didn't want a lecture from him. In fact, at that moment he rang the bell on the pass-through, sending a frowning glance in her direction.

"I have to go. Is there anything else?"

"Yes." He captured her hand. "How about me picking you up after work? We can go—well, I guess it's silly to say we'll go for coffee. We can go for a ride. Have a chance to talk for more than two minutes without being interrupted. Please?"

She shouldn't. But she wanted to, instead of following silly, old-fashioned rules. There was no harm in getting to know someone.

"I can't stay long," she said. "If I'm late getting home, my folks will be imagining I've had an accident."

"Not long," he agreed, giving her that easy smile. "Okay?"

"Okay." She smiled back.

Lancaster County, Spring 1960

Elizabeth stirred, waking slowly from a dream of apple trees in blossom. It wasn't light, but she always seemed to wake automatically in time to get Reuben up for the milking.

She was lying against Reuben, his arm around her, his steady breathing the only sound in the bedroom. She didn't move, wanting to prolong this sense of closeness.

They'd seemed on the verge of losing it altogether in recent months, and something inside her shuddered at the thought. But now . . . as he'd promised, Reuben had joined with his brother in making plans for confronting the zoning board with their concerns. The men had talked all evening, sitting at the kitchen table with coffee and pie, making lists of all the concerns farmers had.

She'd rejoiced in the sight. Surely, if he still cared so much about what happened to farmers here in the county, he wasn't really committed to leaving. She indulged herself for a moment in a rosy dream in which they found the perfect farm within easy reach of their families—one with a farmhouse they could fill with the babies they would have.

That was the only thing wrong with their comfortable bedroom. There was no crib at the foot of the bed. Still, maybe this time . . .

Reuben sighed, turning his face toward her a little. Even in the near darkness she could visualize his dear face. She could see the thick lashes against his ruddy cheeks, the soft down on his cheekbones, the tiny scar at the corner of his eye where Isaac had swung an enthusiastic bat and hit his brother instead of the ball. She loved him so much. Why couldn't they just live and be happy?

The creak of a floorboard in the hall announced that her father-in-law was up. She touched Reuben's cheek, saying his name softly.

His eyes fluttered open, fixing on her face. He smiled. "My Elizabeth."

"You were maybe expecting someone else?" There was a lightness in her voice that had been missing lately.

"Never," he said, and kissed her.

His lips were warm on hers when his daad's knock came on the door. Reuben drew himself back just a little.

"I'm up," he called. Then he kissed her again and swung out of bed.

As usual, she lay still for a few minutes, giving him space to dress. When he'd hitched his suspenders over his shoulders, he bent down to kiss her again, very lightly.

"See you in a bit." He went out, and she heard the rumble of his voice as he exchanged a few words with his brother.

Sliding out of bed, Elizabeth stood on the

braided rug while she quickly washed and dressed. Over the years she'd become adept at getting her hair pinned up smoothly and quickly, smiling to herself as she thought of Reuben winding the long strands over his hand last night.

They'd been so happy. Surely, this would be the month when she started a baby. Then her empty arms would be full.

This was no time to stand here daydreaming, she scolded herself. Already she could smell the coffee that Mamm Alice started first. She should get downstairs and help with the breakfast.

As usual, Elizabeth found Mamm Alice already in the kitchen, measuring oatmeal into a pan.

"Shall I start the bacon?" She reached for the cast-iron skillet. She and Mamm Alice had worked out a routine for getting breakfast on the table smoothly.

"That's gut." Her mother-in-law glanced at her face. "You look better this morning."

Elizabeth blinked. "I didn't know I hadn't been looking all right."

Mamm Alice's glasses slid down her thin nose, as usual. "Ach, well, it's been a hard year, ain't so?" She paused, then gave Elizabeth's hand a quick squeeze, startling both of them since she wasn't a demonstrative person.

The gesture touched Elizabeth's heart. Since Reuben's mother didn't speak of her loss, Elizabeth had thought—well, she didn't know what she'd thought. She'd just instinctively turned to her own mother for comfort.

"Denke," she said softly. "I do feel hopeful today, ja."

Mamm Alice gave a short nod, her eyes blinking rapidly as if to chase away tears.

Should she have confided more in Reuben's mother? The thought troubled Elizabeth. If she had excluded her without thinking, that was unkind. But what could she say now?

Becky clattered down the stairs and into the kitchen, still settling her kapp in place, and relieved Elizabeth of the responsibility of saying anything more. But still, the thought wondered her.

"Ach, I don't know how you two make an early start look so easy." Becky seized plates and began setting the table. "I hate getting up while it's still dark."

"That's because you didn't have cows to milk when you were growing up," Elizabeth said. Becky's father, unlike most Amish, wasn't a farmer. He ran a busy harness shop instead. "You'll get used to it."

Becky darted a look at her mother-in-law's rigid back and rolled her eyes. Elizabeth repressed a smile. She'd had to play peacemaker between Mamm Alice and Becky more than once. How would they get along when Elizabeth and Reuben moved out?

At least, God willing, maybe they wouldn't be

far away. Elizabeth said a silent prayer that Reuben's work on the zoning issue would show him that this was the right place for them. If only it could be so. *Please,* she added. Surely it wasn't wrong to petition the Lord for something she wanted so desperately.

The sun was peeking over the distant line of trees when Elizabeth spotted the men moving toward the house. "They're coming."

She began moving slices of crisp fried pon hoss and bacon to a plate, both of them made right here on the farm after the last hog butchering. She'd rather eat bacon herself, but Reuben loved his mamm's pon hoss, and Elizabeth had copied out her recipe for the cornmeal and pork mixture, thinking one day she'd be the one making it.

The men came in, washing up at the sink just inside the back door. By the time they sat down, the food was on the table and Elizabeth was pouring their coffee.

Elizabeth slid into her chair at the long table and bowed her head for the silent prayer that preceded every meal. In a few minutes, Daad Eli had started the platters around the table and Reuben was pouring cream onto his oatmeal.

"So, the way it's warming up, I'm thinking we can risk planting corn in the lower field this week," Daad Eli spoke between mouthfuls of scrambled eggs. "What do you say, boys? Maybe Thursday, if the weather is right?"

Isaac nodded, but Reuben seemed to hesitate. He glanced at her, then looked away.

"I'm not sure I can do it Thursday, Daad. Would Friday be okay?"

Elizabeth watched Reuben's face, but he'd averted it. Why was he acting so strange? Surely one day or the other wouldn't matter to him.

"I guess," Daad Eli said, frowning. "What's wrong with Thursday?"

Again that hesitation came, and Elizabeth found she was holding her breath. Why didn't Reuben speak?

"That day I'm going with Johnny Stoltzfus and the others to look at land up in the valleys north of Harrisburg. Brook Hill, the place is called. It . . ." His words petered out as he realized everyone was staring at him.

Daad Eli cleared his throat. "Think maybe I've heard some talk of it. It's best you see for yourself, ain't so?"

"Is it really necessary?" Mamm Alice asked, her tone sharp. "You don't need to be in a hurry about moving."

"Reuben is able to decide things without help from us." Daad Eli stared at his wife, and her gaze lowered.

There was an awkward silence. Elizabeth felt as if everyone waited for her to speak, but she couldn't. How could she get any words out?

He hadn't told her. Reuben had made these

plans, and he hadn't said a word to her about it. Last night she'd thought—

Well, what she'd thought didn't matter, did it? Reuben had decided without her, and the chasm between them was wider and deeper than ever.

"Have fun." Ashlee waved as Barbie slipped out the back door at the end of her shift.

Barbie took a deep breath and tried to quell the butterflies that seemed to be dancing in her stomach. It was all very well for Ashlee to talk. She didn't seem to have doubts about anything.

Terry's car was pulled up at the side of the café, near where her buggy was parked. Her mare, Belle, spotted her and came to the gate of the small yard behind the café where Walt let Barbie keep the mare during her shift. Belle assumed they were going home, of course.

"You're really here." Terry leaned a jeans-clad hip against the car door, his eyes crinkling at the sight of her. "I was afraid you'd have changed your mind by now."

"Would I do that to you?" She smiled up at him, relishing the frank approval in his face. At least Terry didn't judge people, like some she could name.

"Well, I don't know." He pretended to be in doubt. "You might have had a better offer since then. After all, the café's a busy place."

"Lots of truckers taking a break, talking on their

cell phones to their wives. And the usual number of older men, solving the world's problems over their coffee."

He grinned, rounding the car to open the passenger door for her. "You've got to watch those truckers. Some of them forget themselves when there's a pretty girl around."

"How about electric company workers?" she teased. "Don't they?"

"Sometimes." His easy grin deepened, and he gestured to the front seat. "Ready?"

"I guess." She took one step, glancing down the alley as she did, and gasped. Without taking time to think, she slid back, behind the steps that came out from the kitchen.

"Barbie?" Terry stared blankly for an instant and then followed the direction of her gaze.

An Amish buggy had stopped at the entrance to the alley, and the couple inside were staring at his car, pulled up beside the buggy.

He caught on quickly. Stretching a little, he reached into the door pocket of the passenger side, pulled out a map, and spread it out, making a pretense of studying it, carefully not looking toward Barbie.

She held her breath. John and Miriam Fisher— it would have to be them. Miriam was the worst blabbermaul in the county, and if she'd spotted Barbie getting into Terry's car, it would be all over the church before she could blink.

The map hid Terry's face from her. What was he thinking? She stayed frozen, afraid to move. Maybe, if she went toward the mare . . .

The map flopped down. "It's okay. They're gone."

She peered cautiously around the corner of the steps. The alley was empty except for them, and only cars moved past the entrance.

"I'm sorry." Her cheeks were probably scarlet. "I guess I acted ferhoodled." The Amish word said it best.

"Fer-what?" Terry grinned.

"Ferhoodled. It means crazy, mixed up, that kind of thing."

"Well, I wouldn't say you were ferhoodled." He took a cautious glance around. Seeing no one, he took her hands in his. "Just cautious. Maybe worried about hurting someone?"

His empathy startled her.

"My parents." How to explain to him what it was like? "They would be very hurt if everyone in the community was talking about their daughter."

"So you don't want to hurt them, but you want to make new friends. They might like me if they got to know me." It was said lightheartedly, but he let go of her hands.

Poor Terry. That just showed how little he understood about how an Amish mother's mind worked. To Mamm, dating led to marriage and family. And that would terrify Terry, she suspected, just as much as it would Mamm to discover her child was dating an Englischer.

"You're very likable," she said. "They would like you. But not as someone to date their daughter."

Terry turned away, accepting it. Then he swung back again. "Hey, why are we giving up so easily? We know we don't mean any harm, right?"

"Sure, but—"

"Look, we weren't too smart trying to get together here, where anybody might see us. But what about the night you came to the bar? When you were in Englisch clothes, nobody looked twice. I mean, except the way guys look at any pretty girl."

"Still, it didn't work out all that well." Not with having to rescue a foolish Mary and getting into trouble with Benuel.

"That was just bad luck," he said quickly. "I like you, Barbie. I just want to spend a little time with you. Ashlee would help out, wouldn't she?"

Barbie's lips quirked. "Ashlee would love it." Her spirits rose. Why not?

"We could go to dinner someplace away from Brook Hill. There's a new Chinese place over toward Harrisburg. What do you say?"

A good Amish girl would say no. "I'll talk to Ashlee."

"Great." Terry beamed, obviously taking that for a yes. "I'll stop by the café to see what you've worked out. See you."

"See you," she echoed, and watched as he slid into his car and backed out.

All the rules she'd been raised by told her she was doing the wrong thing, but rebellion actually felt good to her. Why shouldn't she make up her own mind? She wasn't a child any longer.

Chapter Nine

"Oh, my." Rebecca paused in the process of describing the incoming farm-stay guests to Barbie and Mary the next afternoon. She pressed her fingers to her lips, her face losing its color.

"You're not well," Barbie said quickly, going to put an arm around her cousin. "Why didn't you say something?"

Rebecca managed a wan smile. "I was hoping to overcome it. With guests coming in an hour—" She broke off, a panicked look on her face.

"Just relax," Barbie soothed. "It's fine. Mary and I will take care of everything, won't we, Mary?"

Mary looked nearly as alarmed as Rebecca, but she nodded.

"Komm." Barbie guided her cousin toward the stairs. "You'll lie down until you feel better. We'll take care of the guests."

Once upstairs, Rebecca sank gratefully onto her bed, pressing her head into the pillow.

"You'll be fine." Barbie slipped Rebecca's shoes off and pulled the quit over her. "What can I get you?"

"Nothing. Well, maybe some salty crackers would help." Rebecca seemed to relax a little. "I don't know why they call it morning sickness, when it comes on all day."

"It'll pass soon." She'd heard enough about pregnancies from her girlfriends to know that much. "Just rest. We'll check the guest rooms and get supper started."

Her cousin nodded, obviously too nauseated to argue. "Matt and the kinder should be home around five. He can take over if I'm not up by then."

"I've dealt with guests enough to know what to do, and Mary's a big help." Of course Mary had yet to be confronted with actual guests, but in theory, she knew what to do. "You try to sleep." Giving her cousin a light pat, she tiptoed out of the room.

Barbie hurried downstairs, mentally running through the checklist of things to be done before guests arrived. Fortunately, most of it was done. Unfortunately, the two couples they expected had booked supper, so she'd have to cope with it.

"Is she all right?" Mary still looked upset when Barbie reached the kitchen.

Barbie nodded. "She'll be fine, but we'll have to cope for now. Why don't you go and check the guestrooms while I start getting things ready for supper?"

Mary nodded. "Are you sure Rebecca doesn't need the doctor?"

She grinned. "It's nothing that nine months won't cure." She wouldn't normally talk about it to someone outside the family, but since Mary was working here, she'd have to know.

"Oh." Mary looked gratified at being addressed like one of the adult women. "She and Matt must be happy, ain't so?"

Barbie nodded, smiling when she thought of the way Matt looked at Rebecca these days. She was happy for her cousin. Of course she was. But she couldn't help a tiny pinch of envy. Would anyone ever look at her that way?

By the time Barbie had glanced over the supper plans and begun to organize the meal, she heard the sound of a car in the lane. She glanced at the clock. The guests had arrived earlier than expected, but no matter. At least the Shepards and the Walkers had been here before. They knew the routine and wouldn't expect things that weren't available, like the one guest who'd demanded a high-speed internet connection and left when told that was impossible.

Barbie wiped her hands on a tea towel as she headed for the door. They'd learned a lot last year, but there would probably still be surprises.

"Mary," she called up the stairs. "They're here."

She heard a gasp from Mary, then rapid footsteps as the girl started down. In another moment they were both on the porch, ready to welcome their guests.

The two couples greeted Barbie like an old friend, the women giving her warm hugs. She introduced Mary, glad that the girl's first exposure to guests would be with people so easy to please.

"Do we have the same rooms as last time?" Mrs. Shepard, small, round, and smiling, a little dumpling of a woman who always wore dangling jewelry, embraced her with much jingling of necklace and bracelets.

"Ja, just the same. Mary will . . ." She started to say get the bags, but decided showing the women upstairs was the easier task than arguing pleasantly with the husbands about who would carry the bags. "Mary will show you up to the rooms." She gave the girl a reassuring smile.

Mary swallowed hard and then gestured to the stairs. Tiny Mrs. Shepard and tall, angular Mrs. Walker, her bright scarf fluttering over a cinnamon-colored blouse, followed her.

Barbie headed outside to tease the husbands into letting her carry the suitcases. She could handle the visitors herself if she had to, and with Mary's help, it would be a snap.

Luckily the two couples had already decided to run down to a craft store they remembered from their previous visit. They left as soon as they were settled, the women chatting about what they intended to buy on this trip.

Their quick departure made it easier to get on with supper. Barbie was checking the pot roast when Mary hurried into the kitchen to help.

"I looked in on Rebecca, but she was sleeping, so I didn't bother her. Shall I start the potatoes?"

Barbie nodded, thankful for someone who new her way around the kitchen. Some of the younger servers at the café didn't seem to know one end of a spatula from the other.

"So." Barbie glanced at Mary as they stood side by side at the sink preparing vegetables. "What do you think of our visitors?"

Mary shrugged. "They seem nice. The ladies have pretty clothes, don't they?"

"Colorful, anyway." Barbie suppressed a smile. Amish teen girls were just as fascinated by clothes as any other teenagers. Treading cautiously, she skirted the subject of that night at the bar. "Is that what draws you to the Englisch way?"

Mary shrugged again—typical teenage answer. "Well, it's more interesting than this." She nodded to her burgundy dress and matching apron. "I hate it. I don't see why I can't wear something nice." She frowned. "Or why I should wait on people who have what I want." Her small face set in that sullen look that seemed to drive Benuel to saying all the wrong things.

Barbie wasn't going to make the same mistake. She shrugged as if it didn't matter. "We all have to work for what we want. It's best to make the work fun when we can, ain't so?"

Mary didn't respond for a time. Then she glanced at Barbie. "You always look pretty anyway, even in the same clothes as everyone else. How do you do it?"

If the way to Mary's heart was through clothes, that would be easy.

"Color," she said simply. "We're stuck with the style, ain't so? But that doesn't mean we can't make our dresses in colors that are becoming to us."

Mary mulled that over. "So this." She held out a fold of her skirt. "Does it look nice on me?"

No point in trying to fool her. "Not really. See, you have light, warm skin tones, like me. So we look best in light, warm colors. You just have to try different shades next to your face to see which looks best." She smiled. "You should see me when I go to the fabric store. I look at every piece before I decide what I'm going to buy."

"Sarah gave me this material." Mary glared at the despised dress.

"Well, sure. This is a nice color on her. She probably didn't even realize that it might make you look washed out." She hadn't expected to be defending Sarah, but she had to admit that Sarah always meant well.

"You think that's so?"

"Of course." She hesitated. "Tell you what. Suppose we arrange a trip to the fabric store together. It's always easier with someone else to look at the colors. I'll help you pick out some dress material, okay?"

Mary brightened. "That would be wonderful gut."

To Barbie's relief, that simple offer seemed to brighten Mary's mood. She helped more or less cheerfully right through supper and the clean-up.

By the time Matt and the kinder returned, Rebecca was feeling better. Barbie and Mary were finally able to head for home, nearly two hours later than they'd expected.

Barbie glanced at Mary as they rolled down the road toward home. "I hope your daad won't be worried at me bringing you back so late." She clucked to Belle, and the mare obligingly picked up her pace.

Mary shrugged, as usual. But at least her mouth didn't sag into that sullen expression. "I said I didn't know what time we'd get home. Daad said to stay as long as I was needed." She paused. "I was needed, wasn't I?" There was a hint of longing in her voice that Barbie didn't miss.

"You were definitely needed," she responded. "Poor Rebecca. If you hadn't been there, she'd have insisted on helping. And it wouldn't make the guests feel wilkom to have her being sick, ain't so?"

Mary nodded, looking pleased and amused at the same time. "Did you mean it?" she asked. "When you said you'd help me pick out material for a dress?"

"Sure I did. We'll get a driver to take us one day soon . . . maybe next week. Can you get someone to watch Ben's kinder?"

"I suppose Sarah will." She sounded reluctant to ask. "Or if they're not busy in the buggy shop, Daad and Ben can take over."

"There you go, then."

Mary shot her a look. "You sound Englisch when you say that."

"I guess I picked it up at the café." It wasn't the only thing she'd picked up at the café.

"Or at the bar?" Mary had the air of daring her, and she suspected she knew why.

"I was at the bar that night, but that was the only time." She returned the look. "What about you?"

Mary's face set for a moment, but then she seemed to accept the fact the she'd asked first. "My first time, too." Her eyes flared with defiance. "It wasn't all that bad."

Barbie knew she had to answer, and she wasn't ready. Why had Moses ever thought she was the right person to guide his daughter? She couldn't even guide herself. Well, all she could do was be honest with the girl.

"Judging by the way those boys were groping you, it would have been bad if someone hadn't interrupted."

Mary looked as if she'd like to retort, but she didn't. Maybe she was honest enough to recognize the truth of Barbie's words. If so, that was a good first step.

They went the rest of the way in silence, but it was a companionable one. They pulled up at the back door, and Mary slid down.

She paused a moment, her hand on the seat. "Denke, Barbie. I . . ."

The back door burst open, and Sarah surged onto the porch. "It's about time you're getting here. Daad was took bad with pain in his chest, and you not here to take care of him."

Barbie could read the fear and worry behind the sharp words, but probably Mary didn't.

"Where is he? How bad is it?" She asked the questions before Mary could burst out. Obviously she couldn't just turn around and go home.

"Ben took him to the Urgent Care center," Sarah said. "He was in pain and short of breath. I had to come and stay with Ben's kinder."

"I pray God is with him," Barbie said softly. "I'm glad you were able to be here."

"Well, of course," Sarah said. "But I must get home." She turned to Mary. "You'll have to take over Abram and Libby. They've had their supper."

"But what about Daadi?" Mary's voice shook a little.

"We must wait to hear from Ben." Sarah turned toward the barn. "He said he'd try to call, but I've been too busy with the kinder to check."

Mary didn't wait for the end of that sentence. She darted toward the phone shanty.

Sarah looked after her. "I suppose I'll have to stay. Mary's too flighty to be left."

Barbie bit her tongue to keep from a retort that wouldn't help. Over Sarah's shoulder, she saw Mary come out of the shanty, her shoulders sagging. Clearly there hadn't been any news.

"I'll stay," she said firmly. "There is no point in us both being here. You go on home."

Sarah eyed her as if she'd said something offensive. "I'm Mary's sister. It's up to me."

Well, this was a good chance to live up to her words to Mary about not making things worse. "Ja, of course it's up to you. But my parents won't be worried, since they knew I was working at Rebecca's. And you have the responsibility for your kinder as well."

Sarah hesitated, torn for some reason Barbie didn't understand. "All right. But you don't leave until Ben gets back. And tell him to call me right away."

Still intent on keeping the peace, Barbie nodded and refrained from pointing out that Sarah didn't have to give her orders. She'd stay because of Mary and the kinder, not Sarah.

Ben glanced at his father as the driver he'd called turned into the lane toward home. Daad hadn't quite regained his usual color, but he was breathing easily now. "Feeling okay?" he ventured.

"I'm fine." Daad's tone was short. "Stress— what kind of a word is that to use?"

At least his impatience seemed to be with the medical personnel, not with Benuel, who'd insisted he see the doctor.

"I don't like people fussing over me," he added.

Ben's gaze met that of Clara Nicholls, the Englisch neighbor who loved serving as an unofficial taxi for her Amish neighbors. Clara gave a slight shrug, probably indicating the hopelessness of arguing with a stubborn male about his health.

"I won't fuss, Daad, but I can't say the same for Mary and Sarah, so you'd better be prepared for them." But as Clara pulled up to the back door, he realized that wasn't Sarah's buggy parked by the lane.

Frowning, he slid out, forcing himself not to offer a helping hand he knew would be resented.

Clara leaned across the seat. "You listen to the family and take it easy, Moses. We're none of us as young as we used to be."

Ben suppressed a smile as Daad thanked her for

the ride, if not for the advice. "Denke, Clara. You've been wonderful kind."

"It's nothing." She nodded toward his father. "We have to take care of the good people in this world."

He raised his hand as she pulled around and drove off, and then headed for the door. Whose buggy was that, if not Sarah's?

Mary was already out the door, wrapping her arms around Daad. "Are you all right? Are you sure? We were so worried." Even as she spoke, her eyes filled with tears.

Did she feel guilty, afraid that her misbehavior might have brought this on? But they'd all had a share in the stress Daad felt, surely, not just Mary. He contributed, for sure, and so did Sarah in her way.

"I'm fine, fine," Daad repeated, patting Mary's shoulder. "Just a little tired is all."

Mary must have interpreted that literally, because she kept her arm around him for support as they went into the house, leading him straight to his favorite rocking chair.

"Mary, whose buggy . . ." Ben let the sentence die out as Barbie came down the stairs.

She put her finger to her lips in a shushing gesture as he approached. "Both your little ones are asleep. Abram was determined to stay awake until you got home, but after a story and a song or two, he succumbed." Her mouth curved in a smile that contained a tenderness he hadn't often seen in her. "They are so sweet."

He felt as if she'd caught him on the wrong foot by being here, even by putting his kinder to bed. "I don't understand. Sarah was supposed to stay until Mary got home."

Barbie glanced toward the living room, where Mary was fussing over Daad, insisting that he have a pillow behind his back and a stool beneath his feet. It looked to Ben as if they were both enjoying it.

"We were late getting here, I'm afraid." She gave him a quick, inquiring glance, as if expecting a complaint from him, but he just nodded.

"I suppose Sarah was fretting about getting home to her family, then." And knowing Sarah, that fact combined with her worry over Daad would have made her short-tempered.

"It happens sometimes when you're dealing with guests. You can't always predict how long you'll be needed. As it happened, Rebecca wasn't feeling well, so Mary and I had to take care of the guests until Matt got home."

"I understand that part, but I'm not sure why you stayed on here. You probably had things of your own to take care of."

And he didn't like feeling indebted to her. That was the truth of it, and he'd better confess it to himself, if not to Barbie.

"Nothing pressing," she said lightly. "Mary was a

bit upset, so I thought it best if I stayed with her." Her gaze flickered again toward the living room. "I'm sure you'd rather be on your own to get your daad settled, but if there's anything I can do . . ."

"We can manage. Denke," he added. "I'll walk out with you. I should leave a message on Sarah's phone, letting her know all is well so she doesn't come rushing back to see for herself."

Barbie didn't speak until they were on the porch and safely out of earshot. "How is your daad? I guess it wasn't a heart attack, since he's home."

"Is that what Sarah said? She always jumps to the worst conclusion. He was short of breath and said his chest felt tight." Remembering that moment and his own conclusion-jumping made him cold. "The doctor couldn't find anything physically wrong. He seems to think it was caused by stress."

"I'm sure you're relieved."

He shrugged. "I suppose, except that I don't know how to go about easing his worries."

"No, I guess not." Barbie frowned, her forehead puckering a little. Was she thinking of Daad? Or had her mind switched over to the stress and pain her own actions might cause her parents?

If he were a better minister, he would have just the right words to help Barbie. Unfortunately, all he could seem to do was think about how appealing she looked with that little line crinkling between her brows as she pondered.

The fact that she appealed to him made it all the

more important that he behave as her minister should. But still, the warmth and caring she'd shown today seemed to show she had more depth to her than the frivolous image she often showed him. He found himself imagining how she'd looked when she'd cradled his kinder close and sung to them.

They'd reached her carriage, and he automatically began helping her harness the mare.

"I can do this," she protested. "You should call Sarah and get back to your daad."

"Sarah can wait another few minutes." He settled the harness and began fastening the straps. "And it might do Mary and Daad both good to be together. Besides, there was something Daad wanted me to ask you."

Barbie looked a little surprised, but she nodded. Giving the mare a final pat, she looped the lines in preparation for climbing in.

He stood looking down at her, wondering how best to put the question.

"Well?" she prompted, eyebrows lifting.

"You know worship is here on Sunday. Daad thought . . . well, when the young ones come back for the singing, we wondered if you would stay and help. Mary . . ." He seemed to lose track of the words, not eager to show he needed her.

"He thinks Mary might enjoy the singing more if I were one of the chaperones?" She finished the sentence for him.

"Ja, that's right." Actually, what he'd said was that if Sarah insisted on staying to chaperone, Mary would probably do something just to make her mad.

Barbie tilted her head and seemed to be sizing him up. "And what do you think of me as a chaperone, Ben Kauffmann?"

She'd made him smile, which was probably just what she'd intended.

I think of you a little too much for comfort. "I want you to come. Satisfied?"

"I guess it will have to do." The dimple at the corner of her lips showed for a moment.

She turned, grasping the rail to pull herself up. Before he could tell himself it was a bad idea, he'd clasped her waist, giving her a boost up to the carriage seat.

Was it his imagination, or were her cheeks a little rosier than normal?

"Denke, Barbie. I'll see you later."

Barbie gave a quick, flurried nod and clucked to the mare. Had he put her off balance with his actions? Well, if so, that was only fair, because she put him off balance constantly just by being herself.

Lancaster County, Spring 1960

His companions on the trip to Brook Hill were talking so much that no one seemed to notice his silence. Reuben figured that was just as well.

He glanced out the window, still surprised after a full day and a half here at the amount of undeveloped land there was. In Lancaster County, one farm bordered the next in a peaceful checkerboard of fields. Here the woods came right to the road as often as not, with arable land still wild with growth of pines and hemlocks, sumac and mountain laurel. The laurel on the hillsides was in bloom, its pinky-white blossoms peeping through the stands of trees.

On either side the horizon was defined by the ridges that ran parallel to each other, separated by the valley floor and the inevitable streams, where a man could build a fine farm and raise a family.

But was he that man? The pain and hurt on Elizabeth's face when she'd heard he was coming on this trip couldn't be dismissed from his mind. Was he doing the right thing? Ever since they'd left home early yesterday morning, he'd been praying, asking God to give him a sign, like He had given Gideon. Stay or go? But God had been silent.

Reuben's gaze was caught by a figure moving at a fence line on the farm they were passing. The figure bent, rose, seemed to stumble, and then bent again. It took a second to understand what he was watching. The man—a white-haired Englischer—was trying to lift a wooden pasture gate into place. Even as he watched, the gate fell, taking the man with it.

"Stop a minute." Reuben was already reaching for the door handle. "Looks like somebody needs help."

The driver slowed, pulling over, but Johnny shook his head. "He's up. Must have just tripped."

Their driver consulted his watch. "If we're going to meet that real estate agent at two, we'd better keep moving."

But he had the door open. "You go on. I'll give him a hand, and you can pick me up on the way back, ja?"

"But the property—"

"You can tell me all about it." He slid out, driven by an impulse he didn't quite understand. He wanted out, that was all. He needed to be away from all the chatter about buying and selling and moving long enough to clear his head.

Not looking back, he strode along the fence row, hearing the car pull off as he went. He took a breath, filling his lungs with fresh country air mingled with the scent of growing things. It was a gut place, he felt sure of it, but was this valley the place for him?

The Englischer straightened at the sight of him, eyeing him with a caution that suggested he hadn't seen many Amish. "Can I do something for you?"

He was older than Reuben had thought at first

sight, his face weathered and wrinkled with years spent working outdoors, his shoulders stooped.

"You looked like you could use a hand with the gate." Reuben waited for a response, not sure he'd done the right thing. Not everyone welcomed help, he supposed, and this wasn't home, where he knew everyone in the township, Amish or Englisch.

The elderly Englischer took his time, studying Reuben's face, and then he nodded. "It'd be kind of you." He nodded in the direction the car had gone. "But your friends—"

"They'll stop for me on the way back. They're going to look at a place for sale down the road."

"The Pierson farm, that would be." The man nodded, satisfied he'd placed them. "I heard there were some Amish fellows coming in to look at it. Thinking about settling here in the valley, are you?"

"Could be," Reuben said cautiously. "If we can find places to farm."

"Plenty of good farmland around here." The man bent over the gate.

Moving quickly, Reuben forestalled him, lifting the wooden gate easily and moving it into place between the posts. "If I hold it steady, can you get the hinges in place?"

He nodded, pulling a packet of screws and a screwdriver from the pocket of his overalls. "I'll manage." He shot a glance toward the farmhouse and his leathery face crinkled in a smile.

183

"There's Mother out on the porch, watching to make sure I'm not hurting myself. The way that woman fusses, you'd think I was too old to walk across my own land."

Reuben found himself relaxing at the familiar plaint. "You sound like my daad. Women are always going to fuss, ain't so?"

"Your folks farmers, are they?" He straightened the hinge that had pulled loose from the post and set the new screw.

Reuben nodded. "In Lancaster County. Dairy, mostly, but a good-sized truck patch, too."

"Local talk says you might want to move up here."

What else did local talk say? He'd like to have an idea of how wilkom Amish would be here. The others were so excited at the idea of reasonably priced farmland that they didn't seem to consider anything else.

"There are five families interested in coming." He darted a look at the man, but the weathered face only showed preoccupation with the hinge. "My brother will take over my daad's place when it's time, so I need to find a place I can farm—me and my wife," he added.

The Englischer tightened the screw and gave the hinge a testing yank. Then he stooped to the bottom hinge. "This area could do with some more good farmers," he said eventually. "You and your wife have any kids?"

Reuben's heart winced. "Not yet," he said.

"A farm's a good place for kids to grow up." He spoke softly, almost to himself. "Both my boys loved it. Farm life turned them into good men." He shrugged. "But now they live in suburban houses, and their kids don't know one end of a cow from the other."

Reuben wasn't sure what to say. That seemed a cause for sympathy to him, but an Englischer might not look at things the same way.

Fortunately the man didn't seem to expect an answer. He finished, straightened, and checked to be sure the latch still worked right on the other end of the gate. Then he gave a short nod.

"She'll hold now, I think." He stuck out his hand. "I'm Fred Masters."

"Reuben Lapp." The man's hand, horny with years of work, was still strong, his handshake firm.

"Come on up to the house, Reuben. Reckon we both deserve a lemonade on an afternoon like this one."

He could hardly expect the others back this soon, so Reuben nodded and fell into step with him.

"How many acres do you farm?" Reuben asked, noting the sturdy barn and the various out-buildings, all in good repair. A couple of Jersey cows lifted their heads to stare incuriously at them as they passed.

"There's a hundred and ten acres altogether, but

some of it's in woods." He gestured toward the place where the land lifted to curve up to the forested ridge. "I own all the way up to the ridge, and there's nothing but State Game Lands beyond. Plentiful water comes from springs right off the ridge."

"You're fortunate," Reuben said. That was twice his daad's acreage, and with a good water source besides.

Masters nodded. "Always felt that way. Still, it's getting to be too much for me now. I don't like to admit it, but it's true."

All he could do was show his sympathy. At least Daad knew that his place would be carried on by family for generations, if God willed. It sounded as if Masters didn't have that comfort.

They were near the porch now, and the woman —Mrs. Masters—was looking at them expectantly. "I see you got some help," she said, "and it's a good thing. I don't know what you were thinking of, trying to fix that gate yourself."

"Take it easy, Betty. It's done now, anyway. This is Reuben Lapp. He's thinking of farming around here."

The woman smiled with none of the caution her husband had initially shown. "Well, now, isn't that nice? We could use some young families around here, what with so many young folks moving away. You sit right down, Reuben, and I'll bring you two some cold lemonade."

"Denke," he said, and then corrected himself. "Thank you."

"No trouble." She bustled into the house, only to appear moments later with a tray bearing glasses that she must have had already set out. "There, now. You have a family, do you?"

"Just my wife, Elizabeth." *Who doesn't want to move,* he added silently. "I'm hoping to find a farm for sale that I can afford, so we can settle here." He glanced from one to the other. "I hope we'd be wilkom here."

Masters shrugged. "People here are pretty much like folks everywhere—a bit wary about things they don't understand. But friendly, for the most part. Seems to me you folks could settle down happily here if you didn't mind a few bumps in the road along the way."

"I'd guess it was that way most everyplace," Reuben said. "We always aim to be gut neighbors."

Masters and his wife exchanged glances, and she gave a little nod.

"Well, as it happens, maybe you did yourself as well as me a good turn today," he said. "Betty and me know we have to sell up soon, so this place is going to be on the market. If you're interested . . . well, you'd have some time to check things out before we're ready to sell. But if it looks right to you, we'd give you first chance at it. We'd be pleased to see our place going to a young family who'd farm it the way it should be farmed."

Reuben could only stare at them, his mind whirling. There were questions to be asked, of course. He'd have to have a lot more information before he could make a decision, but looking around, it seemed to him this place already felt like home.

He'd been asking God for a sign, and it looked as if God had answered.

He'd have to pray God would see fit to give Elizabeth a sign as well.

Chapter Ten

Lancaster County, Spring 1960

Elizabeth tried to concentrate on the sunflower seeds she was planting along the edge of the garden, only to discover that she'd dumped a whole handful of seeds in one place and then covered them with so much soil they'd never grow. Annoyed with herself, she removed them and started over, pulling the old rag rug she knelt on along the row.

She hadn't been able to focus on anything all day. Or at least, not on anything but missing Reuben. For the fiftieth time, she stared out the lane, willing the driver who was bringing the men back from Brook Hill to appear. But the lane remained stubbornly empty.

What would she do if they really had to be apart for an extended time? The past two nights had felt like an eternity. She'd wakened half a dozen times each night, reaching out for Reuben across the bed and feeling cold, empty sheets instead of his warm, solid body.

Elizabeth patted down the last of the seeds. Picking up a convenient twig, she used it to pierce the seed packet, sticking it upright in the soil at the end of the row. If Mamm Alice or Becky came out to do any planting, they'd know where the row of sunflowers was planted, even before they'd sprouted.

She was finished, but she continued to kneel, her thoughts tumbling around and around like a pebble in a fast-moving stream. The warm earth and the sun on her back should be comforting, but nothing short of seeing Reuben back where he belonged could reassure her.

They'd parted with coldness between them. She hadn't meant it to be that way. She'd thought she would be able to talk to Reuben calmly, quietly, about how hurt she'd been to learn about the trip in such a way. But each time she'd tried to speak, the tears had clogged her throat. So she'd ended up saying nothing, just looking at him, feeling chilled to the bone, as he'd climbed into the car and left.

Now . . . now she'd give anything just to have him back again. What if something had happened? Panic seized her heart. What if they'd had an accident with the car and no one had known how to reach her? What if he was alone somewhere, hurt?

Stupid. Don't be stupid. Nothing has happened. She planted her hands on the rug and pushed herself up to a standing position. Reuben would be back soon.

And then what? What if he came back all excited about what he'd seen and heard? What if he were even more determined to leave? Was it right to pray that he'd be disappointed?

Elizabeth felt drenched in shame, as if she'd been dunked in a pail of hot water. How could she even think such a thing? If Reuben came home full of plans and excitement for a move she dreaded, she had to remain calm.

She was headed for the hand pump by the back door to wash her hands when she finally heard the sound she'd been waiting for all afternoon. She looked out the lane, shading her eyes against the sun, and her heart gave a little leap. They were back at last.

Hurriedly she washed her hands, brushing them dry on her skirt. When the car pulled up, she was waiting at the edge of the lane, trying not to show what she felt.

The door opened, and Reuben slid out. He met

her eyes cautiously, then turned quickly to raise a hand in farewell to the others. As the car drove off down the lane, he came to her, smiling a little.

"Did you miss me as much as I missed you, my Elizabeth?" He took her arms, pulling her against him gently.

"Even more," she whispered, closing her arms around him, not caring who might come out of the house or barn and see them. "Don't let's ever be apart like that again. I couldn't sleep without you there."

He held her close, and she felt the rumble of laughter in his chest. "Ach, I couldn't sleep either. But at least part of it was sharing a room with Johnny Stoltzfus. He snores."

Laughter chased away the tears that had begun to form in her eyes. "And I thought you missed me," she teased, loving the way his face lit with tenderness when she did.

"Reuben! You're back." Isaac's shout had them slipping apart, but Reuben kept a warm grip on her hand as his brother came hurrying toward them. "Well, how was it? Were the prices really better than here? Was there much land for sale?"

"Ach, let him have a moment with his wife, will you?" Daad Eli came along behind Isaac, chiding him.

Isaac just clapped his brother on the shoulder. "Time enough for cuddling later. We're all eager to hear about your trip."

"Komm in the house, then." Mamm Alice had come out on the porch at the sound of all the ruckus. "No need to be discussing family matters out in the lane that I know of. Besides, Reuben is probably tired and hungry. He needs a chance to catch his breath."

Reuben's eyelid flickered in a private wink just for Elizabeth. "I'm okay, but I could do with some coffee to wake me up after the drive."

They all trooped inside, with Reuben's hand still clasping hers, hidden by the folds of her skirt. It was only when he sat down at the table that he was forced to let go. Becky began pouring coffee into mugs, while Mamm Alice cut into one of the dried apple pies they'd made this morning. Elizabeth retrieved milk and sugar and set out plates and forks.

"Well, let's have it," Daad said, once they were settled. "What was it like?"

"Nice." Reuben nodded, his mouth full of pie. "We all felt that way, I think. Hillier than it is here, but still plenty of arable land. The folks we talked to seemed friendly, though I don't doubt that there would be some who wouldn't like the idea of a bunch of Amish moving in."

Concern crossed Mamm Alice's face, and she reached across the table to pat his hand. "I wouldn't want you settling where people were against the Amish without even knowing you."

"Nonsense," Daad Eli said quickly. "We're just

spoiled because we've been here for so long that everyone is used to us. People are the same no matter where you go. Sounds like they probably just need to get used to the Amish, like the Englisch did when the Leit came here back in the 1700s."

Elizabeth's heart got heavier with every word that was spoken. How could Reuben think of taking her to a place where the neighbors not only weren't kin, they actually bore malice toward the Amish?

"I saw one farm," Reuben began, sending a cautious look in her direction. "Well, I wasn't really intending to look at it. Didn't even know it was for sale. But I saw the owner struggling with a pasture gate that had to be fixed, so I stopped to give him a hand."

Daad Eli's gray eyebrows lifted. "What about the other boys?"

"We were supposed to meet a real estate person who was showing us a farm," Reuben explained. "So I told them to go on and then they could pick me up on the way back. Didn't seem as if all of us needed to be there. So anyway I gave the man a hand, and then he wanted me to come up to the house and meet his wife. She gave me lemonade and sugar cookies, and we talked."

"Sounds like nice, hospitable folks," Mamm Alice said, maybe making up for her earlier comment.

Elizabeth just stiffened, her hands clasping the sides of the chair seat tightly.

"They were." Reuben looked at her with caution. "And it turned out they were actually looking for a buyer for their property. Ach, you should see it, Daad." His enthusiasm seemed to sweep him on. "Plenty of room for a dairy herd, and a substantial barn in good shape. Twin silos, a chicken coop, and the like. It's over a hundred acres, and he's asking half what they asked for the last farm that sold here."

"You'd need a tie barn for milking," Daad Eli observed. "Otherwise it sounds wonderful good."

"Ja." Reuben looked down at his hands, maybe because he didn't want to look at Elizabeth. "There's questions to be answered, that's certain-sure, but this fellow, Mr. Masters, said that he wasn't in any hurry. He won't sell to anyone else without checking with me first."

"Mighty generous of him." Daad Eli looked cautious. "You'll want to check things out careful-like."

"I know. But still—"

Reuben caught back his words as Elizabeth jumped to her feet. They all looked at her. She knew she was making a fool of herself, but she couldn't help it. She couldn't sit here any longer and listen to Reuben making plans for their future without even consulting her.

"I . . . I forgot something in the garden," she stammered, and rushed out of the kitchen.

She'd reached the shade of the big willow tree before her headlong rush stopped. She stood there, hands pressed against the rough bark, grateful for the sweeping branches that shielded her from view like leafy curtains.

How could he talk to his family first? They were his family, ja, but this was something to be decided between husband and wife. It wasn't the family's future Reuben was talking about. It was hers.

Elizabeth sucked in a deep breath, reminding herself that she'd vowed to be calm. To explain quietly, reasonably, what she wanted. Surely she could, and he'd listen—

She'd gotten that far in her reasoning when the green curtains parted and Reuben came into the still, cavelike space beneath the tree.

"Elizabeth? Are you all right?"

She pressed her lips together for a moment, but it was no use. "You talk as if it's all settled. How could you discuss our future like that in front of everyone?"

He didn't speak for a moment, and she sensed that he, too, was struggling to be calm and reasonable. "I didn't mean to, but when everyone started asking me questions, I had to answer, didn't I?"

Elizabeth put her hand to her throat, as if that

would ease the tightness there. "You could have said we needed to talk about it first."

"Well, and so we do need to talk about it. I told you I'd take time in making a decision, and I will." The familiar note of exasperation crept into his voice. "But I can't keep it a secret that I saw a place that . . ." He caught her arm, turning her to face him. "Listen, Elizabeth. If you saw it, you'd see what I did. A good farm, just right for us. A place that feels like home—"

"This is home." The words burst out of her.

His jaw tightened. "I've already explained that we can't stay here. This will be Isaac's place, not ours."

"I know that, but—"

"But you won't be happy unless I produce a home for us close to your family." He snapped the words. "Well, I can't."

"You promised you'd try." Her own control shattered into pieces. "You said you would, but now all you can think about is that farm miles and miles away from anything we know."

"Well, you promised you'd listen. You'd try to understand. But you're not. You're just hanging on to the past."

"I can't do what you want. I can't." She heard herself growing shrill, but she couldn't seem to stop it. "My life is here, my family is here. Our son is buried here."

Reuben jerked back as if she'd slapped him.

He stared at her, his face working. Then he turned and plunged away from her.

Elizabeth's breath caught. The pain in her chest was so fierce it was like trying to bring a new life into the world all over again.

She couldn't get her breath. She pressed her palm against her chest, feeling the thudding of her own heart. How could it still be beating when it was broken?

New life. Her breath stuck on a sob. That was what Reuben wanted. And she . . . she was tearing their present life apart with her resistance.

What were they doing to each other? They'd been so happy together. Now it seemed that happiness was gone forever.

Why? Reuben had never really asked the question. She hadn't even asked it of herself. Why couldn't she consent to this move?

An image of that small grave, just like all the others in the Amish cemetery, forced itself into her mind. That was part of it.

But the rest? She struggled to face it. She was afraid. And the fear was so big, so strong, that she didn't think she could possibly overcome it. But she might have to if she didn't want to lose Reuben.

Barbie stood on the sidelines and watched the heated volleyball game in progress late Sunday afternoon. She was supposed to be the referee, but that didn't seem to stop the good-natured arguments over calls. Each side was made up of the same number of boys and girls, and they were equally competitive. So far she'd treated one black eye, a nosebleed, and a twisted ankle. Amish youth volleyball wasn't for the faint of heart.

The ball came rocketing toward her, out-of-bounds, and she reacted without thought, smacking it back across the net to the far side. Naturally the kids took that for a sign that she was ready to play and hit it right back toward her.

She lofted it back. "Thought you'd catch me off-guard, didn't you? No chance!"

"Bet you can't get this one, Barbie," one of her cousins yelled, sending the ball soaring in her direction.

Grinning, she raised her hands to return it when someone reached over her head and hit it for her.

"Hey, no fair. That was mine," she said, looking up at Ben.

His eyes laughing, Ben took the next shot easily, not giving her a chance. "I can't help it if you're too short to reach."

He really was attractive when his face eased and the laughter filled his eyes. He should look that way more often.

"I'll show you who's short," she said. "Just let me have the next one."

Nodding, Ben took a step back, but when the ball came toward them again he feinted a move, putting her off balance, so that it fell between them.

"Your fault." She gave him a mock glare, making the kids laugh. She bent to retrieve the volleyball just as Ben did, and their heads collided.

He grasped her arm instantly. "Are you okay?"

"I think this game is too dangerous for us," she said, laughing. For an instant they stood close together. Their gazes entangled, and Barbie's breath caught.

"Time out." One of the mothers who'd been setting up supper on a long folding table waved her hands. "Supper is ready," she called over the groans of the more avid players. "Komm, esse." *Come, eat.* Teenagers, especially boys, couldn't resist that.

As the kids flocked to the table, Ben's hand fell from her arm. Faint embarrassment crossed his face. "I'd best see if they need anything," he muttered, and started toward the table.

And better for her to stay where she was for a second, at least until she could be sure no one noticed . . . Well, there wasn't anything to notice, she told herself crossly.

From the corner of her eye, she saw Mary peel off from the group and head toward the house. A problem? She'd been keeping an eye on Mary but hadn't noticed anything. Still, she should find out.

Mary had a head start, and by the time Barbie reached the kitchen, she was firmly telling her father to go and rest while she put the kinder to bed. So that was it. Not a problem, just a responsibility.

"I'll help Mary," she said, when Moses showed signs of arguing. "We'll have it done in no time."

He nodded, and she thought he still looked a bit tired. "Denke, Barbie. Mary. You're gut girls." He sank down in his rocker.

Little Libby had wrapped both arms around Barbie's legs. "Sory," she demanded.

Mary smiled. "She means story. She remembers the stories you told them Friday evening."

Barbie scooped Libby up in her arms. "A story it is. As soon as you're ready for bed." Mary had Abram by the hand, and Barbie followed them up the steps, bouncing Libby a little with each stair so that she giggled.

"I gave them their baths before everyone came, so we just have to do faces and teeth and get them to bed." Mary led the way to the small bedroom that contained a twin bed with a rail for Abram and a crib for Libby. Their night things were already laid out on the bed.

"You're very organized," Barbie said, carrying Libby into the adjoining bathroom to wash her face and hands. "I'm impressed."

Mary flushed a little, as if pleased. "I have to be. There's a lot to do with two little ones in the house."

Surely Ben didn't expect his young sister to do all the mothering. "Doesn't their daadi put them to bed?" She tried to sound casual, not censorious.

"Ach, sure, he does sometimes. But he's usually busy with the stock this time of day. And we're trying to keep Daad from overdoing." Mary efficiently washed the wiggling little boy and reached for a small blue toothbrush. "Still, it's nice to have another woman here." She gave Barbie a shy smile.

Barbie smiled back, but her heart ached, just a little. Naturally everyone in the family would pitch in and help, but it seemed Mary felt extra pressure to be the mammi in this situation.

She couldn't help but compare Mary's state with her own at sixteen. Her thoughts would have been completely occupied with who would sit across from her at singing, and who might want to drive her home. She certain-sure wouldn't have been thinking about putting kinder to bed.

"You do a fine job with the young ones," she said carefully as they bore two clean kinder into the bedroom. "But I can see that another woman in the house would make a lot of difference."

Mary nodded, pulling back the log cabin quilt that covered Abram's bed. "Daad says Benuel's not too old to fall in love and get married."

She shouldn't ask, but she was going to. "What does Ben say to that idea?"

Mary wrinkled her nose. "He says falling in

love is for teenagers, not for a grown man. Really, that's what he says. Isn't that silly? He was telling Daad all the things he wants in a wife, just like he's making up a shopping list."

Barbie could practically hear him. No doubt his list was studded with qualities such as practical, sensible, serious, and responsible— all things notably missing in Barbie Lapp, as far as he was concerned.

Well, she didn't care. She wasn't interested anyway.

"Do you have a shopping list of things you're looking for in a come-calling friend?" she asked, her tone teasing.

Mary shrugged. "I'm not ready to settle down. I'd rather be like you." With a sudden change of tone, she added, "Will you do the story again?"

Barbie nodded. She sat on the bed, snuggling Abram against her side and Libby on her lap. Like her. Mary wanted to be like her. What exactly did that mean?

"Once upon a time, there were three bears who lived in a cottage in the woods," she began, keeping her voice soft and soothing.

She didn't know what Mary had meant. But she suspected that whatever it was, Ben would not approve of it.

Abram and Libby settled down quickly, probably worn out by all the excitement of having the rumspringa group here. She and Mary tiptoed out, leaving the door ajar so Moses could hear if anyone cried.

Barbie studied the girl as they walked back toward the picnic table, where a few of the adults were helping themselves to food now that the teenagers had eaten. It was typical teen food— potato chips and pizza, popcorn and cookies, with a fruit tray brought by some health-conscious mother.

Mary felt the weight of responsibility strongly, maybe because of her nature or because of her mother's death. Was that behind the acting out she'd done with those Englisch boys? As far as Barbie could tell, that had been a one-time thing, but she couldn't be sure. Teens were experts at fooling their elders.

But at least she felt certain that there was a connection. If Mary's home responsibilities could be eased a little, would that help?

Barbie found her gaze seeking Benuel, finding him as quickly as a horse found the barn at feeding time. He was leaning against the barn where they'd had worship that morning, his straw hat tilted at an angle that hid his eyes. The setting sun, striking down on him, turned his reddish-brown beard to flame.

Should she say something to him about the responsibility Mary carried? Or would he think she was inquiring as to his love life? The thought probably embarrassed her even more than it would him.

But Mary was more important than whatever minor embarrassment it might cause her. Anyway, she didn't have to bring up Mary's revelation about his search for a suitable wife. She just needed to point out her concern about relieving some of Mary's responsibilities in the household. Surely Ben could hire someone to come in and help out a few hours a day.

It would have to be the right person, of course. He couldn't turn those precious little ones over to just anyone. Someone gentle and loving and experienced . . .

Now she was the one making up a shopping list. It wasn't up to her anyway. But if she intended to strike while the iron was hot, she'd best speak to Ben now, before the games came to an end and the singing began.

Barbie drifted in Ben's direction, trying not to be obvious, until she ended up next to him. She kept her gaze fixed on the game.

"It looks as if everyone is having fun," she said. Was she being impetuous, bringing this up without thinking it through first? If so, well—that was part of her character, wasn't it? Anyway, it couldn't do any harm.

"Hard to believe we used to enjoy evenings like this, isn't it?" Ben sounded relaxed. "I saw you go in the house with Mary. Is everything all right?"

He was leading right into what she wanted to say. "She didn't want to leave your daad to put the kinder to bed, so I helped her."

He turned to face her. "I had planned to do it, but Daad insisted."

At least he'd had good intentions. "He was still insisting when we got there, but between us, we managed to convince him."

"Denke." A line appeared between his brows. "I should have realized."

She suspected he hated to admit that his young sister had been more diligent than he was in this particular circumstance. "Mary certainly takes on a lot of responsibility for someone her age. I'm sure I wasn't nearly as reliable at sixteen." She darted a look at him. "And if you suggest I'm still not, I'm not going to be very pleased with you."

The slight frown disappeared, and his eyes crinkled. "I wouldn't dream of it." There was a certain warmth in his gaze that flustered her.

"I . . . I started to wonder if Mary might have been feeling overwhelmed." She had to tread carefully, not wanting to suggest that he was at fault. "Perhaps that had something to do with her cutting loose that night."

"If you're saying I expect too much of her—"

"No, I'm not." She snapped the words in exasperation. "That's just what I was afraid you'd think. I'm saying that Mary expects too much of herself."

205

It must have taken a moment for him to absorb the words. He stood looking down at her, his face grim as he struggled with it. Finally he let out a long breath, and his broad shoulders moved restlessly under the fabric of his shirt.

"Before Mamm died, Mary was the perkiest little thing you'd ever want to see." He said the words slowly, looking back into a past that had more than its share of pain. "Then . . . ach, Mamm's death changed everything. And then Donna." His face twisted. "If you're expecting us to be a normal happy family after all that, you're not as smart as I'd thought."

She had the sense that the bitterness in his words wasn't really intended for her. "I know," she said quietly.

The sun slid behind the ridge, streaking the sky with pink and purple. The game in front of them came to an end. In the barn, someone had lit the lanterns on the tables, and their glow filtered out. As if in answer to an unseen signal, the kids began to form two lines—boys in one, girls in the other.

Ben shook his head like a dog coming out of the stream. "We'd best get inside," he said shortly, and turned away.

She followed him more slowly. She still hadn't brought up the idea of finding someone to come in and help with the house and kinder, but obviously now wasn't the time.

In the barn, the tables were arranged end to end to form one long table with benches along the sides. There were chairs placed at either end for the adults, so Barbie moved to her place next to one of the mothers, while Ben settled at the far end.

After a moment, the youngsters began to file in, just as they would for worship. But unlike at worship, this was a cheerful, chattering parade as they came past the chaperones, shaking hands and joking before going to the tables, boys on one side, girls on the other.

Gradually the group fell silent. One of the boys would probably start the singing, and judging by the glances, they'd picked Seth Unser, a shy sixteen-year-old. He looked around, gulped, and began a song in a surprisingly deep voice. The others joined in, and their young voices lifted to the rafters of the old barn.

Barbie was startled to find tears stinging her eyes. They were so young, their voices so pure. When she'd been their age, she'd thought life was such a simple thing. Her worries then had been trivial, almost silly, in comparison to those that confronted her now.

Or those that confronted Mary. She sought out the girl. Her face was lifted, her throat moving as she sang. If only . . .

Well, she didn't know what. She just knew she wanted to make things better for Mary.

Barbie found her gaze drawn to Ben, sitting

almost directly opposite her. He was looking at her, his eyes intent, and she felt the flush rising in her cheeks. What was he thinking? That she had intruded into his family's private sorrows? Or something else entirely?

The singing went on, from one song to the next with barely a pause between them. Now the girls were starting, with the other voices joining in at the end of the first line. Barbie tried to concentrate on the words and the voices, keeping her eyes from straying toward Benuel by force of will.

She'd succeeded fairly well up until the point at which the young singers took a break, heading for the tables where lemonade, soft drinks, and snacks had been put out. They would chatter, refresh themselves, and be ready for another hour of singing.

They would also begin to pair off. She remembered that part of the process only too clearly. Barbie slipped toward the door. If she went outside, she could both keep an eye on any couples who decided to take advantage of the moment and also evade Benuel, who seemed to be working his way through the crowd in her direction.

She tried to tell herself she wasn't being cowardly in avoiding him. But those moments when he'd let her see a small part of his inward pain—she hadn't quite known how to handle it. She still didn't. It was far easier to spar with Ben than to speak seriously with him.

Just a step or two from the barn door the spring evening enveloped her. The breeze was cool enough to be refreshing and carried the faint scent of hyacinths from the spring bulbs that someone, probably Ben's mother, had planted beyond the toolshed. She was near the paddock gate, and one of the buggy horses, displaced from the barn for the day, whickered softly, sensing her presence.

"Hush, now." She moved to the gate and patted the nose that poked over inquiringly.

"Barbie."

She hadn't heard him coming, but she, like the horses, had sensed Ben a second before he spoke.

She turned toward him, trusting the darkness to hide it if that betraying flush returned to her cheeks. What was she thinking of, to let herself be flustered by someone like Ben Kauffmann?

"Just thought someone should take a look around, in case any courting couples decided to make a break for it." She kept her voice light.

"I think we are the only ones out here now." He moved until he was only a step away.

"I guess we can go back in, then, can't we?"

"Not yet." He put out a detaining hand and clasped her wrist in a warm grip. "We didn't have a chance to finish what we were saying. About Mary."

Her taut muscles relaxed. She was perfectly willing to talk about Mary, just as long as it didn't move into dangerously personal territory.

"Mary, ja." She took a breath, annoyed that the touch of his hand could disturb her usual poise. "I . . . was just thinking that maybe it would be good to have a woman come in, even a few hours a day, to help out with the house and kinder, especially now that she's working at Rebecca's."

She paused, but he didn't speak. Didn't give any indication as to whether he was annoyed at her interference or actually listening to her.

"There must be someone—maybe one of the older widows in the community could spare the time. It might ease the need Mary feels to . . . well, to fill her mother's place." Or her sister-in-law's place.

"I have thought of it, you know."

His voice wasn't angry, and his fingers moved absently against her skin, setting up a shiver of awareness that seemed to move right up her arm.

"At first Sarah insisted she could handle things, but that didn't work out very well. So Daad told her we could manage on our own." He shook his head. As her eyes grew more accustomed to the dim light, she could see the way his brows drew together and his mouth firmed.

"Are you concerned she'd be offended if you asked someone else for help?" Once again, she seemed to be treading more deeply into his family affairs than she ought.

"She might." His expression seemed to lighten for a moment, as if he invited her to share his amusement. "But that would not prevent me. The truth is that I didn't see it, and you did."

"You're not going to start blaming yourself, are you?" She kept her voice light with an effort. Little though she might approve of how rigid Ben could be on matters of conscience, she could also understand that it grew out of his sense of responsibility. Maybe even his caring.

"As a minister and as Mary's brother, I should have done better."

Barbie was swept by the desire to shake him. "Stoppe." She actually grabbed his arms. Impossible to shake him, though. He was as solid as a wall. "You can't carry everyone's burdens, Benuel. No one expects it of you."

"But I do," he said. His gaze focused on her face so intently. "Like Mary."

She shook her head, despairing of getting through to him. "You're hopeless, you know that? You'll drive yourself crazy trying to be perfect."

"I'm far from that." His voice was a low rumble. "If I were, I wouldn't be—"

He stopped. Shook his head. And then pulled her against him and covered her lips with his.

For an instant, Barbie was so startled that she didn't react at all. Then she felt the warmth of his firm lips, smelled the scent of his skin, and longing spread through her, fierce and strong. She put her arms around him, leaning into his kiss, ignoring the little voice in the back of her mind insisting that this was wrong, that they shouldn't do this, that she should pull away at once, that . . .

Benuel's lips on hers, his arms strong and secure around her, their surroundings receding into the distance until there was only the circle of his embrace—

He let her go so suddenly that she nearly fell. He stared at her, aghast. "I didn't—I shouldn't—"

Apparently he couldn't find the words. She couldn't, either. He shook his head, clamped his lips together, and marched off toward the barn.

Barbie stood alone in the dark, her lips still trembling from the intensity of his kiss, and tried to find her balance. What on earth was she doing? This couldn't happen. She couldn't possibly have feelings for Ben, not Ben. Not a man who was opposed to everything that made her who she was.

When Grossmammi had told her the story of her terrible fear at the idea of moving away from all she knew and loved, Barbie hadn't really been able to understand. Grossmammi was the bravest person she knew.

She'd always thought she was brave, like her grandmother. Now she felt the other side—the fear. She was terrified of falling in love with Ben.

Chapter Eleven

Lancaster County, Spring 1960

Reuben sat next to his brother in the buggy, trying to clear his mind for the zoning meeting ahead of them. He glanced back. Theirs was only one of a long line of Amish carriages moving along the two-lane township road toward the fire hall where the meeting would be held.

"Looks almost like a church Sunday, ain't so?" Isaac said, jerking his head toward the lineup behind them. "Hope nobody's in a hurry this evening."

"You did a fine job of passing the word about the meeting and getting the Leit to show up."

Isaac *had* worked hard. Reuben just wished he could believe it was going to make a difference to the outcome.

"Denke." Isaac looked almost surprised.

Was it that rare for him to say something positive to his little brother? He'd been so preoccupied with his own worries that he hadn't spared much thought for other people, it seemed. He'd have to do better.

He glanced at his brother, but Isaac seemed

preoccupied, frowning at the horse in front of him as if he didn't see it. Was he worrying about the outcome of the meeting? Or maybe he was afraid he'd be called upon to speak. None of them wanted to push themselves forward or draw attention to themselves, but there was little point in going to the meeting if they didn't make their concerns known.

Isaac cleared his throat. "Is . . . um, is Elizabeth feeling any better?"

"She's all right." The words came out too sharply for anyone to believe them, including him. Elizabeth wasn't all right. She was upset and struggling.

That was part of the problem with so many adults living in the same house. Everybody knew what was going on. He and Elizabeth would be better off on their own. And the least he could do was keep from snapping at his brother.

"You know she doesn't want to move away." It was his turn to stare straight ahead, reluctant to see his brother's face. "It's hard for her to accept the idea that we might have to."

Isaac nodded. "Kind of makes me feel bad that Becky and I get to stay on the farm."

"No need for you to feel that way," Reuben said quickly. "It's the sensible thing to do. Daad will want to keep working for a few more years anyway. You know it as well as I do."

A grin split Isaac's ruddy face. "The problem

will be to get him to slow down when he needs to."

Reuben couldn't help smiling at that idea. "Daad and Mamm both. Somehow I don't see them retiring to a grossdaadi haus any time soon."

"No. Well, I wouldn't want them to, and neither does Becky. She always says she'll be wonderful glad to have Mamm there when babies start coming along."

Reuben felt himself tensing at the mention of babies. The whole subject had become like a sore tooth—just made worse by poking at it.

"So what do you think will happen at the zoning board meeting?" It was an abrupt change of subject, but he couldn't go on talking about some-thing so sensitive. "You've been closer to it than I have."

Isaac's shoulders moved restlessly. "The way I hear it, they'll listen to the folks who want to make the changes. Then, when they're done, we should have a chance to ask questions and say what we're thinking."

"Are you ready to say something?"

"Ja, I guess so. I figure it's not as important how we speak up as that we do. If they could just understand how much trouble it would cause the farmers, I'm certain-sure they'll reconsider."

Isaac didn't sound as if he really believed his own words. And Reuben surely didn't. They'd been seeing which way the wind was blowing in

Lancaster County for a few years now. Progress. That's all the Englisch seemed to want to talk about.

"I hope so," he said. "What are folks around the township saying about it?"

"I heard a few things when I was at the mill yesterday." Isaac's forehead furrowed. "Some folks think the zoning board members have already made up their minds. That doesn't seem right to me. I'd think they should be more like a judge—listen to both sides and then decide."

"Maybe they figure they've already heard everything they need to hear." Reuben tried to think of something encouraging to say. "At least we'll have a chance to show them there's more than one side to the issue."

"Ja." Isaac's frown deepened. "Somebody heard one of the zoning board members saying they'd accommodated the Amish enough." He shook his head. "Didn't make sense to me. I can't see what they've done for us at all."

"I guess they'd say that more people stand to gain if there's a lot of building along that road. Folks in construction, electric contractors, building suppliers—they've all got a chance to make some money off it."

"They have a right to make a living, and I can't argue with that. But does it have to be where it hits us so hard?"

Isaac sounded as if he'd been giving the matter

deeper thought than Reuben would have expected. He kept forgetting that his little brother was an adult, with adult responsibilities now.

"The thing is," Isaac went on, "the farmers have the same right to make a living, and what they're talking about doing will hurt us. If we can just make them see it . . ." Isaac let his words trail off. It sounded as if, despite all his efforts, he didn't have much confidence that they could influence the outcome.

Reuben glanced at the road ahead. They'd been riding along between pastures and cornfields on either side of the road, but all of a sudden houses and businesses started appearing. He waved his hand.

"Look at it. Ten years ago this was cropland, producing food to feed hungry families. Where do they think the food on their tables will come from if they succeed in driving out all the farmers?"

Isaac was silent for a moment. Then he looked at Reuben. "You're going to leave no matter what is decided tonight, aren't you?"

Reuben's hands tensed, gripping the edge of the seat. "I think moving on is right for us. So yes, most likely." He paused, the weight settling on his shoulders. "If I can just get Elizabeth to see sense—"

He stopped abruptly, realizing what he'd said. That sounded so selfish. Was he that confident he knew what was right for everyone else? Somehow he didn't like that picture of himself.

"If we can come to an agreement," he said carefully.

"Well, either way, I'm wonderful glad you worked on this with me. Denke, Reuben."

He nodded. There wasn't really anything else to say. They would try their best to affect the future of the place they loved, and the rest was in the hands of God.

The cement block fire hall appeared ahead of them. He could feel his brother growing tense at the thought of what they were about to face.

As they drew into the gravel parking lot, Isaac spoke quickly, as if there was something that had to be said before he lost his nerve.

"There's something we've been keeping quiet about." His voice was a bit higher than usual, a little forced. "We didn't want to make things any harder for Elizabeth. But the thing is . . . well, Becky is going to have a baby."

Reuben felt the way he had the day he'd fallen from the barn loft and landed on a hay bale. It knocked the breath right out of him.

He should have expected it. Becky and Isaac were a young married couple. Naturally they'd be starting a family. It wasn't their responsibility to fret over how Elizabeth would take it.

Forcing a smile, he clapped his brother on the

shoulder. "That's wonderful gut news, Isaac. I'm happy for you."

"Are you?" His brother's face lit. "I . . . We just worried about how Elizabeth would react."

"Elizabeth will be happy for you and Becky," he said firmly. "There's no doubt about it."

Isaac ducked his head, grinning. "Baby will be coming in November, Becky says. She wants to name him after me."

Reuben kept his smile pinned on his face, determined not to think of his own tiny son. "If he's a girl, that's not going to work too well, ain't so?"

Laughing together, they pulled up at the hitching rail.

Ben peered into the buggy he and Daad were repairing and shook his head. "If this were tricked up any more, the boy might as well buy a car and be done with it."

The youngest Esch boy's courting buggy was done up with every gadget imaginable, from LED headlights to automatic interior lights to shag carpeting and a double mug holder.

"And what does he need with a speedometer?" He glanced at Daad, who shook his head, smiling.

"Maybe the answer to that is how he managed to break the suspension on a buggy he's had for less than a year. Still, it's money in our pockets to fix it." Daad patted the elliptic suspensions that hung along one wall of the workshop. "At least we already have all the parts we need in stock."

"Ja, looks like it." Ben picked up his clipboard and went over the list of what had to be done. "I hope his daad gave him a good talking-to about his antics."

"There's no harm in the boy." Daad always had a generous attitude toward the young. "All this is a young man's foolishness. He'll be putting away such childish things soon enough, like you did."

Ben's eyebrows lifted, and he smiled. "I never wasted money on something as frivolous as a buggy mug holder."

"You were foolish in other ways, as I remember. Luckily Donna wasn't looking for the fanciest buggy."

Ben's smile faded a bit as he thought of the day Donna had agreed to let him drive her home from a singing. He'd been walking on air all afternoon, and by the time the singing was over and they'd headed down the road in the buggy, he'd been so jittery he could barely speak.

"No, Donna didn't care about the buggy. I was the lucky one. I fell in love with the right person."

Falling in love was a dangerous thing. It made a man too vulnerable.

"The right person?" Daad squatted, checking the wheels to see what damage had been done to them. "I thought whoever you loved was the right person."

Ben shrugged, the memory of what had happened the previous night still haunting him. "A man could be attracted to someone who wasn't good for him. Maybe even attracted enough to do something foolish."

Daad straightened slowly, holding on to the wheel as he did. "Do you want to tell me what foolish thing happened between you and Barbie last night?"

"How did you know?" He felt as if he were twelve again, surprised at how on earth Daad could have known he was the one who'd forgotten to latch the stall door.

"I have eyes in my head," Daad said. "And so does Mary. When she says you and Barbie went outside during the break and you came back looking like a thundercloud, she knows something is up. Especially when Barbie couldn't seem to concentrate on where she was or what she was supposed to be doing."

"She said that?" He hadn't noticed Barbie's reaction to what had happened between them. He'd been too busy chiding himself for his own.

"She did. Mary's the sort who sees what folks would rather she didn't sometimes, ain't so?"

"Well, I certain-sure don't want her talking about me and Barbie," he muttered. The shame for his conduct was bad enough when he thought only two people knew what had happened out in the quiet darkness.

"I don't suppose she will," Daad said. "Barbie's a good person," he added.

"Ja." Whatever else he thought, he couldn't overlook the fact that she'd rescued Mary even at the risk to herself.

Daad's gaze, steady and serious, was the one that had always induced a younger Benuel to confess whatever minor offenses were weighing on his mind. Ben sighed. That look still worked.

"I kissed Barbie. I didn't intend to. And I don't suppose she did, either. It just . . . happened." As an excuse, that sounded feeble even to himself.

"You're a single man. Barbie is a single woman. I can't see any reason why you shouldn't kiss if you want to."

Was Daad laughing at him?

"It shouldn't have happened," he said stubbornly. "I shouldn't be kissing anyone unless I'm thinking of marrying her. And Barbie is the most unsuitable person in the world to be a minister's wife."

Daad leaned against the wheel of Thomas Esch's buggy, apparently ready to stand there all day talking if need be. "You know, that puts me in mind of how you got to be a minister. You didn't fill out an application or produce references or even ask for the job."

"No, of course not," he muttered. He could see what Daad was driving at. "People don't choose a minister. God makes the choice."

A slip of paper stuck in one book—and if you were the one who picked it up, that meant God had chosen you for His minister for the rest of your life. You had no say in the matter. The people you would minister to had no say. God chose.

"I don't see how God is going to pick the right wife for me. I'm the one who has to ask. I should use my best judgment, ain't so?"

Daad shrugged. "Barbie Lapp might not fit the picture you have in your mind of the best woman to be a minister's wife, but—"

"She doesn't," he said, interrupting. "She's frivolous and impulsive and far too interested in things Englisch."

"Maybe so. But she has a good heart," Daad said. "She brings a gift of laughter with her wherever she goes, ain't so? And she has been wonderful kind to our Mary."

Daad's words stung, pricking his conscience. "That's true. I haven't forgotten that, but I still wish I hadn't kissed her. She'll be expecting . . ." He let the words fade out, not sure what Barbie might expect after that kiss.

She'd kissed him back—that he knew. He could still feel her arms close around him, smell the fresh scent of her skin, and taste the sweetness of her lips. But that—well, that was desire, wasn't it? At his age, he ought to expect more of himself.

"I guess I should talk to her about it."

Daad nodded. "I guess you should." He turned

away, as if satisfied that he'd made his point, but then he turned back again, his lined face serious. "Benuel, don't be so quick to dismiss falling in love. It wouldn't happen if it weren't a part of God's plan for people. God's ways are not our ways, remember. He may have plans for you that aren't what you think at all."

Maybe so. As low as Ben felt right now, it was hard to believe God had any use for him at all. He rubbed the back of his neck, thinking about Barbie. Wishing he knew what she was feeling right about now. As a minister, it seemed to him he ought to have a little insight into people, but Barbie—well, Barbie was a mystery to him.

Barbie had to force herself to concentrate at work on Monday. She had the lunch shift, which was busy as always, with lots of demands on her attention. Still, Ben's face in the moonlight kept intruding.

She headed for the kitchen pass-through to pick up an order for an impatient pair of truckers. It wasn't as if she hadn't been kissed before. She ought to have better sense than to go on daydreaming about it.

But she couldn't seem to chase those moments out of her thoughts. Telling herself she'd been kissed before wasn't really an answer. Teenagers smooched, of course, and usually that had been as much awkward as it had been satisfying. They'd gotten better at it as they got older, but by then, Amish kids were looking for someone to get serious about—someone to marry and start a family with. And she'd never felt strongly enough about anyone to conquer her restless urge to find a new challenge.

"What's up with you today?" Ashlee paused beside her as they headed back toward the kitchen. "You look as if you're only half here."

"Ach, I'm sorry. I didn't mean to. I . . . well, I've had something on my mind."

"Family trouble?" Ashlee took her time picking up a plate, ignoring the black look Walt sent her way.

"No, nothing like that." Did Ashlee immediately jump to that conclusion because of her own difficulties with her family? Ashlee didn't really talk about them much, but what she did say clearly showed that they didn't get along.

"Guy trouble, then," Ashlee diagnosed. "Don't tell me you're having problems with Terry."

"Terry's fine. In fact, he wants to take me out to dinner someplace away from here. That is, if you wouldn't mind . . ." She paused. Did that make it sound as if she only valued her friendship with Ashlee for what Ashlee could do for her?

"Being your cover? Sure, it's fine." Ashlee grinned. "You should know that by now. I'll let you have a key, and you can use my place even if I'm out."

She flushed, hoping Ashlee didn't imagine she intended to entertain Terry in her apartment. "I'd just need to be able to change clothes, that's all. And I don't really know if I'm going to do it anyway."

"You should. And help yourself to anything of mine you want to wear. It's a good thing we're the same size. My closet is your closet."

"You girls going to chatter or get this food up before it's cold?" Walt's bellow was loud enough to be heard in the dining room.

Barbie hurried to obey, certain her cheeks were scarlet. Ashlee just rolled her eyes and went ahead at her own pace.

It must be nice not to find so many potential pitfalls in the Englisch world. Still, if Ashlee were attempting to put a foot in Barbie's world, she'd probably have just as much trouble, not from lack of experience but from lack of understanding.

Several of her tables finished and left, giving her time to breathe again. She'd diverted Ashlee's attention from what was really bothering her, but she had considerably more trouble diverting her own.

She leaned over to wipe a table, retrieving a straw wrapper from the booth seat. Ben had kissed her. All right. Think about it rationally. A kiss didn't mean anything that serious, did it?

That might be a good argument except for the fact that at their ages, and with Ben being a minister, there was nothing lighthearted about a kiss. Benuel Kauffmann wouldn't go around kissing women unless he had serious intentions toward them.

But she couldn't believe he did, not about her. She was everything he disapproved of in a woman, and he'd made that perfectly clear. Besides, he'd seemed as surprised by that kiss as she had been.

Barbie felt her cheeks grow warm at the thought of how she'd responded to him. She'd practically thrown herself into his arms, and yet it had seemed the most natural thing in the world. Surprising and yet somehow inevitable, as if they'd been moving toward that point all along.

No, they couldn't be. No matter how his touch stirred her senses, Barbie couldn't make herself believe that they were right for each other. Ben was rigid, judgmental, and anything but tactful.

He was also conscientious, gentle with his kinder, and determined to do the right thing. And she was making her own head spin.

Ashlee came up behind her and gave her a nudge. "You're going to wipe the surface right off that table if you go over it one more time. If this isn't about Terry, what is it about?"

The need to talk to someone overwhelmed her. She took a quick glance around, but the café was emptying out, and no one was within earshot.

"You remember Ben Kauffmann, Mary's

brother? The one who's a minister in my church?"

"Sure. The guy who looks like he disapproves of everyone and everything. What about him?"

She lowered her voice even more, though no one could possibly hear. "We were chaperoning a singing for the young people last night out at his place. And we happened to be outside at the same time, and we started talking, and well—we kissed."

Ashlee looked at her a little blankly. "Well, I get that you'd be sorry you kissed a guy who looks like he has as much feeling as a rock, but after all, what's a little kiss between two consenting adults?"

Barbie shook her head. She should have known Ashlee wouldn't understand. There was no way she could. "Ben's a widower with two little kids, and he's a minister besides. He doesn't just go around kissing people. And I—well, I'd have said I didn't even like him but . . ."

"But what?" Ashlee's eyes suddenly lit with amusement. "I get it. You liked the kiss. That just shows you're normal, right?"

"I can't kiss someone like Ben without being serious about him. And I don't want to be."

She nearly wailed the words, or as much as she could while keeping her voice down.

Ashlee considered for a moment. "Is he somebody your parents would approve of?"

Barbie blinked, surprised. "I guess."

"That settles it, then. I'd never go out with a guy my parents approved of." Ashlee, looking as if the matter was settled to her satisfaction, whisked off toward the kitchen.

That might settle things for Ashlee, but it didn't help Barbie in the least. Maybe the best thing to do was try not to think about it, except that she didn't seem able to do it.

A sudden clatter, followed by a child's cry, sent her hurrying to one of Ashlee's tables, where a young mother had a baby in a highchair and a toddler on a booster seat. She was trying to lift the baby, who didn't seem to want to move, when the little boy upset his milk, sending it splashing over the table and his mother's slacks.

"Here, let me help you." Barbie lifted the toddler out of range of the stream of milk and started mopping it up, leaving the mother free to attend to the baby.

But she was staring rather helplessly at her damp slacks and looked ready to cry. "I thought just this once I could treat myself to lunch out, and look what happens!"

"Ach, it's nothing but some spilled milk. We'll get it cleaned up in no time, won't we?" She included the toddler in her smile. He nodded and began vigorously scrubbing at the table with the bib he'd yanked off. "Why don't you go in the ladies' room and sponge it off your nice slacks? I'll watch the little ones for you."

The young woman sniffled once, nodded, and hurried off to the restroom. By then Ashlee had arrived with sponges and a small pail of water, and between them they made short work of the cleanup.

By the time the woman returned, looked subdued but happier, Barbie was entertaining the two young ones with a disappearing napkin and Ashlee had brought a plate of cookies and fresh iced tea.

"On the house," Ashlee said.

The woman's smile trembled a little. "You girls are so kind. I'm sorry I got upset." She stroked the baby's head gently. "My husband's working out of town, and I just get so lonesome some-times I have to do something."

"You can always stop by and say hello to us," Barbie said. "We can use a good helper like this young man."

"Thank you again, so much. Next time I'll remember to bring a sippy cup."

Barbie headed back to her own neglected customers, smiling. No wonder the young woman got upset, with apparently no one to keep her company when her husband was gone. Barbie might sometimes want to escape her ever-present kin, but the alternative didn't seem very pleasant, either. That reminded her of Grossmammi's stories and the trouble she'd had with moving. But if she hadn't, who could guess how that would have changed the lives of her family, including Barbie?

"That's why I'm never having kids," Ashlee murmured as she passed. "Your life isn't your own."

"You'll change your mind one day." Jean, the grandmotherly older server, hearing her, spoke up. "You just have to find the right man. Isn't that right, Barbie?"

Put on the spot, Barbie nodded, escaping to get coffee for a new arrival. Jean, devoted to her grandkids, thought everyone should have children, just as her own mother did.

Would she want to have a family with the right man? She'd always supposed that someday she'd have children, but she'd never given it serious thought. If she did, in an Amish family, there were always people around to help—grandparents, aunts and uncles, and more cousins than a person could count.

For an instant she seemed to feel Abram and Libby snuggling close against her while she told them a bedtime story. A wave of tenderness swept over her. Ben would undoubtedly provide them with a new mother before too long. But it wouldn't be her.

She headed for one of her booths and was nearly there before she realized who was sitting there. Terry smiled, waiting for her.

"Hi." She came to a stop, automatically pulling

out her pad while her thoughts spun. "I didn't see you come in."

"You were busy babysitting, it looked like." He gave her that easy grin, nodding toward the place where the young mother and children still sat. "That was a nice thing you did."

"Just my job," she said quickly, wondering if he had watched her playing silly games to keep the children occupied.

"You went above and beyond duty, I'd say. Maybe that's what I like about you."

Sure her cheeks were growing pink, she glanced at the pad. "Coffee?"

"Sure, coffee. And a piece of whatever pie is best today, as usual. I trust your judgment. And the answer to a question. Will you go out to that Chinese restaurant with me Wednesday night?"

She hesitated, but Terry's frank admiration and simple liking was a welcome relief after Ben's disapproval and her complicated feelings. She liked Terry, and it would be fun doing something she'd never done before.

"Okay," she said. "We'll go out on Wednesday."

Chapter Twelve

Lancaster County, Spring 1960

It was after nine o'clock, and even Daad Eli, who usually went upstairs promptly at nine, was still leaning back in his chair, a newspaper on his lap. Mamm Alice puttered around in the kitchen, and Becky had given up any pretense of sewing and stared out the window for the first glimpse of the returning buggy.

"It's hard to say how long the meeting might last," Elizabeth said quietly, putting her arm around her sister-in-law's waist. "But you know they're always careful on the roads after dark."

Becky nodded, smiling a little. "I'm foolish to worry, I know. Worry won't change anything, like Mamm Alice always says."

"That doesn't stop us from fretting, does it?" She nodded toward the kitchen. "That's why she's still up, ain't so? Let's see if we can help with whatever she's doing."

They walked into the kitchen arm in arm. She'd grown so fond of Becky in recent years that she was almost like a sister. She was yet another person to miss if Reuben insisted on moving.

Mamm Alice was looking in the cabinet next to the sink for something.

"Can we help?" Elizabeth hurried to pick up the dish towel Mamm Alice had dropped.

"I was just looking for the other sugar bowl. Did one of you put it some place?" Mamm Alice looked fretful, a sure sign that she was worrying about the outcome of the zoning board meeting, too.

"The last place I saw it was in this cabinet." Elizabeth knelt, reaching past a stack of dessert plates. Her fingers touched the handle of the missing sugar bowl, and she pulled it out. "Here it is, hiding behind the plates."

"Denke, Elizabeth." Mamm Alice shook her head. "I must need to clean my glasses, ain't so?" She set the bowl down on the counter. "I'm thinking the boys will have some pie and coffee when they come in. Guess we may as well get things ready."

Exchanging glances with Elizabeth, Becky went to the pantry to bring out the two pies that were cooling there. Elizabeth started getting out forks and stopped at a noise from outside.

"The buggy." Her fingers tightened around the handles. "Sounds like they're here."

Mamm Alice nodded, setting the coffeepot on the stove. "By the time they unhitch, the coffee will be ready. You girls can cut the pies."

Elizabeth realized she was holding her breath as

she sliced into the cherry pie, letting the juice spurt out. Would they know for sure yet what the zoning board had decided? She didn't really have a notion of how that worked.

She should be worrying about how Daad and Isaac were going to fare if they couldn't get their produce to the auction. Well, she was concerned for them, but she had to admit that most of her feelings were more selfish. If the decision went against the Amish, Reuben would see that as yet another good reason to leave Lancaster County.

In a few minutes her ear caught the sound of footsteps on the back porch. Too bad a person couldn't judge much from that.

But as soon as Reuben and Isaac came in the door, it was obvious that the decision had gone against them. Elizabeth's heart seemed to sink to the pit of her stomach. One more mark against staying, then.

Isaac crossed the kitchen to where Daad stood, the newspaper still in his hand.

"I'm sorry, Daad."

He shook his head. "Don't feel bad. Things will work out as they should, ja?"

"Well, they're working out the way the Englisch businessmen want, anyway." Reuben's face was tight. "As far as I could tell, every person on the board had already decided before the meeting even started."

"Sit, sit." Mamm Alice pushed him toward a

chair. "You can eat and talk at the same time."

Elizabeth felt a reluctant smile twitch at her lips. Her own grandmother always said an Amish cook thought food was the answer to every problem. Lucky they had plenty of hard work to keep them from getting fat.

Only when everyone was settled at the table with food in front of them did Mamm Alice indicate it was time for conversation.

"What makes you say those folks had already made up their minds?" Daad stirred his coffee vigorously, his spoon clinking. "Aren't they supposed to hear everyone before they decide?"

Isaac shrugged. "It's not like a trial, I guess. They had this study all made up and printed on fancy blue paper that showed how much it would benefit the township to change the zoning. They even predicted how much money would come in as taxes as a result."

"All we had to offer was the fact that farmers would suffer if they couldn't get their produce to market." Reuben stared at his slice of cherry pie as if it wondered him how it had gotten in front of him. "Isaac did a gut job of speaking. So did the others. It just wasn't any use."

"They kept saying they had to consider the needs of most people, not just a few farmers." Isaac sounded as bitter as she'd ever heard him—a far cry from his usual carefree attitude toward life. "But where would any of them be without farmers to grow the food that they eat?"

Daad shook his head. "Mostly they don't think about it, I'd guess."

"If you asked an Englisch child where milk came from, he'd probably say it came from a store." Mamm Alice's tone made clear what she thought of such a lack.

"There's not much we can do about it," Isaac said. "So I guess we'll have to figure out a way around it." He took a big bite of pie, and his expression seemed to lighten. "There's always a way, ain't so?"

"Is there?" Reuben's eyes were bleak, and Elizabeth knew what he was thinking. He was convinced the only answer for them was to move on.

Daad Eli cleared his throat, drawing their attention. "God is still in control." His voice was firm and sure. "Maybe we needed a reminder that we are to depend on Him, not on our own devices."

"We do," Isaac protested. "But it seems like the government is bent on making it harder and harder just to make a living."

Daad Eli frowned at his younger son. "That is the cost of living Amish in an Englisch world. We got through the troubles during the wars, when the government wanted our young men to fight. And we won the right to have our own schools. We survived those trials. We'll survive this one."

"Or we can move someplace where we won't have these problems," Reuben said.

"Ach, Reuben." Mamm Alice touched his shoulder lightly in an unusual gesture of affection for her grown son. "No matter where you are, you'll have problems. You can't run away from them."

Reuben looked abashed. His mother usually left such chiding to her husband.

"I know, Mamm." He held her hand for a moment. "Well, we did what we could anyway, ain't so?" He stood. "I'm ready for bed. Elizabeth?"

She nodded, hurrying to carry plates to the sink. Did that mean he wanted to talk before they went to bed? Or did it mean that his decision, like the zoning board's, was already made?

When their bedroom door closed behind them, she turned to him. He wore a closed-in expression that she wasn't sure how to read.

"Reuben? What are you thinking?" Her chest was tight with all the feelings she didn't want to let out. They couldn't quarrel again. She'd begun to fear they wouldn't survive another argument.

He seemed to be struggling with himself. Then he reached out and pulled her gently against him. He pressed his cheek against her hair.

"I'm too tired to make any sense tonight, I think. Let's sleep on it."

A wave of tenderness swept over her as she

held him tight, and she nodded. "Ja. All right. Sleep is a gut healer, my mamm always says."

Reuben seemed almost grateful. He didn't say another word as they got ready for bed, and he fell almost immediately into sleep, as if it were an escape for him.

Elizabeth lay awake, listening to his breathing, watching the dim moonlight from the window move across his face. They had to find a way forward together. They had to. *Please, God.*

By the time Barbie hurried toward the back room at the end of her shift that day, she'd second-guessed herself about going out with Terry a half-dozen times or more. *Enough,* she told herself firmly. She'd go and enjoy herself.

The room given over to the staff at the café was actually a storage room, with metal shelves along one side, a tiny restroom, and a few lockers. Green-and-white frilly café aprons hung on hooks, though Walt had agreed that Barbie's own plain white apron was okay for her.

Thank goodness Ashlee was still there. Barbie had to confirm Wednesday evening with her. At least once she'd told Ashlee, there'd be no backing out.

Ashlee stood by her locker, frowning at her cell phone, her whole body tense.

"Ashlee?" She let the door close behind her. "Is something wrong? Have you had bad news?"

"What? Oh, this?" She gestured with the phone. "It's nothing."

Barbie drew closer. "You don't look as if it's nothing."

"It's my dad." She dropped the phone in her shoulder bag, looking mutinous. "He's really bent out of shape because I'm not coming home for my mom's birthday."

"I see." Given the strain she knew existed between Ashlee and her family, she'd have to tread carefully. "Do you have to work that day?"

In Amish families, birthdays were important events, and often the whole extended family showed up for dinner. Over forty people had attended her last birthday.

"No." Ashlee snapped out the word, and then she seemed to think something else was necessary. "I just don't see the need to drive all that way to watch Mom blow out the candles on her cake. Anyway, she'll be so excited to have my brother's kids there she won't notice anyone else."

"She's probably thrilled to be a grandmother. I know my mamm spoils my nieces and nephews like she'd never have spoiled us. That doesn't mean she wouldn't be happy to have you there." It sounded as if she were taking the side of Ashlee's parents, so she quickly added, "But she'll under-stand, ain't so?"

Ashlee shrugged, not meeting her eyes. "I guess. I mean, it's not as if I'm ignoring her birthday. I'm sending her flowers and a card. But if I go, they'll just start bugging me about my life. Why don't I go back to school, why am I content to work as a waitress, why don't I move home. It'll be the same old story. I told you that before."

There didn't seem to be anything to say to that, so she patted Ashlee's arm. "I'm sorry. I hate to see you at odds with your family."

"Well, you're not exactly open and above-board with your folks, are you? Did they find out about our night out yet?"

"No," she said quickly. "If I'm lucky, they never will."

The emphasis in her voice brought a smile to Ashlee's face. "Really? So what would they think about Terry?"

Barbie tried to look innocent. "What about Terry?"

"I saw the two of you with your heads together," Ashlee teased. "Come on, give. Did you set a date?"

Barbie nodded. "Wednesday night, if that's okay with you. I can get someone to drop me off for work that day if I can spend the night at your place."

"Sure thing. I told you, any time you want is okay by me." She grinned. "I just hope this time you don't run into any Amish teenagers you think you have to rescue."

"So do I," Barbie said fervently. "Once in a lifetime is enough."

By the time Barbie headed for home, they'd firmed up all the arrangements needed to pull it off. *Needed to lie to your parents,* the voice of her conscience remarked. *Call it what it is.*

This wasn't such a bad thing, was it? After all, she'd eaten with Englisch friends before. Just because this was with a single man, it shouldn't make that much difference. She knew she wasn't going to do anything wrong.

Too bad no one else in her community would agree with her.

When she passed the turn to Grossmammi's place, she realized she hadn't talked to her grandmother in a few days. Grossmammi would be eager to hear about how chaperoning the singing had gone.

Barbie's cheeks warmed at the memories. Maybe it was best if she put off seeing Grossmammi for a day or two. Grossmammi had a talent for seeing the truth.

Her grandmother's stories seemed to linger in her mind after each time they were together. Everything in the dower chest had a memory attached to it, it seemed. The last time, Grossmammi had held a matching sugar bowl and cream pitcher in her hands as she'd talked about those days when they'd lived with Grossdaadi's parents in Lancaster County.

It had been odd to hear of the fear her grandmother once had at the idea of leaving her home in Lancaster County. Brook Hill had been her home for a long time, and Barbie had trouble imagining her anywhere else.

Grossmammi was so brave. She'd faced all kinds of sorrows in her life with courage. Who would have dreamed she'd once been afraid to venture into a new life?

Maybe Barbie's own yearning for adventure, for challenge, came from her grandfather. She welcomed change. It was the sameness of every day that troubled her.

She drew up at the metal mailbox by the side of the road. If Daad hadn't walked down the lane for the mail yet, she could save him the trip. She yanked down on the door.

The box held a handful of envelopes and a newsletter. She pulled them out and leafed through them. A round-robin letter for Mamm from one of her cousins in Ohio—that would please her. Something else that looked like a political advertisement. And then—her heart plummeted at the sight of her name printed in pencil.

She'd nearly succeeded in putting that earlier anonymous letter out of her mind. But it seemed the letter writer wasn't done with her yet.

Barbie ripped the envelope open, finding to her annoyance that her fingers were trembling. Ridiculous, to let it upset her so.

This one was similar to the last.

You can't live Englisch and Amish at the same time. You're a bad influence and soon the whole community will know.

Was that a threat to tell? But tell what? The note wasn't specific. Surely the unknown writer couldn't know about Terry.

Did it matter what he or she actually knew? The suspicion was enough to cause problems. If the person had sent this poisonous note to Mamm or Daad—

Her heart nearly stopped. Many days Daad walked down to pick up the mail. What if he'd done so today?

If he'd pulled this envelope out of the box, he wouldn't have opened it, not when it was addressed to her. But he'd have noticed it. He'd have thought it odd that there was no return address. He'd have asked about it, probably at the supper table. What would she have said then?

Her stomach twisted into knots, and she grabbed the letter in both hands, prepared to tear it into bits. Then she stopped. Ben had made her promise that if she received any more letters, she'd show them to him. Indeed, he was the only person she could show it to.

Her instinct was to destroy it anyway. Ben need never know. But something held her back. No. That was a foolish denial. Besides, what would she say if he asked whether she'd received any more letters? Lie about it?

What had happened last night had changed things between them, and she didn't know yet whether it was for the better or the worse. But she did know that she couldn't lie to him. She stuffed the letter back into its envelope and slid it into her bag. Benuel had complicated her life in more ways than one.

The last thing Ben had wanted was to see Barbie again so soon. He'd anticipated having time to get his head on straight after his foolish actions on Sunday night. But here it was late Monday, and her father had asked him to stop by and check out the lights on David's buggy.

If the opportunity came to speak to Barbie alone, what should he do? Should he bring it up? Apologize for his behavior? Make it clear that he didn't mean—

That brought his mind to a full stop. Face it. A man his age couldn't kiss a woman and pretend it meant nothing. Flirtation was for teenagers, just like falling in love was.

And should he even bring it up? It might embarrass her for no good reason. Maybe she'd rather pretend it hadn't happened.

He'd better decide soon, because he'd already reached the Lapp place, and he could see Barbie and David leaning into the buggy in question.

His heart refused to cooperate in making a decision, and his thoughts felt as if they'd been stirred up with a spoon. He parked his buggy and walked over to them.

Apparently they hadn't heard his approach, because they seemed to be busy arguing. "You must have done something to it, because it was perfectly fine the last time I had it out," David insisted.

"All I did was drive to work and back," Barbie retorted. "That was in the daytime. I didn't do anything to the lights at all, so don't try to blame it on me. And if I had my own buggy, it would certain-sure be a lot nicer than this one."

Despite the fighting words, he had the sense that neither one was actually angry. They were just engaging in the brother-and-sister teasing that must go on regularly with the two of them, as close in age as they were.

"Never mind," David grumbled, leaning under the bench seat so far that he was invisible. "Wait and see what Ben thinks."

"If I could get in there, I might be able to tell you," he said.

David jerked and bumped his head on the seat, and Barbie's eyes met Ben's for an unguarded second before she looked away, a faint flush rising on her creamy cheeks.

"Right, sure thing," David said, scrambling down. He and Barbie looked enough alike to be twins with their fresh, light coloring and lively expressions. "It's all yours. Denke. Glad you were able to get here so fast."

"If you can't fix it, David might have to disappoint Sally King tonight," Barbie said.

"Better watch what you say in front of the minister if you don't want a frog in your bed tonight," David warned, grinning.

"Seems to me I'd already heard a thing or two about you and Sally," Ben said, setting his toolbox into the buggy and climbing inside. "Everyone's looking to see how much celery her daad is putting in this spring."

At the mention of the traditional wedding food, David flushed to the roots of his blond hair. "We . . . we're not that far along yet."

"Maybe you aren't, but that doesn't keep folks from talking," Barbie said. At a glare from her brother, she seemed to take pity on him. "Not that people wouldn't talk whether there was any reason to or not."

"They're interested in the young ones," Ben said. He couldn't remember how old David was, but he knew he was the youngest of the Lapp family. He and Barbie were close in age, coming a fairly long time after their older brothers.

David opened his mouth as if to protest and then closed it again, maybe thinking it wasn't wise to open that subject.

Ben shone the beam of his flashlight along the

wire that ran from the battery to the rear safety lights. Some church districts tried to hold out against the lights and even the orange safety triangle, saying they weren't plain, but with all the motor traffic on the roads, they were necessary, besides being required by law.

"You haven't been tinkering with the lights, have you?" he asked, checking connections. "I thought maybe you'd knocked something loose."

"I don't think so," David leaned in again. "The wires were tucked back against the side so they were out of the way. I thought—" He stopped abruptly at a sound. It seemed a bird was cheeping from somewhere in David's clothing.

David flushed again, backing up, and Ben had to suppress a smile. Like most of the kids who hadn't been baptized yet, he had a cell phone. And he was obviously embarrassed that it had gone off at this moment.

"Sorry," he muttered. He turned away, checking the phone, and then answered it. With a quick, pleading look at his sister, he moved well away from them, around the corner of the porch.

Barbie crossed her arms on the edge of the buggy and leaned on them. "He's embarrassed. I'm supposed to distract you from the fact that he's talking on a cell phone, I guess."

"Do you think you can?" he asked, amused at her directness.

"Probably not. But we've always backed each other. It's automatic by this time."

He shrugged, trying to concentrate on the job instead of on how close Barbie was. "You two are very near each other in age. That makes a big difference in your relationship."

"We are good friends." She hesitated. "Are you thinking that if you were nearer in age to Mary, she'd be more open with you?"

"There's no doubt about that. As it is, she looks at me more like another father than her brother."

"That's natural, I think. I remember that James—" She stopped abruptly at the mention of her oldest brother, the one who had jumped the fence.

He studied her face, thinking of the sense of loss she'd betrayed the last time they'd spoken of him. "You must have been pretty small when he left."

Barbie nodded, her bright blue eyes shadowed. "I was eight, but I couldn't possibly forget my big brother. And you're right. He was more like another daad to me. Maybe that's why it hurt so much when he left." She focused on him. "Do you remember much about him?"

"Not much," he admitted. "He was one of the grown-ups to me, too." Ben wasn't actually much older than Barbie in years, even though he felt about a hundred in experience.

Her fingers twisted together. "I always thought

there must have been something wonderful gut out there for him never to have come back. Never to get in touch with us, even."

"I'm sorry." That was the hardest thing for a family to bear—the empty seat at the table.

Barbie gave a curt little nod, as if to accept his sympathy and at the same time to close the subject. Well, there was no reason she should talk about her brother to him if she didn't want to, but it seemed as if she wanted to talk to someone about him.

"So you're not going to get after David for having a cell phone," she said.

"The Ordnung has accepted the use of cell phones by those not yet baptized as well as for limited business use where necessary. Did you think I'd be stricter than the Ordnung?"

Her smile flashed, her dimples appearing and then vanishing. "Well, you are known for taking a fairly rigid interpretation of the rules."

A loose connection—there it was. He focused on that, but he couldn't quite let go of Barbie's comment.

"I have concerns about cell phones, ja, but people say they want their teenagers to have them for safety's sake. Maybe, if Mary had had one, she could have called for help when she got in trouble."

That thought bothered him more than he wanted her to know. Neither he nor Daad had even thought about getting a phone for her. Maybe they should have.

He could feel Barbie's gaze studying his face, probing for how he really felt. She made a tiny gesture, as if to reach for him, but drew her hand back quickly.

"I don't think it would have made a difference." Her voice was soft. "By the time she'd had something to drink . . . well, I'm not sure she'd have called."

"No." The word had a bitter taste. "I guess she wouldn't."

"I'm sorry." She drew back. "Maybe I should let you get on with the job."

Now or never. He forced himself to meet her eyes. "Before you go or David comes back, I wanted to say . . . about last night." This was harder than he'd expected. "I shouldn't have done it. I don't know why I did."

That wasn't true, was it? He'd kissed her because she attracted him in a way he'd never experienced, even with Donna, and didn't welcome. He didn't want to feel this way, and he didn't know what to do with it.

The silence between them had lasted too long. Barbie wrapped her arms around herself.

"We should forget it." Her voice was tense, and her eyes suspiciously bright. Before he could find anything to say, she was gone.

Chapter Thirteen

Lancaster County, Spring 1960

Elizabeth was doing one of the things she enjoyed most—spring cleaning the grossdaadi haus next to her family home with her two sisters. Grossdaadi had been gone for several years, but Grossmammi still loved being a part of everything that went on in the family. She had her own place when she wanted privacy, but all she had to do was open the door and walk through the enclosed porch to be in the house with Mamm and Daadi and whoever else was around.

"It's wonderful simple to spring clean Grossmammi's house," Anna said, wiping the baseboards energetically. "If my house stayed this clean, I'd have lots and lots of time to do other things."

"Except for the dirt from the coal furnace." Lovina was washing around the heating vent, where the white wall was tinged with gray. "And what would you do with all that time anyway?"

"She'd be sewing, I think." Elizabeth lifted one edge of the mattress to turn it, and Lovina dropped the rag she was using and came to help her. "Turning out dresses by the dozen."

"What I can't figure out is whether she likes to make the dresses or to wear them," Lovina teased.

"No, no, she just likes the material," Elizabeth said. "Haven't you seen the way she strokes every bolt when we go to the fabric store?"

"That's how I tell if it will be easy to sew. And wear," Anna added, getting up from her knees. She picked up her bucket and cloth and moved to the next wall to start the baseboard there. "You don't understand. You have to get a feel of the fabric."

"It's a gut thing you had daughters so you could make some dresses. The boys' clothes aren't as much fun to make," Lovina said.

Elizabeth felt the familiar twinge in her heart. How she would love to be making clothes for a child of her own right now. But she didn't want her sisters thinking they had to be careful of what they said around her.

"We all know why you put such deep hems in your boys' pants," she said, keeping her voice light. "You want to keep letting them down as long as you can."

Lovina chuckled. "My secret is out. Who wants to be sewing another pair of broad-fall pants when I could be quilting?"

Both of Elizabeth's sisters were experts with the needle, and she'd always thought it odd that their passion was so specific. But Lovina just seemed to have an artist's eye for the quilts she made. Her patterns were always traditional, but with a little something different that was her own.

"You're both so talented that you put me to shame." She smoothed a clean mattress cover over the mattress of Grossmammi's bed. "I do wish I had a little more space for sewing at Mamm Alice's, though. Whenever I want to cut something out, I have to work around all the other people who want to use the table."

"It'll be easier when you and Reuben have a place of your own." Lovina's tone was comforting. "Has he looked at any more places lately?"

"No."

That came out too sharply, and Lovina glanced at her with that assessing, big-sister look.

"I mean, there haven't been any new places up for sale." Except far away, where it seemed the farm Reuben wanted would fall right into his hands. "Anyway, he's been busy helping Isaac with the zoning board."

They were all silent for a moment, as if they mourned something lost. Maybe they did—another good farm lost to development, and another obstacle put in the way of Amish farmers.

"That was a shame, that was," Lovina said finally. "It seemed like the least they could have done was listen. I heard Isaac did a real fine job explaining."

"That's what Reuben says." That was about all Reuben said about it. Sometimes she thought he'd never expected them to succeed.

"Isaac turned wonderful responsible," Anna said. "I remember thinking a few years ago he'd never settle down, and look at him now, about to become a daadi."

Elizabeth's fingers froze on the double wedding ring quilt they were pulling up on the bed. She tried to think, but her brain seemed to have gone numb. "What . . . what did you say?"

Lovina and Anna stared at her, and Anna's mouth formed an O of distress. "Elizabeth, I thought you knew."

"Maybe it was wrong, what we thought," Lovina said quickly. "We just assumed, from something Becky said before worship on Sunday, that she is expecting. But if you don't know, then we must be mistaken."

Her brain finally started to work, presenting her with a number of small indications she hadn't even put together, despite living in the same house with Becky. Her late arrivals in the morning, the way she often had just toast at breakfast, even the look in her eyes when she and Isaac were near each other.

Becky, expecting. And she still wasn't.

Somehow she had to put up a good front. "I think you're right," she managed. "I didn't realize it until you said it, but I think she is expecting."

Her throat was tight. "She and Isaac must be so happy."

Lovina and Anna exchanged glances. "We shouldn't have spoken," Lovina said, her voice soft. "It will be you soon. I'm certain-sure of it."

"Ja." Elizabeth forced a smile. Becky hadn't told her. Naturally they wouldn't talk about it when the men were around, but women in a family usually shared a secret like this one.

Becky hadn't wanted to upset her, she supposed. But she had to know.

Before she could stop them, tears welled in her eyes. Lovina made a wordless sound of sympathy. She took a step toward her, and Elizabeth shook her head. She had to be by herself for a minute.

"I'll go check on Grossmammi," she murmured, and fled.

She hadn't thought she'd actually seek out Grossmammi, but found she'd headed straight for her. Grossmammi was one of those people who made you feel better just by being there.

Her grandmother wasn't resting, as they had hoped. She was in the kitchen, heating up two quarts of the beef vegetable soup they'd made and canned for her last fall.

"You must think we are very hungry," Elizabeth said, forcing a lightness she didn't feel.

"You've been working up an appetite, ain't so?" Grossmammi's faded blue eyes studied her face. "Are your sisters ready for lunch yet?"

"No, I . . . I just wanted to take a little break, and . . ." The words seemed to leave her. She pressed her lips together, shaking her head.

"Tell me." Grossmammi turned from the stove to put an arm around Elizabeth's waist. "Is it this plan of Reuben's to move on?"

"Ja. No." She shook her head again. "I try so hard to have faith. To accept what happens as God's will. But now Becky is going to have a boppli. And still I'm barren. Why?"

Grossmammi held her and patted her as if she were a small child. "Ach, we never know the whys in this life, child. Someday we will know."

Rebellion rose in her. "I would be a gut mammi. And Reuben—he never says anything, but I know he longs for a child as much as I do."

Grossmammi didn't answer, but Elizabeth felt the love flowing in a healing stream from her touch. When she did speak, her voice was soft. "Do you remember when I gave you my dower chest? You were so young, so happy as you planned your life with Reuben. And I said to you that the chest would hold a lifetime of memories for you—some gut, some bad."

Elizabeth nodded. She'd heard, all right, but then she'd been too swept up in her own happiness to listen.

"That's what life is—good and bad, happy and sorrowful, all mixed up together. We don't get to have one without the other, but together they make up a life. And when you near the end of your time, as I do, you know that you would never trade any of them, even the sad ones." She drew back, cupping Elizabeth's face in her hands. "You don't see it yet, but you will."

She wouldn't contradict her grandmother, but she didn't see how she could ever accept losing their little Matthias. She sucked in a deep breath, trying to compose herself.

"If Reuben insists on moving, at least I won't have to go through Becky's pregnancy with her," she muttered.

"Elizabeth." Grossmammi's tone held a warning. "Don't move on thinking that you can escape life. You can't. But if this move is right, well, then, you must have courage. Think of those who came here. They escaped the persecution in the old country, ja, but they found new challenges here. Still, we're thankful they found the courage to do it." She smiled and patted Elizabeth's cheek. "Maybe, one day, some of our people will be equally thankful to you and Reuben."

Barbie pulled on the top Ashlee handed her, took one look in Ashlee's full-length mirror, and promptly pulled it back off again.

"That looked great," Ashlee protested. "That coral color is perfect for you."

"It's not the color." Barbie slipped the top back

onto its hangar. "It's too snug and too . . . bare." She thought of the amount of skin exposed by the sweater and felt herself flush at the thought of Terry looking at her in it.

"I wear it." Ashlee sounded a bit nettled.

"You look great in it." Barbie hastened to reassure her. "But I just wouldn't be comfortable wearing something like that when I'm used to Amish clothing."

Ashlee held the top against herself for a moment, looking in the mirror with approval. Then she hung it up and pulled out another—this one in a shade of light aqua that reminded Barbie of the color of a pool deep in the woods.

"Okay, try this." Ashlee smiled, her good humor restored. "If it works, I'll do your hair." She glanced at her watch. "We don't have much time if you're going to be ready when Terry gets here."

Nodding, Barbie slipped the aqua sweater over her head and sucked in her breath with pleasure at the way she looked. The color was perfect, making her cheeks rosier and accentuating her blue eyes. And it was cut modestly enough that she wouldn't be longing to cover herself up all evening.

"Great," she said. "Isn't it?" She was suddenly doubtful. Would Terry like the way she looked?

Ashlee grinned. "It's perfect. Come into the bathroom. I have the curling iron heated up.

We'll make you look like a girl going on a date."

Barbie unpinned her hair, feeling it ripple down her back, and winced a little as Ashlee approached it with the curling iron.

"Relax," Ashlee said. "It's not going to hurt."

"I know. I'm just not used to it." That was a gigantic understatement. She wasn't used to anything that was going on tonight. The thought of going out alone with a man—and an Englisch one at that—made her stomach queasy.

To distract herself, she said the first thing that came into her mind. "Did you decide yet about going home for your mother's birthday?"

Ashlee's hand jerked on the curling iron, and it snagged on her hair, pulling.

"Ouch. I thought this wasn't going to hurt."

"Just don't bug me about my family. I get enough of that from them."

The snap in her voice had Barbie meeting Ashlee's eyes in the mirror.

"I'm sorry. I didn't mean anything. I just—"

"You just thought I should go home and be nice to my family," Ashlee interrupted and finished for her. "What is it with you and families?"

Barbie tried to find an answer that would be accurate without further irritating her friend. "The Amish consider the family to be one of the most important parts of our lives. Even when I get irritated by the things they expect, I still don't want to hurt them."

Ashlee mulled that over for a moment or two, frowning as she concentrated on Barbie's hair. Barbie watched, fascinated, as her straight blond hair began to take on long, loose curls that lay against the soft aqua of the sweater.

"Would they really be all that hurt? From what I hear, lots of Amish young people don't stay Amish. They must be used to it by now."

"Not lots," Barbie protested. "I'd guess ninety percent, at least, stay in the faith. And even if there were a lot . . ." She hesitated, thinking of her mother's words about grieving the one who wasn't there. "My parents already lost my oldest brother when he jumped the fence to the Englisch world. I don't know how they'd stand it if they lost another one." The familiar weight settled on her heart.

"But your brother's still part of the family, isn't he?"

Barbie felt tears sting her eyes. "He could be, I guess. He wasn't baptized yet when he left." Ashlee wouldn't understand about the perils of making baptismal vows and then breaking them. "But when he left, he disappeared. It's been years and years, and we haven't heard a thing from him. We don't even know if he's still alive." Her throat tightened as she thought of James the way she'd seen him last, hugging her fiercely before he'd walked out the door.

Ashlee snapped the curling iron off, frowning. "Haven't your parents tried to find him?"

"How? He hasn't been in touch with anyone, not even the people who'd been his closest friends."

"There are other ways." Ashlee drew the brush through Barbie's hair, blending the strands so that it shone in the light, curling softly.

Barbie stared, amazed at the results. "I look like a different person."

"That's the idea, isn't it? But your brother—if he's living like a normal person now, you could probably find him with a simple Internet search."

Normal. Did that mean she thought Barbie and her people were abnormal?

"I don't know that that would be a good idea. If he wanted to be found, surely he'd get in touch with us."

But Ashlee seemed seized with enthusiasm for her idea. She flitted to the sofa and pulled the computer onto her lap.

"At least we can look. What was his full name?"

"James Frederick Lapp," she said. "But I'm not sure—"

Ashlee was already typing the name. "At least we can try. He might pop up at the first shot." Her fingers moved on the keys.

"Don't." Barbie grabbed her hands, making Ashlee stare at her. "Please. I appreciate it, but I'd have to think about it first. Okay?"

Ashlee paused, her eyes narrowed. Then she shrugged. "Okay. Have it your way." Her head came up. "I hear a car. Maybe it's Terry."

It was Terry. He tap-tapped at the door a moment or two later. When Barbie opened it, he stood for a moment, his eyes widening with admiration. He gave a low whistle.

"You look great. Ashlee's clothes suit you."

The obvious pleasure in his face gave her a lift that almost canceled out any apprehension.

"Thanks." She tugged at the bottom of the aqua top. "Ashlee's very generous."

"That's me." Ashlee set the computer aside and came toward them. "Have a good time, you two."

"We will," Terry said. He clasped Barbie's hand. "Let's go. And don't get worried. No one you know is going to see you."

"You can't be sure of that, can you?" She kept the words light. "We'll take the risk, though."

"Way to go." He held the door of the car while she slid into the seat. "If I see a buggy coming, you can crouch down until they've passed us."

"That's a deal." *Keep it light,* she reminded herself. *And don't start feeling guilty again.*

That had been easy enough when she was seventeen and slipped out for an unsanctioned party. At her age now, she ought to be beyond it.

Terry had pulled his car into the driveway between Ashlee's building and the one next to it. He glanced in both directions and then leaned toward her.

"Alone at last." He said the words as if it were a joke she should recognize, so she smiled. "Now I can do something I've wanted to do since the first time I saw you."

He tilted her face toward his and kissed her.

Terry's kiss was pleasant. Enjoyable. And flattering to think that he'd been longing for this moment. It was nothing like Ben's kiss had been. It stirred up no unwelcome turmoil.

Terry drew back a little, smiling, and two things occurred to Barbie almost simultaneously. One was the troubling thought that Terry might soon expect more from her than she wanted to give. And the other was the fear that she had only said yes to Terry as a reaction to Ben.

After a couple of days had passed, Barbie's unease had largely disappeared. She and Terry had had a great evening together. She'd enjoyed the restaurant, and they'd both laughed as they'd tried to eat their food with chopsticks before giving up and using a fork. He'd kissed her good night at the door but hadn't pressed to come in. Maybe he was sensitive enough to realize that going out with him was a daring step for her.

Ashlee moved around her to the coffeepot. The lunch rush was over, with only a few stragglers left lingering over their coffee. Jean waved, already heading out the door, eager to get home to her grandchildren.

Ashlee nudged her. "You daydreaming about Terry?"

Barbie shook her head. "Just thinking I'll be able to leave soon." She was off after the lunch shift today, but she'd have a longer workday tomorrow.

"Why aren't you thinking about Terry?" she persisted. "Did you fight? Is that why he hasn't been around?"

"You're giving me too much credit. He hasn't been around because he was sent out to do storm damage repair in New Jersey."

She eyed Ashlee, wondering what kind of response she'd get to the question she had to ask. With Ashlee it was hard to tell.

"By the way, my mother wants me to invite you to have supper with us. Any night is fine. Just name it."

Ashlee turned, a mug of coffee in each hand. "Nice of your mom. What about you? Do you want me to come?"

There was something a little challenging in her question that startled Barbie. Well, maybe she had been thinking that it would be easier to keep her friendship with Ashlee and her relationship with her family separate. She pressed down her slight apprehension.

"For sure I want you to come. My mamm is a

good cook. I promise you'll enjoy it." She hoped her words rang true.

Apparently they did, because Ashlee smiled and nodded. "Sounds great. I could use a home-cooked meal. How about tomorrow? I could drive you home after work."

She nodded. Would it be possible to suggest to Ashlee that she dress a little more modestly than usual? Probably not without hurting her feelings.

"Good. We'll plan on it."

It would be all right, wouldn't it? Ashlee understood that her parents couldn't know about her dating Terry. She'd be careful what she said.

The assurances didn't entirely allay her fears. Ashlee wouldn't understand how self-contained the Amish world was. Everyone knew everyone, and often everything about them.

The Englisch seemed able to inhabit different worlds if they wanted to—different groups of friends at work, school, play, and home. It wasn't so for the Amish. The people you worked with were the same ones you saw on Saturday and Sunday, and more than likely were related to you.

Her only taste of the Englisch way was her work at the café, and even there, she couldn't be entirely separate from the Leit. That was why she couldn't avoid Benuel, no matter how uncomfortable the aftermath of their kiss.

The phone by the register rang, and Ashlee

moved to answer it. After a moment, she gestured to Barbie.

"She says she's your cousin," Ashlee said, handing her the receiver.

"Rebecca?" Rebecca was the only cousin she could imagine calling her.

"I'm sorry to phone you at work." Rebecca sounded a bit flustered. "I just heard from the family that was supposed to come in this weekend. They're going to be here tomorrow instead."

Barbie ran through her work schedule mentally. "I'm supposed to work—"

"Ach, no, I wasn't saying you should come. I just thought you could stop on your way home and ask Mary to do it."

There was silence on the line for a moment. But of course she couldn't say no, even if it meant running into Ben again. "Ja, sure I will. I'm leaving soon."

Maybe he wouldn't be there. Maybe he'd be busy in the shop. She could hurry in, give Mary the message, and be on her way.

Barbie was still telling herself that an hour later when she turned into the Kauffmann lane. As she neared the house, she knew she'd been kidding herself. Mary was nowhere in sight, but Ben was in the yard behind the house with the two kinder and the half-grown puppy.

The pup was the first to notice her arrival. He came rushing toward her buggy horse, yipping loudly. Belle, unmoved, took her place at the hitching rail and lowered her head to scrutinize the pup. He backed up, whined, and abruptly raced back to Abram.

Ben chuckled, bending to ruffle the pup's ears. "She scared you, ja?" His laughing eyes met Barbie's. "Wilkom, Barbie. What brings you by?"

She slid down, reminding herself to act natural —as naturally as he did. "A message for Mary from my cousin Rebecca. Is Mary here?"

He shook his head. "She went with Daad to pick up a package of parts at the post office. He kept insisting he would go alone, so she had to make up an errand to go with him."

She nodded, understanding the subterfuge that was sometimes needed to save a person's feelings. "Your daad isn't one who wants to be fussed over, ja?"

"That's certain-sure."

By this time Abram and Libby had reached her, both tugging on her skirt for attention at the same time. Laughing, she knelt to greet them.

"Abram, your puppy is growing as fast as you are, I think."

"Faster." His face puckered a little. "Why does he grow faster, Barbie? I want to get big, too."

"You'll always be bigger than he is," she assured him.

Libby held out a chubby pink palm. "Owie," she declared. "Barbie kiss it."

Barbie solemnly planted a kiss on the soft, warm skin. "All better, ja?"

"Ja," Libby said, dimpling.

"Show Barbie how the puppy likes to chase you two," Ben suggested. "She wants to watch."

"Shep, komm." Abram clapped his hands and darted across the yard, the pup in pursuit. Chortling, Libby trotted after them.

"That will keep them busy for a minute or two," Ben said. "You want me to tell Mary something for you?"

"Denke, that would be fine." This was getting easier. Given a little more time, she'd be able to look at Ben without feeling his lips on hers. "Rebecca's weekend guests are coming in early. She hoped Mary could come in to work tomorrow to help get ready, since I'm tied up at the café."

"I don't see why not. I'll tell her." He hesitated, and she imagined she read something that might be embarrassment in his eyes. "I wanted to say that I took your advice."

She found she was looking at him blankly, thinking only of how the sunlight brought out the gold flecks in his eyes. "My advice?"

"Getting a woman to help out with the house and the kinder."

"Oh, ja. That's grand."

He nodded, still with that trace of embarrassment. "I think it's going to work out fine. She can come most days for several hours, and that way Mary doesn't have to feel it's all on her."

"Fine. Who did you get?" She'd know who-ever it was. She knew everyone who was close enough for the job.

"It's . . . um, Linda Esch."

Linda Esch. Barbie had been picturing an elderly, grandmotherly figure who'd tell stories to the kinder and make them cookies. Not that Linda couldn't do those things. She'd probably do them very well, and besides that, she was young, pretty, and had been a widow for a bit over a year.

"That . . . that's very nice," she managed. "Linda would be perfect for the job."

Perfect for Ben, too. Just the kind of woman a young minister should have for a wife, around thirty, widowed, childless. Also sensible, modest, and with a spotless reputation. Perfect.

"She doesn't have to be perfect," Ben pointed out. "I'm just hiring her, not marrying her."

Barbie's head jerked up. "I didn't—"

The puppy, with Abram racing after him, charged between them. Trying to avoid them, Barbie stepped aside, stumbling a little.

Ben grabbed her arms, steadying her. His hands were warm and strong, and the impact of his touch ricocheted along her skin, traveling straight to her heart.

Barbie's breath caught, and she struggled to hide the rush of feelings. No, it seemed she wasn't back to normal where Ben was concerned. Not in the least.

Chapter Fourteen

Lancaster County, Spring 1960

"We're hoping to have you and Elizabeth with us, but the rest of us have decided. We're moving to Brook Hill by fall."

Johnny Stoltzfus's words didn't come as any surprise to Reuben, but they pointed even more sharply to his own state of indecision. He rested an elbow on the mailbox at the end of his lane, where Johnny had caught up with him.

"Gut," he said firmly. "I'm wonderful glad you all found the places you wanted there."

Johnny's lean face was split by his grin. "I'm like a kid on his birthday about it, that's certain-sure. The others feel the same. It's a whole new beginning for us." He hesitated, his face sobering. "What about you?"

Reuben blew out a deep breath. "I wish I had a definite answer for you. Soon. I'll know soon."

"Ja, I understand. My wife's none too keen on leaving her kin, either, but she's so busy with the kinder . . ." Again he paused, awkwardly this time. "Well, that makes it different, ain't so?"

Did it? Reuben wasn't sure. If they already had

the kinder they longed for, would that make it easier for Elizabeth to agree to the move? Or would it be just another reason to stay? But he nodded, since he certain-sure wasn't going to talk about it with Johnny.

"You'll let us know." Johnny spoke when the silence had lasted too long. "Five families would be better than four to form a new church district, but either way, we're going." He clapped Reuben's shoulder. "We hope you'll be with us."

Reuben nodded, stepping back out of the way of Johnny's buggy. "I'll be talking to you soon."

He raised his hand and then stood watching as Johnny's buggy moved off down the road. He'd talk to him soon, ja. But what would he have to say? Everyone, it seemed, wanted a decision from him.

Glancing at the envelope he still held in his hand, he started back down the lane toward the house. He'd hoped to hear about the farm he'd visited in Brook Hill. He just hadn't expected the elderly couple would make their decision so quickly.

He glanced down at a few lines of the letter.

My wife says you should show your wife these pictures of the house. She says a young woman is sure to be more interested in the farmhouse she'd be moving into than the barn and the pigsty.

The woman was probably right about it. They'd be taking out the electric and phone, but even so, Elizabeth should be pleased with the farmhouse's fine big kitchen and four bedrooms. That's if she was capable of feeling pleased about any place that wasn't right here in Lancaster County.

He'd already memorized the letter's ending.

We don't want to rush your decision, but we'd like to be out by the end of the summer. So if you can let me know by the end of the month, we'll hold it until then for you.

Folding the letter around the photographs, Reuben stuffed them back into the envelope. No one else must see this before Elizabeth did, no matter how much he longed to share his news. She'd already been upset enough by the fact that he'd broken the news about the farm in front of everyone. He couldn't make that mistake again.

He just hoped he'd be able to get Elizabeth alone quickly, because otherwise he was going to burst with his news.

This farm was the right choice for them—he was convinced of it. She must see it.

And if she didn't, what then? His stomach twisted into knots. He loved Elizabeth with all his heart. Could he bear to hurt her by insisting on this move?

As he neared the house, he spotted her in the

rhubarb bed again, pulling the largest stalks, removing the leaf from each, and dropping the stalks into her basket. She moved gracefully, bending to the task, her green dress seeming to blend into the foliage. Absorbed in the task, she didn't notice him approaching.

"Rhubarb sauce for supper?" he asked. "Or will it be a pie?"

She glanced up, her gentle smile warming her face. "A pie this time, I think. In another week, there should be enough to start canning it."

"Gut." He paused, trying to find the words and failing. "How was your grossmammi today?"

"Fussing over us like always. You know how she loves having us girls over." She straightened, staring down at the basket she held. "Did you know that Isaac and Becky are going to have a little one?"

"I . . . Isaac just mentioned it to me yesterday." And already he was in the wrong. He hadn't told her. What would she think?

"Why didn't you tell me?" Her face tightened. "You should have told me so I wouldn't hear it first from someone else. Didn't you consider me at all?"

The unfairness of the accusation stung him. "You know I do, Elizabeth. Can you really blame me for not wanting to tell you? I knew you'd take it hard, and I didn't want to hurt you."

Her gaze fell. "I . . . I'm sorry. I shouldn't have

said what I did. I just . . . I want to be happy for them, but all I can think is how much I wish we were the ones. I know it's selfish."

Reuben's heart wrenched. He took the basket from her and set it on the ground so he could clasp her hands. "I know. And it's not selfish to long for a child of our own." He took a breath, trying to calm himself. "And there is something else I must tell you before anyone else knows."

"What?" Her gaze lifted, startled and wary, to his. "Is something wrong?"

"No. At least, I don't think it's wrong." Now it was his turn to evade her eyes. He focused on the envelope instead as he pulled the letter and the photos out. "I received this today from the man in Brook Hill who showed me his farm. He says his wife insisted he send some photographs of the inside of the house for you to look at."

He held the handful of pictures out to her. For a moment she just stared at them, and then her fingers closed around them.

"That was wonderful kind of her." Elizabeth's voice was toneless, but at least she'd taken the photos.

"See here?"

He leaned closer, his enthusiasm getting the better of his judgment. If only Elizabeth could share his feelings about the move. They could be planning it together, the way they'd planned everything together when they'd first married.

He had a sudden image in his mind of the afternoon Elizabeth had sneaked him up to her bedroom in her parents' house, just so she could show him the set of quilted placemats her sister had made for them. They'd talked about how their kinder would love the bright appliquéd rooster on the place-mats.

"There's the kitchen. Look how nice and big it is, and with a good-sized pantry, too. And there's a separate room for the laundry. That would be handy, ain't so?"

Elizabeth seemed to make an effort. "It's nice." Her neck bent, and she was very still for a long moment. "Maybe . . . maybe it would be for the best." Her voice was strained. "I just don't know anymore."

Hope surged through him. "Do you mean it?"

Still she didn't look at him, and he wasn't sure she even saw the pictures she stared at. "It might be better to go than to stay here and have to watch Becky and Isaac's happiness." She stopped abruptly, as if she'd just heard what she'd said. Her hand flew to her lips. "Ach, no. I'm sorry. How could I think that?"

He hesitated, sensing he had to move carefully. "It's all right. I know you don't really mean it."

Elizabeth's eyes met his, and they glistened with unshed tears. "I'm afraid. That's the truth of it. Afraid there won't be another baby, afraid I can't get along without family near. Afraid my jealousy will show. And I'm ashamed of myself."

"My sweet Elizabeth." His heart ached. "I wish I could make everything better."

"I know." She managed a tremulous smile. "I'm really wonderful glad for them. I know I have to find the courage to do this."

His throat was tight as he nodded. "I'll help you. It will be all right as long as we're together."

"Rueben . . ." He realized she was blinking back tears. "Could you make one last effort to find a place here first?"

There wouldn't be anything. He already knew it. Still, making another round of properties was a small price to pay for Elizabeth's cooperation.

"I'll try. But if I don't find something in the next couple of weeks, we've decided, ja? We'll be moving to Brook Hill."

Barbie studied her grandmother's face as she leaned back in her chair. Grossmammi loved telling her stories, but this morning she seemed more tired than usual. She closed her eyes, fumbling a little with a hand-quilted placemat she'd taken from the dower chest.

"Are you all right, Grossmammi?" Barbie put her strong young hand over her grandmother's thin fingers. "Have I tired you out, coming in the morning this way?"

Since she was working the lunch shift today, she'd had time to visit her grandmother before heading to work. Her brother would drop her off at the cafe, and then Ashlee would drive her home and stay for supper. She found herself tensing with the hope that the get-together would go well. What would Ashlee think of her family? Just as important, what would they think of her?

Her grandmother opened her eyes, smiling a little. "I'm fine. I'm wonderful glad you came, busy as you are." Her gaze seemed far away. "I don't know that I appreciated how happy being busy makes a person until I wasn't able to do things."

Barbie wasn't sure how to respond to that comment. She certain-sure didn't want to make her grandmother sad over this whole business.

"You must have been kept very busy on the farm back in Lancaster, ain't so?"

"I suppose I was. It didn't seem so at the time. With Becky and Reuben's mamm both working alongside me, we usually talked so much the time flew by."

Barbie smiled. "That's why we call them work frolics, ain't so? The work is play if you have people to do it with."

"Maybe that was part of my reluctance to move when your grossdaadi wanted to." She said it slowly, as if it hadn't occurred to her before. "I was used to having other women around all the time, sharing the chores. Moving sounded like a lonely business."

"It sounds like an adventure to me." Barbie couldn't help the lilt in her voice. Anything out of the ordinary seemed exciting to her.

"Ach, that's because you are a bold spirit." Grossmammi's smile brightened her face, taking away the fatigue. "I was never like you."

Barbie found that hard to believe. "I've always thought you were the strongest person I've ever known. You're the one who keeps the family together."

"Ach, no. I'm just the story-keeper, that's all. It's people like your grandfather who will brave the unknown to make a better life—they are the strong ones."

Barbie patted her hand, relieved to see her returning to normal. "I'm not so sure. After all, you've always been the one we turn to when we need advice. Or even just comforting."

Grossmammi laughed softly. "That's the best part of being a grandmother, my Barbie. You'll know it one day when you are one."

"I'll have to have some kinder of my own first," she said lightly. She rose, putting the quilted placemat back in the dower chest. "David is driving me to work. And one of the Englisch girls I work with will drive me home and stay for supper."

"You'll have a gut time, then." Grossmammi kissed her cheek gently as Barbie bent over her. "We'll talk again soon."

With a good-bye wave, Barbie crossed from the dower house to the main house, just a few steps away. She popped her head into the kitchen to say good-bye to her aunt.

"Grossmammi seemed a little tired this morning. I hope I didn't keep her talking too long."

Her aunt turned from the sink, drying her hands. "It does her good to visit with you, that's certain-sure. She loves telling you girls her stories. I'll just check and see if she wants anything."

Grossmammi was in good hands, for sure. All of her daughters-in-law would do anything for her. Barbie headed outside to where Belle stood patiently in the shade of the big oak tree, waiting.

Before she could climb into the buggy, Barbie heard someone coming down the lane. She turned in time to see Ben Kauffmann's buggy draw up next to hers.

Life certainly seemed to keep throwing them together. She pinned a smile on her face, determined that this time she wouldn't allow Ben to so much as quicken her pulse for a moment.

He slid down, giving the buggy horse a pat. "Barbie. Been visiting your grossmammi, have you?"

She nodded. Probably the entire church knew by this time that Grossmammi was passing on her family stories to her granddaughter. There were few secrets in an Amish community.

Well, there was one, at least. The one she and Ben shared.

"What brings you here?" she asked.

"Your onkel is thinking about putting new upholstery in the family carriage. I brought by some samples for him to look at. How is your grandmother?"

"A little tired, I think. Usually I come by on my way home from work, but I'm working later today." To her annoyance, she felt a slight fluttering as his golden brown eyes studied her face. "How are things going with Linda helping at your place?"

There, that mention of Linda Esch would remind her that Ben Kauffmann was out-of-bounds for her. Wouldn't it? With such a perfect woman around taking care of his house and children, he was bound to become interested in her.

"Linda?" For an instant it seemed that he had forgotten the name. "Oh, right. She's fine, I suppose." He paused a moment and then shrugged, the faintest hint of a smile teasing his firm lips. "It seems strange having her around, that's all. I keep wondering if I remembered to wipe my feet before I came in."

She kept a firm hold on her unruly imagination at the image that presented, not looking up into his face. "I'm sure Linda believes in keeping a clean house," she said.

"She has all the virtues," he said, seeming to agree. "She's neat, a good cook, gentle with the children, efficient in getting things done."

"What else could you ask for?" She kept her gaze fixed on his shirt front.

"She does seem to be a little lacking when it comes to . . . well, to fun."

Barbie couldn't help it. She looked up, finding that his eyes were laughing at her. A gurgle of laughter escaped her. "You mean she's missing my only gift?"

"Exactly. Abram says she's very nice but not as much fun as Barbie."

"And here I thought you didn't approve of fun," she teased.

"Maybe I've learned to appreciate it lately," he said. His fingers brushed hers, making her want to clasp his hand and intertwine her fingers with his.

"It's never too late." Or was it? If Ben knew she'd been out on a date with an Englischer, kissing in a car even, he'd soon decide that all the fun in the world wasn't worth an association with a woman like her.

That was what she wanted, wasn't it? The sensible part of her brain told her so. But his fingers were holding hers, and just his touch was far more powerful than Terry's experienced kisses.

"I hope it isn't." His voice deepened. "I

want . . ." He stopped, seeming to assess what he was about to say. "I want what's best for those I love," he said, and she sensed those were not the words that had been on his tongue a moment ago. He drew his hand back slowly.

He was coming to his senses, obviously. Realizing that giving in to temptation where Barbie was concerned would be a serious error and one he'd regret.

And she didn't want to be anybody's regret. She cast around for something to say and realized she'd never told him about the second note, even though she'd promised.

"I . . . There's something I've been meaning to tell you." Since when did she start stammering around a man? As Ashlee would say, she'd better get a grip. "About that note."

He was instantly alert, his eyes narrowing, his expression growing serious. "What about it?"

"There's been another one. Not at work this time. This one had been put into our mailbox at home."

"What did it say?"

She shrugged. "About the same as the last one. Nothing very specific. I have it in my bag if you want to see it."

"If? For sure I want to see it. If a soul in my care is sending anonymous letters, I must deal with it."

There was the uncompromising Benuel she

knew. Good. It should be easier to resist her feelings for him, although this time he seemed intent on defending her.

Reaching into the buggy, Barbie retrieved her bag and took out the note, handing it to him. "I thought of destroying it, but you said to tell you if any more came. I've been trying to get to the mailbox before Daad every day, but there hasn't been anything else."

"When did it come?" He was staring at the note, an intense frown drawing down his eyebrows. His jaw was tight, and a little muscle seemed to twitch at the corner of his mouth.

"A couple of days ago, more or less." She watched him reading it, feeling cold despite the warmth of the day. "I hate the thought that someone is watching me with . . . well, with ill will."

He was so intent on the note that he didn't immediately respond. And when he did look at her, his face had tightened into a mask that gave away nothing at all. "I want to keep this. Will you trust me with it for now?"

She nodded, wondering what he saw in the words that would make him look so stricken. And then she knew. He wouldn't look that way unless he had a very good idea who had written the note.

Alarmed by his expression, she reached a tentative hand toward him. "Ben, what is it? Who . . ."

He shook his head with a curt movement and turned away. Whatever he was thinking, he didn't intend to tell her.

Ben was hardly able to keep his mind on the discussion of the upholstery samples, and he couldn't escape soon enough. That note Barbie had received seemed to be burned into his brain.

As soon as he was on the way home, he pulled out the letter. The envelope had not been through the postal system. Someone had dropped it in the Lapps' mailbox. Only Barbie's name appeared on the outside.

Letting the gelding have his head, Ben pulled out the note. The wording was similar to what she'd remembered of the first one. But the writing—he couldn't be mistaken, could he?

He took a deep breath, trying to focus his thoughts. To accuse someone groundlessly would be a terrible wrong. But to allow one of his own flock to continue in an action that was hurtful and unkind was also wrong.

Especially if that person was family.

His heart wanted to reject what he was thinking. But he couldn't. He couldn't, because he had a terrible certainty that the person who'd written it was his own sister. Sarah.

He offered up a silent prayer for guidance. Then he picked up the lines and turned the horse toward his sister's place.

This was actually a good time to stop by, since he must talk with Sarah privately. Her husband would be at work with the construction crew, and the children would be at school. He certain-sure didn't want anyone to hear what he had to say to her, whether he was wrong or right.

He pulled up by the kitchen door and stepped down, pausing for a moment's silent prayer—for guidance, for tact, and especially for kind-ness. He couldn't allow the fierce anger he felt for this persecution of Barbie to influence how he spoke to Sarah, either as a brother or as a minister.

The back door opened. "Ben." Sarah's wel-coming smile turned quickly to a look of alarm. "Is something wrong? Daad?"

"No, no, Daad's fine."

"Mary, then. What has she done now?"

He'd long-regretted letting Sarah know any-thing at all about Mary's teenage rebellion. At least she didn't know the whole of it. Only he, Daad, and Barbie knew that secret.

"Mary is well. Working hard at the farm-stay, according to Rebecca, and they're pleased with her." He let Sarah usher him into the kitchen, where she automatically turned to the stove and began pouring coffee into a mug.

"Still seems silly to me for Mary to be working at someone else's place while you have to hire someone to help out at home. I've told you and told you that I can spend more time at home now that my kinder are all in school."

She had offered her help, but he and Daad agreed it just wouldn't do. No matter how fine her intentions, Sarah just couldn't help bossing people around.

"Daad wanted Mary to have some experience working for someone else." He skirted around the fact that the idea of relieving Mary of some of her responsibilities at home had actually come from Barbie. "Anyway, I didn't come to talk to you about Mary."

He put the coffee mug down, the coffee untasted. "Sit down, please, Sarah."

Surprised, and not exactly pleased, his sister took the chair across from him. "Well, what is it, then? If it's not bad news . . ."

"If you can be still a moment, I'll tell you." Anger flared, and he fought to control it. He pulled out the envelope addressed to Barbie and laid it on the table between them. "Did you write this?"

Ben saw the truth in her face before she even began to deny it.

"What is it? A letter to Barbie Lapp? Why should I be writing to Barbie Lapp, of all people?"

"That's a gut question. Did you write it?" He attempted to hold her gaze, but she looked down dismissively at the envelope.

"No." She blinked several times, evading his direct gaze.

He shook his head. "It's no use, Sarah. You look the way you did as a little girl, assuring Daad you'd remembered to close the chicken pen. You were lying then, and you're lying now."

Sarah pulled herself up. "That's a fine thing to say to your own sister. Accusing me of lying. Next thing you know—"

"It's your printing." He threw the words at her. "Do you think I don't know it after all these years? You wrote threatening notes to Barbie."

She stared down at the envelope, her face set. Finally her gaze met his, defiance in every line of her face. "What if I did? Someone has to make that girl see how far she is straying. You should be doing it. You're the minister."

That hit close to home, as she must have known it would. But his responsibility and her guilt were two different things. "Blaming someone else doesn't make your guilt any the less. What do you think the rest of the Leit would say of such an act? It's not your job to judge a sister in the faith."

"A sister in the faith?" Sarah's face reddened. "And how long is she going to be one? Anyone who looks at her can see that Barbie Lapp is well on her way to jumping the fence, just like her older brother did. She'll break her parents' hearts and never look back."

"Stoppe." He barked out the command. "You don't know what you're saying. You don't know anything at all about Barbie, and you've no call to say such a thing."

"Don't know? I know what half the church knows." Sarah's voice rose. "There she is, working in an Englisch business, making Englisch friends. Flirting with the customers. For all you know, she's probably going out drinking with them."

Going out drinking. Barbie had certain-sure done that, but if she hadn't, only the good Lord knew what might have happened to Mary that night. But Sarah didn't know that part of it, and he couldn't tell her.

"Gossiping. Spreading rumors. Thinking ill of a sister. I wouldn't have thought it was possible for you to behave that way. And if you want to talk about a parent's hurt, think about how Daad would feel if he knew."

She moved uncomfortably on her seat. "Daad is just as blind as you are." Her lips twisted. "Let a pretty woman smile and talk sweet, and you're ready to believe anything she says."

There'd been nothing sweet about the way Barbie talked to him. Tart, maybe. "That's foolishness, and you know it."

"It's not foolish." Her anger seemed to propel Sarah out of her chair. She stood, hands planted on the table, fury distorting her face. "It's the truth. And this is the person you picked out to guide my little sister. Barbie Lapp! She'll guide

Mary right out of the faith with her if you're not careful."

He stood as well, equally angry.

"You're wrong about Barbie. And even if you were right, it doesn't excuse what you did." He grabbed the note, shaking it at her. "This is not how we solve problems. Do you want me to share this with the bishop? The other ministers?"

"Go ahead." She folded her arms across her chest. "I'm not ashamed of anything I've done, which is more than Barbie Lapp can say."

Ben tried to pretend this wasn't the sister who had guided his first stumbling steps. What would he say if this were any other of the Leit?

The question helped him regain control. "You must make amends. Tell Barbie you wrote the letters. Ask her forgiveness."

"I won't." Sarah seemed to bite off the words. "And I don't think you'll be eager to tell the bishop about this, will you? That would let everyone know what your precious Barbie has been up to."

"You have made a grave error already, Sarah. Don't compound it now by stubbornness." When she would have spoken, he held up his hand. "No. Don't say anything more now. Think about this, and pray. We'll talk again when you've done so."

He turned and walked away, anger and pain battling in his heart. This might be a breach between them that would never heal.

Chapter Fifteen

Barbie had to smile at the picture Ashlee made, sitting at the supper table that night between Daad, at the end of the table, and her brother David. Ashlee had, without any prompting, worn a pretty but buttoned-up blouse with a denim skirt. She seemed a bit in awe of Daad, but David was getting her to warm up quickly.

"So how is our Barbie at work?" he asked her with a mischievous glance at Barbie. "Is she flirting with all the men?"

"Well, I . . . I wouldn't exactly—" Clearly Ashlee didn't know how to answer that one without incriminating anybody.

"It's okay, Ashlee," she said. "My little brother isn't happy unless he's teasing me. And it's not flirting to smile and be friendly to customers, is it?"

David grinned. "It is the way you do it. You don't have to answer, Ashlee. We all know Barbie's been flirting since she figured out she could get Daadi to pick her up if she batted her big blue eyes at him."

"Ach, and who wouldn't want to pick up a pretty

little daughter after all those rough boys," Daad said.

"Besides," her brother Zeb put in, "David got spoiled plenty by Mammi, being the baby."

"I never spoiled any of my kinder," Mamm said, not quite accurately. "Now, who has saved enough room for pie?"

"I'll get it." Zeb's wife, Esther, got to her feet and gathered her three daughters from the end of the table with a quick glance.

Anna, Debbie, and Katie obediently started removing plates. Hard as it was to believe, Zeb and Esther's three girls were in their early teens already. Pretty as they were, Zeb was going to have to beat the boys off with a stick in a few years.

"Your pretty girls look so much alike it's hard to tell them apart," Ashlee said.

"That they do." Zeb couldn't seem to help a little pride in his voice. "Like their mother."

"What about us?" Sammy, the youngest boy, piped up.

"You don't want to be pretty," his next older brother informed him from the wisdom of his seven years. "That's for girls."

Barbie leaned over to give little Sammy a quick hug. "Boys are strong."

"I'm strong, Aunt Barbie," he said, returning the hug. "See how big a hug I can give."

"You sure can." She dropped a kiss on his flaxen

hair, feeling a rush of tenderness. Funny. She hadn't given a thought to having kinder of her own until the past month or two. Now it seemed to keep intruding on her when she didn't expect it.

"There's snitz pie, cherry pie, and rhubarb pie," Mamm announced. "Just tell the girls which kind you want. Ashlee, you're first. You're our guest."

Barbie suspected Ashlee didn't have a clue what snitz pie was, but she didn't ask.

"I'd love to try the rhubarb. My mother makes that kind."

Mamm reached across to pat her hand. "Well, you'll like your mamm's pie best, that's certain-sure. But maybe ours will make this seem more like home."

Given how Ashlee felt about her parents, Barbie was surprised when Ashlee looked touched.

"Thank you," she murmured.

All the grown-ups relaxed over dessert and coffee, while the kinder were only too eager to finish and run outside. Zeb's kinder loved to visit their grossdaadi's farm, even though it wasn't much different from their own. Finally they were allowed to depart, tugging David along with them for an impromptu game of ball.

"Better not make Onkel David run around too much after that big meal he ate," Barbie called out to them. "He might burst."

Grinning, David shook his fist at her.

Daad and Zeb departed for the barn to look

over the new heifers, leaving the women with the dishes. Barbie glanced at Ashlee. "You don't have to help. You're company."

"I can dry dishes." Ashlee carried dessert plates to the sink. "Even though we have a dishwasher at home, I've done a few."

Mamm handed her a dish towel. "Around here, when someone has a baby girl, we're like as not to say that so-and-so has a new little dishwasher."

"Don't boys take their turn with the dishes?" Ashlee sounded as if she were about to defend women's rights, and Barbie held her breath.

"They do if it's needed," Mamm replied. "When I had all those boys before I got my daughter, I pressed them into service. But if we have daughters, it just seems natural to send the boys out to do chores in the barn while the girls help in the house. I guess it's not that way in your family."

Ashlee looked a little disconcerted. "We didn't have a lot of chores, since we lived in a modern suburban house."

"There's always work to be done when you're raising a family," Mamm said, rinsing a plate before setting it in the rack.

"That's for sure," Esther said. "I wouldn't trade my six for anything, but they do make messes. So it's best they learn to clean them up while the messes are still small."

"It's hard to believe those girls of yours cause

you any trouble. They are as sweet and helpful as can be." Mamm was obviously proud of her granddaughters, whatever the church might say about pride.

Esther smiled affectionately at her mother-in-law. "They're extra sweet when it comes to their grossmammi. No wonder you think they're special."

Ashlee nodded. "I guess I've always been extra sweet to my grandmother, too, maybe *because* she thinks I'm special."

Barbie relaxed, hearing the familiar women's talk flowing easily and including Ashlee. After all, women weren't so different, whether they were Englisch or Amish. They all wanted the same things, didn't they?

Well, home and family, that was the same. Some women wanted more—careers or jobs of their own. Maybe that was more common for the Englisch, but many Amish women felt that way, too. Then there was the freedom Englisch women enjoyed.

She found she was watching Ashlee as she talked easily with Esther. Ashlee had plenty of freedom—that was certain-sure. But was she enjoying it? That question made her wonder.

When the dishes were finished, Ashlee glanced at her watch. "I think I'd better head home. Barbie, will you walk out to the car with me?"

Barbie nodded. Did Ashlee have something to say she didn't want others to hear?

Ashlee made the rounds, thanking everyone for making her so welcome. When Mamm hugged her, she looked surprised for an instant, and then she hugged her back, blinking a little.

Finally they were standing out by Ashlee's car. The sun had made its way behind the ridge, and twilight settled in, deepening shadows by the outbuildings. David and the kinder disappeared into the barn to help with chores.

"I hope you had a good time."

Ashlee's smile flashed. "Who wouldn't? Your family is great. I can see why . . ." She let that trail off, but Barbie knew the ending anyway. Why she wouldn't want them to be disappointed in her. That was it, wasn't it?

"They liked you, too," she said quickly. "You'll have to come again."

Ashlee nodded, but she thought her mind was elsewhere. "Listen, Barbie, I have to tell you. I did something I'm afraid you won't like."

Barbie eyed her. "You haven't been setting up dates for me, have you?"

"If only," she said, grinning. Then she sobered quickly. "I know you didn't want me to do it, but I couldn't help myself. And I think you'll be glad, really. I found your brother James."

She couldn't have heard what she thought she had. "James?" Was her voice as empty as her mind seemed to be?

"Right. James Lapp, your brother." Ashlee's

nervousness betrayed itself by how fast she was talking. "He wasn't really hard to find. He's living in Ohio, near Columbus, not all that far away. He's married, he has two kids, a boy and a girl who are ten and eight, and he works for a construction company. He . . ."

"Wait, wait." She held up her hand to stem the flow of words. "I can't take it all in. You actually found him. Are you sure it's my brother?"

"Certain. He didn't make any secret about his family. In fact, he said—"

"You talked to him?" Her thoughts were tumbling in her head, so quickly she couldn't process them. "You actually talked to James?"

"Well, I e-mailed him first. But when he found out I knew you, he said he wanted to talk, so we did." Ashlee looked at her, anxiety plain in her face. "Are you mad?"

"N-n-no, I guess not. It's just a lot to take in. After all this time of not hearing from him, to have him suddenly pop up like this . . ."

"I guess. That was kind of what he said, too. But he sounds nice." Ashlee blew out a relieved breath. "Anyway, I'm glad you aren't mad." She hesitated. "He left a message on my phone for you. Do you want to hear it?" Ashlee held up the phone.

Barbie stared at it. Then she nodded.

A moment later, with the phone pressed against her ear, Barbie heard her brother's voice for the first time in years.

"Hi, Barbie. I guess your friend told you how she got in touch with me. I just wanted to say— well, I'm sorry about leaving that way. I've always wanted to reach out to the family, but I figured maybe they wouldn't want me to. Or maybe I was just scared. Anyway, I'd love to talk with my little sister. Your friend has my number and address, so if you want to call or write, it would really make me happy. I know I let you down, but I never stopped loving you." The recorded voice broke on the last few words, and Barbie thought he was holding back tears as he hung up.

As for her—well, she wasn't holding them back at all. Her face was wet when she handed the phone back to Ashlee, and her heart felt strange— as if a piece that had been missing was pushing itself back into place.

Lancaster County, Summer 1960

Elizabeth could hardly keep still as the car turned into the lane. She knew she'd been smiling the entire ride from the doctor's office in Lancaster, and the Englisch neighbor who had driven her probably wondered what was going on.

She couldn't tell Mrs. Forbes, as nice as she was. She couldn't tell anyone until Reuben knew.

Elizabeth clasped her hands together over her belly. A baby. At last, the news was good. Reuben would be so happy. All of the darkness between them would be turned to light, and their marriage would be as happy as it had been.

If only she could find him alone. She knew she couldn't contain herself long, and this was news that deserved privacy.

Mrs. Forbes stopped at the kitchen door, and Elizabeth leaned forward to hand her the money she had ready. "Denke, Mrs. Forbes. I don't know what we'd do without our kind drivers."

"It's my pleasure," the woman said, as she always did. And Elizabeth felt sure she meant it. With her children grown and away and her husband at work all day, she seemed to enjoy every opportunity for an outing, almost as much as she liked the extra money it brought in. "I hope you got good news from the doctor?"

Her tone made it a question, and the twinkle in her eyes suggested that she'd already guessed. Barbie just smiled and nodded. Whether she'd guessed or not, Mrs. Forbes could be trusted not to talk about anything she saw or heard when she was driving. That was one of the reasons she was everyone's first choice for a driver.

Elizabeth slid out of the car, scanning the farm quickly. Mamm Alice was out in the garden, bending over the row of young lettuce, and she could see Reuben's daad and brother in the far field, fixing fence. Even as she began to wonder where her husband was, Reuben came out of the building they used as a workshop.

She waved, and he came toward her quickly. It had been his idea that she make an appointment with the doctor. He'd grown increasingly concerned about her lately.

She'd known he was worried about her, and she'd struggled to hide her pain. But he knew her so well, he'd seen past every façade she tried to put up. But now—now everything was different.

"What did the doctor say?" Reuben took her hand, his gaze studying her face.

She glanced around, afraid someone else would notice she was here and start toward them. "Let's walk down toward the stream, so we can talk by ourselves."

With a quick look at his mother in the garden, Reuben nodded. Together they crossed the lawn and went down the path to where the huge weeping willow overhung the stream. They could be private there, surely.

Reuben turned to face her, taking both her hands in his. "So, what did the doctor say? Did he give you something to make you feel better?"

She began to smile and felt as if she'd never stop. "He gave me something, ja. He gave me gut news."

"News?" Reuben didn't seem to understand what she thought was so obvious.

"A baby, Reuben." Happiness bubbled through her, needing to spill out. "We are going to have a baby."

A look of incredulous joy spread across his face. "Really? For sure?"

She nodded, tears springing to her eyes. "For sure."

"Ach, my Elizabeth, that is wonderful. I'm so happy." He threw his arms around her, lifting her off her feet in a huge hug. He pressed his warm cheek against hers. "Praise God."

"Our prayers have been answered." She wrapped her arms around his neck. "This is all I need to make me happy—you and a baby to love."

"And me." He cradled her face in his hands, looking intently into her eyes. "But what exactly did the doctor say? Is there anything we must be careful about?" A shadow crossed his face, and she knew he was thinking about little Matthias.

"That's what I asked him, and he was so kind and understanding. He explained again that it wasn't anything we did or didn't do the last time. He said there was nothing that would have made a difference, and he told me that there's no reason at all to think something will go wrong this time."

"That's wonderful gut to hear. But still, you must take it a little easy. Don't push yourself to do too much, and . . ."

He let that trail off, and Elizabeth read his thoughts easily. He was thinking of the proposed move.

"Reuben." Her voice trembled when she said

his name. "I know I said that I agreed to the move. But it's different now. Please understand. Now, of all times, I need the love and support of family around me. How can I go so far away from all the people who would want to help me? From the doctor who would take care of me? I . . . I don't want to disappoint you. But everything is different now. Don't you see?"

He seemed to go inward for a moment, as if searching for answers. Then he gave her a tender smile and touched her cheek. "I know, Elizabeth. I understand. I won't ask you to move away, not now."

She went into his arms again, with thankfulness this time. "Denke, Reuben. You . . . you know I would if I could. But I just can't."

"It's all right." He drew back a little to look in her face. "You and the baby are what's important now. We'll . . . we'll find a house we can rent, so we can be on our own but be close to family. And I . . . well, I'll start looking for a job."

Her heart contracted. "I don't want you to give up farming. It's what you love."

"I love you and this baby more, so I will do what I must do. Someday, maybe things will be different, ain't so? For now, I'm content."

The words were what she wanted to hear. But she couldn't fool herself when it came to the defeated look in his eyes. He was giving up the very thing he'd been born to do for her sake.

• • •

Waving good-bye to Ashlee, Barbie headed out the back door of the restaurant at the end of her shift the next day, moving quickly. If she hung around, Ashlee would surely be nagging her about why she hadn't called James yet.

Her stomach seemed to turn a somersault. She'd been on the verge of calling a half-dozen times, but she couldn't quite make up her mind. Was it better to talk to him first, and then break the news to her parents that they'd been in touch? Or should she tell them about it first?

Telling them would mean admitting that she'd confided in Ashlee and that Ashlee had taken the initiative in finding James. She wasn't sure how they'd react to it. It would also put the decision to contact him or not in her parents' hands, and she wasn't sure she wanted to do so. After all, James's message had been to her.

She turned down the alley toward her buggy and came to a sudden stop. A car was pulled up next to it—Terry's car. And Terry was getting out, smiling at her.

"Hi. You're back." That was a silly thing to say, but he'd taken her by surprise.

"I just got in and came by to see you first." He grinned down at her. "Did you miss me?"

"Maybe a little," she said, teasing automatically.

"Aw, come on. You're hurting my self-image if you didn't miss me a lot."

"I don't see anything wrong with your self-image," she replied. "It seems pretty healthy to me." Smiling, cheerful, uncomplicated—there weren't any unexpected depths to Terry to make a woman's heart twist with hurt and longing. Not like some people she could name.

"I'm back in town for the next few weeks, at least." Terry stretched out his arm along the roof of the car, leaning toward her with frank appreciation in his face. "You think we could set a time to go out to dinner again?"

She should have known this was coming and been prepared for it. Another date would be fun, but it would also be dangerous. Each time she ventured beyond the boundaries, she risked being caught and hurting those she loved.

"I think . . ." she began.

"Barbie Lapp."

At the sharp voice she jerked around toward the street. She'd been so involved in her thoughts she hadn't heard the buggy approaching, and now it was too late. Thomas and Miriam Miller stared at her, their faces wearing identical expressions of shock and disapproval. Two of their teenage boys peered out at her from the carriage, less disapproving but probably equally shocked.

"Miriam, Thomas." She nodded, her mind racing. "I . . . I was just leaving work."

"So we see." There could be no doubt about the condemnation in Miriam's voice.

Thomas put a restraining hand on his wife's arm. "We have bad news, Barbie. Your grossmammi—she has had a fall."

Grossmammi . . . The sudden pain in her heart felt as if someone had hit her with a hammer. "How . . . how bad is it?"

"They don't know yet." Thomas's tone gentled with sympathy. "We saw the ambulance taking her to the hospital, so since we were on our way to town, we said we'd let you know. Your aunt thought you'd want to meet the family there."

"Ja, ja, of course. Denke. I . . . I will do that." Her mind raced. She'd need a ride to the hospital, she'd have to do something about her buggy—

Thomas had the same thought. "My boys will take your buggy home for you, ain't so? You won't want to be worrying about it." He jerked his head, and the two boys jumped down.

"Denke," she said again, turning to the boys. "The mare is back there." She pointed. "You'll find everything . . ."

"We'll take care of it." Young Thomas, the older boy, patted her arm awkwardly. "Don't worry." They hurried off as Thomas turned his mare and drove on.

For an instant she just stood there, trying to organize her thoughts. Grossmammi . . . Surely this couldn't be the end already. Grossmammi hadn't finished telling her all the stories in the dower chest. She had to finish, didn't she?

Barbie became aware of Terry, still standing there, looking completely at sea. What was she thinking? He wouldn't have understood any of the conversation, conducted in Pennsylvania Dutch as it was.

"Something's wrong, I guess, but I don't know what." He looked as if he didn't know whether to go or stay.

She took a deep breath, trying to steady herself. "It's my grandmother. She's fallen, and they've taken her to the hospital. I don't know how bad it is." Her voice broke on the last few words, and she held back a sob with a determined effort.

"So sorry. I didn't realize. Look, at least let me drive you there. You can't go out on the highway in a buggy."

She hesitated. Accepting a ride from Terry would only put her deeper into trouble, but that hardly mattered at the moment. Her problems seemed petty in comparison to her grandmother's health.

"That would be great. Thanks so much."

"Good. Hop in. I'll have you there in no time."

Apparently Terry considered this an emergency calling for speed, because he took the corner at a rate that would have caused an accident had anything been coming. She gasped and clung to the armrest.

"Sorry. I guess it wouldn't help if I got stopped by the cops." He proceeded a little more decorously until he reached the highway.

Barbie stared straight ahead, trying not to let herself imagine the worst. Incoherent prayers jumbled through her thoughts, mixing with visions of Grossmammi—laughing, telling stories, baking cookies, listening—always there, in the background, a solid part of her life. Barbie wasn't ready to lose her yet. Maybe she never would be, but not now. Not now.

"She seemed tired when I visited her yesterday. I told my aunt." The words spilled out. "I should have done more. If we'd taken her to the doctor, maybe this wouldn't have happened."

Terry shrugged. "Maybe, maybe not. You can't blame yourself. She's pretty old, isn't she? It's just fate."

Fate? That wasn't something she could cling to. God's will, that was what they would say. What Grossmammi herself would say—that life was made up of good things and bad things, and all of it God's will.

But she nodded to show she'd heard. Terry was trying to be comforting, she supposed.

They turned off the highway at the sign for the hospital. He cleared his throat. "Do you want me to wait for you?"

"No, no, you shouldn't. I don't know how long we'll be here, and I'll be with family anyway." She glanced at him and summoned up a smile. "Thanks so much for the ride."

He grinned. "It wasn't quite the welcome back

I'd hoped for, but you have to do what you have to do. I'll be around. Maybe we can plan that dinner later."

She nodded absently, her mind racing ahead as he drew up under the portico at the main entrance. What was she going to find?

Once inside, a helpful pink lady at the front desk directed her to the third floor. Grossmammi had been admitted, then. She tried to tell herself it didn't necessarily mean anything dire, but it didn't seem to work. By the time the elevator stopped, her fingernails were biting into her palms.

Barbie followed a murmur of voices speaking Pennsylvania Dutch to a room just down the hall—a waiting room, by the look of it, currently crowded with family. She went swiftly to her mother, to be enfolded in a comforting embrace.

"We don't know anything yet," Mammi said, before she could ask the question. "Your aunt heard a thud and ran over to find her on the kitchen floor. It didn't look as if she'd tripped over anything. She just . . . fell." Mamm's voice held pain mixed with fear. "All we can do is wait and pray."

Pressing her lips together, she nodded. Her brother David appeared in the doorway with a cardboard container of coffees. He passed them around as far as they would go and then stopped beside Barbie.

"Shall I get you a coffee, then?" His ruddy young face was pale.

"You don't need to. You just got back."

His face seemed to twist. "I'd rather go for coffee than stand here waiting." He gave her hand a quick squeeze and hurried back out the door.

David had the right idea. It was hard to stay, to hug her aunt and listen to her murmurings that she should have checked more often, to see the grave faces her father and uncles wore.

The room slowly filled up as the word spread. Rebecca came in with their cousin Judith, and the three female cousins clung together for a long moment. Grossmammi had entrusted them with her family stories. Rebecca and Judith would understand, without her saying it, how tragic it would be if Grossmammi didn't have a chance to finish the stories for Barbie.

Benuel slipped into the room, greeting each of the brothers first and offering words of comfort. He began moving around the room, his quiet presence seeming to spread a measure of peace.

Barbie watched him. How did he do it? And how strange that he didn't seem to understand what a good minister he actually was.

He'd reached her, and he touched her sleeve lightly, the gesture hidden from those around them by his sturdy frame. "She is in God's hands, as we all are."

Barbie nodded, her throat closing. She wanted

to say she knew, to tell him the family appreciated his presence, but the words wouldn't come out.

Before she could find her tongue, there was a stir in the room. Everyone turned to face the door. Ben moved in close beside her. His hand touched her elbow as if in mute support.

The young doctor who stood in the doorway seemed taken aback by the size of the group waiting for him. "Family of Mrs. Lapp?" he asked.

They all nodded, and Daad and his brothers stepped forward.

"How bad is it?" Onkel John, Rebecca's daad, asked the question that was in all their minds.

The doctor gave a second glance at the chart he held, as if to be sure of the facts. "Mrs. Lapp is conscious now." His lips twitched in what might have been a smile. "In fact, she's telling us she wants to go home, but we can't allow that yet."

"Her injuries?" Daad said.

"A slight concussion and a badly bruised arm, probably from where she tried to break her fall. Apparently she became dizzy, so we want to do a few more tests to find out why. Preliminary indications are that her blood pressure is low, but we haven't found anything else yet. If nothing else turns up, we should be able to let her go home in a day or two."

A babble of talk burst out. Barbie sagged with

relief, and Ben gripped her firmly. She could feel the warmth and strength of his hand right through her sleeve.

"You're all right now," he murmured. "Everything is fine."

For a moment longer she leaned into his support, and then she straightened. Grossmammi would be all right, but everything else was all wrong. Unless she was badly mistaken, Ben and the other ministers would soon be hearing from Thomas and Miriam Miller about her behavior.

A cold hand clamped over her heart. Once he heard the truth, Ben would turn away from her. She knew it as well as she knew her own name. She just hadn't realized until this moment how much it would hurt.

Chapter Sixteen

"I hear Elizabeth Lapp is doing much better." Benuel's father put his newspaper aside to comment the next evening. "You saw her today, ain't so?"

Ben sank down in the rocking chair and leaned his head back against the pad. Some nights he felt as if he ought to go to bed the same time as the little ones did.

"I stopped by to offer support." That was part of his responsibility as a minister, to say nothing of his duty as a friend.

And he hated to admit he'd felt a pang of disappointment to find that Barbie wasn't there. He was thinking too often of those moments in the waiting room when she'd seemed to rely on him. To say nothing of that episode in the moonlight when she'd been in his arms.

"So?" Daad prompted. "How is Elizabeth doing? A fall can be serious at her age, ain't so?"

He nodded, trying to keep his errant thoughts under control. "It can, but she escaped with a sore wrist and some bruises. She can't wait to be home, and the family hopes that tomorrow will be the day."

Daad folded his paper, the better to focus on Ben. "Do they know for sure what made her pass out that way?"

"From what I heard, her blood pressure was low, and that might have made her dizzy when she stood up. The tests they've done so far have been fine. That's why the doctor has kept her longer, for the test results. Now he wants to adjust the medicine she's taking."

Daad nodded. "That sounds wise, but I'm sure Elizabeth is impatient. She's not one to lie around when she thinks there are things to be done."

"Better to be safe . . ." he began, but stopped when he heard the clop of horse's hooves and a harness creaking from the lane outside the living room window.

Daad was up and at the window before he'd gotten out of his chair. His father seemed to freeze, his hand on the pane.

"Daad? Who is it?"

His father turned toward him, his face paling. "The bishop. Ezra King and Jonas Fisher are with him."

Mary. Ben didn't say the name aloud, but he knew that's what Daad was thinking, too. Had they found out about Mary's misdeeds? If so, Mary would not be the only one in trouble. He had known, and he had ignored his duty as a minister and kept it secret.

He realized his hands were clenched into fists, and he deliberately relaxed them, forcing himself to calm. "Komm. We'd best go to greet them."

By the time the knock came on the back door, he'd managed to compose himself. They would deal with whatever happened together as a family. That was all he could be sure of.

Ben opened the door and nodded to the others as they filed in. There was no point in pretending this was an ordinary visit when they all knew it couldn't be.

Bishop Caleb Esch greeted each of them, his lined face giving nothing away. After he'd refused the offer of coffee, he turned to Daad.

"We have church business to talk over with Ben, Moses. Will you excuse us?"

Daad's relief was written on his face for all to see. "Ja, ja, for sure. I'll just take my newspaper upstairs with me." Nodding to them, he went quickly toward the front of the house, his step light.

"Please, sit." Ben's thoughts scrambled over likely possibilities for this meeting. It had to be a serious matter to be brought up in this fashion. He took the chair at the foot of the table, opposite Bishop Caleb.

"This is a grave matter," he said, echoing Benuel's thoughts. "I hate to say it, but I've heard disturbing news about one of our people. More than rumors. Fact." He gave a heavy sigh, his face drawn down with regret. "I have learned that Barbara Lapp has been going out with an Englischer."

His first instinct was denial. "No. Surely not. I don't believe she would do so."

The bishop shook his head sorrowfully. "I don't want to believe it, either, but when Thomas and Miriam Miller went to tell her the news about her grandmother, they found her with a young man. She seemed to be leaving the café where she works with him."

"She might have just been talking with someone. One of her customers at the café, or someone who asked for directions." Even as he said the words, Ben knew they didn't sound very convincing.

The bishop sighed. "They say they heard something said about another date. She will have a chance to explain herself, but we have to act." He folded his hands on the table, his face grim. "Don't think I come to this point easily. There have been other rumors about her actions—rumors I have been reluctant to believe without more evidence. But it seems now we have it."

Ben wanted to protest, but he had a sinking feeling that it would do no good. Barbie had been skirting the line lately; he knew that as well as anyone did. Now it seemed she had crossed it. Maybe that night at the bar hadn't been the only one. Maybe she made a habit of it.

Then he thought of how good she'd been with Mary, with his own kinder, and he rejected the thought. Surely this couldn't be as bad as it looked.

"She's not a baptized member yet, of course," Ezra reminded them. He rubbed his forehead as if to wipe away the task ahead of them. "But she's not a teenager. She's of an age to be married and have a family."

"Well, she's still young," Jonas said with a touch of indulgence. He had daughters nearing their twenties himself. "Girls seem to want to work awhile these days before settling down. But I agree. We can't ignore it if Barbie has gone so far as to be dating an Englischer."

"What do you plan to do?" Ben forced the words out, looking at Bishop Caleb's weathered face and dreading the answer.

"We must go together to ask her if this is true," he said firmly. "That's what scripture commands. If so, and if she is willing to submit to the church's discipline, we will proceed to impose the penalty. Since it was a public act and one that could influence younger people, I think some-thing more than private confession is needed. Public confession before the members meeting is warranted in this case."

Jonas stirred. Perhaps he would press for the more lenient private confession to the ministers. It was what Benuel himself wanted to say, but he was tied by the conflict between his duty as a minister and his relationship with Barbie.

But all Jonas said was, "Sitting or kneeling confession?"

The stages of church discipline were well-known to all of them. Private confession. Sitting confession before a members meeting. Kneeling confession. And in the end, if there was no other way to bring the offender to his senses, expulsion.

"Sitting," Bishop Caleb said. "I see no need for kneeling for this offense."

Ben's jaw was too tight for speech. Surely it would be enough for Barbie to confess privately. To humiliate her before the congregation was a serious blow.

But he knew what the bishop would say to that argument. The aim of confrontation, confession, and repentance wasn't to humiliate. It was to bring the penitent back into the fold.

The bishop looked a question at the others. One after the other, they nodded, with Ben a reluctant last.

His mind was beginning to work again, but his thoughts were in turmoil. He knew, none better, what Barbie had been doing. After all, he'd seen her in those Englisch clothes the night she brought Mary home. But as he'd gotten to know her recently, he'd begun to change his initial opinion of her. He'd started to believe that behind that pretty face and pert manner was a warm, caring woman just waiting for someone to love.

And where had that search for love taken her? Into an Englischer's arms? Pure jealousy shot through him.

"We're agreed, then. Best to get it over with right away, before rumors begin to spread." Bishop Caleb's glance at Ben was filled with a kind of pity. "We all know that you have become . . . friends with Barbie. There is no need for you to go with us."

It was tempting. He'd give a lot to be spared this ordeal. But Ben shook his head. He couldn't shirk his duty just because the person in question was Barbie. He could only pray that she would see he wanted what was best for her. Imposing public confession was a loving act on the part of the fellowship, a desperate effort to retrieve the straying sheep.

But he feared Barbie wouldn't see it that way.

She should have been expecting this, Barbie knew. She watched as the men filed into the kitchen, and wished for the floor to open up and swallow her. She didn't want to see Mammi and Daadi standing there, shock in their faces, glancing at David as if to ask what he had been doing. But it wasn't David the ministers had come to see, she knew.

Ben was the last man through the door. Her heart sank even further. Was he responsible for this visit? It was hard to believe that he would sacrifice Mary in order to report her. If he had . . . Her hands clenched. If so, how did he rationalize his own actions?

Bishop Caleb greeted each of them. Then he looked at her brother. "David, we need to speak in private with your parents and your sister. Will you leave us, please?"

David sent one startled, scared look toward her before nodding and slipping out the back door.

Daad's face was stricken. He nodded to the seats around the kitchen table. One by one they sat down, until she was the only one left standing.

Bishop Caleb's steely gaze rested on her. "Sit down, Barbie. We must talk."

Wordless, she sat, feeling so stiff that it was a wonder she could get her knees to bend. She couldn't look at Ben. Wouldn't look at him.

But she found herself stealing a glance. He sat nearly as rigidly as she did, his face so tight it might have been carved of stone. The man who'd laughed with her over Abram and Libby's antics with the puppy had vanished, leaving behind this censorious stranger.

Bishop Caleb cleared his throat. "We come in response to the Biblical injunction. If a brother is in error, two or three must call on him to give him the opportunity to repent. Tonight the erring soul is our sister Barbara Lapp."

Daad's expression didn't change, but Barbie heard a stifled sob from her mother and thought she felt her own heart begin to break. How could she have been so heedless as to bring them this pain?

An unexpected little flare of anger lit in her. But who were they to judge her, especially Benuel Kauffmann? She hadn't done anything so terribly wrong, had she?

"Barbara, word has come to us that you have been seeing an Englisch man." Bishop Caleb frowned, and Barbie dropped her gaze, studying her hands as if she'd never seen them before. "There have been other rumors, but in this case you were actually seen with him."

Thomas and Miriam, of course. They had told

the bishop, but they obviously hadn't told Mamm and Daadi. If her folks could have been prepared, it wouldn't have come as such a shock.

But she couldn't very well blame Miriam for not telling. She was the one who should have told them, who should have prepared them. Instead, she'd let herself hope she could get away with it and that no one would know.

Silence. She clenched her hands together.

"Do you wish to say anything in your own defense, Barbara?" The bishop's tone had gentled slightly.

For one wild moment she considered denying it. They didn't really have proof of anything. Obviously no one had seen them that night she'd dressed in Ashlee's clothes and gone to dinner with Terry.

But lying would only compound the offense. And she might have bent the truth a little when she'd told Mamm and Daad that she was spending the night with a friend, but she couldn't sit here and tell an outright lie.

Everyone knew what happened when the bishop and ministers called to bring you to a sense of your own misdeeds. You either repented or you rebelled, and rebellion seemed inevitably to lead away from home and family and everything you loved.

"No." She swallowed the lump in her throat. "There is nothing."

She thought he breathed a little easier. "Will you tell us how far this offense has gone?"

Her fingers gripped the edge of the table. She couldn't look at any of them. She couldn't bear to see the pain in her parents' faces. And she didn't want to know what was in Ben's eyes right now.

"I met him—the Englischer—through friends." If she were being completely honest, she'd tell them about going to the bar, dressing in Englisch clothes. But if she did, any questions would lead inevitably to Mary. "He started coming to the café where I work. We talked."

When she didn't go on, the bishop stirred. "And then?"

She sucked in a breath as if she couldn't get enough air. "He wanted to take me to dinner. To get to know me better. So I went."

"How many times?" The questions were inexorable.

"Just once."

"This man—did you let him kiss you?"

She could feel her cheeks grow hot. "Yes." She dared to flash a quick look at the bishop. "But that's all. Nothing else."

Mamm pressed her hand against her mouth. Was she thinking about James? Had the ministers come to call about James, too, before he left? She'd been too young to know.

"Are you prepared to confess your wrong before the members meeting? To show repentance and agree that the offense will not be repeated?"

Rebellion flared again. To go before the whole church, to make such an admission—it was unfair. Why should she be singled out in this way?

But she sensed the tension that held Mamm and Daad motionless, not even breathing. Unless she was ready, here and now, to leave the faith and her family for good, she had no choice. The only answer she could make was the expected one.

"I am."

"Gut."

She could feel the wave of relief that went around the table, and even with her heart sore and bruised, she recognized that there had been no malice from anyone. They truly believed they were doing the right thing.

Even Ben? Did he believe? Could he really be free of malice toward the woman he'd kissed, the woman he'd begun to trust with his family?

"After the next worship service, then. We will all be wonderful glad to put this behind us." The bishop stood, and they all scrambled to their feet. "We'll pray silently now for the true repentance that will restore Barbara to her place in the com-munity."

Bowing her head, Barbie tried to pray, but her thoughts bounced around her head. If this had to happen, maybe it was just as well that it happened now, before she'd gone any farther in defiance of the Ordnung.

But would she have? She honestly didn't know.

A shuffling of feet announced that the prayer was over. In a moment the visitors were heading out the door. She held her breath, not knowing what she'd do if Ben tried to speak to her.

He didn't. He walked outside without a backward glance. Obviously whatever had been growing between them had now been destroyed for good. She was left to face the wreckage of her relationship with her parents.

Lancaster County, Summer 1960

Reuben stood on the sidewalk outside the carpet plant. Did he look as discouraged as he felt? Most likely.

"We're not hiring right now, but we'll be in touch if we have any openings."

"We'll keep your application on file."

"We don't hire anyone who doesn't have a high school diploma."

Those answers, or variations of them, had been repeated everywhere he went, it seemed. Not that he felt especially qualified to run one of those big machines in the factory, but he was young and strong, and he could learn. But not unless someone gave him the opportunity.

He smacked his hat against his leg in frustration, then clapped it back on his head. The gelding waited patiently under the shade of the only tree that overhung the parking area. The fact that there were no facilities for horses and buggies should have told him that Amish workers weren't welcome here.

That probably wasn't fair, but it was how he felt. Some of the other places where he'd put his name in were more accustomed to employing the Amish, but even there, no one seemed to be hiring. He'd made the sacrifice of moving willingly for the sake of Elizabeth and the new babe, but he hadn't dreamed it would be so hard even to find a job. And if he did get a job at one of those places, he'd have to ride with someone, since they were too far away to go by horse and buggy.

He knew what that meant. A long day, gone from early morning until suppertime or later, little time to spend with family or to train children by working alongside them. So many of the things he valued in life would have to be sacrificed.

The sorrow and frustration rode with him all the way home. He'd made a promise to Elizabeth, and he meant to keep it. Still, even now, it might not be too late to find a place to farm here in the area as an alternative.

But even as he'd gone through the motions— reading all the ads, scanning all the auctions, searching the bulletin boards at the hardware store and the lumberyard—he was losing hope. He'd keep looking—that was certain-sure. If—when—

he found a job of some sort, he could continue to look. That didn't console him much. Land prices would go nowhere but up, and the restrictions on farmers increased daily. Would there be any farms left in Lancaster County in ten or twenty years?

When he turned into the lane, Reuben straightened. He shouldn't let Elizabeth guess how worried he was. She had enough to trouble her, with the memory of losing little Matthias affecting her every thought about the new baby.

Elizabeth came out of the house as he pulled up at the barn, walking across the grass to join him. She was smiling as she neared him, and the color in her cheeks cheered him. It had been some time since he'd seen her looking so well.

"Have a gut day?" He asked the question quickly, before she could say the same to him.

She nodded. "A little sick this morning, but that's nothing."

Nothing compared to the joy she felt over the new life within her, she meant. He wouldn't taint that bright happiness with his own discouragement.

"Has my mamm guessed yet?" He moved smoothly about the unharnessing, trying to delay the inevitable moment when he'd have to confess he'd come up with nothing.

Elizabeth chuckled softly. "She hasn't said anything, but with both her daughters-in-law going pale at the scent of coffee in the morning, I think she knows. Becky guessed, and I couldn't resist telling her."

The slight constraint she'd shown before when speaking of Becky was gone now.

Elizabeth leaned against the buggy, watching him without, he suspected, really seeing him.

"Becky feels that she can ask me things now. With her own sisters so far away, I'm glad to be of help to her." She hesitated. "Because of Matthias. She thinks I know everything about being pregnant."

He studied her face, fearing what he might see there. But she seemed surprisingly serene. "It doesn't trouble you, speaking of him?" he ventured.

Her gaze dropped. "A little, I guess. But not the way it did before." Her blue eyes met his again. "It's as if now I can remember the happiness of being pregnant with him. I feel a little guilty about it. I don't want this new baby to take his place in my heart."

"Ach, Elizabeth, it could never happen. Our firstborn will always have his own corner of our hearts. But it's not wrong to rejoice over a new life."

Her eyes sparkled with tears, but she was smiling. She tenderly rested her hand on her stomach. "If this babe has let me feel thankful for what we had of Matthias, then I'm doubly happy."

Heedless of who might be watching, he put his arms around her, drawing her close, love swelling his heart. He pressed his cheek against hers.

"Then I'm happy, too. Whatever life brings."

She drew back a little. "But I'm forgetting to ask you. How did it go today?"

He forced a smile. "Nothing yet. Maybe the next time."

She touched his cheek. "I'm sorry. I know how hard you're trying. Nothing new about land for sale, either?"

"No." He tried to drum up some hopefulness. "It doesn't have to be forever. Even if I get a job, we can still be on the lookout for a farm, ain't so?"

She nodded, studying his face a little doubtfully. "You're sure it's . . . well, all right?"

He clasped the hand that was against his cheek and pressed a kiss on the palm. "As long as we're together, everything is fine."

He wasn't sure she altogether believed him, but it was all he could find to reassure her.

And it was true. Whatever God sent them, they would endure together, knowing it was His will and for their eventual good.

Chapter Seventeen

"I still don't understand why you have to quit." Ashlee dropped the stack of paper napkins she was holding and they fluttered across the counter. "Honestly, Barbie, that's ridiculous. Nobody has a right to tell you what to do."

Whatever God sends, we endure, knowing it is His will and for our eventual good. Barbie reminded herself of the words her grandmother had spoken to her, wanting to believe they were true.

She'd waited until the morning rush was over to tell Ashlee what she'd already told Walt. She'd work another week, but then she had to leave.

Walt had been annoyed by the upset to his routine, but he'd hauled out the *Help Wanted* sign to put in the window. Ashlee was a different story. Not only was she angry, she acted as if she'd been betrayed. And Barbie didn't know how to explain it to her so she'd understand. Or if that was possible.

Still, she had to try. Ashlee was her friend, and she owed her an explanation.

"It's not a question of anyone forcing me to quit." She took a step back toward the hall, hopefully out of earshot of any of the lingering coffee drinkers. "When you're Amish, you know from the time you're born that you live in obedience to the Gmay—the local church district in which you live."

"Even when their rules are unreasonable? Why isn't it enough that you say you're sorry for going out with Terry? Why do you have to quit work, too? Did those ministers demand it?"

"No. They didn't even mention it. But they knew if I was truly sorry, I'd . . . well, get away from the place that tempted me to do wrong."

"How can it be wrong to go out to dinner with a guy? It's not like you're going to marry him or anything. I sure don't think about marrying everybody I go out with." Ashlee flung out her hands in an extravagant gesture, seeming to throw potential dates to the wind.

"I know that's how it is for you." A smile tugged at her lips at the thought of Ashlee getting serious about anyone or anything. "But I told you before, we don't see it that way. If we single someone out, we're looking at all the possibilities. That doesn't mean an Amish girl marries the first guy she goes out with, but she does look at him as a possible husband. That's why we have time to do a little running around before we settle down. To figure that out."

"Well, then, I still don't get why what you did was so wrong. Your folks were really nice to me, even though I'm not Amish."

"They liked you." Her smile faltered. They had, of course. Ashlee was very likable. But they must suspect that Ashlee had at least helped her to go out with Terry, if not outright encouraged it.

Ashlee frowned at her for a moment. "This business of quitting your job—is it because they want to get you away from me?"

"No, no, nothing like that." She clasped Ashlee's hand. "It's just that if I keep on working here, my folks would be wondering all the time if I was doing something improper. I don't want to hurt them any more than I already have."

"You really mean it, don't you?" Ashlee went on before she could answer. "Is this because of what your brother did?"

Again Barbie saw herself hugging James, watching as he left the house, only half-comprehending that her big brother was leaving forever.

"A little, I guess. My folks would still be upset, no matter what. But I saw how much it hurt them when James left. How can I do that to them again?"

Ashlee's eyes widened. "You mean you've actually been thinking of leaving?"

"No. Well, maybe sometimes I think of it, but not seriously."

Ashlee didn't speak for a moment. Then it was her turn to grasp Barbie's hand. "Listen, if you decide . . . Well, whatever you decide, I'm still your friend. I'll help you, no matter what."

"Denke." Her throat was tight. "Thanks."

"I'll be around. Although . . ." She hesitated. "Well, I'm going away this weekend. Home, for my mother's birthday."

"I'm so glad." She'd never felt it right for Ashlee to be so separated from her people. "I'm sure she'll be wonderful glad. What made you decide to go?"

Ashlee shrugged. "You, mostly. Well, your family. Seeing you with them reminded me of the good times I've had with my own family. So I figured this trip was one small step I could take."

Barbie blinked, surprised by the longing in Ashlee's eyes. Apparently Ashlee wasn't enjoying her independence quite as much as she claimed. "I'm glad," she said again. "Families can cause you grief, but they can bring a lot of joy, too."

"If that's really what you believe . . ." Ashlee took hold of her arm and steered her toward the back hall. "Then you need to go in the break room. Now."

"What? What are you talking about?" A thought struck her—so unreal a thought it just wasn't possible. She could only stare at Ashlee. "What have you done?"

"Not me, not exactly." Ashlee actually flushed. "But your brother called me back. He really wants to see you. So . . ."

"You mean he's here? I can't. I don't . . . I'm not

ready to see him." Not now, when her thoughts were in such turmoil.

Ashlee gave a little shove. "He drove all this way. The least you can do is talk to him for a minute. Go on. I'll square it with Walt."

Her breath caught. She'd been so preoccupied with her own troubles that she hadn't even thought of James, off somewhere waiting for a call back and finally coming to see for himself.

She took one step, then another, her heart thudding in her chest. She'd longed to see her brother again, but at a time like this . . .

Barbie stopped at the door, hardly breathing. One little turn of the knob had the potential to change a number of lives for better or worse. She opened the door and stepped inside.

The man who turned toward her looked like any other Englischer at first glance—a stocky figure, clean-shaven, ruddy, wearing a pair of jeans and a polo shirt. Then he gave her a tentative smile, and she saw her brother again.

"Barbie?" James's voice, just as she'd heard it on the message, but actually here. "Is that you? You're all grown up."

She had to swallow before she could speak. "Hello, James."

"I'm so glad to see you." He'd slipped into dialect, but he sounded a little rusty at the language. He took a tentative step toward her. "How are you?"

"I'm fine." She hoped he couldn't read the doubt in her voice. "Everyone is fine. Well, Grossmammi had a fall, but she's okay now. Just a little bruised."

What was wrong with her? Why was she sounding as if he were a stranger? This was James, after all these years.

"I miss her." His voice thickened, and he took another step closer. "I remember all the stories she told when I was little."

"She's still telling her stories," Barbie assured him. "Things don't change much here, ain't so?"

He shook his head. "You did. You're different." His face twisted, and she knew he was holding back tears. "You've grown up, and I missed it all."

The depth of loss in his voice went straight to her heart. No matter who had caused the rift between them, James was here now, wanting to be her brother again.

"Ach, James." Her voice broke on his name, and she ran into his arms as if she were eight again.

James hugged her fiercely. "My little sister. I've missed you so much."

Mopping the tears that persisted in spilling over, she drew back and looked at him, seeing the familiar lines of her brother's young face in this mature man. "Why? Why didn't you get in touch with us? Why did you just disappear?"

His face seemed to quiver, and he turned away slightly, as if not wanting her to see him cry. "I . . . I'm sorry. It was stupid, I guess. I wanted to see everyone. I nearly came back dozens of times over the years."

"Why didn't you?" She shot the question at him, and his face suddenly crinkled into a grin.

"That's my little Barbie. Always wanting to know why."

"Well, I do." She adopted Mamm's scolding tone. "You should have written, at least."

"I was afraid, I guess." He looked as shame-faced as if he were a kid again and Mamm was scolding him. "Afraid I wouldn't be welcome. I guess, as long as I didn't know for sure, I could believe everybody still loved me."

"Ach, you make me want to swat you. Of course everyone loves you. There's a hole in the family waiting for you." She knew, quite suddenly and without the need to ask, that it was true. Mamm and Daadi still missed him. Still loved him, Englisch or not.

"You think, if I went to the farm, they'd want to see me?" He sounded so uncertain, as if life had taught him that he didn't have all the answers.

She hugged him again. "There's only one way that I know of to find out." She hesitated. Would it be better if James just appeared on his own? Or if he went home with her? She honestly didn't know.

"Will you . . . Is it okay if I hang out in town until you finish work and go home with you?"

It seemed so odd to have her big brother actually

needing her help. His uncertainty made the decision for her.

"Sure it is." She patted his cheek. "It will be all right. You'll see."

He blew out a relieved breath. "So how is everyone, really? The boys, are they married? Not David, I hope. He'd be too young."

"David is having too much fun courting to think of settling down." How much did David remember of James? She'd never asked him. He'd been even younger than she was when James left. "The others are married, with families of their own."

"Even little Zeb?"

"Married with six kinder—three girls and three boys. What about you? You have a family?"

"My wife, Andrea, and I have a boy and a girl, eight and ten." He hesitated, then pulled out a cell phone. "I have pictures, if you want to see."

"Of course I do." She grabbed the phone. Her heart seemed ready to burst at the sight of the two little figures. The boy held a baseball bat proudly on his shoulder, and his face had the look of Zeb's boys. And the little girl's blond hair and blue eyes made her look as if she'd fit right in with the other nieces. "So sweet." She touched the faces gently. "I love them already."

James blew out a breath of relief, it seemed. "I'd sure like them to meet their grandparents before—well, before it's too late. Have you said anything to the folks about me?"

"Not—not yet." She should have; she saw that now. "I meant to, but there have been some things going on. But don't worry. It'll be all right."

After all, James had left before being baptized, so he wasn't under the bann. There was every reason to believe the family would be happy to see him again. They certain-sure wouldn't be the only family in the church to have Englisch kids back to visit.

"We're just in Columbus, Ohio." James's voice took on a lilt. "It's not a bad drive for us. Maybe, if the folks think it's okay, they'd let us come for a visit this summer, once the kids are out of school."

"That would be wonderful good." She glanced toward the door. "I should get back to work, but I have to ask. Do you ever regret it? Leaving, I mean."

He didn't answer right away, frowning a little as if trying to decide what to say. "At first a lot," he said at last. "I had my head all stuffed full of notions of being free to decide things for myself." That almost sounded like something Ashlee had said. "I saw pretty fast that it wasn't exactly like I'd imagined. And I missed all of you so much I'd lay awake at night and think of you."

She was about to ask why he hadn't come back, but he was going on.

"Then I met Andrea, and it got better. Now I have a wife I love, a good job, and two great kids.

I'm happy. But sometimes . . ." He met her gaze. "Sometimes I still miss it—that sense of belonging, of being part of a community that's more important than what any one person wants. You know?"

"Ja," she said softly. "I know."

Ben glanced at Mary, sitting next to him on the buggy seat. She hadn't said a word during the drive to Rebecca and Matt's farm-stay, and she'd said very little even before that. She'd heard something of what was going on with Barbie, clearly.

He shouldn't talk about it with her. The details of what went on between the ministers and the penitent were meant to be private.

Still, news tended to spread. Someone would have seen them going to the Lapp place. Or Miriam had let something drop—even with the best of intentions, she was one who liked to talk, and he didn't place much reliance on her discretion.

Thinking of discretion reminded him of his sister Sarah, and his jaw tightened. He hadn't resolved things with her after he'd confronted her about the letters. He probably should have left that to the other ministers.

If she didn't come to her senses soon—well, he was already holding on to too many secrets. He'd have to turn the matter over to the others. Writing anonymous letters was as grievous a transgression as going out with an Englischer, at least in the eyes of the Lord, and especially if it was motivated by malice or jealousy. He would hate to believe that of his sister, but maybe he was too close to understand.

As for his part in this whole situation with Barbie, he was too close to that, too. He was caught in a web of indecision and pain. He couldn't have refused to go along with the decisions of the bishop. But he had hurt someone he'd begun to care for, and in doing so had hurt himself as well.

Still, he couldn't forget what Barbie had confessed—dating another man. How did she feel about the Englischer? Was she attracted to him? In love?

But this jealousy was his problem, not hers. She'd done wrong and knew it. The course ahead was clear enough—the Ordnung, developed over years through the accumulated wisdom of the Leit, spelled it out.

He drew up at the hitching rail near the back door and managed a smile at Mary—a smile that wasn't returned. "Here you are. Have a gut day."

Mary nodded, her face averted, and slid down. In a moment she'd disappeared into the house.

Ben was turning the buggy in preparation for going back out the lane when he spotted another buggy headed toward him. He backed the gelding out of its way and waited. The lane was only wide enough for one, and he didn't want to go through the grass when it was still wet from last night's shower. With a jolt as if he'd been struck, he saw that the approaching driver was Barbie.

What could he expect from her? Was it better simply to nod and drive away? Somehow he couldn't, even if it might be the wisest reaction.

Instead, he waited until she'd stopped at the hitching rail and climbed down, looping the lines. "Barbie, I . . ."

Ignoring him as if he weren't there, she busied herself with getting down, averting her face from him. It was no good. He could still envision the dimples when she smiled and the way her blue dress reflected the blue of her eyes.

"I know you're angry with me." He fought to keep his voice firm. "But I had no choice. I couldn't refuse to impose the appropriate punishment when the bishop brought it up."

"No, of course not." Her tone was brittle, and she still refused to look at him. "You must have been glad it was taken out of your hands, so you could clear your conscience."

"That's not so." Wasn't it? He couldn't be sure.

"Well, it's out in the open now, isn't it? I suppose you'd like me to leave the farm-stay, so I don't contaminate your sister with my presence."

Her words sparked the complex mix of feelings she alone seemed to bring out in him—anger, frustration, desire . . . He grabbed her arm, pulling her around to face him, and realized too late that he shouldn't have touched her.

She stared at him, her eyes wide, the blue seeming to darken, and he leaned toward her—

The screen door slammed, making the gelding toss his head. Mary erupted onto the porch, her attention only on Barbie.

"You're here." Her hands clenched. "How could you? How could you act like you were setting an example for me? How could you expect me to obey the letter of the law? When all the time you were doing what you wanted to and probably laughing at me for swallowing all of it!"

"Mary, no." Barbie took a step toward her. "That's not true. I only wanted the best for you, always."

"Am I supposed to believe that? You preached one thing to me and did something else yourself."

Barbie's face lost whatever color it had. "It's not the same. I'm older than you, and I—"

"Ja, you're older." For a moment Ben let his anger have free rein. "You should be setting an example for the younger girls, not running around with Englisch men."

"Leave her alone!" Mary turned on him with a startling reversal of sides. "You're a fine one to talk. For all your preaching about what I should do or shouldn't do—you don't care about me. All you care about is what other people think!"

Whirling, Mary ran into the house, the door slamming again behind her.

Frustrated, Ben swung on Barbie. "I should have known better than to rely on you to guide my sister. You're the last person in the world to serve as a good example of what an Amish woman should be. It's a wonder to me that you haven't left already."

Barbie's head went up, and her blue eyes seem to spark dangerously. "Really? Well, maybe you should look to yourself when it comes to setting an example. Because I think Mary is right about you. You don't care about people. You just care about what people think of you."

Ben glared at her, defying her to see that her words had hit home. Then he flung himself into the buggy and slapped the lines, sending the horse jolting down the lane as if he could run away from what he feared was the truth.

Such a short time ago he had accused Sarah of being driven by jealousy and malice. Maybe he ought to accuse himself of the same thing.

Rebecca was waiting in the kitchen when Barbie burst in. Instantly she put her arms around Barbie as if she were one of her own kinder.

"I'm so sorry. Do you want to talk about it?"

Barbie dabbed at the tears that persisted in

overflowing. "You must have already heard, haven't you?"

"I don't listen to gossip." Rebecca led her to a kitchen chair and pulled another one over so that she could sit close to her. "I only want t hear what you want to tell me."

"Mary?" Barbie glanced around, but the girl was nowhere in sight.

"I sent her upstairs to make up the beds. She'll be a while."

Barbie wiped her cheeks with the backs of her hands, trying to think through the misery that swamped her. "I should try to make things right with her."

"Not now." Rebecca patted her hand. "Give her time to think. She flew off the handle, and in a bit, she'll be feeling sorry and ashamed."

"I don't blame her." But she was relieved to have time to gather her thoughts before coping with Mary. "I let her down. Maybe Ben was right about me. How can I guide Mary in the Amish way when I'm so restless with it myself?"

"Ach, Barbie, you're young yet. It's natural enough to have questions and wonder. That's what you're supposed to do when you're young. It doesn't mean you're not meant to join the church and take your place in the community." Rebecca spoke with quiet maturity.

Barbie rubbed her temples. "I just wonder if maybe I'm like James."

"James?" Rebecca clearly took a moment to realize Barbie was talking about her brother. "Just because James disappeared . . ."

"Not any longer. He came home for a visit." Her voice trembled as she thought about the moment she'd seen him after all those years. "I . . . I got in touch with him." There was no point in bringing Ashlee into it.

Rebecca blinked, her eyes growing serious. "Has James been influencing you to leave?"

"No, no." She shook her head in emphasis. "He was just eager to make peace with the family. Ach, Rebecca, you should have seen him—scared as a kid at the thought that Mamm and Daad might not welcome him."

She seemed to be back in that moment when she and James had approached the house, watching Mamm turn, surprised at the sight of a stranger, and then recognize him and hold out her arms. And Daadi, wiping his eyes unashamedly at seeing his son again.

"They must be so happy. And dear James." Rebecca's lips curved in a reminiscent smile. "He was a few years older than me, but I remember him so well. He broke a lot of hearts when he left, and I don't mean just the family. Half the girls in his rumspringa gang were crazy about him."

"Really?" she asked, diverted for a moment. "I never knew that about him. He was just . . . my big brother."

"Ach, what am I thinking? We must go and welcome him. Will he have time to come for a family picnic, do you think?" She looked ready to start preparing immediately.

"Not this time. He's over at your folks' visiting Grossmammi, but then he has to head back to his family in Ohio."

Rebecca glanced out the window toward her parents' farm. "Ach, how happy Grossmammi must be. Will he come again soon? He's married now, is he? An Englischer, I suppose?"

"Slow down," she said, smiling. "Ja, she's Englisch. Her name is Andrea, and they have two kinder. You should have seen my mother crooning over the pictures."

"He'll come back and bring them, ain't so?"

Barbie nodded. "They're making plans already for a visit." She smiled, thinking of James's astonished joy at his welcome. "He really was worried, you know. After all, he was the one who disappeared. Never getting in touch—he thought they might find it hard to forgive."

Rebecca gave her gentle smile. "Then he underestimated a parent's heart."

"I'm thinking seeing James again mended their hearts a bit after I broke them. It would be ironic if James came back and I . . . and I left."

"Left?" Her cousin seized her hands in a fierce grip. "No, Barbie. You can't be serious."

"Why not? Isn't that what people say about

344

me?" Ben's words sounded in her heart, stabbing like broken glass. "That I'm too rebellious, too restless. That I'll jump the fence?"

"People are saying that you've been foolish, going out with an Englisch boy." Rebecca seemed to choose her words carefully. "But if you confess, you'll be forgiven. It will be forgotten. That's what you want, ain't so?"

"I don't know," she muttered. "Ben said—"

"Ja, I heard what Ben said through the screen door. He was loud because he was angry and hurt, I think." Rebecca patted her hands again, her touch comforting. "And you were hurt, too, because you love him."

"Love?" The word frightened her. "I don't . . . Surely this isn't love. It hurts too much."

Rebecca nodded. "If you didn't love him, it wouldn't hurt so much," she pointed out.

"I should have known better." She was talking to herself as well as to Rebecca. "Everybody knows what Ben's like. He's so strict, so determined to obey every little word and thought of the Ordnung. According to him, there's no wiggle room. You're either obedient or you're on your way out. And he made up his mind a long time ago which camp I'm in."

"Funny," Rebecca said innocently. "I got the impression that he had trouble keeping his mind off you. Are you saying he never did anything to show that he cared?"

Heat flooded Barbie's cheeks. "No, I can't say that. He kissed me, and it was . . . it was like nothing I ever felt before." The memory flooded back. "But then he looked like he'd committed the biggest sin in the book. He made me feel like I was some kind of temptress."

Her cousin chuckled, and the sound coaxed a reluctant smile from her.

"I don't imagine he thinks so. And I'd guess he's so upset about you seeing someone else for other reasons besides the Ordnung."

"No, I can't believe it." The weight of all that happened landed on her again. "He sat there with the other ministers while the bishop questioned me. He was condemning me, I know. He left with-out even looking in my direction. And you heard him just now. He made it pretty clear what he thinks of me."

"He'll calm down. Once you are forgiven in worship, he will forget all of it. You'll be able to go on."

Barbie shook her head slowly. "No. I knew from the beginning that if I cared for him, he'd break my heart." She pressed her hand against her chest, imagining she could actually feel the sharp edges of the shattered pieces. "The worst of it is, he's right. How can I ever commit to anybody when one day the call to leave might be too strong to resist? What if I disappear, too, like James did?"

Chapter Eighteen

Lancaster County, Summer 1960

Elizabeth stooped to pick the strawberries, the skirt of her dress flaring out around her. First the ones that were exposed—the birds would be swooping down on them as soon as they saw the flash of red. Then she brushed the full green leaves gently back to find the hidden berries, choosing only the ripest ones. The sun warmed her back, and the earth beneath her hands was warm as well, seeming to pulse with life.

"It's going to be a fine crop this year, if only we get another shower or two." Mamm Alice cast a practiced gaze at the sky. "Maybe a shower this evening, ain't so?"

Elizabeth followed her glance at the western horizon, mentally measuring the darker clouds there. "Looks like it." She brushed the earth from a particularly ripe berry and popped it into her mouth, where the sweetness seemed to explode. "Best be sure we get all the ripe ones, in case it comes down hard."

Mamm Alice nodded, knowing that a hard rain could bruise any overripe berries, pounding them into the earth. "If you don't have room for a strawberry patch at your new place, you must come here next spring and share with us. We can put up the jam while the babies play together."

Elizabeth smiled at the baby comment while her mind busied itself with the rest of what her mother-in-law had said. "I'm sure Reuben will want to have a garden and berries, no matter where we are."

Straightening, Mamm Alice put one hand on her back and stretched. "Ja, I'm sure he will. But if you have to move someplace close to town for his job, you might not have much yard. Some of those places the yards are so tiny it wouldn't take five minutes to cut the grass."

"I hadn't thought about it that way, but I suppose Reuben will want to be close to his work, wherever that is." She reminded herself that as long as they stayed here in Lancaster County, she'd be happy. Even if she had to give up having her own garden.

But Reuben would miss that even more than she would. She looked at her mother-in-law again, but couldn't make out any opinion from her expression. "What did you think about Reuben wanting to go out to central Pennsylvania to settle?"

Mamm Alice shrugged. "Ach, you know full well I'd hate having all of you so far away. Still,

I suppose the way things are going here, there will be more and more of the Leit moving out to the valleys."

The valleys. That was the popular term among the Amish for that central area of the state, probably because of the alternating lines of ridges and valleys running northeast to southwest across the area.

"You really think so?"

She nodded. "I hate thinking it, that's certain-sure. But things are changing here, and I guess we'd be foolish not to see it."

"I wish things didn't have to change." She rose, picking up her basket.

"I know." Mamm Alice looked at her with what might have been pity. "We've been settled here for a couple hundred years, and I guess we got used to it. Maybe we shouldn't have. God's people have always been wanderers, ain't so?"

"Like Abraham and Sarah, you mean," she said. "I guess so."

"I think sometimes God wants to remind us that we aren't meant to find our home in this world, no matter how happy we might be."

Elizabeth blinked in surprise at the words coming from her mother-in-law, always the most practical of people. "I haven't heard you talk this way before."

"Usually I leave the preaching to the ministers, you mean." Mamm Alice's smile was wide. "But just because I don't say anything doesn't mean I don't have opinions."

Elizabeth couldn't help laughing at that comment. Everybody knew that Mamm Alice had an opinion on just about every subject.

Her mother-in-law caught her eye, and she chuckled. "You've never noticed me being shy and retiring, ain't so? I guess I do speak out a bit. And you don't need to tell me that everyone knows it."

They were laughing together when Reuben drew near. "What are my best girls finding so funny?" he said.

Mamm Alice fanned herself. "Ach, I was just being foolish, that's all. I think I'll take these berries in the house now. It's getting hot out here."

Still smiling, she went off.

"Are you going to let me in on the joke?" He lifted an eyebrow at Elizabeth.

She shook her head, still smiling. "You'll have to be content with the berries." She selected an especially ripe one, wiped it with her fingers, and popped it into his mouth, feeling his lips brush her skin.

"Sehr gut," he said. "Is there a strawberry-rhubarb pie in my future?"

"If I can persuade your mamm to let me make one instead of using them all for shortcake."

Reuben put his arm around her waist, and they walked together toward the house. "I predict our little son or daughter is going to like straw-berries," he said.

"I hope so." *Please, God, let this babe be healthy.*

"I have some news," Reuben said, fitting his steps to hers. "I have a job offer."

She stopped, turning to face him. "Really? That's wonderful gut news. Where? When do you start? Do you like it?"

He held up a hand to stem her questions, laughing a little. "One at a time. It's with Harper Construction. Ted Harper hires a lot of Amish, and he agreed to take me on for a job. If it works out okay, he'll keep me."

"Reuben, I'm so glad. And you'll be working with others of the Leit, so that will make it easier."

Her heart danced in celebration. They could stay here, they'd find a house for themselves, not far off, with room for a garden and a small stable, and they'd be happy.

"Harper plans to begin a new house in a couple of weeks over toward Bird-in-Hand, so I can start then. And he has a van to take his Amish workers back and forth. The only thing is . . ."

He hesitated, and her breath caught as she waited for something bad.

"Well, it will mean some traveling, I think. The brothers I talked to said last season they were on the road most of the summer and fall, often staying away all week. And then laid off in the winter, with no money coming in."

"We'll manage," she assured him. "We can save, and I'll still preserve most of our food." She was too delighted at the prospect of staying here to let a few problems get in the way.

"I hate to think of you alone, that's all. Especially in a place of our own, where you won't have family right there to call on in case of trouble."

Trouble. He meant with the baby, of course.

"It will be all right." She linked her hands with his. "At least we won't be far away from our families. And maybe someone could stay with me at night." She couldn't help smiling. "Ach, Reuben, I'm so relieved."

"Gut. I'm glad you're happy," he said.

He didn't say he was happy. Even though he smiled at her, Elizabeth could see the regret deep in his eyes. He was still mourning that farm he'd fallen in love with up in Brook Hill.

He'll get over it, she assured herself. *He'll settle in to the new job and be happy.*

But somehow the words didn't make her feel as relieved as she expected.

Ben arrived at the site for worship on Sunday with a heavy heart. If only he could be sure about his motives, then he would still grieve over Barbie's troubles but at least not feel responsible.

Where was the single-hearted devotion he'd imagined he had the day he'd been chosen as minister? He was beginning to understand why folks were more likely to offer condolences than congratulations when the lot fell on the new minister.

Leaving the buggy in the hands of the young boys whose job it was to be hostlers for the day, he walked toward the barn where worship would be held. Then he saw Bishop Caleb, alone at the paddock fence, and veered in his direction.

He couldn't carry this burden alone. It was time to share it with someone who would surely understand. There couldn't be many quandaries Bishop Caleb hadn't faced during his years of ministry.

"Benuel." The bishop greeted him with a nod and a searching gaze. "You look like a man who didn't get much sleep last night."

"No, I didn't." Ben grimaced. "Did you know I'd be wanting to talk to you this morning?"

"I thought you might. You're struggling with the issue of Barbie Lapp, ain't so?"

He nodded, planting his elbows on the top fence rail and looking out across the paddock where the boys were putting the visiting buggy horses. It was easier than looking into the bishop's wise old face.

"I know we had to act. I know it's for Barbie's own good."

Bishop Caleb leaned on the rail next to him. "Your feelings for Barbie are causing you doubts."

"Not about your decision," he said quickly. "But about my own motivation in agreeing."

The bishop was silent for a moment. Then he heaved a sigh. "It's always difficult. The Lord bids us to act always in love, but I won't deny that sometimes other feelings come into church discipline." He glanced at Ben. "What are your intentions toward Barbie?"

"None," Ben said quickly, backing away from that idea. "I mean, it was Daad's idea to have Mary working with Barbie and Rebecca at the farm-stay. He thought they would be gut examples for her. I was afraid . . ."

"Afraid Barbie was a little too frivolous to serve as anyone's pattern?" There might have been a touch of humor in the bishop's voice.

"Something like that," he muttered. He'd done enough to Barbie already. He certainly wasn't going to talk about the night she'd brought Mary home.

"But your feelings started to change," Bishop Caleb prompted him when he didn't go on.

"I suppose they did. Being around Barbie, I couldn't help but see that there's a loving heart behind her foolishness. But I never intended—I mean, she's completely unsuitable to be a minister's wife."

"I don't know that we have any requirements for being a minister's wife." His tone was mild. "You might say that God picks the woman, just as He chooses the man."

"Ja, well, anyway, I didn't mean to be drawn to

her," Ben added hastily. "Now I wonder about my own motivations in imposing discipline on her."

"It's never easy, no matter who the person is." The lines in Bishop Caleb's face seemed to grow deeper. "It's especially hard when the person doing wrong is a member of the family or another person you care about."

"That's certain-sure." Ben thought of Sarah. What was he going to do about his own sister?

"I'm not sure we can ever have a single purpose in that case. We just have to do our best and leave the rest to the Lord. Our feelings don't matter as much as our obedience."

Ben nodded, accepting the rebuke. "I'll try."

"I will be taking the text of the Good Shepherd for the long sermon today. I think that you should do the short sermon on the Prodigal Son."

Ben was left gaping at this unexpected assignment. "I don't . . . Given my own doubts, I don't think I'm worthy to preach today."

"None of us are ever worthy to preach God's word," the bishop said.

Ben grimaced. It was surely truer of him than of someone like the bishop, who had given his life to God's service. "The way I've been feeling, I should be sitting in the penitent's seat today."

Bishop Caleb put a hand on his shoulder. "You know, sometimes I think every one of us should be reminded of that. Remember, if we got exactly what we deserved, we'd all be sitting in the penitent's seat."

For a moment Ben let the words sink in. Then he nodded slowly. He would try. He'd have to ask for God's grace, because he certain-sure couldn't do this thing in his own strength.

Too soon it was time to file in for worship. The service moved on in its usual way. Church discipline would come during a members meeting at the end of worship, after all the kinder and non-members had been excused. He glanced to where Barbie sat in the back row of unmarried women. This must be hard for her, sitting through the service and knowing what lay ahead. He didn't bother to deny the longing he felt to comfort her.

When Bishop Caleb rose to speak, Ben found he was watching his sister Sarah. Should he have spoken to the bishop about her actions? He'd rather she confessed on her own, but that seemed unlikely, given her attitude. At the moment her face was stony, as if she dared anyone, especially her brother, to hint that she'd done wrong.

To hear Bishop Caleb speak of the lost sheep was to be moved, in some cases to tears. Ben sat with his head bowed, not daring to look at Barbie. By this time the whole Gmay would know who was coming forward for discipline today. People would try not to look at her, and he prayed they were listening with a whole heart to

Bishop Caleb speak of the rejoicing at the restoration of one who was lost.

Too soon, it was his time to speak. He stood, filled with misgivings, but as he stepped forward, the longed-for grace seemed to flood through him. He didn't have to wonder what he was going to say. He knew.

Barbie had to force herself to remain sitting upright when Ben rose to speak. If her posture reflected what she really felt . . . well, she wasn't sure anymore just what her feelings were. She seemed to feel her mother's gaze on her back, and lowered her face to look at her hands.

It was possible that she was doing this for herself. She was sure she was doing it for her parents, especially for Mamm. The grief and pain and self-blame her mother tried to hide had pierced her heart over and over again in the past days. Even the joy of having James back hadn't been able to blot it out. Hurting her still more was unthinkable.

Painful though it was to listen to Benuel's voice, Barbie couldn't help being caught by his words. She'd never heard him speak this way before—impassioned, caring, obviously longing to get through to his hearers.

He didn't spend time on the prodigal's sins, to her relief. Instead, all of his passion was for the forgiveness of the father, for the rejoicing of the community over the return and restoration of the lost. He spoke with such power—she had never heard him so passionate before. The barn was absolutely still, with none of the rustling and movement that was common. Even the babies were silent.

She dared to raise her eyes enough to see his face. His eyes seemed to glow, and he leaned forward as if to reach each of them and demand their attention. "The father didn't even allow his son to say the words he'd prepared. He didn't need to. It was enough that he'd returned, and his father welcomed him with open arms."

She saw Mamm, opening her arms to the son who'd hurt her so much; Daad, wiping away tears of joy at his return. Her heart twisted, and tears began to spill down her cheeks.

She wasn't the only one. There was a stifled sob from somewhere behind her, and others besides her wiped their eyes.

"Never forget," Ben said, looking from person to person as if he spoke to each one of them. "If all of us received justice instead of mercy for our sins, each one of us would be sitting in the penitent's chair this morning."

Ben sat down. There wasn't a sound in the place. It was as if his words had struck them all to silence.

Bishop Caleb, not waiting for any response, stood to pray. Then he cleared his throat. "All children and unbaptized persons are now dismissed. Baptized members should remain in their seats."

Silently the kinder and teens filed out. Some of the older girls would automatically take on the job of watching out for the little ones during members meeting.

Barbie took a deep breath, knowing what was coming. It was so quiet that no one could possibly believe there were still seventy-some people sitting on the backless benches in the barn.

Bishop Caleb spoke again. "Remember, 'where two or three are gathered in my name, there I am in the midst of them.' Our decisions here must be pleasing in God's sight."

Having ensured that members were taking this business seriously, he nodded to Barbie.

She rose, knowing full well what was expected of her. Somehow, her legs managed to carry her to the front of the barn, where she sat on the chair that had been placed before the members. Now for the words, used over and over in confession.

"I have sinned." Her voice shook, but she kept going. "I earnestly beg God and the church for patience with me, and from now on I will carry more concern and care with the Lord's help."

She longed to keep her face buried in her hands, but when the bishop spoke, she forced herself to look at him. She could read nothing but sympathy in his lined face.

"Have you gone out with a man who is not Amish?"

"Ja." She breathed the word.

"Did you fail to tell your parents what you did?"

"Ja." Her voice broke on the word. She sensed him look to the other ministers, as if silently asking whether they had other questions.

When no one spoke, he bent over her, giving her a reassuring smile when she managed to look at him. "You may go out now," he murmured. "It won't be long."

She nodded and fled.

Standing outside the barn, she dried her face, fighting to compose herself. But the questions lingered. Had she done the right thing for the wrong reasons? If she repented because she didn't want to hurt her family, was that true repentance? If she accepted she'd been wrong . . .

Barbie's breath caught. It was wrong to lie, even by implication, to those who loved you. But did she really mean to spend her life obeying the rules? She rubbed her forehead, tired of the thoughts. Maybe she really belonged in the outside world, like James. Maybe her longing for adventure was a sign that she should heed, telling her that she didn't belong.

The door opened behind her. Smiling, her mother gestured her inside, hugging her. "It's all right," she murmured. "It's all over."

Barbie moved forward, uncertain now of what

to expect. But when she reached the front of the gathering, Bishop Caleb's wife waited to give her the kiss of peace.

Bishop Caleb, smiling, held up his hands. "Our sister has confessed her wrong and been forgiven. The matter is buried and may never be brought up again in either word or thought."

In another moment Barbie was surrounded by family and friends, taking their turns to hug or kiss or offer words of encouragement. Even Moses joined the group.

But not Benuel. He stood apart, his head lowered.

Lunch after worship went on as usual. Nobody stared at her, and if there was any whispering in corners, she didn't detect it. So it really was over. She'd finish up her next two days of work, tell Walt and Ashlee and the others good-bye, and try to be content with working at the farm-stay. People would forget.

If only . . . She found herself glancing in Ben's direction, and she resolutely turned away to talk to her cousin Judith. Whatever might have been with Ben was over. Still, her decision hung in the balance. Was she meant to be Amish? Could she be happy if she stayed, or would the regret taint her future?

She was helping to carry serving bowls to the kitchen when Sarah, Ben's sister, came out. Sarah stopped, staring at her. Barbie stared back, not sure what Sarah expected of her. If she intended to add her two cents' worth to how she was an unfit example for Mary . . .

"Can we . . . Can I talk to you for a moment?"

Barbie stiffened, wondering if she ought to remind Sarah of what the bishop had said. The wrong, once admitted and forgiven, must be forgotten as well.

"I need to take these into the kitchen." She gestured with the bowls she carried.

"I'll wait," Sarah said. She moved to the side of the porch, out of the stream of traffic into and out of the kitchen.

Apparently there was no help for it. Barbie took the used bowls to the sink. When she went outside, she found that Sarah had moved a bit farther away, as if eager that she not be overheard.

"What is it, Sarah? I said I'd help with the dishes." She glanced toward the door. Even dish-washing sounded better than a little chat with Sarah.

"I had to talk to you. I have to tell you . . ." Her voice died, and to her astonishment, Barbie realized Sarah was fighting back tears.

"What is it?" Moved, she put her arm around Sarah in a comforting gesture.

But Sarah pulled away, shaking her head. "I didn't think it was wrong. I told Ben that when he spoke to me. I was angry and stiff-necked. Then I heard what he said today." Her face twisted as she fought back tears. "I should have been the one confessing in front of the church. I wrote you those letters."

For an instant Barbie didn't even grasp what she was talking about. Then it came to her. The letters . . . the ones accusing her of being a bad example to the youth. Sarah had written them.

"But why, Sarah? Why? What could you know about me?" Well, she knew more now, but she couldn't have then, not when she'd found the first note.

Sarah blotted tears from her face. "I don't even know why I did it. Mary kept talking about how nice you were and how she could talk to you, and I guess I felt . . . I felt jealous. I wanted her to think that about me."

Barbie's heart twisted. Mary certain-sure didn't think that about her now. And that wasn't Sarah's fault. She had lost that by her own actions.

"You don't need to be jealous," she said. "I'm glad Mary thought of me as a friend, but you're her sister. Your bond is for life. She'll always need you."

"Do you really think so?" All of Sarah's confidence seemed to have deserted her, and she was pathetically eager for reassurance.

"I'm sure of it." She patted Sarah's arm. Any anger she'd felt at the revelation vanished before it could blossom. "Don't worry about it anymore. Just forget it."

What was the point of being angry with Sarah?

Everyone in the church now knew too much about what she'd been doing. The notes hadn't done any harm. Maybe they'd even helped by making her think about the pain she could cause her family.

Sarah shook her head. "You're generous. I didn't see it before. Maybe . . . Well, anyway, I'm sorry and ashamed of what I did. If you want, I'll confess to the bishop."

"No, don't. That's not necessary." She didn't want to put anyone, even Sarah, through what she'd just endured. "It's enough that you've spoken to me. We'll forget about it now, ja?"

"Denke, Barbie." Sarah studied her face. "I think I understand why Mary is so fond of you. I hope you'll keep helping her."

She tried not to wince. "I'm afraid Benuel might have something to say about that. He's not likely to want me around his little sister after everything that's happened."

And Mary wouldn't want her friendship, anyway. That hurt more than any of it.

"I doubt it." Sarah smiled and patted her hand. "I wouldn't take Ben too seriously. And after the sermon he preached today, I don't see how he can hold anything against you."

"Maybe you're right." But she suspected Ben would find some way to rationalize keeping her away from his sister. And away from him.

Chapter Nineteen

It was Barbie's final shift at the café, and as it turned out, Ashlee wasn't there. She'd worked breakfast and lunch today, but Barbie had agreed to do the supper shift. It felt strange, not to be checking in with Ashlee every few minutes.

Still, she'd better get used to it. Although they'd promised to stay in touch once Barbie left the café, she knew what would happen. Once they weren't seeing each other daily, and Ashlee couldn't text or call at a moment's notice, she'd drift out of Barbie's life.

Moving behind the counter, she refilled coffee for the three local guys who sat finishing their desserts, knowing already how they liked their coffee and who would want to switch to decaf. Listening idly to their talk, she glanced up at movement and saw that Terry had come in.

Another person she should be saying good-bye to, she guessed. Still, she hadn't seen much of him since that day she'd learned that Grossmammi was in the hospital. Maybe the reminder of how different her life was from his had discouraged him. Pulling her pad out, she approached his table.

"Hi. What can I get for you tonight?"

He slid the menu back into its holder. "Just a cup of coffee. Is it true? Ashlee says you're quitting your job."

She nodded, wondering how much Ashlee had told him about it. Did he realize he was the inadvertent cause of her trouble?

Not fair, her conscience insisted. She'd brought her problems on herself.

"Listen, is all this because of me?" He caught the hand holding her pencil. "Because those people saw us together?"

"It wasn't your fault," she said quickly. "I should have known better."

"I'm sorry." He gave her a rueful smile. "Guess this means we won't be going out again. At least, not as long as you're . . ." He let the sentence fade, gesturing to her clothing.

"Afraid not." And if she did, at some point, decide she was leaving, it wouldn't be because of Terry, nice as he was. "I'll get your coffee."

She was smiling a bit when she reached the counter. Terry wasn't heartbroken at seeing the last of her, not that she'd thought he would be. There must be something he took seriously, but she didn't know what it was. He'd be off smiling at the next pretty face he saw, with never a passing thought for the Amish girl he'd once gone out with.

"All I'm saying is, don't take that road out by

the reservoir tonight," one of her three customers was insisting. "There's going to be a big teenage bash out there, and you know what they're like once they get a few beers in them. Lucky if they don't drive anybody into the ditch."

"Celebrating school being out soon, I guess," his buddy commented. "Still, a few quiet beers isn't anything worse than we did at that age."

"Quiet beers, nothing. They've got half the high school coming by what I heard. Some of the boys were bragging that they're bringing a few Amish girls. They'll get an education, I guess."

His friend elbowed him, nodding toward Barbie.

"Hey, I'm sorry." His face reddened. "I didn't mean anything."

"You're sure of that—about the Amish girls?" Barbie asked. It wasn't the first time, and it wouldn't be the last, but it sounded as if this party might be wilder than anything they'd be ready for.

He shrugged. "That's what I heard. Maybe it's not true. Just kids talking big about the fun they're going to have."

"Not as much fun as they expect," the man sitting farther along the counter put in. "Way I hear it, the cops know all about that party at the reservoir. They've messed around out there one too many times, and tonight they're going to get raided."

Barbie's breath caught.

"Well, it's not so bad," the other man said.

"Maybe if their folks have to come down to the station and pick them up, they'll keep tabs on them better. And like Gus said, it's nothing we didn't do in our time, but our folks sure got after us for it."

Maybe it meant nothing for the Englisch kids. Maybe it was even a good lesson for them. But if there were Amish girls at the party, caught by the police—

She could imagine the headlines in the newspaper only too well. The misdeeds of Amish teenagers always made news. Their families would be shamed—the whole community would be.

Pressing her hands against the counter, she tried to think what was best to do. If she knew which girls were involved, she might be able to reach them. Warn them. She glanced out the window. It was dusk already, which meant the party would start soon. It might be too late for warnings to help.

The thought hit her like a sledgehammer. What if Mary were one of those girls? She'd care about any of them—want to help any of them. But if Mary were in trouble, she'd be guilty of contributing to it. Guilty of letting down the vulner-able girl who had depended on her.

Once the idea took possession of her, she couldn't let it go. If Mary were at this party, if Mary were caught by the police . . . Her heart cringed painfully, and she felt for a moment as if she couldn't breathe. She had to do something, but what?

Think, Barbie, think. As far as she knew, Mary didn't have access to a cell phone. But David did, just as she had when she'd been younger. She'd given hers up when the last of her rumspringa gang had settled down. What was the point of it then?

But David might know about the party. Might even have heard who was talking about going. And he wasn't really all that good at keeping secrets from her.

She hurried to the phone in the back hall, leaving her customers to fend for themselves. Luckily she'd memorized the number, even though this was the first time she'd had occasion to use it.

Pressing the receiver to her ear, she listened to it ringing. *Please, pick up.*

Finally the ringing stopped, and a cautious voice spoke. "Um, who's this?"

"It's Barbie," she snapped. "Listen to me. I'm at the café, and I just heard there's supposed to be a big teen party out by the reservoir tonight. Are you there?"

"No!" He was indignant. "I'm too old for that stuff."

"Well, I hoped you were. Do you know anyone else who is planning to go?"

There was a long hesitation before David spoke. "Why . . . why would I?"

He was trying to protect his friends, she

supposed. "Never mind trying to protect anyone. According to some of my customers, the police know about the party. They're going to raid it."

His gasp was audible. At least now she had her brother's attention.

"Listen, they also said there may be some Amish girls there. Do you know anybody who that might be?"

She could almost sense the struggle going on in his mind. He was still enough of a teenager not to want to tell on his friends.

"David, the only way to protect them is to stop them, or at least get them out of there, fast. Now tell me."

"All right, all right," he said, giving in. "Sadie Esch and her sister were saying they'd been invited. And . . ." He paused again, and she thought she knew why. "And Mary Kauffmann," he added reluctantly. "But, Barbie, it's too late. They'll have gone already. I'd go after them, but a buggy isn't going to make it out to the reservoir in time."

"I know." Anxiety pooled in her stomach. "You can't make it, but maybe I can. I'll do it."

She clicked off and stood for an instant, holding the phone. She could call the Kauffmann place and leave a message, but what would she say? Anyway, by the time they listened to it, they wouldn't be able to do anything, any more than David could. It was up to her.

She hurried back into the dining area, going straight to Terry's table. He looked up with a smile, but she couldn't return it, not now. "Terry, I don't have any right to ask you this, but I need help. Will you drive me somewhere?"

He looked startled, and for a moment she feared he'd refuse. But then he stood, pulling keys from his pocket. "Sure thing. Where are we going?"

"Some kids I know are at a party out by the reservoir. They're going to be in big trouble if they're caught by the police."

He grinned. "I guess we'd better hurry, then."

"I'll meet you outside." She didn't wait to see his reaction, but hurried to catch Jean before she could go to another table.

"Jean, I'm sorry, but I have to leave. It's an emergency. I don't have time to explain . . ."

Jean's startled look was quickly replaced by sympathy. "That's okay. You go. I'll handle everything."

Everything but Walt, who'd be furious, Barbie thought as she hurried out the door. Well, she'd tell Walt how sorry she was later, but this was too important to waste time arguing.

Terry's car was parked at the curb. Hand on the door, he looked at her. "Speaking of trouble, isn't this going to get you in trouble if you're caught?"

"Yes."

More trouble than he could imagine. For the first time she actually looked at what it would be like to leave the community. Really looked, not just daydreamed and wondered. In that moment, she knew what she wanted for her future. An Amish life. A life she was putting in jeopardy by what she did tonight.

She yanked open the door. "Hurry."

Lancaster County, Summer 1960

It was the rarest of evenings for Elizabeth—a chance to have supper alone with Reuben. The rest of the family had gone off to enjoy a meal with Becky's parents, while she and Reuben stayed home to finish up the chores.

She couldn't remember the last time they'd had supper by themselves, and Elizabeth wanted to treasure every minute of the evening. Not that she didn't enjoy being part of a big family—of course she did. But living here meant that their alone time was precious.

Lifting the lid from the chicken potpie, she inhaled the rich aromas of chicken broth and homemade noodles. Just the smell of the coffee had turned her stomach on her breakfast, but now she felt as if she could eat a horse. That was one of the oddities of early pregnancy that had slipped her mind.

The rush of running water from the sink in the back hall announced that Reuben was coming in, and she hurried to set the potpie on the table.

Everything else was ready, so she could turn to him with a smile when he came in.

"Mmm, smells wonderful gut in here." He came over to plant a kiss on her cheek. "And I get to have supper all alone with my wife."

"You're saying just what I was thinking. It's nice, isn't it?"

Reuben nodded, taking his daad's seat at the head of the table. "Unusual, you mean." With a quick smile, he bowed his head.

She followed his lead, knowing why he'd smiled. This must be the first opportunity he'd had to be the leader in the prayer before meals, since it was always his daad's right.

Reuben reached for the potpie, and she started the dish of pickled beets. "This is what it will be like when we move into our own house, ain't so?"

"It won't be just the two of us for long, though." Joy bubbled up in her, and she laid a gentle hand on her stomach.

"You'll be busy once the boppli comes." He frowned slightly. "I hope it won't be lonely for you in the house all day when I'm at work."

Elizabeth realized she'd been so preoccupied with her joy that they didn't have to leave Lancaster County that she hadn't thought much of what it would be like when Reuben was working construction.

"I'll be fine. After all, our families won't be far away." She took a slice of fresh brown bread.

"Do you know what the hours will be at the job?"

"From what I hear, we'll be working as long as possible while the weather is fine. A builder has to take advantage of summer while it's here. Then it will slack off in the fall and winter."

Something about that worried him, she could tell. Was he fretting about leaving her alone for long hours? Or was it that he still wasn't reconciled to the choice he'd made?

The choice you've pushed him to, a small voice said in the back of her mind.

"It's not so different from farming, ain't so? You can't stop making hay when it's ready, no matter how long it takes." But she wouldn't be there, couldn't hurry out with a jug of cold water or lemonade for a quick visit. She wouldn't see him at all from the time he left in the morning until he came home at night.

"I guess." He reached across the table to squeeze her hand. "But I won't be able to pop in for a kiss."

Her cheeks grew warm. "Ach, you don't do that now."

"Because I never get you alone." His voice was teasing, and whatever the reason he'd been worrying, it seemed to have slipped away. "How can I cuddle my wife when my mamm is always here?"

"So that's the real reason you're ready to move to a place of our own." She could tease, too.

"For sure." He grinned, relaxing.

Reassured, she settled down to enjoy their time together. Surely Reuben wouldn't be able to laugh so easily if he were blaming her or regretting his decision.

They were clearing the table together, laughing over some foolishness or other, when she caught a glimpse of a buggy coming down the lane. She leaned forward to peer out.

"The family couldn't be home already. Not unless something went wrong."

"It's not the family." Reuben's voice had a tone she didn't understand. "That's Johnny Stoltzfus and his wife. And it looks like Daniel and Etta King are with them."

Elizabeth's fingers tightened on the plate she was holding, and she put it down carefully in the sink. "Did you know they were coming?" *And why are they here? To talk us out of our decision?*

"No." Reuben spoke firmly, looking at her. "I didn't."

She was conscious of a strain between them, as if something were pulled so tightly it might break.

She let out a breath. "I . . . I think there's enough cake left to serve them. I'll put the coffee on."

Without another word, Reuben went out to greet them. Her hands trembled a bit as she started the coffee. What had possessed her to ask him that in such an accusing manner? She hadn't meant . . . Well, she'd thought . . .

That train of thought didn't seem to be comforting her much, so she concentrated on arranging her face in a welcoming smile as the two women came in the back door.

"Etta, Ruth. How nice to see you. Wilkom." She exchanged hugs with Etta King, who'd been in her grade in school and in her rumspringa gang. Ruth, several years older, she hadn't known as well, although of course she knew everyone in the church district.

"I hope we're not intruding." Ruth took off her bonnet, hanging it on one of the pegs by the back door. "I told Johnny we'd be interrupting your supper, but he was anxious to get on the way."

"It's just fine. You'll have coffee and cake."

Etta came to lean over her shoulder. "Your mother-in-law's chocolate cake with peanut butter icing? Nobody will turn that down."

"Actually I made it from her recipe," Elizabeth confessed. "Are you still willing to risk it?"

Etta's grin made her look like the freckled ten-year-old she'd once been. "Are you better at cooking than you were that day we made the peanut butter fudge?"

"The batch that ran so much we had to eat it with a spoon, you mean? I was only nine or ten then. I hope I'm a better cook now than I was then."

Ruth smiled at the banter but didn't join it. "I'll get the plates and cups ready." She reached out to the open shelves to take down coffee mugs. "These okay?"

Nodding, Elizabeth set a cream pitcher and sugar bowl on a tray so it could be carried into the living room.

"When we move, I want to have open shelves like these in my kitchen," Etta announced. "Daniel says he'll do up the kitchen however I want, since he'll have to take out the electrics that are in there anyway."

"So you and Daniel . . . you've bought a house up in Brook Hill already?"

"Ja, it's a nice place, Daniel says. He's that excited he's like a kid on his birthday. It's right next to . . ." She hesitated and glanced at Ruth. "Next to the farm that Reuben had a chance to buy, Daniel says."

"Our place is a bit farther along the same road," Ruth said. "And the Esch brothers bought a place that's not far, either. They're going to share the farmhouse until they can get another house built. Hopefully by fall, they say."

Elizabeth set plates of cake on a tray. "Don't you . . . Aren't you at all upset about going off to a new place like that where you don't know anyone?"

Etta glanced at Ruth, as if telling the older woman to go first.

Ruth seemed to consider her words carefully before she spoke. "I'll miss family, that's certain-sure. But Johnny is right that it's more and more difficult to live as we want here. We thought about it and prayed about it, and I feel content that God is directing our path."

The words seemed to strike her, despite being delivered in Ruth's usual calm, measured tones. When had she prayed about this decision? Oh, she'd prayed all right—but only for what she wanted.

Etta put her arm around Elizabeth's waist as if they were girls again. "It would be easier for me if you were going to be just across the field, but I have good feelings about this move. How often do we get to have an adventure?" Her eyes danced. "Remember how we learned about those Amish who set out for a new world, not knowing what they'd find? Well, this is a chance to be like them, ain't so?"

It seemed to echo something her grandmother had said about having the courage to move ahead. Inner panic took a grip on her, making it hard to breathe. Courage.

But she'd been willing, hadn't she? Before she'd learned the baby was coming. She'd agreed to go, but the new baby changed everything. Reuben understood that.

The men came in then, talking, seeming to fill the room to overflowing. Ruth picked up one of the trays, leading the way to the living room, while Etta took the other and Elizabeth picked up the coffeepot.

"Komm," she said. "We'll have cake and coffee while we visit." Somehow she managed to sound normal, despite the way her thoughts tumbled and bounced in her head.

Once everyone was seated, she fussed over serving them, trying to keep her thoughts at bay through busyness. Finally she settled in her usual rocking chair, realizing that Reuben was watching her, frowning a bit. He knew her so well—maybe better than she knew him.

That idea troubled her. Was she really that selfish? He had grieved over their lost little boy, too, but he had put his pain aside in order to comfort her. And now—now he had the chance at the life they truly wanted, and he was giving it up. For her.

Johnny had begun talking about his plans for the move, complicated by the distance and the need to transfer animals as well as people and household furnishings.

"Ach, I don't know what I'm complaining about," he said. "After all, the Bible tells us that Abraham packed up everything he owned, including his flocks, and traveled where the Lord told him even though it took years. We can manage a trip that just takes a couple of hours."

"I'd guess that Sarah did most of the packing," Ruth said. "That hasn't changed." Ruth and Johnny exchanged the glances of two people who knew each other too well to need speech to confess their feelings.

Elizabeth laughed along with the others, but her heart felt sore. If they had come here tonight to make her think, they were succeeding, but she didn't have to enjoy it, did she? She wanted to go back to the joy she'd felt at the double news of the coming baby and the decision to stay, but she couldn't.

"Well, we won't deny that we'd rather have you along with us in Brook Hill," Daniel said. "But you have to do what you think is right. Sure you won't think again?"

She looked at Reuben and couldn't turn away. His face was set, the lines in it seeming to make him older than his years. He was willing to sacrifice all he wanted for her. What was she willing to sacrifice for him?

Before he could speak, she grasped his hand. "Komm. We must talk."

His startled gaze met hers. Then, without a word, he got up and went out with her, through the kitchen and onto the back porch.

Elizabeth stood for a moment, seeing the rays of the setting sun turn the land to gold around them. Her heart filled. This had always been home for her, but how could that be? Home wasn't a place. It was wherever her heart was, and Reuben held her heart.

"I think we should go." The words coming out

of her mouth startled her. She expected to feel pain, but instead relief flooded her. This was right. She knew it.

"Elizabeth?" Reuben looked at her as if he couldn't be sure he'd heard correctly. "What are you saying?"

"We should go," she said. "Can you find out if the farm is still available?" Fear assaulted her— fear that because of her delaying, Reuben could have lost the farm he wanted.

Reuben took both her hands in his, his intent gaze studying her face. "He said he wouldn't accept an offer from anyone without checking with me first, so that's all right. But are you sure? You said . . ."

"I know." She blinked back tears as she looked into his dear face. "I was letting my fear speak for me." She smiled shakily and said what she'd begun to see so clearly now. "I thought it would take courage I didn't have. But now . . . now I see. It's not courage. It's faith."

She reached up to place her hand against his dear face, loving the joy that slowly dawned in his eyes.

" 'Whither thou goest, I will go. Whither thou lodgest, I will lodge.' I don't think I'm brave, but like Ruth, I have faith . . . Faith in you, and faith in God, who guides our steps."

Reuben's face seemed gilded with gold, too, and his smile was so very tender. He drew her into the circle of his arms. "My sweet Elizabeth. I promise I will make you happy. I promise . . ."

She shook her head. "You don't need to promise. You already make me happy. And wherever we are, our future is together." She smiled, joy bubbling up inside her. "Let's go and tell our friends we are ready for our new adventure."

Barbie glanced at Terry as he turned onto a two-lane country road. "You seem to know exactly where to go."

"I have to admit I've been to a party out here myself a time or two." He grinned. "Not lately, though. I'm past the stage of finding it fun to sit on damp ground to swill beer."

Barbie gasped and braced her hand against the dash. "There's a police car up there." Had she gone this far only to be too late? That would be ironic.

"I see it." Terry made a quick turn onto a dirt road. "Looks as if we'll have to take the back way in."

She asked the question on her mind. "Do you think the police are already there?"

Terry considered for a moment. "Probably not. It looked to me like that car was just waiting. And I think we'd see flashing lights through the trees if anything was happening." He pointed slightly to the right ahead of them. "The clearing kids usually use for parties is that way. There's a fire ring where they can start a fire."

And drink. This was likely to be a wilder party than any of those girls had bargained for, regardless of the probable intervention by the police.

"If the police are there . . ." she began.

"Then I can't go in," he said flatly. "If I got involved, get my name in the paper for being involved in underage drinking, it could cost me my job." He glanced at her. "Sorry. But I'm no hero."

"It's good of you to do this much. I appreciate it." There were lines he wouldn't cross, obviously, and she didn't blame him. But she couldn't help thinking of Benuel, who would do what was right whatever the cost.

The road turned into a lane, then a grassy track. The car bumped and jolted and finally came to a halt.

"This is as far as we can drive. You can see the campfire through the trees over there. You'll have to walk the rest of the way."

"Right." She started to slide out, but he halted her with a hand on her wrist.

"This is really important to you, huh?"

She nodded, pushing the door wide. "I'm afraid a . . . a friend of mine is involved. I feel responsible for her."

Terry's smile flashed. "See, that's why I don't take on responsibility for other people. Too likely to lead you into trouble."

"You're here, aren't you? That seems plenty responsible." She got out. "But if you see the police coming, go ahead and leave."

He shrugged. "We'll hope that doesn't happen. I'll turn and be ready to take off when you get back here with the kids. Make it fast. The cops could come any minute now."

He didn't have to remind her. The cold feeling in the pit of her stomach was already doing it. She hurried away from the car toward the glow of the campfire, brushing through the high weeds, the pounding of her heart increasing with every step.

Easy enough to cover the ground in the open, but as soon as she entered the undergrowth, she had to slow down, even as the need to hurry beat in her brain. Brambles reached out, catching at her skirt as if they were malevolently determined to delay her. She pushed on, wincing when one caught at her unprotected wrist, drawing blood.

Finally she was into the belt of trees, where the going was easier. Breathing quickly, she sped along, trying to shift her gaze between the ground in front of her and the campfire. She could hear voices and laughter now, smell the wood burning. Music blasted for a moment and then was turned down.

At the edge of the trees she stopped, hand on the slender trunk of a locust tree, and scanned the area in front of her. The flames leaped, burnishing the faces of kids and reflecting off the black shimmering surface of the reservoir. While she watched, a couple of guys pulled down a *No Trespassing* sign. They tossed it into the flames to the cheers of their friends.

It wasn't easy to pick out the three Amish girls, dressed as they were in jeans and T-shirts. Finally she spotted Sadie Esch a little way back from the fire. She chugged from a can of beer, then offered it to her younger sister, Becky. Becky took a swallow, made a face, and passed it on to the girl next to her—slight, small, with long blond hair. She turned slightly to drink, and Barbie saw her face. It was Mary Kauffmann.

Her stomach clenched. She'd been hoping it was all a mistake—that Mary wasn't here. But she was, and Barbie had to get her and the others out of here before their night out turned into a possible lifetime of regrets.

She walked toward them, trying to move unobtrusively enough not to attract the attention of the rest of the crowd. Fortunately the others were grouped around the blaze, feeding the fire with small branches so that the flames leaped higher. Didn't they realize how much attention they could draw? Maybe they didn't care.

Reaching out, Barbie grasped Mary's arm. The girl spun and saw her.

"You! What are you doing here? Go away and quit bugging me."

She tried to pull free, but Barbie held on. "Listen to me, Mary. And you two, as well." She rounded on the two Esch girls, who had started to back away. Not wanting to start a panic, she kept her voice low. "The police are going to raid this party. We saw one car already, and there'll be more coming. If you don't want to end up in tomorrow's headlines and have your folks bailing you out of jail, come with me now."

Sadie, who'd looked ready to sass her, blanched at the mention of the police.

"How?" She tossed the can away.

"I have a friend waiting with a car. Komm. Schnell."

Without waiting for an answer, she tugged Mary along with her and ran for the trees. The rush of footsteps told her the others weren't far behind. Back through the trees again, but with no firelight to guide her this time. Mary stumbled once, and Barbie helped her up and got her moving again.

When they emerged from the trees, Terry saw them right away. He flung the doors open, turning on the overhead light. The motor was already running. Even as they cleared the brambles and hit the grassy area, she heard the sound she'd been dreading. Sirens wailed in the distance, and someone shouted.

Barbie shoved the girls into the backseat, slammed the door, and jumped into the front. "Okay, go."

Terry didn't need a second invitation. He roared back down the lane before Barbie could even get her door closed. She managed to slam it just as he reached the dirt road.

He glanced toward the backseat. "You three better crouch down in case they've left a cop car out on the road. I'll tell you when it's clear."

White-faced, they did as he said. The younger Esch girl stifled a sob. They were scared, as well they should be. If they got out of this without a major scandal, they'd be fortunate. She could only hope they'd also learn a difficult lesson.

Mary . . . She hurt for all three of them and their families, of course, but Mary was her responsibility. It didn't matter that she hadn't wanted to take it on, and it didn't excuse her, either. She'd known the girl looked up to her, and she hadn't cared enough not to let her down.

They neared the blacktop road, and she held her breath. If there was a police car there, if they were stopped with three teenagers in the backseat—

Terry made the turn, slowing so as not to attract any unwelcome attention. The police car was still there, farther down the road, but the officer standing next to it didn't even glance in their direction. He was focused on the road ahead of him, probably here to make sure no one ran out through the woods to the main road to get away.

They rounded another turn, and the police car vanished from sight.

"Okay," Terry said. "You can sit up now. It's over."

Over. Relieved as she was, Barbie knew nothing was done with, not yet. She still had to cope with the repercussions of what had happened tonight.

Chapter Twenty

Following Barbie's directions, Terry dropped the Esch girls at the end of their lane. They'd have to figure out for themselves what to tell their parents.

Sadie paused by Barbie's window. "Barbie . . ." She looked thoroughly chastened and at a loss for words. "Denke," she said finally. "We won't forget what you did tonight."

Barbie nodded. If the two of them were smart enough, they'd take a lesson from the wailing sirens that would keep them out of trouble, at least for a time.

They drove on down the road, and Barbie gestured toward the lane to the Kauffmann place. "You can just let us off at the end of the lane."

Terry glanced at her, the light from the dash just enough for her to see his expression. It seemed to linger between relief and regret. "How will you get home?"

"Someone will take me." She managed a rueful smile. "Believe me, it won't help for you to be seen."

The relief seemed to win out. "I guess this is good-bye, then."

"Yes." There wasn't much she could add to the word. It was definitely good-bye. "Thanks for your help. I couldn't have done it without you."

He shrugged. "Hey, it was an adventure. I hope everything goes okay with you and your friend."

She slid out quickly and waited while Mary climbed out of the backseat, her head bowed. They stood by the sign that read *Kauffmann Buggy Repairs* and watched as Terry's taillights disappeared down the road and around a bend.

Barbie started walking, her thoughts revolving around the word Terry had used. "Adventure," she said, as much to herself as to Mary. "I always thought I wanted adventure, but if this is what it's like, maybe it's not so great after all."

"I know. I've never been so scared in my life."

Mary's voice took her by surprise. She'd thought the girl was going to give her the silent treatment, since she hadn't spoken since they'd bolted for the car.

"You want to know the truth? Me, either." She smiled at Mary, who gave her a trembling grin in return.

The lighthearted moment slipped away quickly. "I guess I'm really in trouble now." Mary looked ahead at the lights from the farmhouse, growing closer with each step.

In contrast the darkness seemed to press around them, isolating them. Aside from a few faint rustles in the grass of the hedgerows and the call of an owl in the distance, the night was still. It provided a kind of anonymity, in a way. It was easier to say difficult things when you couldn't see the other person's face, Barbie decided.

"It would be worse if they'd had a police car coming to the door," she said, keeping her tone practical. It wouldn't help for Mary to lose control and fly out at her father and brother over this incident.

"I know." They took a few more steps. "I'm not sure why you bothered with me." Mary's voice was tearful and miserable. "You could have gotten in big trouble yourself."

She considered passing it off lightly, but that would only compound the wrong she'd already done. "Listen." She stopped and faced the girl, just short of the porch. "I was responsible, that's why. Everything you said about me was true. I was telling you to live a life I wasn't willing to live myself. That was wrong, and I had to do what I could to make it right." She glanced at Mary, adding, "Besides, I'm fond of you. I didn't want to see a headline about you in the newspaper."

Mary caught her arm. "Wait. Before we go in—denke. And I'm sorry. I . . . I care about you, too. I don't want you to get into trouble because of me." Her voice wavered a little, and in the next moment, she was hugging Barbie desperately. "I've just been so lonely since Mamm—and Ben doesn't understand—and I don't want to disappoint everybody, but what if I can't do what I should . . ."

She dissolved into tears at that point. Barbie just held her, rocking her back and forth a little as if she were a baby. That's what she was, really. Just a baby, missing her mammi and not sure what to do about it.

"It's going to be all right." She patted the shaking back. "Everything will work out. No one expects more of you than you can manage." How like Ben she was—trying so hard to meet everyone's expectations. How strange that neither of them seemed to see it.

Mary drew back at last, mopping her face with the backs of her hands. She took a deep breath. "Okay. I'm okay. But you'll go in with me, won't you?"

Barbie put her arm around Mary's waist. "That's certain-sure. Let's go."

It felt like a replay of that first time she'd brought Mary home, but there was a difference. She hadn't understood, then, just how much she had to lose.

Brook Hill, Pennsylvania, Fall 1960

Elizabeth hurried to give her mother another hug before the group from Lancaster County climbed into the van to go home. So many people had come for the weekend they'd had to farm them out to the neighbors to have enough beds.

"I'm wonderful glad you all came to help with raising the new tie barn." She pressed her cheek against her mother's, memorizing the feel and warmth of it.

"It was a treat for us," Mamm said. "The tie barn looks grand, ain't so?"

They both glanced at the raw new structure next to the sturdy old barn that already stood on the property when she and Reuben bought. The barnraising had been accomplished in a single day, thanks to their small church community, the family from Lancaster County, and some of their new Englisch neighbors.

"Reuben's sehr happy with it. Maybe now he'll have time to finish the cradle he's making for the boppli."

Mamm smiled, laying a hand on Elizabeth's burgeoning belly. The babe kicked just then, and they both laughed. "A fine, strong babe, ain't so?"

"That's what the doctor says. I hope it's another boy, for Reuben's sake, but he insists he'd be just as happy with a girl who looks like me." She blushed a little at repeating the compliment. Still, it filled her heart with warmth and gratitude each time she thought of it, and she suspected Mamm understood.

"You're not worrying, are you?" Mamm's gaze searched her face. "Because of Matthias, I mean."

"Not too much." She couldn't say it hadn't crossed her mind, and her smile was bittersweet when she thought of their first son. "The doctor is reassuring. He's convinced all will be well."

"I'll be back to help when the time comes," Mamm reminded her. "It's not such a long trip as it seemed at first."

"We'll look forward to it." She'd told her mother several times that she needn't make the trip for the babe's birth, but Mamm was determined.

"Ach, your father is looking impatient. He wants me to get in so we can start." She gave Elizabeth another searching look. "You are happy here, ain't so?"

"Very happy." She walked with her mother to the van and saw her safely inside. She was happy, but it wouldn't be surprising if she shed a tear or two when they drove away. They'd brought a sense of family with them when they came, and the weekend was over too soon.

Reuben came to put his arm around her as the van drove away. He touched her cheek. "Tears?" His face grew anxious. "You're not feeling regrets?"

"No. No regrets." She turned into his embrace,

laughing a little when the bulk of her stomach came between them. "This place seemed strange to me at first, but now . . . well, now it feels like home. We have the farm and the life we've always wanted, with gut friends and church members nearby."

Reuben's expression relaxed. "And the church will be growing, if all I've heard is true. There's been talk of another two or three families joining us in the spring. Soon Brook Hill will have a big Amish community."

They turned to go in the farmhouse. *This is home,* she thought. *Not the place where you grew up, but the place where you raise your family.*

"My grossmammi was right." She thought of her grandmother and smiled. "She said that one day the Amish of Lancaster County might see us as pioneers, carrying our community to a new place."

Reuben stopped on the porch to kiss her cheek. "Your grandmother is a wise woman. I think that one day, you'll be just like her."

She pictured herself an old woman, surrounded by children and grandchildren and maybe even great-grandchildren. The image seemed to glow with promise.

One day, she thought. One day she would tell those grandchildren their story—the story of what it was like to be Amish in a constantly changing world.

Saying a silent prayer, Barbie tapped and then opened the kitchen door. Ben was in the act of rising from the table, a cup in his hand. He looked at her as if he couldn't believe what he was seeing.

His father came in from the living room as Ben moved toward the door. "Was ist letz? Is something wrong?"

"Not exactly." She stepped inside, once more tugging Mary along behind her. She could understand the girl's hesitation to face the music. After what had happened the last time, this would be like reliving a nightmare for all of them.

Speechless for a moment, Ben stared at his sister, taking in her jeans and her tearstained face. Barbie put her arm around Mary's waist again and gave a little squeeze for courage.

At the same time, she tried to look a warning at Ben. *Don't overreact. Don't drive her further away with what you say now. Please.*

Did he get the message? In any event, he didn't say anything. He might just be saving it up, intending to vent it on her.

"I'm sorry." The words burst from Mary on a wave of tears. "I'm so sorry. Please forgive me."

It was the best thing she could say. Her father held out his arms, and Mary rushed into them, sobbing. He held her, patting her, making soothing sounds. Ben looked at Barbie, who lingered, not sure what to do next. They'd want an explanation, and she didn't think they'd get anything coherent from Mary for the time being.

"You'd best come in, I think." Ben's face didn't soften when he looked at her, but at least he didn't bark.

"Barbie, komm, sit." Moses looked shaken, but he managed to sound fairly normal. He led Mary to a chair and sat down close beside her, still holding her.

"I'm sorry." She sat down, glancing from one to the other of them. She really was. If she could have seen a way to spare them, she would have. "Mary, do you want me to explain?"

The only answer was a small affirmative movement of her head.

"All right." She forced herself to be calm, but her hands twisted together in her lap, as if they would independently protest.

"I was working the supper shift at the café. My last shift," she added quickly, wondering if Ben would question what she was doing back there after her confession. "I overheard some talk at the counter about a big party the teenagers were having at the reservoir tonight. Apparently there had been talk that they had some Amish girls coming."

Ben didn't speak, but he seemed to wince. Of course it would hurt him. As a minister, he felt responsible.

"And one of the other men said that the police

knew about it and were going to raid it. So I knew I had to do something." She struggled to condense the events of the evening into as short an account as possible. "I called . . ." She paused. "I called someone I thought might know what our young ones were doing."

Ben could probably translate that with no difficulty. He'd guess that she would have called David as her closest insight into what the teenagers were doing. But she was determined not to name anybody she didn't have to.

"He gave me three names," she said carefully. "It was too late to try reaching the families, and I didn't know who else to turn to. So I got a . . . a customer at the café to drive me out there. We were able to get the girls away before the police arrived." That was really a shortened version, but she hoped they'd be satisfied and not inquire too deeply.

Silence for a moment. Maybe they were thinking, as she had, how close they had come to open scandal, with Amish teenagers' exploits trumpeted in the newspaper.

"Ach, Barbie," Moses said at last. "You could have been caught up in it yourself."

If he knew how close she had come to failing . . . well, that would have been disaster, for her as well as for the other families.

"I know, but . . . I couldn't just let it happen without trying to stop it."

Moses glanced at Mary and then at her. "You followed your generous heart. We're thankful."

"She was just in time." Mary looked up, her face shining with tears. "We could hear the sirens as we drove away."

"It's over with now," she said quickly, not wanting to bring on another bout of weeping from Mary.

"You are a gut friend, Barbie Lapp. And a kind person."

She could feel her color rise at the unexpected praise from Moses. The silence from Ben seemed to indicate that he didn't agree, but that didn't surprise her, did it?

Not surprise, no. But hurt. Still, she ought to say the rest of what was in her mind. If it hadn't been for her actions, Mary might never have been in that position tonight.

"I let down a lot of people when I went outside the boundaries, and Mary was one of them. If I could do something to make up a little for it, I'm wonderful glad I had the chance."

"Denke, Barbie." Mary's eyes swam with tears. "You won't have to rescue me again. I promise."

She smiled at the girl who was so quickly growing into a woman. "Gut." She stood before she could start crying herself. "I'd best go."

"Do you have a way home?" Ben glanced toward the window, as if wondering whether a car was waiting there.

She shook her head. "I told the driver he should go. We'd already imposed enough on him."

"I'll take you, then."

"I can try to reach David and ask him . . ." she began, but Ben was already out the door before she could finish. Well, maybe he wanted the privacy of taking her home. Then he could tell her how wrong she was to involve an Englischer in their troubles.

"Good night." She went around the table to hug Mary. "It will be all right," she whispered.

Mary clung to her for a moment. "Denke," she murmured.

Barbie walked out into the scented darkness, irresistibly reminded of the night Ben had kissed her. She could hear the jingle of the harness as he hitched up the buggy horse, but since she didn't have a flashlight, she waited where she was until he drove up and stopped next to her. He reached out a hand to help her up, and she grasped it to pull herself to the seat next to him.

It was no use thinking about how his touch made her feel. She'd lectured herself on that topic more than once, and it didn't seem to help. Funny, that she'd had so many men interested in her and the only one she could fall in love with was the man who was the least likely match for her in the world.

Folding her hands in her lap, Barbie pressed her lips together. She'd said and done all she could with Mary to undo the damage she'd done. There was nothing left to say, and if Ben wanted to chide her, she'd let him speak first.

That worthy resolve lasted only to the first bend in the road. Then she couldn't stand the silence any longer.

"Well? If you want to lecture me, go ahead and do it. I can take it."

He turned toward her, but she couldn't make out his expression in the shadow cast by the trees. "Why would I lecture you?"

"For starters, Mary wouldn't have gone to that party tonight at all if I hadn't let her down by preaching something I wasn't practicing. And then there's the fact that I got one of my Englisch friends to drive me out to the reservoir. That should be worth a few words."

The horse's hooves clopped several times, and they moved from shadow into moonlight, bright enough that she could see him. The pain on his face was enough to shock her into silence.

"Ben . . ." Instinctively she reached out to him. He glanced at her hand and then wrapped his around it, holding on as if he'd never let go.

"How can I blame you when I'm the one at fault?" The grief in his voice shook her. "I'm the one who's been driving a wedge between myself and my sister by being so rigid she can't turn to me with her troubles."

"Don't." The feelings she'd been trying so hard

to suppress seemed to burst to the surface. She put her other hand on top of his, holding it with both hands. "You're blaming yourself needlessly. Feeling responsible for Mary and everyone else in the church. You can't carry all that burden yourself." She shook her head. "Mary is just like you, you know. She's been trying to fill your mother's shoes and blaming herself when she fails."

That got through to him. He stared at her, letting the lines go slack, and the horse plodded on without his guidance. "Mary thinks that? But none of us expect that of her."

"Of course you don't. Any more than the church expects you to take responsibility for every problem that comes along. But that's how you're made, and Mary is just like you."

He looked down, staring at their hands. "Mary has no cause. But I . . . I know I failed. I couldn't deal with it when my wife died. I felt as if I had nothing left to give."

"You needed time. That grief was too overwhelming to allow you to do anything else. People understand, just as you understand about Mary."

She held her breath. He did understand what she was saying about the girl, didn't he? Poor Mary. She needed help and support, not more rules.

That was what Ben needed, too, but he'd probably never admit it.

"Daad said you had a generous heart. It's also an understanding one." He drew to a stop at the pull-off by the entrance to the farm they were passing. "I have to ask you. Why did you go after the girls tonight?"

"I told you. Because I wanted to protect the community. Because I knew I'd let Mary down by my actions." Her brow furrowed. Didn't he understand that much?

"I know." His fingers moved against hers. "But what did it mean to you, to take that risk?"

He was asking for honesty, complete honesty. And he deserved it. He'd spoken to her about his own private struggles in a way he probably hadn't talked to anyone else.

"For the last year or so I've been struggling." She spoke slowly, looking back, trying to find the beginning of her doubt. "I began to think that maybe I was like my brother James. That my dreams would lead me to the outside world." There was a lump in her throat, and she tried to swallow it. "When I thought about what might happen tonight, I knew I could be risking my future in the church. It hit me then. In my heart, I am always Amish. No matter what discipline I have to face. No matter if it means giving up my dreams of adventure. I am Amish."

His taut face relaxed. "Ja. You are." He raised her hand to his lips. "I know I have said some foolish things in my time. But one thing I see clearly now. You really are that perfect Amish woman you accused me of looking for."

Her heart was beating so loudly she could hardly hear herself, and the ripples from the kiss he brushed on her hand spread up her arm, seeming to suffuse her whole body with awareness.

"Not perfect," she managed to say. "But at least headed in the right direction."

Ben seemed to study her face. He lifted his hand to stroke her cheek with one finger, and she trembled.

"You wanted adventure," he said softly. "Living Amish in an Englisch world is always an adventure, I think."

She thought of tonight's escape from the wailing sirens and smiled. "It is."

"And there's another adventure you might want to take on." He pressed his palm against her cheek, and her breath caught. "Loving. Risking your happiness on marriage and children. That's an adventure, ain't so?"

"A grand adventure," she managed to say. "But no one has asked me yet."

His smile seemed to contain all the sweetness in the world. "Ach, Barbie, how many ways can I say it? I love you. You bring joy and love into our lives just by being yourself. Will you be my wife?"

The happiness seemed to bubble through her,

dancing along veins and muscles until she felt as if she'd float right off the buggy seat. She reached up to pull his face down to hers.

"That's the way that counts. I love you, too."

She was going to say more, but his mouth covered hers, and anything else was lost in the delight of that kiss. It wasn't a surprise this time, but it was just as exciting as that first kiss had been.

Better, because this time it came with love and a promise. She leaned into his arms, knowing she was in the right place at last.

Ben's arms tightened around her until she thought he'd squeeze the breath right out of her. Finally he drew away just a little, still close enough that she felt his breath on her lips when he spoke.

"I don't think I can wait until November to be married to you. Maybe we can convince the ministers to let us have an out-of-season wedding."

Her laugh was interrupted by a light kiss. "Since you're one of them, that might just be possible." She sighed, relaxing against him, content to stay there, feeling the rise and fall of his chest as he breathed.

Her thoughts drifted to her grandmother's stories. She'd wondered, hadn't she, what insight her gift would bring to her. Maybe she knew.

She'd listened, and she'd learned that adventure didn't necessarily come from what you did.

It came from living and loving in accordance with God's will.

He stirred. "I'd better take you home before your parents worry. Do you think they would like to be consulted?"

"I think they'd be delighted," she said, longing to hear cool, reserved Benuel expose his feelings to Mamm and Daad. "Let's go home."

Ben picked up the lines with one hand and wrapped the other around hers on the seat between them. He clicked to the gelding. Hands clasped, they rode toward home together.

Epilogue

They were lucky Grossmammi's birthday was a warm day for October, Barbie thought, because the whole family couldn't possibly fit inside the house at the same time. They'd overflowed the daadi haus and the main house into the backyard at Rebecca's parents' place. Everyone was here, and she and Ben seemed to be getting almost as many good wishes on their recent wedding as Grossmammi was getting birthday wishes.

"Do you think it's too chilly out here for Grossmammi?" Cousin Judith paused next to her, carrying a tray of glasses. Judith was a bit of a worrier.

"I think I wouldn't want to tell her she needs to go inside," Barbie said, and Judith smiled.

"Coward," she teased.

"That's right, I am." Barbie helped herself to a glass of lemonade from the tray. "Besides, she's well wrapped up, isn't she, Rebecca?"

Rebecca, her infant son cradled in her arms, nodded. "As well wrapped up as young Matthew," she said.

Barbie bent over the infant, crooning to him. The baby's wide, milky-blue eyes tried to focus on her face. "Ach, he's a fine boy. But he's not going to let you enjoy the party for long without demanding something to eat."

She was abruptly tackled around the legs. "Boppli," Libby demanded. "See the boppli, Mammi."

Barbie scooped Libby up in her arms, still sweetly surprised when Ben's little ones called her Mammi. "See? But don't touch." She caught the chubby hand that reached for the baby's face.

"I want one," Libby announced. Barbie flushed as her cousins laughed.

"Soon enough," Rebecca said. "Give your Mammi some time."

A ball bounced past, kicked by her brother James's little boy, and Libby wiggled to get down.

"Will you roll the ball to your cousin Libby, Kevin?"

The boy, who looked like James, grinned,

showing his missing teeth, and nodded. "Okay, Aunt Barbie."

"James's kinder seem gut with the little ones." Ben stood next to her, his smile warm when she looked up at him. "I'm glad to see them fitting in so well."

"I think they're amazed to find they have so many cousins." She threaded her fingers through his. "It's wonderful gut to have James and his family here." They'd become fairly regular visitors, and even James's wife, Andrea, now felt like one of the family.

Barbie's heart seemed to expand. Her family was growing before her eyes. And loving Ben seemed to have given her even more love in her heart to share, instead of less. She looked up at him, eyes dancing.

"I just heard my aunt saying how fine your sermons are since we've been married. Do I get any credit for it?"

He squeezed her hand. "Everything in my life is better now that you're my wife. Does that satisfy you?"

"It does. Just don't forget it," she teased.

Rebecca nudged her. "Not to interrupt the newlyweds, but I'm thinking if the three of us talk to Grossmammi, we might convince her to move inside for a bit."

"We can try." Judith set down the glasses.

"We're her favorite granddaughters, aren't we?"

With a glance at her husband, Barbie went with her cousins to the spot where their grandmother, well wrapped in shawls, sat in a rocker that had been brought out for her. A number of the younger children clustered around her.

The three of them paused at the fringe of the group, listening. Grossmammi was telling the story of the first Lapp family that had come over from Europe to build a new life.

Barbie found herself blinking back tears. Their grandmother seemed more fragile since she'd come home from the hospital in the spring, but she could still hold listeners enthralled with her stories.

As Grossmammi spoke, Barbie seemed to see the family spreading out in time and space—back into the past, forward into the future, and encompassing more and more members. The same spirit linked all of them—the spirit that lived so strongly in Grossmammi. It was based on the promise of faithfulness. The family would survive, because no matter where they went, they would follow the Lord.

Recipes

Barbecued Venison

Many Amish enjoy hunting, not only for sport but also for the addition of meat to the family larder. This recipe is especially suited to the end pieces of venison.

2 pounds venison roast
1 tablespoon shortening
1 teaspoon onion flakes
¼ cup ketchup
2 teaspoons sugar
1 teaspoon mustard
1 teaspoon Worcestershire sauce
2 teaspoons apple cider vinegar
1 teaspoon salt
¼ teaspoon pepper
¼ cup water

Brown the venison roast slowly in the shortening in a heavy pot or Dutch oven. Mix the other ingredients and pour over the meat. Cover and simmer very slowly for at least 2 hours or until the meat begins to fall apart. It can also be roasted in the oven in a covered roasting pan at 275°F for 2 hours. Makes 8 to 10 servings.

Ham Loaf

⅔ pound ground ham
1⅔ pounds ground pork
1 cup dry bread crumbs
¼ teaspoon pepper
2 beaten eggs
1 cup milk

Combine the meat, bread crumbs, pepper, eggs, and milk. Mix thoroughly, preferably with a mixer, until the combination is very fine. Form into a loaf in an 8½-inch loaf pan. Bake at 350°F for 1 hour. Makes 6 to 8 servings.

Savory Pot Roast

This recipe is a shortcut version of sauerbraten, since it doesn't require the lengthy marinating that sauerbraten does.

3 pounds beef chuck or rump roast
1 tablespoon shortening
⅓ cup grape jelly
2 large onions, sliced
2 bay leaves
2 teaspoons salt
½ teaspoon allspice
½ teaspoon ginger
¼ teaspoon pepper
¼ cup water
⅓ cup apple cider vinegar

Brown the meat slowly on all sides in the shortening in a heavy pot or Dutch oven. Spread the grape jelly over the surface of the meat, top with the onion slices, and sprinkle with the seasonings. Mix together the water and vinegar and pour over the meat. Cover and cook very slowly for 2 to 3 hours until the meat begins to fall apart. Makes 8 to 10 servings.

Dear Reader,

I'm so glad you joined me for the final story of my Keepers of the Promise series. I've been building up to telling Barbie's story for a long time, and I'm happy to see her on the page at last.

The three stories of the Lapp family, while fictional, are very similar to what actually happened to the Amish settlements in Pennsylvania. In *The Rebel*, I've taken on the period during which increasing pressures from the outside seemed to threaten the very existence of the Lancaster County Amish, leading to migration into other areas and the establishment of daughter communities to that original group. Over time, each of the daughter colonies has created its own identity as it responds to the area in which it settled, so that we now find variation in customs among each of the groups, even as they maintain their tradition of living simply and separately in accordance with God's will for their lives.

Interestingly enough, the settlement in Lancaster County didn't disappear, despite their fears. The Amish have adapted and strengthened, and even though groups still move out, both the mother and daughter settlements continue to thrive and grow.

I hope you'll let me know what you think of Barbie's story. You can find me online at martaperry.com and facebook.com/MartaPerry Books, e-mail me at marta@martaperry.com, or write to me in care of Berkley Publicity Department, Penguin Random House, 375 Hudson Street, New York, NY 10014. If you'd care to write to me, I'd be happy to reply with a signed bookmark or bookplate and my brochure of Pennsylvania Dutch recipes.

Blessings,
Marta

About the Author

A lifetime spent in rural Pennsylvania and her own Pennsylvania Dutch roots led **Marta Perry** to write about the Plain People who add to the rich heritage of her home state. She is the author of more than fifty inspirational romance novels and lives with her husband in a century-old farmhouse.

Visit the author online at martaperry.com and facebook.com/MartaPerryBooks.

Center Point Large Print
600 Brooks Road / PO Box 1
Thorndike, ME 04986-0001 USA

(207) 568-3717

US & Canada:
1 800 929-9108
www.centerpointlargeprint.com